How To Marry and Keep a Supermodel

Lessons From a Mid-Wife Crisis

Herman Franck

A Kit Media production

ISBN: 0-9843-9620-9
ISBN-13: 9780984396207

dedication: This book is dedicated to all men who are suffering, will suffer, or have suffered through the unstoppable force of nature known as a mid-wife crisis.

This book is further dedicated to Mr. David Byerley, husband of the illustrator Maria Byerley, who sadly passed away at the age of 39. David posed for the scenes in The Dance of ISIS. He leaves behind a loving wife and a beautiful three year old daughter.

Table of Contents

List of Songs

acknowledgements: Diane lucas of lucas illustrations designed the front and back cover for me. see www.lucasillustrations.com for more information about diane's book cover illustration work.

The photo credits for the front and back photos on the covers belong to some person that took the photos on my camera. i don't know who it is, but thanks.

Maria byerley did the illustrations and page design for *the dance of isis.* we call the theme "dreamscape."

Jamie Blair of Dixon, California did a wonderful job of proofreading the manuscript. She also wrote a review of the book, which included: ". . .wonderfully written and very dramatic. The conversation that develops between the author and the reader is thrilling and intense, but so natural. It's truly as if two friends are catching up after a long hiatus." And, ". . . enjoyable, dramatic and humorous. The lighthearted tone that the author uses to deliver such serious messages is what makes this book so hard to put down. It's not as if the reader is simply reading another book, they are having a conversation with Herman Franck about his wild and spectacular wife!"

about this story: *How to Marry and Keep a Supermodel* is a frictional tale based on an actual made up story of incomplete truth.

What?

This means the characters and events are make believe but are inspired by real events.

I ask that the reader think about this hybrid of reality and fiction like this: do you think I would have been able to write this book if something like this didn't really happen to me?

To get an idea of the real story, please see Appendix B to this book, *I Remember.*

about the author: Herman franck, esq. is a mild mannered attorney at law practicing in the field of civil trials and appeals. he owns his own law office, franck & associates, in sacramento, california.

He grew up on a ranch in scottsdale, arizona, where he learned to dig holes, put in fence posts, and how to install barbed wire and chicken fencing. he also learned a rule of life there, "the animals eat first." during his tenure as a ranch hand he managed to let loose into the wild a group of 9 peacocks, whose offspring can be found atop telephone poles in the scottsdale area even to this day.

Mr. franck attended high schools in scottsdale, arizona before returning to woodside, california, and graduated from the often overlooked woodside high school in 1976, at the bottom third of the class.

After a second, third and fourth chance at several california community colleges, he managed to gain entrance into u.c. berkeley, and received his b.a. (*honors*) from u.c. berkeley in political economy in 1981.

Equally miraculous was his admission into the Georgetown University Law Center, Washington, D.C., where he received a juris doctor in 1985. He also received a Master of Arts in Economics from Georgetown University, and did a masters thesis in Anti Trust economics.

He recently self published his first economics book, *U.S. Grown, To Survive a Nation Must Feed Itself* (Booksurge 2009).

He is a member of the State of California Bar, and is admitted to practice before the Federal Courts of California (where he sometimes goes and argues cases), the State Courts of California (where he spends roughly each day arguing cases; the Court has considered charging him rent), the United States Court of Appeals for the Ninth Circuit (where he is occasionally found arguing a dispute to be a published case typically in the field of prison civil rights), and the United States Supreme Court (which has yet to invite him to argue a case).

He was formerly admitted to practice in Ukraine (1992-1995) under its foreign attorney program. Mr. Franck resided in Ukraine during 1992 in connection with an agri-business project, and from that, gained some insights from traveling throughout Eastern and Central Europe, Central Asia, and other far off locations.

Mr. Franck was admitted to practice before the U.N. Tribunal for War Crimes for Former Yugoslavia (but alas, never got a case).

Mr. Franck is the founder of The Entrepreneur Center of Sacramento (www.entrepreneur-center.net), and is the author of a book entitled *Entrepreneur by Necessity* (XLibris 2008).

Mr. Franck is a co-founder of the food labeling company, U.S. Grown LLC, Williamson, New York. See www.usgrown.com for more information about this company.

Mr. Franck is a weekend writer of books and screenplays. *How to Marry and Keep A Supermodel* is his twentieth book. His 19th book, *Supernatural CSI, Dead People Make Excellent Witnesses* (Booksurge 2008) received a positive review from the Sacramento Book Review (June 2009). ("This was an enjoyable read written by an author with an invigorating imagination.")

Mr. Franck lives in West Sacramento with his real life loveliest wifee-poo, Sabrina Q. Chen, their real life children, Adam and Alex Franck, and two Dalmatians, Spots and Diamond.

A new arrival, Ms. Lo Qin Romano of Turino Italy, is now with us, from Sabrina's first marriage to a handsome blue-eyed Swiss Italian by the name of Mr. Igor Romano (who is still very much alive and well).

What do you do when your wife falls in love with another man?

A. Dump her; or,

B. Start a campaign to win her back.

This is a story about a man who chose Plan B.

other works by herman franck, esq.: Herman Franck is the author of the following other books, comic books, and screenplays:

Supernatural CSI. Dead People Make Excellent Witnesses. (Booksurge 2009) Trips to the otherworld reveal evidence of crimes here on earth.

Ice Dragon. [XLibris 2007] *Book I. Battle of the Longheads.* [google longhead and see what you find] Kit Media produced a completed 32 page English/Spanish language color comic book based on Episode I of the book. Comic artwork, layout, lettering by Atlantis Studios, Atlanta, GA. Online comic: www.icedragon.biz

Ice Dragon [XLibris 2008] Books II and III: The Case of the Stolen Cartoons; The Case of the Missing Toys. Vincent and Ice Dragon solve the most important crimes in the history of the world.

Star Boy. [XLibris 2007] Novella. Kit Media produced a 32 page Spanish/English color comic of the first third of this novella. An ET visited earth and left a little hybrid boy for somebody to take care of. Artwork, layout, lettering of the color comic by Atlantis Studios, Atlanta, GA. [Starboy's song: *I know it's true, I'm part ET, but please, don't hate me.*]

Katie Cranberry [XLibris 2008]. Novel. Traveling fruit characters attend Katie's world university of diplomacy. Bow and Arrow recommended. Book I: *Katie's Silk Road Adventure;* Book II, *Katie's Preview in South America;* Book III, *American Stonehenge* Completed Telescript for one hour series pilot, How to Earn a Kingdom.

Katie Cranberry IV: Katie's North American Peace Adventure. [BookSurge 2009] Katie Cranberry and her entourage of worldly friends set out on a mission to eliminate the white man's annihiliation of the Native Americans.

Juan Bonderello Quatro Cinco Seis. Novella Book I: The Case of the Stupid Food. [XLibris 2007] Juan Bonderello is the perfect peoples' spy to save the United States from its first bout with agro terrorism.

Second Life [XLibris 2006]. Novella. Success and failure are but two sides of the same page. A failed alcoholic doctor's soul is transferred into the body of a totally successful doctor.

Cheetah Kids [XLibris 2007]. Novel. Two infants are raised by a family of Cheetahs, and become the fastest humans on earth. A Dubai sheik with a heart of gold, as in Olympic Gold, shows them the path to glory. In the process, they find the tragedy that left them with without parents. How fast can you spell revenge.

The Post Debutante [iuniverse 2001] Novel. An innocent deb gets on the wrong side of a murder case. In the process she becomes an expert on injustice and disloyalty, even among family.

The Politician [Kiwe Publishing] Novel. A new country is formed on a series of super barges. And that's not treason.

The Family Business. [Emerson-Adams Press 2002]. Novel and screenplay. Between organized crime and corporate America, will the real criminals please stand up. Introducing Tina, Mafia spy girl, the story of Tony, who thinks he is leaving the criminal world for so called legitimate business.

The Nobel Prizener [iuniverse 2004] Novel and feature length screenplay. Rape is a hard charge to beat, especially when you're innocent.

Franck Tails. [Kiwe Publishing 2003] Collection of animal stories. *Winnie and Thunderose, The Lonely Leopard, Ca Ca Boy, Wolf's Law.* Also wrote a script for *Winnie and Thunderose.*

Relationship Agreement [Iuniverse 2005] A code of conduct for lovers. Example: you can say no, but you can't say no all the time.

Just Add Water [Kiwe Publishing 2001]. Novel. There had to be revenge for this killing.

Entrepreneur by Necessity [XLibris 2007] Booklet on how to start a business when you have to. No Ice Dragons, Starboys, or fruit characters in this one.

U.S. Grown. To Survive a Nation Must Feed Itself. The Impact of Food Imports on American Food Producers. Okay, so I wrote an economics book.

Reptile Man [*Homo-Reptilius Criminalis*] Eliminate this specie and you eliminate crime. Completed 125 page feature length screenplay.

OOPS. Out of Prison Inc has a run in with the Christian right. Completed 95 page screenplay. Where is Martha when you need her?

The Conversation. They all died and lived happily ever after. 52 page script for a poltergeist/legal drama.

The Tehachapi Militia. Ex- military turned Prison guards plus mowed over by state bureaucrats equals militia that takes over a prison. Completed 120 page feature length script.

The Debt. Its like waking up and learning that you were Hitler in a past life. Completed 135 page feature length script. Received honorable mention in Film Makers screenplay competition, 2001.

The Shanghai Twins. Its nighttime in Shanghai, do you know where your children are?
Two part mini series [95 pages each] based on author's grand-parents' tragic experience of losing male twins in Shanghai during the 30s. We never did find them. Written in China [in English].

Mayflower. These are not the pilgrims we learned about in grade school. Completed 120 page scandalous feature length script.

Red Card, script. If you take the time to help a stranger. Geek American engineer attempts arranged marriage in Gobi Desert China. Oops, in the process he gets arrested for lying to Chinese immigrations authorities. His defense never worked before, but this is a new Red China.

The Family Business. Feature length script based on the author's novel.

The Nobel Prizener. Feature length script based on the author's novel.

Katie Cranberry. Script for a one hour pilot for a tele-series based on the author's novel.

Winnie & Thunderose. Script for a tele-movie based on the author's short story.

Illustrated Stories

Winnie and Thuderose is being produced into an illustrated book [forthcoming][Artwork by Maria Byerley].

The Dance of Isis [artwork by Maria Byerley].

New Books in Progress

Ultimate Revenge [in progress]. A man's fiancée is raped. The man captures the rapist, and uses hormone therapy to turn the rapist into a woman. Unspeakable things happen.

The Fake Family [in progress]. Everything about this family is 100% fake, until something terrible happens that teaches them how to be real.

More coming . . .

Chapter 1
SO YOU WANT TO MARRY
A SUPERMODEL

Let's first begin by analyzing the question, "Will you marry me?" This question is a shorthand version of the following series of promises: Do you take this man to be your lawfully wedded husband, to have and to hold, in sickness and in health, rich or poor, and to forsake all others, until death do you part?

Is that not one of the most obnoxious promises a man could ever possibly request of a woman? Amazingly, every day women of all types and sizes say yes to this request. What are the true odds that the promise will actually be performed? Will she stay with you if you're sick? Will she stay with you if you're poor? Will she "forsake all others"? Get real.

Add to this a woman who happens to be a supermodel, and you have the goal of this book, how to marry and keep a supermodel.

Chapter 2
MY CREDENTIALS

The reader may naturally ask how on earth the author has any basis to write such a book. The lessons I have learned from marrying a supermodel by the name of Sassafras are chronicled here. How I found her, how I met her, how I initially wooed her, how I convinced her to marry me, how I lost her, how I wooed her back, and how, I amazingly managed to keep her, are all part of my own history from which many lessons can be learned. I do not pretend to have the only answers to these quests; these are simply my answers based on my own experience.

Sassafras first shot to fame as one of the key bikini barely-clad women in the *Sports Illustrated Swimsuit Edition.* She is a stunning Chinese/Anglo mix, and as is typical of mixed race women, the results were out of this world. She wore an emerald two-piece which looked gorgeous against her darkish skin. What set her apart from so many of the beautiful Asian women were her Anglo features, combined with the Asian exotic. *Sports Illustrated* found it first. *Vogue, Cosmopolitan,* and the rest of the fashion world followed. She became the Lancôme girl, the Chanel girl, and graced the pages and cover of just about every fashion magazine in Europe, America, and China.

One of the least publicized aspects of her extremely public life is the simple fact that she was married to a very simple person, me.

Chapter 3
RULE NUMBER ONE: ANYONE CAN MARRY A SUPERMODEL

There has never been a recorded incident in the history of the world where a female and male supermodel got together, got married, and had children. It's never happened, and probably never will happen. Instead, and this good news for all you regular guys out there, supermodels tend to marry ordinary humans that have absolutely nothing to do with the supermodel world. Qualified psychologists could remark on several theories to explain this behavior. I would tend to the notion that the supermodel world is filled with short-lived flashes in the pan, followed by long periods of depression, drug use, and instability. The last thing the errant supermodel wants is to hook up with another flash in the pan having various psychological issues, mental shortcomings, and a general shallowness permeating their entire lives.

Instead, the supermodel seeks what most women naturally seek, solidity; stability; the long haul; a man who is for real, is not effeminate, and is and acts like the male counterpart in a heterosexual relationship. Naturally, most male supermodels do not fit the bill, thus opening the field of competition to ordinary humans like you and I. The further you are away from that world, the higher your chances are of wooing a supermodel. So shine your shoes, cut your hair, pick out the dangling nose hairs, lose some weight, look your best, and summon your courage, as all things are possible.

Chapter 4
RESEARCHING YOUR SUPERMODEL

The odds of a particular woman falling in love with a particular man are astronomically low, in the range of one in a billion. There are some methodologies that men should be aware of to heighten their success rate, probably from one in a billion to the much more comfortable odds of one in a million. I thus announce rule number two: women tend to want to marry a man that is like their father. The qualified psychologist would no doubt have several reasons to analyze this fact of life. For our purposes here, let us not concern ourselves with the why of this rule; instead, let us simply understand that this is the rule.

An initial first step would be to look at yourself in the mirror, analyze how you look outwardly and inwardly, and come up with a bit of an inventory. I do not suggest the geekish practice of actually writing down this inventory. Instead, make a mental note of how you look and how you are. Do a self-assessment.

Step two is to research supermodels' family histories and find a supermodel who, as a total coincidence, happens to have a father that looks, acts, and appears not exactly like you, but close enough that you will get her attention. This will be a subliminal effect. She won't even know why she likes you, she just will.

So where do you find information on the family background of a supermodel? In my case, I happen to be an attorney that handles immigrations cases. As it would have it, I have access to a substantial database of immigrants coming into the United States. In the immigration application papers, one of the requirements is to set forth data and information about the immigrant's parents. I can access this database, learn the names and identities of just about any immigrant parents, and then begin a process of researching those parents.

As it would happen, many supermodels are also immigrants. They come from the small farms of Ukraine, the backward villages of China, the little towns in Italy, the hamlets of Germany, and the many unknown cities that dot Eastern Europe, Central Europe, and other completely unknown places. They are born absolutely gorgeous, tall, thin, with lovely cheekbones. Most of them realize at a young age that they are destined to leave that little farm village for places like Milan, Shanghai, Paris, and when they finally arrive, New York City.

There is a kind of brotherhood of immigration attorneys that exists. Most people don't know about this. I have contacts all over the world that are engaged in the practice of immigration law. For example, if there was a particular Polish woman a person was interested in, and the Polish woman, let's say, never immigrated to the United States but instead immigrated over to Paris, I would not have access to the French immigration database. But, my French friend, Pierre Lefonte, a busy immigration attorney in Cannes, France, has complete and total access to those databases. One phone call to Pierre and I can give you a complete readout on the Polish princess that you are interested in, including who her father was, what he does for a living, where he lives, and how he looks.

What you need to do is access this database, find out about her father, and see if you are anywhere close to a match to him. Let's suppose he is a farmer with blonde hair, blue eyes, round face, and a head full of hair. Let's suppose you are a dark-haired, tallish, balding strapper of a man, without any Polish blood. Probably isn't going to work. But you need to realize the world is filled with immigration trends, and in Poland there are people that are related to Romanians, Mongols, Hungarians, French, Lithuanians, you name it. So, if you have a darkish blend of tones, and you see a Polish girl that is bright, sunny, blonde, blue eyes, do not give up. There is a high probability that somewhere in her bloodline is a Romanian, a Mongol, or some other swarthy member that gives her a certain inkling toward the dark.

In the same way, if you are a lightish toned person, and in the natural order of things are attracted to roughly the opposite of you, this same challenge will persist. You need to find a darkish supermodel who happens to have a lightish father. The good news, in the order of things, it happens that opposites do indeed attract. Thus, the odds that a beautiful blonde woman got together with a darkish swarthy man, or vice versa, are often high.

The moral of these rules is to not focus on what the supermodel looks like, and to instead focus on what her parents look like and are like. In particular, look for what her father looks like, how he is, what he does, and who he is. The closer you are to a match with him, the closer are the odds of catching the supermodel.

Chapter 5
HOW I MET MY SUPERMODEL WIFE

It is perhaps a truism that you find love when you are not looking for it. Notwithstanding my access to considerable immigration databases, I happened to find my supermodel through fortuitous means. It went like this: after my day job of attorney at law, I'm a book writer. I was in the process of writing a book called *The World Food Atlas*. This book sets forth maps of the world, and shows where the different foods of the world come from. Don't worry, I won't explain it in any further detail other than to state that the preeminent database on the sources of food production is an entity known as the United Nations Food and Agriculture Organization, FAO for short.

It happened that this agency of the United Nations is headquartered in Rome, Italy. They have a database system that maps out annual food production of every crop, country by country. They also have maps of every country, and a database of photographs of the various farms that are scattered throughout every country. It was a one-stop shopping spree for me to go to the FAO in Rome, and to purchase the rights to this database, the rights to the photographs, and the rights to the net. By combining them all together, I was well on my way to prepare the world's first world food atlas.

At the time, I was in San Francisco, California, where I had a modest law office. I decided to fly to Florence first, to visit an attorney friend of mine there by the name of Alfredo La Guzzi, an immigrations attorney. Alfredo had provided me with quite a bit of data on a group of supermodels in Italy, most of which came from former Eastern Bloc countries. I wanted to pay him a visit as a way of saying thanks. Alfredo is a large, portly man, looking a little bit like Pavarotti, except his tenor has less amplitude. He is a soft-spoken large man, a gentle giant.

As a precursor to the ensuing events, we had dinner in a Chinese restaurant located in the outskirts of Florence.

Chapter 6
THIS IS NOT MY FIRST SUPERMODEL

I will spare you the details of my experiences dating other supermodels. For now, we will focus on the woman whose family background was chronicled in a manila file brought to the dinner by my good friend Alfredo. Of course I had to ask:

"Did you bring it?"

"It?"

He was playing coy.

"You know."

"I think you mean her."

"Do you refer to your files as people?"

"This file is about a person."

"Did you bring her?"

"I did."

He brought out his small briefcase. Ironically, it was not Italian, and was made of fake rubber. I was not the only moderately incomed attorney on the planet. He unlocked the combination, as though there was some great state secret enclosed. He opened it, and produced a file. Just before he gave it to me, our waitress appeared. She was Chinese, and as the Chinese do in Italy, she spoke perfect Italian. She knew Alfredo by name, and stood outside his reach. He moved his chair over to her, and held her hand as though reading her fortune.

"You will meet a handsome Italian man. You will fall in love with him and you will live happily ever after."

Yeah, right, I thought to myself. The woman, a gracious host, rolled her eyes up and announced,

"Can I get you a drink?"

Alfredo looked at her.

"Oh, you can give me so much more than that."

She was fairly attractive, if you like light-skinned Chinese girls. Me, being the fairly light-skinned mix of English-Dutch heritage, and due to the fact that opposites attract, I prefer the more darkish girls. Alfredo, being an olive-skinned and hot-blooded Italian, appreciated the light-skinned exotic Chinese girl. The only problem with this equation is that this nice girl, for whatever reason, did not appreciate him. I could see this was not his first time hitting on her. She left with our drink orders, a bottle of sangria, and we got down to business.

"Really, Alfredo. Your hunting of a Chinese girl strikes me as being a little bit ridiculous."

"Oh? Any more ridiculous than you hunting for a Hungarian woman in Italy?

He produced the file of Marguerite Hisonyi, formerly of Budapest, and now, thanks to Alfredo's good legal work, the owner of a permanent resident's card in Italy. She was quite obviously a supermodel. I was holding the file with great excitement. I'd already seen her photos in *Vogue*. The file had a photo of her family, which is exactly what I wanted to see. He had a couple of Post-its stuck on the pages of the Italian immigration papers that included data about the family. As I was going to say it out loud, Alfredo predicted me,

"Her father?"

Alfredo showed me his photo.

"It's kind of strange, but he kind of looks like you."

"Thank god for this amazing coincidence of finding a supermodel who has a father who's a lawyer and who happens to look a little bit like me. Okay, he has brown eyes, I have blue eyes. He's Hungarian, I'm English-Dutch. But he has darkish hair, a square jaw, similar cheekbones, and small ears. This has got to be the one."

My next question was rather obvious.

"Where is this woman?"

Alfredo laughed. It's nice when you're with a lawyer who happens to know the whereabouts of a supermodel whose father looks like you.

"She's right here in Florence. Would you like to see her?"

Just before I was about to say, of course I would, our waitress reappeared with a bottle of sangria and two glasses. She was about to pour, Alfredo took over.

"May I?"

She allowed him. He took the cork off himself, something he was quite experienced with. He poured a small amount into a glass and handed it to me as though I would know good from bad. I played along. I took a sip.

"It's absolutely lovely."

Alfredo then ordered all the food for us. Knowing that I was a bit clueless, he took over. He spoke of Chinese food in Italian, which I clearly did not understand. The waitress took it all down, and repeated the order back to him in perfect Italian. I trusted him to order us a nice hopefully light in cholesterol dinner. Fat chance of that. I pored through Marguerite's file. She was educated at the University of Hungary, where she studied liberal arts. Because her dad was an intellectual, no doubt she had a little bit of a brain. Her mother was quite beautiful, as would be expected of a supermodel. These cheeks don't come from nothing. She had two brothers, one of which had become an attorney in Budapest.

So far so good.I continued reading every millimeter of the page of her file. She had come to Italy three years ago. She was referred to Alfredo, the great and fearless immigration attorney of foreign tutelage, by another friend of hers who had made a similar path, without the supermodel career. Alfredo managed to get her an Italian green card.

Our dinner arrived. Some form of a pasta dish with pineapple and bits of ham.

"This like a Hawaiian pizza without the pizza."

Alfredo laughed.

"It's one of my favorites. I love pineapple."

Interesting how Italians don't like Italian things. As I explored this entertaining dish, the waitress brought a Greek-looking salad. I say that only because it had goat cheese. My idea is anything with goat cheese in it has to be Greek. It also had those little funny-shaped olives. Next she brought out some slices of fatty sausage, something that Alfredo had ordered a thousand other times. I had to ask,

"So, Alfredo, I see you watching this Chinese girl. With all these beautiful Italian women, you're here chasing down a Chinese girl. How come?"

"It's simple. Italian women, for whatever reason, they just don't like me."

"Oh, and this girl does?"

"Well, it's all relative. Comparatively speaking, she dislikes me less than the Italian women."

"Oh, marvelous. So, why don't we harass her some more?"

I intercepted the check before it was placed on the table.

"Allow me."

"Okay."

He did not put up much of a fight.

"Our next stop is a private disco club called Apollo."

"Okay. And what might we find at Apollo?"

Alfredo picked up his file.

"Her."

We left the Chinese restaurant for a downtown disco club called the Apollo.

Chapter 7
THE APOLLO

Rather than riding like rich famous people in a limousine, we hopped aboard Alfredo's only form of transportation, one of those annoying motor scooters that populate all of Italy. Add to that the fact that he's a typical Italian driver, with more than half a bottle of sangria in him. That, combined with a little angry male testosterone over being once again jilted by his favorite Chinese waitress, and I was in for a harrowing ride down the small streets and alleys of Florence.

I would've never found this place in a million years. It was left, right, down a cobblestone street, down another one. It actually looked like a fairly rough area. Finally we approached what appeared to be a warehouse. It had a rear front, a long line of people waiting with velvet roped enclosure at the front door, and a couple large Ethiopian style bodyguards in front. I wondered without fear how we would get in. I just figured Alfredo had probably handled the immigration application of virtually everyone in the place. The Ethiopians in front knew him well and hugged him.

"Alfredo! Alfredo!"

He gave them a cursory hug and ushered me to go in. The people in the line seemed a little bit miffed that we got this advance forward, but I ignored them. I had issues to deal with, the issue of a Hungarian supermodel inside. We walked up a flight of stairs and then another flight of stairs. I could hear the low bass thumping of New Age music. The disco had a 1970s style globe mirror on top with different colored lights flying out everywhere.

The place was packed with energetic dancers, sexy as all get out.

I saw a small stage, and there she was. Why did she have to be so damn sexy? She was a hot one. Long dark blonde hair, lengthy thin arms twirling upwards to her circular twists. Marguerite was stunningly beautiful. She was quite a dancer, her arms up in the air showing her naked armpits. I looked at her, thinking how on earth could I ever meet this girl? Alfredo made it quite simple. She jumped off the stage, ran to see him, and hugged him. She did not speak English, and spoke with him in her second language, Italian. Her first language was Hungarian.

"Hello, Alfredo," was the effect of her untranslated remark.

She gave him a big kiss on the cheek, and I was green with envy. I couldn't help but think, wow, it's nice to know these Italian immigration attorneys. Alfredo then spoke with her in Italian. I had no idea what he was saying, but she was listening keenly. The music was quite loud, so she had to cup her ear. I heard my name, so somehow whatever they were talking about involved me. She looked to me and smiled. Wow, what a smile. The Hungarians are a mix between Slavic, Germanic, and other tribes of people that collected in the Central Volga region of Russia long ago, and for some reason decided to leave and form the Magyar country, now known as Hungary. The women can be extremely tantalizing, as shown by Marguerite.

One of my favorite songs came through the disc jockey, "American Woman, Stay Away From Me":

"American woman gonna mess your mind
American woman, she gonna mess your mind
American woman gonna mess your mind
American woman gonna mess your mind
Say A,
Say M,
Say E,
Say R,
Say I,
C,
Say A,
N,
American woman gonna mess your mind
American woman gonna mess your mind
American woman gonna mess your mind

American woman, stay away from me
American woman, mama let me be
Don't come hangin' around my door
I don't wanna see your face no more
I got more important things to do
Than spend my time growin' old with you
,
American woman, listen what I say.

American woman, get away from me
American woman, mama let me be
Don't come knockin' around my door
Don't wanna see your shadow no more
Coloured lights can hypnotize
Sparkle someone else's eyes
Now woman, I said get away
American woman, listen what I say.

American woman, said get away

American woman, listen what I say
Don't come hangin' around my door
Don't wanna see your face no more
I don't need your war machines
I don't need your ghetto scenes
Coloured lights can hypnotize
Sparkle someone else's eyes
Now woman, get away from me
American woman, mama let me be.

Go, gotta get away, gotta get away
Now go go go
Gonna leave you, woman
Gonna leave you, woman
Bye-bye
Bye-bye
Bye-bye
Bye-bye
You're no good for me
I'm no good for you
Gonna look you right in the eye.
Tell you what I'm gonna do
You know I'm gonna leave
You know I'm gonna go
You know I'm gonna leave
You know I'm gonna go, woman
I'm gonna leave, woman
Goodbye, American woman
Goodbye, American chick
Goodbye, American broad..."

She held my hand and walked me up to the dance stage. Oh my goodness, I thought. Am I actually going to be dancing with this woman? Indeed. As the music yelled out, "Hey, don't come a'hangin' around my door," she gyrated in a way that they would never allow on a runway. Rather than walking with that expressionless straight line, heel to toe, heel to toe, she had pure erotic pleasure on her face, and wild gyrations in her shoulders, arms, hips, and legs. She was quite a good dancer, which made me look a bit awkward as I am not.

I was wearing a coat, something that apparently bothered Marguerite. She took it off. The whole idea of this girl undressing me, even partially, was quite exciting. She walked it over to a nearby chair, empty of its dancer, and carefully draped it on the back. She held my hand and brought me back to the stage. I must be dreaming. The music continued to roar, her hips continued to gyrate, and my mind was spinning outside the orbit of Pluto.

After a couple of songs, we sat down at a table. Here was the one showstopper between me and this girl, and generates yet another rule about meeting supermodels: you need to find one that speaks the same language as you. She spoke perfect Italian, but zero English. Alfredo had to serve as a translator. I actually had been to Hungary several times, part of my adventures in the agribusiness world. I thought she might like to know of my adventures. I explained to her how I was in Szabolcs County, at the Ukrainian-Romanian-Hungarian border. It is an ag country where the primary fruit was apple.

Here's the thing about immigrant girls. The last thing they want to know about is their own country. Most of them thank their lucky stars every day that they found a way to escape, especially the farm girls. I had misjudged the situation and thought that she would be curious about my several visits to Hungary. Instead, she was much more curious about California and the USA.

Alfredo explained,

"Enough about Hungary. She doesn't give a shit about that country."

He looked at me as though I was the stupidest guy in the world, which when it comes to women, and especially supermodels, is an apt title. I then got with it. I explained to her in English I had been to the Statue of Liberty, which caught her attention. She wanted to know about that. I described the process of coming to New York, when I was in law school in Washington, D.C., coming down to the tip of Manhattan and taking a ferry over to Staten Island that allowed us to go up into the Statue of Liberty and look out into the harbor at the many boats coming in. This made her dreamy with wonder about whether someday she would make that trip as well. Only it would not be by boat; it would be on a first class ticket on Air Italiano.

Her modeling career had not quite catapulted her to the A-list venues in the world. She remained ambitious, and I could see it in her eyes. One day she would be there and see the Statue of Liberty from the air. She would walk down a runway, people would clap, photographers would snap photos, thousands of flickering flashes would go off. Later the pictures would adorn magazine covers. I explained all this to her. She was so happy to hear someone vocalize her own dream, and in her heart of hearts, I could see there was no doubt about it: she would make it. She would get there and become a super-supermodel.

Which generates yet another rule about supermodels: they are dreamers. One must remember to help fuel those dreams. They probably are a bit on the narcissistic side of things, so don't be surprised if they aren't interested in your dreams. They probably don't even consider that the men of the world have dreams as well. Don't get your feelings hurt; talk about their dreams. Talk about how they will reach their dreams. They may get the notion that you can assist them in that process. Of course with me, nothing could be further from the truth, as I had zero connections in the fashion industry.

This actually turns out to a good thing. It generates another rule: don't pretend to be some kind of connected up person in the fashion industry. For the most part, there are a lot of fake people in that world, people that think or want to think that they know people, when in reality they don't know anything or anybody and will never be able to help anyone achieve anything. It's actually an advantage to be a refreshing outsider, having absolutely no connection to that world.

Me being a lawyer was perfect for this. Lawyers are seen as more solid, more professional, and of particular relevance here, more like her father.

Don't fake that you are in a world that you really aren't in. Be in your world. Be yourself and show her that your world is one that will accentuate her world. She gets enough fashion industry all day long. When it comes to you, it is better to show her a completely different world, a world where people are solid, regular, normal, apple pie Americans with feet firmly planted on the ground.

This is what a supermodel wants, not another dreamy wannabe supermodel.

And I remind the reader of one of the untold tenets of this story: every supermodel wants a regular solid guy. This is nothing but good news for all of us men out there who are far from supermodel status. We have a shot at the supermodel.

Chapter 8
LATER THAT NIGHT

Amazingly, she invited me into her hotel room. Normally, I would never even think of approaching a girl in this way on a first date. But she was openly hot to go. I may be pathetic, but I am not a dweeb.

"Of course."

Alfredo smiled and explained to me I would be losing my translator. I was confident that somehow I would manage. Perhaps the most surprising aspect of her passion was how needy she was. These supermodels walk down the runways looking like cats, skittish, vacant stares, beautiful eyes that never connect, and lovely lips that don't form any kind of kiss or other expression. For some reason, they choose to look dead when they walk on the runway. But this one had a completely different side, as shown on the dance floor, and now artistically exhibited in the bed. Like any other human, she was needy, needed a partner, a lover, a confidante, someone she could hold and trust and adore. It was an amazing night.

To keep the story at a near-PG rating, I will not get into the acrobatics of the evening, other than to say that she looked even more stunning undressed. As I had a very early train to catch the following morning, I bid her farewell and left her asleep in her hotel. I left her my business card and dreamed of a day that she would call. Of course that would never happen, but even lawyers have dreams.

Chapter 9
FIRENZE TRAIN STATION

I had a 7:19 a.m. express train to Rome. One of the first things I noticed about the Florence train station were two American girls that I had seen the night before at the disco. They looked absolutely exhausted, hungover and ready for their next adventure and travels through Italy. They recognized me as a fellow American, and seemed a bit embarrassed at their out of control dancing the night before. I smiled. They ignored me.

I walked out to the train platform and immediately saw a very confusing situation. There were no fewer than nine trains having a dangling sign over the platform reading, "Roma Espresso." An elderly gentleman with his lovely Italian wife of similar age stood below one of these signs. I asked him a question that made me seem rather stupid.

"Is this the Roma Espresso?"

He looked up at the sign, which couldn't be clearer, looked at me and tele-pathed his clear thought: are you the stupidest American on the planet? It was just then that I met the next supermodel of my trip, the Chinese beauty by the name of Sassafras. She was darting across the platform carrying two bags. She had an assistant, a boyish looking girl, that carried three other bags. She was running towards the same train. Worried that she was going to be late, she ushered her friend forward. She spoke perfect Italian, which is a rather odd thing to be hearing a Chinese girl speak, but this is what happens to a Chinese girl that lives in Milan. They learn Italian.

She yelled out something in Italian which probably meant, "Come quick, we're about to miss the train," perhaps more elegant than that. I watched as she darted by and saw the first glimmer of an opportunity. As she sped by the plat-form, she managed to slightly bank off another man, striking him in the shoulder. She didn't knock him down or anything, but it caused him to be pushed away. He was wondering what had hit him, and saw the tracks of Sassafras into the train.

Here was my opportunity: the slight jolt caused one of her earrings to fall off. It was not a fancy expensive earring. It was made of jade, had some Chinese character in the middle of it. I'm not sure how it got dislodged, but I saw it fall off her ear and onto the platform. While the man held his shoulder, wondering what had hit him, I walked up just next to his shoe and picked up the earring. I then asked this man, as though he would know:

"Is this the 7:19 a.m. Espresso train to Rome?"

To my delight, the man spoke perfect English.

"Yes, it is."

This was quite a nice opportunity for me. I saw that Sassafras jumped like a gazelle from the platform into the train, missing the first two stairs. This girl could have a career as a track star if the modeling thing didn't work out. Her boyish friend, who was actually a female, walked up the stairs behind her.

I was not too far away and walked right behind them. They took a seat in first class, which actually isn't that big of a deal on an Italian train. It had four seats and a table. I walked to the seat. Sassafras was putting her bag up above and had to stretch her back a bit, with her arms raised above, which gave me a glimpse of her impressive physique. She was somewhat athletic, not one of these emaciated, heroin addicted-looking models. She was darkish, which struck me as exotic and highly desirable.

I tried to keep my mouth closed as I watched her place her items up there. She had no idea I was gawking at her until she had finished placing her bags up there and turned around to sit down. She then saw me. I showed her my safe nature by opening the palm of my hand, which held her jade earring. She didn't know she had lost it. She put her hand up to the first ear and saw that it was still there, and then to her second ear and saw that it was still missing. She spoke to me in Italian. I don't really look Italian, but somehow people in Italy just figured I was. I told her politely,

"I'm sorry, I don't speak Italian."

Happily, she spoke English, though in a strange Asian-Italian accented way.

"Thank you for finding my earring. Did not know it was lost."

Interestingly, she didn't take it from my palm. By her mannerism she suggested there should be some other gesture by me to offer it to her, so I did. I held it closer to her. She smiled beautifully, took it out of my palm. As she did so, her fingers slightly tickled my palm. I hate to sound wimpy, but it sent shivers down my spine, radiating out to my hips, down my thighs, my legs, and all the way down to the bottom of my big toe.

"Ooh," I thought. "I love her touch."

Unfortunately, the post on the earring was lost. She explained to me.

"These earrings are very important to me. They were given to me by my grandmother."

Was that cool or what? Right away, I'm a hero for saving the family's irreplaceable heirloom, to a supermodel, and on top of that, I'm on the same train all the way to Rome with her.

Here was my most immediate problem, though. All the seats in the neighboring areas were full. The only available seats, if I were to be in that train car at all, were the two of the four at the table where she was sitting with her friend.

I did not want to be forward about it and attempted to elicit an invitation. I pretended to start to walk away and looked hopelessly for a seat. I showed to her that I could see all the seats were taken. She could see the same, and at last she gave me the offer that would spark the entire relationship that would now begin.

"Would you like to sit with us?"

Even a gay man would say yes to that. I smiled and nodded yes. I sat down, right in front of her, and hoped that the train would somehow be taken over by terrorists and held hostage between Florence and Rome for a decade.

Chapter 10
THE SPELL OF SASSAFRAS

The Italian word for witch is *strega*. Somehow Sassafras had *strega* all over her face. It had to do with the dark hair, dark eyes, dark eyebrows, and dark skin. There was a bit of magic about her, the bigger question being was it black magic or white magic. Perhaps shades of gray applied to all things, including witchcraft. Today's white magic, as will be seen, can become tomorrow's black magic. But make no mistake about it, I became subject, irretrievably, to the spell placed on me by this *strega*.

One of the nice things about having gone out the night before with Marguerite and being in a completely satiated state is that I was a perfect gentleman in my discussions. I did not make any type of suggestion about anything of a sexual nature. I think this is an important rule for dealing with supermodels. They know that they're beautiful, they know that men like beautiful women, and they like to see a man who wants them not for their beauty, not for their sexuality, but for their heart and soul and who they are. I was able to arrive at that state because I was so spent out by the night before. I had no thoughts of erotica bouncing through my brain. Had it not been for my chance encounter with the Hungarian princess, it would have been a very different discussion.

She asked me about the purpose of my trip to Rome. I explained to her, a rather odd ambition, to make a world food atlas. Now, you may think a supermodel has heard every story on the planet, and then some, but I can assure you that Sassafras had never heard of anyone trying to make a world food atlas.

"Really? I've never heard of such a thing."

"Indeed, that's because one does not exist, which is exactly the reason why I am setting out to make one."

"But who needs a world food atlas?"

I paused. The reality is the answer may very well be that nobody needs such a book. But I couldn't help to think for some funny reason that the world needed such a book, and I was going to be the guy to put it together. She thought it to be a rather interesting ambition, and shook her head in dismay. I had caught her attention with this plan. She was also pleased to learn that I was a lawyer. This has kind of an international appeal. People just figure if you're a lawyer, you know what you're doing, you're a professional, you're official, smart, and you make a good living.

Unfortunately, it is not the case with all lawyers that they are rich or even near-rich. I always like to downplay anything having to do with wealth because I don't want to disappoint a girl later when she learns that I get by—barely—each month with a bunch of clients that pay, and don't pay, and things in between. I try to skip the whole subject of rich or money or anything like that and show instead a simple man with an Anglo red-blooded American look, blue-green eyes, a young-ish looking face, filled with ideas and ambitions on many different subjects.

In other words, I show her me. Which is the number one rule for supermodels or any other woman: you have to show the girl who you are—who you truly are, not the person you wish you were, not the person you may someday become, but the person you are right then and there, the true you. And don't be embarrassed about who you are. It's all you've got to offer. If they don't like who you are, tough luck. You'll have to find somebody else. But if you fake them into thinking you're somebody else, obviously later the truth will come out. So, don't try to kid anybody with, "I am this, I am that," when you really aren't that at all. Be real.

This was always back in the days when I used to eat quite a bit of junk food. As it happened, I had stopped by McDonald's at the train station and picked up a Big Mac meal. Interestingly, it was number one on the list in Italy, just as it is in the USA. I became a bit hungry and pulled it out. She looked at it, recognizing the golden arches, and laughed.

"American food for the American."

I knew right away that it would of course be rude to eat this without offering it up to her. But on the other hand, I was actually quite hungry. The bright and early morning did not allow me enough time for breakfast, so this was my first meal of the day. Then I figured a safe idea would be to offer it up to her. I held it out.

"Would you like this?"

She looked at and laughed. Yeah, right. A supermodel's going to eat a Big Mac, right? Not on your life!

She shook her head no and gave me a green light to eat it myself. Which generates yet another rule about supermodels: if you have a hamburger when you meet one, don't be afraid to offer her the entire hamburger. Chances are 99.9 percent she will say no. You will then appear to be a gentleman, and at the same time will be able to eat your entire hamburger.

The entire time that I spent eating the Big Mac was filled with her discussions about her own travels from China to Italy, where she came from, how she had her own dreams of leaving China, her own concept that she felt she was a gypsy meant to be traveling the Seven Seas, how she arrived at the shores of Milan, was noticed in the fashion world, made her first fashion debut on the runways of Milan, and was attempting to progress in her career, all the way through to her present adventure in Rome, where she was due for a runway near the Coliseum.

I listened intently as I gobbled down this three-decker disgusting hamburger. Why do I eat this garbage? I offered both of them French fries; they both declined. These girls would not eat a French fry if they were starving to death in the middle of the Sahara Desert. They live on bottled water and sliced apples. She had a baggie of these, and started munching on them. She offered me one. I felt it was not right for me to eat any part of her meager lunch, but the fact was the apple looked quite good. I took a slice. I smelled it. Very appley. She was a bit surprised to see me smell it, but for some reason I always smell my food. It's one of the reasons why I think Big Macs are disgusting. Have you ever smelled one?

I ate the apple. It felt so good and healthy, especially when compared to the Big Mac. I looked at her, a thin beauty, and thought, she knows the right way. I decided not to finish my Big Mac. There was still about a third left. I put it back in the box it comes in and put it in the bag. I would not eat the rest of my French fries. There would come a time later in my life when I would stop eating this junk food altogether, but that would be another day. For now, I listened intently to her tales of travels through the Orient and to Europe, and her path toward becoming a world-famous supermodel by the name of Sassafras.

Chapter 11
ROMA

Terrorists did not take over the train and hold us hostage for even a couple of hours. Drat. And I'm sure the Italian trains never get anywhere on time, except the day when you want them to be delayed heavily. The train was express, non-stop, and arrived in Rome perfectly, like a German train would. The conductor stated it loudly, "Roma! Roma!" as though we didn't know. We came to a stop and I found myself wanting to cry. I thought, gosh, I'll never see this girl again. I got a little nerve up and asked her something.

"Can we meet later?"

To my permanent surprise, she said, "Yes."

She gave me her cell phone number. Perfect, I thought. I actually did not have a cell phone; one of the few attorneys on the planet who didn't. But never mind that. I took her number and put it in my top pocket.

"I need to go to the United Nations Food and Agricultural Organization. It's over by the Coliseum. I'll be there for several hours. I could meet you later, say, around four o'clock?"

I explained to her. She explained.

"I'll be over in the Spanish Steps area,"

She answered simply. And there it was, I arranged my first date with Sassafras. We bid farewell at the train station. I took a cab in one direction, over to the Coliseum area, she took a cab in another direction, over to the Spanish Steps area.

My next stop was the rather large bureaucratic-looking office known as the United Nations Food and Agricultural Organization. It was a very successful visit. I noted in the lobby there was interestingly a map of the country of Iran, and a depiction of all of the foods grown there. In the southern areas they had pomegranates, in the northern area they had apples and oranges, in the middle and on the edges they had grapes. I studied it and thought to myself, isn't this exactly what I'm trying to create? I looked around as though I were engaged in some kind of illicit espionage. Indeed, it was exactly what I wanted to do, except for every country on the planet.

I had previously organized a meeting with the head of the Data Division, which had a system of data showing food production for every single country. The official there confirmed my own suspicion that there was no such thing as a world food atlas. When I explained to him how I wanted to go about to make one, the first thing he said was, "You'll become a millionaire."

I thought, "How cool is that?"

He also pointed out that they had a whole system of maps, so this was truly a one-stop shopping spree for me. The CD that gave an access to the production data, country by country, was available for six hundred dollars, but there was one catch: you had to go to Rome to get it. I was happy to do so, and put the six hundred on my Visa card. The man was nice enough to give me a sample of fifteen maps. He also booted up the data system and printed out several exemplar pages. There I was with this fantastic idea of a world food atlas, and within moments I could see several pages of it actually coming together. I had one example country of Iran, I had food production data printed out for fifteen countries, and a group of maps ready to go.

He asked me if I'd like to have a nice view of the city of Rome from the rooftop of the FAO building.

"Sure."

We walked up there. It was quite a sight, not something your typical tourist would get to see. The FAO building is right by the Coliseum and gives quite a view of all of Rome. Unfortunately, I did not have a camera with me, or I would have recorded this unique experience.

All of these items were packed into a handy little United Nations bag, with the insignia of the United Nations. It looked very official. I was gliding on air walking out of there. Here I was with the beginning of my new book, and a next stop on my first date with Sassafras, the Asian supermodel. I was loving life.

Right across the street from the FAO is indeed the Coliseum. Any American that goes to Italy has to be a bit of a tourist and see this great structure. I personally was rather disgusted with what I knew had gone on in the Coliseum. The whole idea of feeding people to lions is hardly impressive. This was a form of entertainment to the ancient Romans, which I thought was quite bizarre and suggested some kind of a mental defect.

On the sidewalk in front of the Coliseum there are several art vendors that sell lovely paintings of various scenes of Rome. I spoke with one of the vendors about a picture he had of the Coliseum. He wanted to know where I was from.

"San Francisco, California."

"I love the idea that my art travels to far corners of the world."

I hated to disappoint him. I explained.

"This won't actually leave Italy. It's going to a girl who lives in Milan, so it won't be going too far away."

He laughed.

"Milan is a lovely city too. It is the place of the world of fashion."

I gave him a "tell me about it" look. He charged me the equivalent of about twenty-eight dollars for the painting. I slipped it into my United Nations bag between the country maps of Italy and Germany. I then hailed a cab. The driver asked me where I was going and I said with great excitement,

"Spanish Steps."

He, of course, knew what I was talking about and drove me over there in a matter of twenty minutes.

Chapter 12
SPANISH STEPS

A beautiful set of stairs cascades down a small hill to a large piazza with a gorgeous fountain in the middle. Several horse drawn carriages drop tourists there. The horses had those little side blinders so they would only look straight ahead and not be waylaid by the sights to the left or the right. The horses were still.

I got out of the cab and saw the Spanish Steps for the first time. I now understood why Sassafras would be in this area. The surrounding stores were a who's who of fashion: Gucci, Chanel—you name it, the boutiques were there. I did not immediately see Sassafras until one of the horses walked away. There, to the side of the horse, was the gorgeous girl that amazingly enough had shown up for our first date. She was wearing a Chinese outfit, black and white, pants and shirt with long sleeves. It did not show much skin, which was her style, but it did show her. "Wow," was all I could think, and probably said out loud.

We said hello to each other. We couldn't help but compare our set of shopping bags. Hers had all the fashion marks on them and included a new purse and new shoes. Mine showed the United Nations insignia and had a bunch of maps and agricultural data. I explained to her how I obtained all this from the UN. After I explained my cache of maps and food data, she made an interesting remark.

"You make the impossible possible."

I thought about that and knew, of course, that she was right. I was on an impossible mission, and would probably fail at both. We went to a small bistro and had tea and soup. She ate maybe half of the soup and continued with her discussion of her gypsy ways, her dream of being a supermodel, and how she made some fairly good progress in this endeavor.

Toward the end of this meal, she invited me to see her at tomorrow's fashion show. Unfortunately, I actually had a schedule which couldn't permit that. I explained to her rather sheepishly that as much as I would like to, I could not see her at her show. I explained to her that I had a flight out the next morning, and had to get the train back to Florence. It was as though I had stood her up on something and it made her a little angry. But the reality was I was helping myself by not being such a lapdog looking for any crumb that she would throw out.

Which brings me to another rule of meeting supermodels, a rule that applies in many other aspects of life: keep them wanting more. She walked me over to an area where taxis collected. I had to go to the train station. A nice Italian cab driver opened his door for the two of us, but I had to explain that it was only me that was going. He was disappointed. She took her camera out and asked him to please take a photo of us. I did a somewhat forward act and put my hand around her shoulder. I don't think she even noticed. The Italian took a photo and nicely handed the camera back. I then bid farewell and told her I would be calling her every hour. She laughed.

I got in the cab and drove away, en route to the train station. The cab driver couldn't help but ask.

"How come you no kissa the girl?"

"I just met her today," I explained.

He looked quite confused at this response.

"I ask again, how come you no kissa the girl?"

I shook my head as we made it to the train station.

Chapter 13
BACK TO CALIFORNIA

That morning before I left my hotel in Florence, I called her to say good-bye.

"Thank you for such a lovely day."

I have never been more serious about a woman in my life.

"I enjoyed myself very much. Thank you," she was sweet enough to tell me.

"Good luck in your show today. I hope it all goes well."

"I *know* it will go well."

Of course she knows, and of course it will go well. I was overcome with emotion. This meeting was unexpected, unplanned, and completely perfect. I was under her spell, hook, line and sinker. I had written poetry since the age of 4. On the way back, a poem, perhaps a ballad, came to me. I wrote like a crazy man on the plane and penned one of my best ever, "Love in a Day."

Love in a Day
by Herman Franck, ESQ.
July 23,1998, on Return from Florence, Italy
Dedicated to my lovely, lovelier, loveliest wife Sabrina Q. Chen
I go away, as you stay, always away, it is your way. I fall in love in just a day.
You can't imagine love, like a song, it must unfold on its own, still you can't stop love, like a song that must be told, written on its own.
The whirlwind leaves blow away from the trees, not stopping for anyone. It takes the stormy rain, with rushing water up to my knee. This brings the leaves back to the tree.
Remember I am a gypsy magro, just as you are a gypsy strega. I travel all the time, born to find a view, in a calming port, the land of you. I make the impossible possible. The cold wind blowing becomes still, tropical.

No is on your lips, yes is on your mind, at least some of the time. I see the conflicting signs.

Yes, no, maybe, I don't know, maybe no. All answers are good from your lips to me. I imagine this idea, please let me tell. True love can be, even for just a day, even if never realized. Don't fight it away. You can't stop your heart; you can't break our small start.

Our way to meet to know to connect our hearts was such a tiny chance, like finding the same star. You were born a gypsy, always to go away, as was I, and so here we are, two swimming fish in the ocean. A million times no, but for me, maybe.

I return with thoughts of you. The clouds remind me of my hope for your feelings. I will try to bring you to you.

You may always be away, but remember with me, you were swept away. Like the windy leaf blown into the fountain.

So now you stay. The water can be poured on you, as I ask for your heart, kissing your hand. Not for your answer, but just to show you my thought.

Strange how love goes, it isn't up to you or me. We do not choose who we are, how we meet or our matching chemistry. We do not choose love; our hearts do.

You must be calm and gentle as I work to be. Relax, trust your heart, and allow our small start. Your gypsy way, away with me you find it all, love, in just a day.

When I arrived in San Francisco, I rewrote the poem in neater handwriting. It took six pages. I called her and asked if she had a fax number. She gave me her hotel fax number in Rome. One hour later, she called me in tears.

"That is the most beautiful poem I've ever read."

To me it seemed incredible, impossible, that I was actually getting to this *strega* supermodel. Which brings me to another rule about supermodels: if you have an artistic side, and virtually all of us do, show it. They are artists and will always appreciate a fellow artist. Don't be afraid. Be brave enough to show your vulnerable side, the side that men rarely show. I did it, and it totally worked.

Chapter 14
HOW TO MARRY A SUPERMODEL

The first thing you have to understand is that while you are away from the supermodel, she will be busy doing some fairly extraordinary things. As I toiled away at a rather mundane existence in my small law office, new lawsuits, green card applications, and the like, she was busy jetting all over Europe, attending fashion shows, traipsing down runways, being photographed by thousands of magazines, gracing the covers of them as well, and of particular note, being chased by all kinds of super-wealthy men.

So, how does a mild-mannered attorney win the heart of such an extraordinary woman? The first thing to know is you can't compete on the same basis as her multi-gazillionaire friends. They can fly her to Paris, end up in the five star hotels, limousine around France, purchase Cartier watches, expensive Gucci gowns, and the like—an endless showering of gifts that were well beyond my meager means. So, just don't. Don't even think of trying to compete with that. Imagine how ridiculous it would be to send her, say, a one hundred dollar present, when during that week she had received up to, say, forty thousand dollars in gifts. Just forget it. You'll only embarrass yourself.

What a person needs to do is turn inward and find their own skill sets to exploit. Coupled with this is the added challenge of conducting a romance campaign, on limited funds, from thousands miles away. She was in Milan, I was in San Francisco. The first thing I decided to do was to find a way to stay in her mind. Out of sight, out of mind, it is said. Unfortunately, it is a very true saying. So, don't be out of sight. Don't be out of mind.

Now, if I were a painter, which I'm not, I would've painted a picture every single day and I would have mailed it to her. I would've made it so that each day she would come home after meeting these millionaire guys, none of which in a million years would ever paint her anything, but from me she would receive a painting. I would hope that of all the gifts she received that week, she would set them aside and instead look at my painting and think, wow, this guy is special.

So, if you're a painter, paint. For me, I'm a poet, I'm a writer. So, what did I do? I wrote poems, an endless series of poems. My first poem to her was literally written on the plane flight home, and is called *Love in a Day*. Every day in the mail she would receive another one. These weren't poems that were going to rock the literary world to stop and take notice of me. None of these are going to be literature. These were poems for her. They weren't for the rest of the world. They were for Sassafras, and it touched a chord with her. She read them. I received a phone call back from her.

"Thank you for the lovely poem. I truly enjoyed it."

It made me feel as though I had a shot at this. At the same time, though, I couldn't help but notice the photographs in the newspaper. I saw one of her in France, under the Arc d'Triomphe, with some handsome Italian man. Oh boy, I thought. Look at that guy. Right next to him was his Ferrari. Great, I drive a truck. I'm thinking to myself, I've got to try to earn more money. But then I'm thinking, I'd have to earn enough for ten lawyers in order to even get close to what these guys are making. Unfortunately, I don't have star looks, I don't have connections to Hollywood, I don't have a chance of being in a movie, or getting any of my scripts into the right hands.

So, here's another idea. I thought about this and I went ahead and went for it. I knew that she had a further dream. She was excited about her modeling career, she loved to see her picture on the cover of all these fashion magazines, she loved the fancy clothes, all the attention; it is the ultimate career for an egocentric, narcissistic beauty. But there was something she wanted that it wasn't giving her: she wanted a role in a movie. Hmm, I thought, why don't I develop a screenplay that would be perfectly tailored to Sassafras? Something she could star in, something that she would love to read about, something that would catapult her from the runway to the red carpet of Hollywood.

Okey dokey, I thought. So, what's the story? What's the script? Then I thought about it. I had the perfect story. It's a story that is based on a family event that happened to my grandparents back in the 1930s. They lived in Shanghai, China. It's a rather sad story, but it had action and mysterious moments. My grandparents lost a set of male twins while in Shanghai. They were stolen. They never did find them. We never did know what on earth happened to them.

So, I thought about it and I came up with an idea. Why don't I write a story about what might have happened to them? I will tell a fictional tale. I called it, The Shanghai Twins. Oh boy, here we go. My first step was to write a synopsis of the story. It involved my grandparents, a humble professional couple from the Pacific Northwest. My grandmother was a pioneer attorney, my grandfather was an accountant. He took a job with a very wealthy aristocratic English family that run a tea empire in China. In all of the wealth of England, there was still somebody that needs to count it all up. That somebody was my grandfather, Robert Emmett Franck, CPA.

I came up with the idea that the aristocrats, last name Edwards, had a black sheep in the family that had married a psychotic aristocrat wannabe by the name of Alice. Alice Edwards had a major problem: she could not have children, and it drove her nuts. The other problem she had is back then, you couldn't adopt children in Shanghai. The further problem was that she married the black sheep of the Edwards family and the practice was to send the black sheep off to the Hinterlands, where they would be Burma, Singapore, or in Henry's case, to Shanghai, China.

They were stuck in China without children and it made Mrs. Edwards bonkers. In the same way she saw my very humble grandparents, they were everything she never was: regular, American, not pretentious, hard-working, professionally educated, simple, salt of the earth people. I say this with one sub-note, that my grandmother was intensely preoccupied with the notion of social climbing. She would love to get out of her small town law roots and arrive into a more aristocratic plane. However, you don't become an aristocrat; you are born one. My grandmother would sit idly by with jealousy over all the aristocrats that she was constantly dining with. My grandfather really didn't care that he was a modest man. He was proud of who he was, and he would be the first to tell them that he didn't own even half an acre of farmland. Instead, he was a man of genius capabilities, could add nine columns of numbers by just looking at them, and had a way with all matters of finance. He was the perfect quiet, type B, hardworking, detail-oriented, totally organized, down to earth professional to be employed by a black sheep psychotic aristocratic absolutely nuts couple from England.

My grandmother became pregnant. The Edwards were intensely jealous of her. Here they were with mega-millions, my grandparents making a small salary and having no assets, and the Edwards were jealous of the Francks. Imagine that. They wanted those children, and they actually made a rather odd contract with a local mafia group to arrange a nurse to fake the death of the Franck child. She would bring in a corpse from another baby that had recently died. They kept that baby in the refrigerator so that he would not decompose. When the Franck child was born, she took the child out of the birthing room, and upon her return noted that the child was dead. In fact, the Franck child had not died, and had been cleverly skirted out of the hospital by other co-conspirators, into the awaiting Rolls Royce purring in idle in the alleyway behind the hospital. Mrs. Edwards opened the door, her gloved hands came out, the child was placed in. She drove away with great happiness. At last she had that which God would not give her, she would take herself.

Well, a little problem happened to Mrs. Edwards that day. Nobody knew it, nobody could predict it, but things like this happen in life. My grandmother, three hours later, had a second child, a twin. This child was not pronounced dead at birth and was born exceptionally healthy, handsome, blue-eyed, blondish-brown hair; everything was absolutely perfect, all ten toes and all ten fingers. When news of this twin got to the Edwards, their faces turned ashen. This was a big problem. My grandparents lived in the British sector, even though they were American.

This was because they were employed by Brits. You couldn't really have one twin growing up across the street from the other twin. These were identical twins. You could not tell them apart.

You might wonder where in all this is a role for an Asian woman. I had a simple answer for that: my grandmother later would live in Japan and befriended some aristocratic Japanese of the Mikimoto Pearl family. She managed to become very close friends with them and enjoyed their company immensely. I transplanted this concept into a noblewoman by the name of Qin, who was married to a former ambassador. She and her ambassador husband would have a supporting role in this story, and would provide the indigenous Chinese element that would assist Mrs. Franck in the process of uncovering this terrible crime. It became a whodunit, following the death of her second twin—once again a fake death was planned and orchestrated.

The Francks went to an opera. When they returned, their house had burned down, and in the living room was the corpse of a young child. My grandmother was consumed with agony. It was already a huge devastation for her to have lost her first twin, but now to have lost her second, she became catatonic. Oddly, sitting in the driveway watching the flames go up, for some reason she decided to take the ashes from her house and throw them onto her face and hair. She looked a mess, black ashes over her white, white face; she was obviously in need of some serious psychological intervention.

Luckily, she got just that and was taken to the hospital for a lengthy regimen of psychiatric analysis, diagnosis, and treatment. She suffered a huge bout of depression. Unfortunately, back then they didn't have a lot of medicines like we do now to battle depression. They tried therapy—thank God this was before the days of electroshock therapy. She went into a quiet mode, which was much contrary to her general yakkity-yak way. But this tragedy had shut her down and would keep her down for a period of years.

It was this Chinese noblewoman who would bring her out of her shell. She would cuddle her, would hold her, would sing to her. She treated her almost like a young daughter, even though my grandmother at the time was a full adult, in her late 20s. During the ensuing dialogues between my grandmother and Qin, held at the hospital, figments of clues started to arise. The first was the birth certificate, oddly described as one even though it was more of a death certificate. It showed that the baby had died of toxemia, which is where the entire womb becomes toxic.

What was odd about that? It's sort of like having a vat of poison, then you put two animals in the poison and one dies but the other doesn't. How would the other child have survived? The answer, according to the doctors there, was that it would be simply impossible for the other child to survive toxemia. Thus, there were two possibilities. The first baby did not die of toxemia, and if it didn't die of toxemia, then what was the real story?

The next clue came in a rather tragic way. The corrupt nurse, with her own sense of right and wrong, committed suicide.

Right away, Qin smelled a rat. What was that about? Nurses don't commit suicide. They're among the most solid people out there. They know how to take care of people, they work hard, they have a no-nonsense career; they just don't do that. Right away she started checking things out. Later, my grandmother would approach Mrs. Edwards to find out where they had adopted that child. Mrs. Edwards explained that they were able to arrange it through a process in Singapore. She made up a trip that they had gone there. Qin had some good contacts in Singapore, as her husband used to be the Chinese ambassador there. Upon investigation, it was learned that the Edwards had never gone to Singapore and had never adopted any child there.

Aha! they thought. The process of Qin and my grandmother coming forward as a team of modern day detectives during the 1930s had all the elements of a psychological thriller. She brought my grandmother out of her shell, allowed my grandmother to re-find her legal abilities, and began a fairly tricky forensic process of uncovering every stone and piece of paper, all the crumbs of which led to the door of the Edwards' mansion in Shanghai.

The end of the story, of course, was full victory for the Francks. The twins were reunited with their parents, the Edwards were brought to jail, and my grandmother became an everlasting friend of an impressive Chinese noblewoman, to be played by Sassafras.

So, I wrote this script. Again, if I was a painter, I would've sent Sassafras a painting a day. I was a writer, and I wrote the script. I wrote it a little long. It was supposed to be one hundred and twenty pages, but leave it to me to end up with three hundred and thirty pages. But this was a real story—well, half real, half made up—I had a huge motivation in writing my heart out to chase down this model. I couldn't compete with diamonds, I couldn't compete with Gucci dresses, but if I could give her a script that gave her not a starring role, but the first supporting role in an American-Chinese drama set in the opulent Shanghai of the 1930s, this would get her hand in marriage. I was sure of it.

So, I sent her the script. Oh, my god. After she read that, I'm telling you right now, she was mine. She cried on the phone, she told me it was the most beautiful, incredible story ever, she told me she had no idea that I had this connection to China. This is just incredible.

"My own family is from Shanghai. In fact, I have about one-fourth British blood in me. There was a little incident involving a British family with one of the hired help, and there was a payoff for her to basically disappear and have the baby. That baby was my great-grandmother."

Several generations later, Sassafras was born in a hybrid mix of mostly Chinese, Cantonese, Shanghai-nese, accentuated by some lovely Anglo features from her one-fourth British blood. She had a slightly different kind of mouth, more elongated, less round; her face had more Anglo features, which was perfect for a Chinese model. As it happens, the Asian looks become more powerful when blended with a bit of the Anglo.

I had connected on several levels here. Sassafras had a goal to move beyond her modeling career into show business. I had connected up with her own family background in Shanghai, connecting up with my own interesting roots there as well. These common grounds and the allure of a phenomenal story by the name "The Shanghai Twins" began the process of winning over Sassafras's hand in marriage.

Chapter 15
HOLLAND

I rarely have to go to Europe, but as it would happen, I had a mission in The Hague. It is where my grandfather's family came from back in the 1890s. But I was not going there on a family reunion. Instead, I'd become registered with the United Nations International Court established for the prosecution of war crimes in Yugoslavia. This was before the United Nations set up a permanent war crimes court.

There is a process by which attorneys from all over the world can become, in effect, licensed to practice before that court. Part of the process is showing documentation that you are an attorney in good standing in your own country's jurisdiction. Part of it includes an interview process. I had gotten through phase one by completing all my documents, and I now needed to complete phase two, an interview with several of the judges. For this reason, I needed to travel to The Hague. I contacted Sassafras about this.

"Darling"—I love calling her that—"I need to go to The Hague, Holland. Any chance you could meet me up there?"

I was so happy to hear her respond immediately.

"Of course! Just tell me when and where and I will be there."

This was a wonderful opportunity, as our entire relationship had subsisted on just one chance meeting in Florence, a bunch of poems, and one screenplay called "The Shanghai Twins." On top of that, I called her every day and spoke with her at length about absolutely nothing. But we needed to see each other. The physical part of our relationship had not happened, and it needed to happen. We were well past the introductory phase and needed to progress to the next level. I was very excited about this.

"Let me organize the hotel search."

I figured I would agree with this. She knew her way around Europe.

"Why, certainly."

I told her the date, which was in just two weeks. She didn't even ask me why I needed to go there, and I figured I might as well not even explain it. It's just kind of a strange thing to explain to somebody. "I'm trying to represent a person indicted for killing six thousand people." How obnoxious is that?

I flew out from San Francisco to Amsterdam. I would meet Sassafras there. Oh my god, I just can't believe how beautiful she is. I decided to do something before I left. Generally speaking, it is not a good idea to be pushy with women.

You should proceed slowly but deliberately. You should proceed unambiguously, though, not as a friend interest, but as a romantic interest. But if you get too pushy, they'll get turned off and it won't work. So far I had been very slow; writing poems, writing a screenplay, talking on the phone. Nothing was forward about that. But this time, I decided it was time to make a move. So, before I left, I did something a little bit obnoxious, shall we say: I bought her a wedding dress.

Oh my god, like I could possibly choose what wedding dress she would want. As though I even had a right to buy her such a dress, and as though I would ever pick one out that she would actually like.

I went down to Union Square. One of the great stores there is Saks Fifth Avenue. I found a perfect wedding dress for her. It was a size 2, which would be a little bit big for her, it was white, of course, long, without sleeves. It was elegant, it was simple, it was made of satin, and the good news, it was on sale. Oh my goodness, I could actually afford this little item! I will not brag about how little I paid for it. The good news is that it looked extremely expensive. It would match even the gifts of all these Ferrari-toting Euro men that had been chasing her throughout Italy, France, Germany, Belgium, and probably somewhere in Holland.

I arrived in Amsterdam first and went to the hotel. I checked in. The room was absolutely gorgeous. I thought right away, I can't afford this. But I was only staying there for a couple of days, so I thought, what the hell. Let's splurge a bit. I returned to the airport to pick her up. I waited and I was reminded of this idea of a man waiting at an airport or waiting at a train station for the woman of his dreams, and she never shows. I thought, oh God, what's going to happen? She'll be a no-show, I'll be crushed, I'll have to go down to The Hague by myself, have my war crimes interview, and then return with my tail between my legs back to San Francisco.

Just as I was having these rather pessimistic thoughts, who gets off the plane from Milan but Sassafras. Oh heavens. Will you look at that. She was absolutely gorgeous, wearing pants and a simple shirt, carrying a small round bag. So elegant, so simple, and she had this beaming smile. She came up to me and did something that melted my spine. She put her hand on my cheek. I don't know what it is, but when a woman does that to a man, we just turn into water. I was already under her spell; now I was infused in her spell. She had me from that pawing, until death do us part.

When we got back to the hotel, I walked into the room and I couldn't help but tell her.

"Sassafras, I have a present for you."

"Oh, really? What's that?"

She saw a big box sitting on the bed. It was white with a red bow around it, compliments of the free gift wrapping service that accompanies even sale items at Saks Fifth Avenue. How cool is that?

She was an elegant woman, but the way she opened that box was like an animal. That ribbon was not neatly untied, it was ripped off. My goodness, I thought. The box was torn and came off in an abrupt manner. She didn't place it to the side, she threw it across the room Frisbee-style. It went in several circles, landed near a chair, bounced onto the ground, and came to a rest at approximately a forty-five degree angle. I thought, okay, this is the way she's going to open the box.

She brought out the dress. This is where I was actually scared to death. She could've seen that dress and thought, what a piece of garbage, and who the hell do you think you are buying me a wedding dress, as if you would know anything about it, and as though I would ever marry a little peasant like you in the first place. These were the thoughts that went through my now frozen spinal cord.

But I was quickly relieved. Oh my goodness, she loves it. She, right then and there in front of me, took off her clothes and put that dress on. I was thinking, oh God, are you going to strip naked for me? But she didn't strip naked. She had this beautiful bra and panty set that I'll never forget in my life. The lace was something that they probably only sell in Italy or France or somewhere like that. It probably cost more than my sale rack special wedding dress.

I pretended to turn around, but she said, "Oh come now, we're all adults."

She put the dress on. She turned her back to me and said, "Would you please zip it up?"

But of course, I thought. I zipped it up. She walked over to the mirror. She turned to the side, she turned to the other side, she turned full frontal, she turned back, and then she looked at me and said some words that still send a chill up my spine whenever I think of it:

"Am I pretty enough for you?"

Oh God, by about seven thousand miles. Are you kidding? Looking at her in that white dress with this glowing smile, I could see in two seconds amazingly enough she didn't just like it, she LOVED it.

She held her arms out and gave me this huge kiss. Then, to my permanent amazement—and believe me, things like this never happen to me—she took it off and began the process of—well, you know. I'm going to keep this a family rated story, so we won't get into the details of what happened. But suffice it to say that at that point, I was so hooked on this girl that if she were ever to dump me, and of course she would, I would just die.

Chapter 16
THE HAGUE

We traveled by train to The Hague. It's not a very long ride. It's quite beautiful going through all the tulip lands of Holland. I explained to her the rather odd purpose of my trip. This was so out of her world that she found it puzzling and yet still, happily, a little bit interesting. She did not mind that I would be representing some of the most evil people on the planet. For her, it was the notion of doing something important that mattered.

"It sounds like very high level international law."

I looked at her and thought, wow, that's exactly what it is, and this is exactly why I wanted to do it. I was trying to get out of my own meager practice of law, in the trenches of green card applications, and get into the more high-falutin law of war crimes trials. This was a million miles from San Francisco, and yet I was there. I was a contender. I was getting in.

But as I would also later learn, there are high-falutin aspects in the international realm of American green card law. More on that later.

We drove by the Queen's palace in The Hague. Very impressive. The cab driver was a little bit grumpy about the prince of the castle. Apparently he was thought of to be a bit lazy. He didn't have a job, he didn't really do anything.

I said to the cab driver, "What is a Prince supposed to do?"

He responded rather grumpily, "He can clean my taxi."

Sassafras and I both giggled at this disdain for royalty and understood it to be simply the opinion of a person who had little, concerning a person who had a lot.

A day later, we were back in Amsterdam. We walked around this Venice style city with canals and waterways throughout. For some reason, she was tantalized by the red light district and would stand and watch the odd display of women standing before a window with red light on, showing themselves to would-be customers.

The next day we would have to part again at the airport. She would fly to Milan, I would fly back to San Francisco. Her plane left first. I held her hand. I wanted to cry, but I was trying to be strong. I kissed her. She was in the process of leaving when suddenly she turned back and asked me a question I'll never forget in my life:

"So, are you going to marry me or what?"

I was stunned at that. I could only say one thing: "Of course I am."

She kissed me again. I told her for the first time, "I love you."

She responded, "You better."

She got on the plane and flew away while my head spun. On the flight home, I penned another poem.

Of Course I'll Marry You
Written October 14, 2008 in Amsterdam and en route back to San Francisco
Well of course I'll marry you,
I love you through and through
I'm always going to stay with you,
For all of my life,
as husband and wife.

Wherever we are, no matter how far,
I'm going to be there for you.
I'm going to love you now and forever
I'm going to stay with you.
I'm never going to let you slip away.
I know how to seize this chance.
To bring you over to be mine.
Such a lovely, lovelier, loveliest find.

Of course I'll marry you.
I love you through and through.
In everyway, everyday.
We will always stay.
I'll never let you get away.
For all my days with you.

Take my cold house.
Lights off all the time, no rugs on the floor.
Can you warm it for me?

The lights are on again
And now I see myself.
No so alone at my home,
With your love in me.

I'm never turning back.
Now I'm never going to die.
With you love always to my side.
The glow on your cheek
I feel so weak.

As I look to your warmth.
You don't have to speak
You say it all in your looks to me
Your ways with me. You wave me.
Hold me in my arms, wrap your legs a around me.
Touch my cheek. Take away the harm.
Hold my face with your soft way,
I feel the trust in you this way.
Nobody touches this way unless they are in love.
Only somebody in love can be this way.

This glow, ambient, such enchantment
The warm touch of love
Knowing its presence, its force,
Its calming still, slow the rain,
Ease the terrain, sleep sleepy sleep.
All night till morning again.

I cannot imagine it
Any other way.
There is really nothing else to do.

I look to see, I listen to hear.
I speak to say to such my precious dear:

YES of course
Without a doubt
Positively certain, forward and clear,
Of course I'll marry you.

I wrote that on one of the postcards they provide on the airplane. When I arrived in San Francisco, before I left the airport, I put stamps on it, put it in a mailbox, and knew it would get to her in a matter of three or four days. Amazingly, my dream of marrying Sassafras was becoming a reality.

Chapter 17
CHRISTMAS IN SAN FRANCISCO

I belong to a social group here in San Francisco called the Guardsmen. It's a very nice group of professional gentlemen, generally aged 28 to about 40 or so. We are engaged in various philanthropic projects, the core of which is a Christmas tree store that we operate during the Christmas season. The profits of this store fund a program to pay the summer camp fees for inner city youth who would otherwise never in a million years get to go to summer camp. We had sent thousands and thousands of kids from the inner cities of Oakland, San Jose, San Francisco, and elsewhere, off to places where pine trees replace sky scrapers. They come back and face their environment again with the benefit of having seen the gifts of Mother Nature. It doesn't solve all their problems, it doesn't replace or reduce the poverty, but it helps.

It was during this Christmas season that I had my next date with Sassafras. She came to San Francisco, thank God, and spent the Christmas holidays with me. I had purchased a diamond ring. Actually, not exactly a ring; I bought a diamond from an estate. Okay, it's a used diamond, but what's the difference? A diamond lasts, what, a million years? So, the fact that someone else owned it before, does that really matter? I bought a new setting, shiny as can be, and had the ring attached to it by a jeweler. It is the kind of ring that you could have spent seven thousand dollars on, but in my case, doing it in this crafty manner, it cost just a matter of a couple thousand. This was in my meager budget.

I had a big plan to propose to Sassafras while she was here in San Francisco. Do you think that made me nervous? She stayed at my house, which was probably the lowest kind of living arrangement she had experienced since living in China, but I wanted her to know who I was and what I was. One of my friends had already accused me of lying to her and saying I was rich. No, I didn't do that. She knew what was up—at least, I hoped she did. I didn't want to disappoint her into thinking I was some rich megabucks American lawyer, when in fact, I was a lawyer trying to make a living working with clients some of which could pay, many of which could not.

I took her to the tree lot. Now, this is a fish out of water story. Here's this international supermodel walking in an indoor tree lot. It was a bit like an indoor forest; all the trees were upright, my fellow Guardsmen were wearing our green jumpsuits, heavy gloves, and boots. We would take trees out as they were selected by customers, cut off the base, put a new base on, and put the tree onto the cars. It was hard work, to say the least, and we did it all for free.

She was not that interested in this process. First of all, as a Buddhist, she didn't really understand the whole concept of Christmas. She never had a Christmas tree and didn't realize what an important symbol it was to many in the United States and elsewhere. Second, she despised the whole notion of manual labor. Her world, of course, was a pristine existence. She didn't mind my world as a lawyer, that would be okay, but when she saw me working as a manual laborer, even if for a philanthropic purpose, she became negative, disenfranchised. I sensed her silence when we went home and tried to understand it.

"Oh, nothing's wrong."

"Yet you're so quiet."

"It's okay."

"Well, what is it?"

"I don't like that place."

"Oh, I'm sorry. I thought you would."

"You thought wrong."

She got snappy at me. Wow. Is this our first fight? I realized, of course, we're always going to have an argument at some point, but over a Christmas tree, or ten thousand Christmas trees? I tried not to pursue the discussion and took note of the fact that she simply didn't appreciate Christmas trees. Fine, I thought.

I then saw the first exhibition of the dark side of Sassafras. There are plenty of songs written about the whole notion that every rose has a thorn. I might add to it that the sharpness of that thorn could very well be directly proportionate to the extremeness of the beauty of the rose. The most beautiful, gorgeous rose on the planet was now one dangerous thorn. And for Sassafras, her thorn was a psychological defect of some sort that would send her into an oblivion of anger, depression, and darkness over absolutely nothing.

The rest of the night, she sat in my living room, silent and angry. She refused to say a word to me. I tried to get her talking again, but it was no use.

"Sassafras, please, don't close me out."

"I am not closing you out. I just don't feel like talking."

"Okay, okay."

It continued like this for the rest of the night. The next morning, the day I had planned on proposing to her, she organized all on her own to leave. A cab pulled up, she had her bags all packed, she looked at me, didn't say goodbye, turned, got in the cab, and drove off to the San Francisco Airport for a flight to Milan.

I sat there with my two thousand dollar used diamond ring in my pocket. I don't usually do this kind of thing, but I couldn't help but cry. I thought, she's gone, I'll never see her again. I shook my head and went back to bed, crying my way to sleep and realizing that the biggest dream of my life had just walked out.

Chapter 18
THE HOOKER AND THE LAWYER

There are those times when the best therapy is a hooker. I am not above it or below it, and I know where to find it. It's simple, really. You walk down to where the massage parlors are. Oh my goodness, what those girls can do with their hands!

This gal, her name was Ieato, was quite hot. She was a Filipina, about late 20s, small proportions as they often are, and having a facial structure with poised lips ready to go. She was actually sleeping. I felt kind of bad. The mamasan had no problem waking her up.

"Gosh!"

"Let the poor girl sleep," I said.

"No, she go with you."

Okay, I thought. The girl dutifully woke up, took me by the hand, and walked me back to her massage room. There was nothing but a table, some oils, and a pillow. The massage, of course, is about one-twentieth of the experience that is paid for. The rest is something that we won't get into, in order to keep this story with a PG rating.

The surprising part was in the aftermath. Most of these girls are wham, bam, thank you, sir. They are profit seekers and, since they receive a flat rate, the quicker they get you off (excuse the phrase), the quicker they can get a new customer in. It's the same principle that restaurants use, turn those tables. But this one was different. Afterwards, *she spoke to me*. Ooh, I thought. How interesting.

"You look sad," were her first words.

I'm not a man that cries often, but for some reason those words made me cry. Not like a baby, but tears came down. There's something about a man being in a vulnerable state that makes him quite attractive to women. Most men might incorrectly think crying is a sign of weakness and that the last thing any woman wants is a big crybaby. We must not forget the nurturing side of women. They love to take care of people. This is an innate quality of the Filipino girls who, when they don't occupy themselves at massage parlors, are more commonly occupying positions as registered nurses.

She could sense my sorrow. I don't know what it was to her. Big deal, some guys that's sad and gets a hooker. Who cares? But she cared. She wanted to know,

"What happened?"

"I got dumped."

"Oh, poor guy. Did you think she was the last girl on the planet of Earth?"

"No, of course she's not."

"Did this happen a hundred years ago? Or yesterday?"

"It happened yesterday."

And then she said, at the same time I said it.

"But it seems like a hundred years ago."

A hundred years of sorrow, all compacted in a twenty-four hour period. She soothed me,

"Look, the girl is gone, there'll be another. You know how it goes. Life goes on."

"Pick up the pieces."

That was my remark. Indeed, pick them up, move on. I knew I could make it forward, I just needed a little crutch, a helping hand. The Filipino hooker is better than a bag of cocaine or a vial of heroin.

As I dressed, I pulled out my wallet. She thought I was going to give her a tip, an amount past what I had already paid.

"Oh, please don't. It's not necessary. I know you enjoyed yourself," she told me with a smile.

I smiled. Actually, I wasn't going to give her a tip at all, cheap guy that I am. I was going to give her my business card in some kind of weird hope that somewhere, somehow, on some imaginary planet, this girl would call me. Yeah, right.

You know what they say, be careful what you wish for. The following day my phone rang. "BRRING. BRRING." My favorite sound. You never know what's going to happen when the phone at a law office rings. A new prisoner case? New criminal case? Immigrations appeal? Or, as it was in this case, a Filipino massage girl calling up for some interesting and a bit of titillating legal advice.

"Hi," she said, as though I would know who she was.

"It's me."

"Oh sure, me, I know you."

But I did know her. I knew the voice right away. It was very hard to understand her. Her accent was rather pronounced. I knew who it was.

"Hey, how are you?"

"I'm good. Can you help me on something?"

Like I was going to say no to that.

"What's the problem?"

"I have a problem with my husband."

"Oh?"

\ "He got kind of rough with me the other night."

"I see. What did he do?"

"He slapped me, he pushed me on the bed, he told me to get out. I didn't want to go out. Then he left."

"Did you call the police?"

"No. He didn't hurt me that bad this time."

"Has he done this before?"

She was quiet for a second, then she responded.

"Yes. Several times."

"I'm sorry."

"I don't feel like starting a whole criminal case against him. I also don't think what he did was enough to be a crime. It was just a slap. But I don't want him back."

"Okay."

"Can you help me get some kind of restraining order?"

"Okay, I can help you on that. You have to come into my office."

"I think it would be much better if you came to *my* office."

I thought, okay, great. I'll show up with my briefcase, tape recorder, pad and pencil, and take copious notes of the terrible events that transpired the other night at this nice hooker's home.

"Okay."

"Let me look at my schedule."

"Oh, I was thinking you could come over right now."

"Right now?"

"Yeah. Unless you're busy."

"Oh, no. I um, I um—I'm not busy. I mean, I am busy, but I can, uh, you know, I can come over."

"I don't want to put you out if you've got other more important things to do..."

"Oh no, this is very important. I want to help you. So yeah, let's get together, say, in fifteen minutes."

My office was not that far from hooker land and I figured I could use a good walk. So, I picked up a tape recorder, which is my way of taking notes, and strolled down a few streets to the Mirage Massage Parlor. I just hate overdressing. Showing up in my blue pinstriped suit, Brooks Brothers button down white shirt and yellow tie, and black leather shoes was a ridiculous example of overdressing for a massage parlor.

As I was walking in, I tried to telepath to everybody watching me go in, "It's not what it looks like." Yeah, right. I rang the bell. I was let in by the nice mamasan, who was puzzled to see me in this outfit. The night before, I was much more casually dressed.

Ieato walked out and brightened my day in the dark lobby of the massage parlor. She was wearing a short silk negligee. She lived in sleeping clothes. She had those clear heeled shoes, pumps I think they call them, the sort that they like to film women with in porno movies. I don't know what it is about a girl that wears shoes in bed, but somehow it makes it more exciting.

She held my hand and walked me back to one of the massage rooms. I decided to make this a more professional meeting and kept my clothes on. I sat on the bed, took my tape recorder out, and explained to her,

"You talk, I listen. I tape, you talk, I listen, I tape. Are you ready?"

She nodded her head. She was quite somber and serious in this process. This was no joking matter for her.

"We have been married two years. He is gone a lot. When he comes back, often drunk, he's mad at me. He knows my job. He knows what I do."

I stopped her.

"He's jealous?"

"Yes. I try to explain, these men, their business is nothing, it's no emotion, but he never believes it."

I looked at her mouth as she spoke. Just business, I thought.

"So, tell me what happened."

"It was two nights ago. He was drunk. He slapped me."

"Okay, stop right there. Tell me what part of his body came into what part of your body."

"The back of his hand. He did a backhand."

She motioned like a tennis player.

"It hit me right here in the cheek."

I took my glasses off and examined her as though I were a medical doctor of some sort. I could not find a mark. She saw that I was looking for one and explained,

"As I said, it wasn't that hard of a hit. That's why I didn't call the police."

"Okay."

"Then he threw me down on the bed."

"You didn't hit the floor?"

"No."

"Did your head hit anything?"

"A pillow."

"So, you didn't get hurt by this?"

"No."

"Tell me how he pushed you."

"He just pushed me."

She pushed her hands out, showing his movement.

"Show me on me."

She takes her hands and pushes my shoulder. She was actually kind of a strong girl. I remarked.

"Wow, you work out?"

"Are you kidding? Every day for three hours at the Nautilus."

I looked at her legs and I could see this was not some lay about gal. This was an athletic, well-toned sex machine that used her body to earn a living, and there's nothing wrong with that.

"Then he left."

"And that was it?"

"Well, after he left he called me and he said something. It was terrible."

She got super serious. She started to cry. I was thinking, what could it have been?

"He said—"

And she went into tears and crying and emotions. I turned off my tape recorder and tried to console her. I patted her back as though that would help. Men are so un-nurturing, or at least this man is. She looked up with her red eyes, tears rolling down her cheeks, and explained to me,

"He said he was going to kill my children."

Ooh. This was a bit serious.

"Your children?"

"Yes."

"They live with you?"

"No."

"Okay, does he know where they live?"

"He does. They're in El Cerrito."

For those of you not from the San Francisco Bay area, it is an East Bay city that no one would ever have a reason to go to, other than to find real estate less than a million dollars.

"So, your children—I'm sort of thinking out loud—they don't live with you; I'm guessing they live with, what, their father?"

Gee, go to the head of the class. But oh, when we assume, we get things wrong.

"No," she said. "They're with a couple."

"A couple?"

"Yeah."

"A couple of what?"

"A couple of people."

"Oh, what's that about?"

"The father's gone."

"Well, if the father's gone—look, maybe I don't need to know this, but why aren't you having the kids?"

She looked at me again and started bawling, this time much more extreme than before. I turned off my tape recorder again and patted her on the back. I held her. She kept crying and crying, her head on my shoulder.

"I'm sorry, I get so upset."

"It's okay. Don't worry, I'm here. I don't need to know. It's really not—"

And then she explained.

"They hate me."

"Oh. They hate you?"

"They hate me. When I left their father, he turned them against me. He told them what I did, that I was a whore, that I was a bad girl, that I slept with many men, that I use my body to make a living. They were young. They shouldn't have even learned of these things at that age. He knew it would turn them against me. He said, 'Mommy is dirty. Mommy is bad.' And now they hate me."

"Well, where is he? I mean, if he's going to destroy your relationship with him, I don't understand why he would not be there for them."

"Because he's an idiot and a loser. He can't hold a job, he can't afford a house, I don't even know where he is."

"Okay, so this couple, are they adopting them?"

"No. I pay them."

"You pay them?"

"Yes."

"You pay them to raise your kids that hate you and their father is gone?"

She looked at me and realized how awful that sounded. She continued crying. I felt bad, as though I had judged her, and who am I to judge this poor girl? My goodness, she's a nice girl, a pretty girl, trying to make a living, trying to take care of her two boys, trying to deal with the fact that they hate her for what she is, who she is, even though she really isn't that person. I didn't see her as a whore. I didn't see her as dirty. I saw her as a gorgeous, athletic, well-toned beauty with untold talents, a beautiful soul, a lovely heart, and a set of lips to die for. And here I was judging her?

"Oh, I'm sorry, dear. I didn't mean to say it that way. Please forgive me."

"No, it's okay. I know, I know."

She continued crying.

"No matter what, I will protect them. I don't want him to kill them. Please, will you help me stop him?"

Can you imagine how utterly pathetic you would have to be to not take this case?

"Of course I'll help you. I need to prepare a petition to enjoin harassment, and in it I will include your two children. They're boys?"

She nodded. There was a small wicker box by the candles. She opened it up and in it was a framed photo. It was her, looking quite motherly, with her two sons.

It's interesting seeing someone in one environment, a massage parlor, and then seeing them glow in motherhood in a completely different environment. She had a nice navy blue dress on, her hair was combed back, and the boys looked like they adored their mother.

"I'm sorry, I don't see hate here. I see love."

"It is love and it is hate. They know I'm here for them, I take care of them."

"Okay, listen. I have enough information. I will prepare the documents. You need to come by my office tomorrow to sign them, and we will file them with the court. A restraining order will issue the same day. I need to serve him, then there will be a hearing about ten days later to see about having a three year restraining order. That's the procedure."

"Thank you so much."

I have to say that the tenderness of the emotions that I saw with this girl made sex with her the furthest thing from my mind. She had gone from sex object to, well, what do you call this? Beautiful mother? Protective mother? Protective mother over sons that hate her for knowing who she is, but not really knowing who she is. If they did know, they would love her. Maybe somehow there would be a way to explain this to them. I don't know. Maybe someday I'll meet them and I'll tell them myself, "Boys, your mother is a wonderful woman."

By two o'clock the next day, a family law judge has issued a temporary restraining order against Huey Chong, restraining him from coming within one hundred feet of Karen Stamos. Okay, guess what, her real name isn't Ieato. We listed her two boys, Thomas and Robert. Their father, formerly an enlisted man in the Navy, was white and met her in the Philippines, so the kids had this Filipino-white mixed race situation going on. One was 7, one was 8.

I sent the temporary restraining order out to my process server. She found him at work. He was a golf professional, of all things, working in the pro shop at a somewhat elegant country club. To protect everyone at that club, many of whom knew Ieato, or Karen, quite well, I will not mention the club's name. It's a rather embarrassing thing to be served with a restraining order at any place, but especially in a shi-shi country club. The process server asked for ID. He showed him a driver's license.

"What's this about?"

"We're serving some papers on you. You've been served."

Others in the club turned. They knew what that meant. Many of them had been served with something at some point. He opened it up and read it. He was pissed.

"That bitch!"

The club members looked up at him. He realized he was out of line.

"Excuse me."

The hearing was eleven days later. It was a Tuesday, the nine o'clock calendar. It's always kind of interesting going to family law court. You never know who you're going to meet. As it happened on this delightful day, one of my debutante friends happened to be there on a divorce hearing in her own case. This girl was actually super cool, super beautiful, and was sitting on the bench in front of the courtroom.

"Hello, Herman!"

"Oh hi, Carol, good to see you! Oh God, you're here on your case."

She looked sheepishly embarrassed.

"Yes. It's a support order hearing."

"Well, good luck."

It was kind of awkward for me because I was friends with her husband as well. He was sitting a few benches away. I waved at him. He waved at me. Karen saw this right away and showed me a little something also innate in Filipino women. I suppose I shouldn't limit it to them.

"Who's that girl?"

"Oh, she's a friend of mine."

"Really? She's got a court case? Is it like mine?"

"Uh, no. It's nothing like yours. It's just a hearing, she's getting divorced and it's a spousal support motion. So, it's nothing too dramatic."

"So she's a single woman?"

I looked at her. I started to see where she was going with this.

"Look, she's just a friend. Don't worry."

"Why don't you marry her?"

"No, no, no. I'm not going to marry her. Don't worry. She's just a friend."

"Are you sure?"

"I'm sure."

She smiled at me. Carol looked over, seeing what appeared to be, and indeed was, an inappropriate relationship between attorney and client. I didn't need to say a word about it. It was kind of one of those "a man's got to do what a man's go to do" situations. I mean, she could see right away why I'd be attracted to this girl. She was devastatingly gorgeous. She could also see that the girl had a little something nasty about her.

The courtroom doors opened. We all went in. It was rather interesting; my case got called first. So there's Carol dying to hear what this is about, and I've got to put on this whole story about this night in question. He was there, Mr. Chong, wearing some kind of golf pro outfit. He looked pathetically preppy. Asian preppy is something I'm still not used to, but it exists in a big way. He walks in like he just got off an eighteenth hole, as though he didn't have a care in the world. The way it works is I get to first explain to the judge what the issues are. The judge then gets to ask questions.

"Ma'am, is this your petition?"

She looked at me. I looked at her and ushered her to answer.

"Yes."

"Are the facts stated in this declaration true and correct?"

"Yes."

"Did he hit you?"

"He slapped me. He pushed me on the bed."

"Did that hurt you?"

"No, it just scared me."

"And then he made a threat?"

"He called me and made that threat."

"He threatened to kill your children?"

"Yes."

"Anything else?"

"Nothing further, Your Honor."

It was now Chong's turn.

"Mr. Chong, you may cross-examine the witness."

He came out blasting.

"Are you a whore?"

The courtroom was aghast.

"Objection, relevance."

The judge thought about it.

"Sustained."

"Don't you make your living with your body?"

"Same question, objection, relevance."

"Sustained. Look, Mr. Chong, you are not allowed to ask questions that have no bearing on whether this wife of yours became a victim of your assault on her. I don't care if she's an astrophysicist or a street person; you don't have the right to hit her. Do you understand? So, here's the real question, sir: did you hit her? Yes or no?"

Now, if you want to deny something in court, you'd better deny it immediately, forcefully, and convincingly. Don't be silent, put your head down, and look at your toes, and then sheepishly say, "No."

"What? I didn't hear that."

"No, Your Honor."

"Oh, that's pretty convincing. 'No, Your Honor'?"

The judge mimicked his slight whisper.

"Look, I don't know if 'no' means the same thing in your language as it does to mine."

The judge was sounding a little bit racist here. He was one of these white-Irish San Francisco judges kind of poking fun at this Asian guy. I thought it was a little bit funny. Others giggled.

"No means no."

The guy got a little tough with the judge.

"Watch out."

"Oh, okay. Now you're coming right out and denying it. Now, that's a denial. I mean, hey, Mr. Chong, if you're going to deny something, by all means come out and deny it! Don't leave me wondering if maybe you're lying. Mr. Chong, are you lying to me?"

Again, the poor guy looks down at his feet and sheepishly says, "No."

"Okay, next question."

"Did you push her on the bed?"

You know, these cases you can get like a half confession, and then the whole thing is confessed.

"Maybe I pushed her a little," he said.

Ooh, I thought, there you go. Green light. Bingo. The bell rang. Case closed. Convicted, wrongful human bad guy beat up his hooker wife and shame on you."

The judge took it all in.

"Maybe a little, huh? Maybe a little or maybe a medium amount or maybe a lot? Which is it?"

"I pushed her a little."

"Okay. And then you left?"

"I left."

"Did you make a phone call to her afterwards?"

I studied his answer. This would be interesting.

"No, I did not."

Now, that denial was almost convincing.

"Okay, so you deny the slap, you admit the push, and deny the death threat. Is that what we've got?"

"Yes, Your Honor."

"Counsel, do you have any questions of him?"

I could see the judge was ready to rule on my side. I could've prolonged the situation by asking all kinds of questions. I didn't want to press my luck. There were another thirty cases waiting, including Carol's. But I thought I should ask one question:

"Do you respect your wife?"

Oh, I got him there. If she's a whore, he doesn't respect her, and if he doesn't respect her, he'll hit her. He realized he couldn't say he didn't respect her because he knew I had him in this little trap. It was a nice little checkmate. If he said he respected her, then that means his question to her about being a whore was a total lie. So, either he's a liar or he's a hitter, and either answer, I win. He gave the middle piss-ass answer:

"I don't know."

The judge shook his head. He didn't really care if the guy respected her or not. He'd heard enough.

"Counsel, matter submitted."

This is a code word in court meaning I've heard enough, I'm ready to decide, you're going to win, so sit down and shut up and let me hand you your victory.

"Matter submitted, Your Honor."

I knew the right thing to say.

"All right. I find there is sufficient evidence to issue a three year restraining order. Respondent, Mr. Chong, I want you to know you are hereby ordered to stay one hundred feet away from Karen Stamos and her two children, Robert and Thomas. You are restrained from calling them, contacting them, harassing them, molesting them, striking them, or hurting them in any way, shape, or form. Do you understand these orders?"

"Your Honor, I do, and I have no reason to ever see this woman again."

"Very well. As long as you obey the order, we're all going to be fine."

He started to walk away.

"Mr. Chong, don't leave just yet. My clerk is preparing the order and will be serving it."

The clerk was typing as the judge was talking, filling out a court form, printing it out, making a copy, handing one to the bailiff. The bailiff walked over, handed it to Mr. Chong, and then gave me a copy. Mr. Chong abruptly walked out.

I walked out. I had to look at Carol one more time. She looked at me with this kind of "I know what you're up to" look. I smiled. She smiled, and her husband, my fairly good friend, just shook his head. The lawyer and the hooker in court. Isn't that just swell.

There's a rule that the woman generally gets to leave first, and they hold the man back about five minutes so that the two don't see each other outside of court, but Chong left so quickly that we didn't even have a chance to get in front of him. So, the bailiff asked us to wait a bit. We waited right outside the courtroom door with the bailiff. She looked at me. Oh boy, was I ever her knight in shining armor, her hero, her savior, protector of her children, do-gooder. That was me.

When the bailiff finally walked away, she gave me a big smooch right on the lips.

"Oh, thank you! Thank you! Can I see the order?"

"Why, of course."

I handed it to her.

"Show me where it says my kids are protected."

I showed her the language right there.

"Protected persons, you see it right there, Robert and Thomas."

"Oh, thank you! Thank you!"

She hugged me again. We walked out of the courthouse. I had this feeling I was in for a reward. We didn't even need to talk about it. We got into my car, a Mercedes SUV, and drove to my house.

Inside, she did something that distinguished me from her customers: she kissed me on the lips. Hookers don't kiss customers on the lips. It's too loving, too caressing, too thoughtful, too sensitive. I knew that. I was now special, how about that.

What happened next is obvious enough and will not be detailed here. I shook my head at the oddities of life, the ebb and flows, tragedy, miracle, sadness, happiness, love, hate; you just never know what's going to happen.

Chapter 19
JUST AS I WAS ABOUT TO GIVE UP ON HER

The following day, my doorbell rang. It was a FedEx deliveryman. Hmm, I thought, what could this be? The sender address was Milan, Italy. I opened it to find two items: a cell phone with a Post-It note:

"Call me."

Attached to the cell phone was an envelope. I opened the envelope. Inside were airplane tickets in my name, San Francisco to Milan, leaving in four days. Oh, I guess we're back on? She had placed her name and number as the only contact phone number on the cell phone. Of course, I called her.

"Bongiorno."

"Hello, Sassafras. It's me, Herman."

"Oh, thank you for calling me."

"How could I not? I got this fancy cell phone."

Indeed, the phone was far fancier than my crummy little phone, which had become disconnected due to my unfortunate failure to pay the phone bill. I would fix that later, as soon as I received a little money from one of my many non-paying clients. It wouldn't take too long, so I wasn't too worried. I guess she got fed up trying to reach me.

"I have been calling you."

"Oh? I didn't know."

"That's because your phone is turned off."

"Oh, sorry. It's a problem with the phone."

"I have solved the problem by mailing you a phone."

"Yes, I'm talking on it right now."

"Will you please come to see me? I sent you an air ticket."

"Yes, I have it. Thank you so much for that."

"Can you tell me?"

"What is wrong?"

"Nothing's wrong."

"Well, it seems like there's an emergency or a crisis."

"No crisis, I just want to see you."

What a supermodel wants, a supermodel gets. I will never know what would have happened had I said no to this invitation. There were obvious signs in favor of a no. She was becoming abusive in an emotionally distant manner; hot and cold, dark and light, a theme that would carry forward in our ensuing relationship.

"Of course I'll come. I see I'm leaving in four days?"

"If you can come."

"I can."

"Thank you, darling. And please will you bring the ring?"

I had to laugh to myself. Here we go again. The ring, indeed.

"Yes, I will bring the ring."

"Okay, I will see you in Milan. I love you."

And she hung up the phone. The "I love you" part was stated in such a casual way, in a way that she might even say to a close girlfriend. I did not take that to heart to mean that she loved me in a way that I would like her to love me. I don't think it is realistic to require a supermodel to actually love you. If this was the premise of a relationship, such a relationship would probably never occur. There's something about the tallish super-attractive roses with super-sharp thorns that makes true love a fantasy never to be realized. I say this now, having been with this supermodel for more than ten years, two kids later, so I know what I speak of. But at that point in my life, hearing "I love you" didn't convince me of its truth at all; in fact, just to the opposite, I knew that that truth would never be caught.

But don't let a lack of love stop you from chasing the woman of your dreams. Maybe the love will come later; maybe it will never come. Perhaps this was one of my biggest mistakes in life; I was willing to pursue a woman that I knew didn't love me, would probably never love me. And yet there I was, standing in the long line at the international terminal of the San Francisco Airport, headed on a roundtrip flight to Milan. In my pocket was a small box with a secondhand diamond attached to a newly minted engagement ring.

Would she take it this time? Would I return with or without this ring? Stay tuned. As will be seen, it was anything but smooth.

Chapter 20
THE JEALOUS HOOKER

The first problem I ran into was Karen. She became the jealous hooker.

"What do you mean, you're leaving?"

"Oh, I just have to go out of town. It won't be long, don't worry."

"Where are you going?"

I thought, oh gosh, I can't really tell her the truth, can I?

"Washington, D.C."

I came up with this city first because I used to live there. It was where I went to law school, Georgetown University. So, if anyone were to quiz me about the city on my return, I could provide full details, names of bars, hotels, streets, the works. I also could describe the friend I stayed with when I was there and could provide an extremely credible alibi for my whereabouts. It also was credible in that I could discuss a law project that would take me to D.C. So, it was the perfect answer, or so I thought.

"I want to come with you."

Oh. I was not expecting that. How can I talk my way out of this? I can't very well bring a hooker to a high-level law seminar, now can I? Well, I can't say that. That's so insulting she'd probably kill me on sight. So, I had to come up with another excuse. Oh, I know, the perfect answer.

"Listen, darling, I'd love to take you, but where I'm going I can't have you there. You have to understand –"

"It's because I'm a hooker?"

"No, it's because I'm staying with a friend of mine, one of my good buddies from law school. If you'd like, I can get him on the phone and you can talk to him, and he'll confirm it."

She balked at that.

"Forget your buddy. I'll get you a hotel."

One thing about this hooker is she had a lot of money. She pulled out of her purse last night's take, over four thousand cash. It was wrapped up in hundred dollar bills. Wow, I thought. Look at all that. She pulled out a thousand.

"How much is a hotel in Washington, D.C.?"

"Oh come on, hon, you don't need to do this."

"I'm sure we could get one for a thousand."

"Oh my God, we could get one for one hundred. What are you talking about?"

"How many days are you staying there?"

"I need to go four, five days, basically one week, and then I'll be back."

"Okay, two hundred a night times five is one thousand. Here's two thousand so you have some left over. So, when do we leave?"

Oh great, I thought. How am I going to shake this?

"Listen, hon, I have to be in a conference all day long. You can't go to this law conference, so what are you going to do all day?"

"Oh, don't worry. I'll get some customer over there."

"Nice. While I'm going to my law conference, you'll be out trolling for men? No, I can't really do that. I hope you understand, dear. It just isn't going to work."

With that conclusion, Karen went off on me. I was completely unprepared for her violence. She smacked me with her open palm right on my ear. I didn't have a second to duck. It left a ringing sound, nearly knocking me down. Wow, I'd never had a woman do that before. She was, to be sure, quite athletic. Right after stinging me with that slap to the ear, she picked up one of my chairs and threw it at me. I caught it, so it didn't break over my head or anything. I was rather proud of that.

Unfortunately, holding the chair with both of my hands left me vulnerable to her next line of attack, throwing the phone at me. My house phone came lunging at me like a small torpedo. I blocked it with my forehead. Great. It really smacked me. I got a little bit caught up in the wires of the phone. She approached me with the look of a crazy woman. Her mouth was wet, salivating like a rabid dog. I could see the hate in her eyes, the vengeance in her hands. This woman was going to kill me.

I grabbed her from behind, trying to calm her down. She bit my arm. I threw her forward. Over on the table there were a couple bottles of port wine. One of my clients likes port and knows I like port, so he was kind enough to give me two bottles. One of them came flying right at me. Now, the thing about a port bottle is they are made of thicker glass. If one of those bottles were to hit me, it would cause some serious damage. It missed, hit my wall, and fell down to the ground. Amazingly, it did not break.

Then came the second bottle, rather predictably. Flying through the air, I caught it like a football. I used to play football, and I am quite agile with my hands, with excellent eye-hand coordination. She was quite surprised that I caught it. Now, I was pissed.

"You don't come into my house and start tearing this place apart. Get the fuck out of here right now."

She looked at me and saw that I was coming at her. I took two seconds and turned myself into a monster. The first thing I did was to slap her right across the face. Now, a girl like that, no matter how strong, she still only weighs about ninety-eight pounds. Me, I'm kind of heavy, near one hundred ninety, so one slap from me knocked her right to the ground. I then picked her up and unceremoniously threw her like a sack of potatoes up against the wall. She landed on the ground, causing a kind of injury to the tailbone. I picked her up, walked her to my front door, and tossed her out to the street. I locked the door and yelled,

"Get the fuck out of here and don't you ever come back!"

I locked the door. Now, this is not the kind of girl that's just going to lightly walk away. Instead, she stood out in front of my door screaming her head off.

"You motherfucker! I'm going to make your life miserable! You wait to see how much trouble I can make for you."

She called 911. Within minutes, the police arrived. Oh great. Now what? They took a look at her. She had a bloody lip, she had a sore butt from the throw, her arm got scratched up on a collision with my door on the way out; they knew right away they had a domestic violence case. Two cops entered my house. Two other cops brought her down the road a bit to interview her. While one set was interviewing her, the two others came to me.

"Please show us your identification."

I had my drivers license, which I showed them. Without saying a word, I showed them my arm. I showed them the bite marks. I showed them the phone that had been shattered by her toss. I showed them the chair that was upside down. I showed them the two port bottles that were still intact but had obviously been thrown. They looked around and saw all this damage, but had one simple question for me.

"Did you do this or did she?"

I looked at them.

"I don't trash my own house. She did."

"And in response you beat the crap out of her. Mr. Franck, I'm putting you under arrest for domestic violence."

They cuffed me, walked me out to the police car, and in front of my neighbors stuck me in the back. Oh great. I just hope I get out in time to get to Milan. Of course, they didn't do a thing to her; she was the poor damsel in distress. The way the domestic violence laws are, the women can go off, can commit all kinds of crimes and wrongdoings against the man, but it is the man who goes to jail. I proceeded through the booking process at the San Francisco County Jail. Swell. They photographed me, fingerprinted me, searched me, took off my street clothes, put me into jail garb, and put me into a cell filled with a bunch of white guys.

I posted bail and got the hell out of there. The good news is that I would get this hooker out of my life. Probably not a good idea for a lawyer to be dating a hooker. Generally speaking, bad idea. The bad news is I would have to face some pretty serious consequences: a misdemeanor conviction, zero jail time, three years probation, and an anger management program. But all that would happen later. The important thing for me is that I was released in time to get onto my plane and make my way to my supermodel in Milan.

Chapter 21
ENGAGEMENT, TAKE TWO, AND ACTION

I told you this would be anything but smooth. I must have been on some kind of bad luck streak. I got off the plane in Milan and guess what, no Sassafras. Mind you, I have never been to Milan, so I don't know anyone. I get out of the airport, I look around, searching for a beautiful supermodel, and find none. I call her on my cell phone, the one she gave me. I get her message.

"Sassafras, hi, I'm here. Where are you? I don't know where to go."

I hang up. I'm thinking to myself, I don't want to sound so pathetic. My goodness, she'll just think I'm an idiot. I have to take action. Okay, step one, like it or not, you're in Milan. I have no place to stay, so let's find a place to stay. I take a cab into town. As I'm driving by, a hotel catches my eye. It's called Hotel Adrian. It is nothing famous, nothing exquisite, no place that anybody of substantial means would stay in a million years. Why did I like it? For one simple, somewhat silly reason: Adrienne is the name of my mother. Well, this was Adrian, which was the male version of it, but for me on that day, lonely in Milan, it was close enough. Plus, it was fairly cheap, the cost equivalent of seventy-five dollars a night. Some of the other fancier places, of course, would be in the neighborhood of three hundred a night, which was well beyond my means.

I checked in. The nice man smiled at me, asking for my passport. Thank God the DA didn't ask me to forfeit it. They were okay with me traveling around. I guess they figured a lawyer would not become a fugitive over that little piss-ass case. I smiled, handed him my passport, gave him my address.

"How long are you staying?" he asked me.

"Good question. I'm not sure. A couple days."

I figured, what, I'll stay here two days, and if I don't hear from Sassafras, I'll go. The room was modest but perfectly adequate. It had two of these small European sized beds. I don't know why they make them so small. Are people smaller in Europe? I put my bag on one of the beds and my body on the other. I was jet lagged, tired, depressed, screwed up, and went to sleep. I did not awake until my cell phone rang. It was Sassafras.

Jet lag is a strange thing. I'm still on California time, which means I'll be completely awake even though it is in the middle of the night. I can't sleep. I call

Sassafras on her phone. Again, no answer. How frustrating is this? Here a girl sends me tickets, has me come out, and then what, she just splits.

I decide to take a walk on the streets of Milan. It's a lovely city, one of Italy's most beautiful, and I'm happy to just be alive. I am in a part of town that is not the nicest part, but it's not far from the fancy area, so I just start walking. I am a walker. I will think nothing of walking one mile, two miles, even four miles, so I just continue walking. I'm looking around, enjoying the sites. The last thing I need to be is a tourist, but here I am, stuck in the middle of Milan with nowhere to go, no one to see, and nothing to do. So, I walk.

At around four o'clock in the morning, my phone rings. Oh goodness, it's Sassafras at last.

"Hello?"

"Heeeyyyy yyyyooooouuuu..."

Her voice trailed off. Now, this was a strange tone. I had not heard this from her before. She had always been rather snappy, rather quick, not this kind of de-layed talk.

"Whhhhaaaat's ggoooinnngg onnn?"

"Hey, Sassafras, I'm here."

"Ohhhh yess, I knowwww. I gooottt yooour messsaaaage."

Her speech was slurred. This girl was either drunk as a skunk or on some kind of drug or, as I would later learn, both. I could hear in the background there was some kind of live music going on. There were men talking.

"Hey, babe! Come back, it's your turn!"

I'm thinking, your turn? What's that about? The guy sounded British. What were they doing?

"Hey, Sassafras, what's up? What's going on? Where are you? I flew here, you wanted me to, I'm here, you don't pick me up, and now you call me at four o'clock in the morning and it sounds like you're drunk, you're at a party, you're with some guys; what are you doing?"

Click. She hung up the phone. One of the lessons with supermodels: do not interrogate them. They won't answer, they will not cooperate, they will invoke their right to remain silent.

So, I'm sitting there in the middle of the street knowing that my dream girl is at some kind of late night party with God knows what rock stars doing God knows what, high as a kite, angry for some reason at me, total blowing me off and leaving me high and dry in the middle of Milan. Swell. I think to myself, how the fuck did I ever get myself in this position? I'm angry, of course. I'm hurt. I am a broken puppy.

I turn around and decide, fuck this, I'm going back to my hotel, I'm going to arrange for a new airplane flight, I'm going home and I am going to give up on this dark ass bitch. Who needs this kind of crap? As I'm walking back to my hotel, she calls again.

"Helloooo, honey? Do you remember me?"

"Hi, Sassafras. It's now five o'clock in the morning. Are you still up?"

"Oh, dear. I'm a night owl. I'm up all night long. I'm having so much fun with my friends."

I can hear in the background some guy talking to her as she's saying this to me. He's kind of mumbling; it sounds like he's really high as well. I hear the sound of a smooch.

"Sassafras, is that someone kissing you while you're talking to me?"

"Yeah, just a minute. William, please, I'm talking to Herman. Will you just stop for a second?"

And I thought, yeah, for a second, but not for an hour, not for a day, not for a week, not for a lifetime. Just stop for a second.

"Sassafras, look, I'm going back to my hotel."

"Oh, tell me dear, where are you staying? I will send a car."

"You'll send a car? What am I, a piece of luggage?"

"I will send for you. I will have him pick you up and bring you here where I am."

"Where are you?"

She paused for a second, and then her own emotion came to her. She started thinking, yeah, where am I? And she realized the sad truth was she didn't know. It made her cry.

"I don't know where I am. I'm somewhere, maybe on the moon, maybe on Mars. I don't even know if I'm in Italy."

She was so high she couldn't even tell where she was. I gave her an idea of how to figure it out.

"Is there a phone in the room?"

She turned and saw in her hotel room that indeed there was a phone.

"Go take a look at the phone. What does it say?"

Right on the phone was the name of her French hotel, Hotel Fontainebleau, in Cannes.

"Oh, wow. I'm in Cannes."

"Well, that's a nice place to be. I'm in Milan, at your invitation."

"Oh, I'm so sorry, I just forgot about it. I've been so busy, there was a big fashion show up here, and I just got distracted. I hope you'll forgive me."

"Uh, look, Sassafras. I've never had something like this happen to me before, so you'll have to allow me to adjust to it. Let's go like this; don't worry about it, I'm going to go back to my hotel room. I'm just going to reorganize my airplane flight and go home tomorrow. You and I can talk later. Good night."

I just hung up the phone on her. How ridiculous was this? I go back to my hotel room. The nice manager's wife was up. She smiled at me. I can't even fake a smile. I go back and begin making phone calls.

"Air Italia, hi. I have a flight for this coming Saturday. Is there any way I could advance that to tomorrow?"

"One moment please."

I hear the sound of someone typing on a keyboard. She brings up flight information.

"I'm sorry, the flights for tomorrow are all booked, but the following day, Wednesday, that's available."

"Okay, I'll do that then."

And so it was, I changed my flight from that Saturday to that Wednesday. I would spend the following Tuesday walking aimlessly around the streets of Milan. I looked at all the fancy shops, places I would never go into in a million years. I went into them anyway, realizing of course that this was Sassafras's world. I thought at least if I could be here physically, even just this one moment, I would share her space, even without her.

One of the stores had a cover of a magazine article, showing Sassafras wearing one of the dresses from the store. I was transfixed by it. The store manager walked up to me.

"May I help you, sir?"

I looked at him. I looked at the photo. I shook my head.

"I don't think anybody can really help me right now."

I walked out of the store dejected, humiliated, depressed. It was time to go home.

Chapter 22
PEOPLE VERSUS JUANITA CARNEROS

My friend Rolo Ramos, a Filipino immigrations attorney, had asked me to assist him in a case. Ramos is somewhat of an institution among the Filipino community, and has had his office in the neighborhood for several decades. He is also a politician, having been elected to several county and educational boards over the decades. He has an impressive set of photographs of him shaking hands with various other political luminaries, including several presidents of the country of the Philippines.

But today was no social call. In his office was his associate attorney, Donna, a thirty-something single mom, Ramos, and their client Juanita Carneros. They introduced me.

"Herman, you know Donna."

"Hello, Donna."

"Hi, Herman."

Donna did not hide her interest in me. I'm sure I'm guilty of provoking her flirtations by my own suggestiveness. Perhaps I should be more rude, but it just isn't my style. Especially to brown girls with dark eyes. Donna explained,

"Juanita has a pending deportation proceeding."

"I see. When is it set for?"

"Three weeks. October 15."

"We would like to obtain a stay of those proceedings pending state court criminal law proceedings," Ramos explained.

"Oh, and what are those proceedings?"

"That's where you come in," Donna explained. "The problem is Juanita managed to get a felony conviction. This is the basis of the deportation proceedings."

Indeed, a felony conviction will undo a green card.

"What did she get convicted of?"

"I have no idea."

So far, Juanita had not spoken a word. She was a demure Filipino gal. She remained quiet, still, as though she had no idea what was going on. She wasn't pretty, but she wasn't ugly, a Filipino plain Jane.

"Felony child endangerment," Donna explained.

Ooh, I thought. That sounds rather wicked.

"How many kids do you have?"

At last she spoke.

"Two."

"Boy or girl?"

"One boy, one girl."

"How old?"

"One is 5, one is 6."

"Are you divorced?"

"Yes."

"Okay, so Donna, what happened?"

"Her ex-husband was an abusive alcoholic. He lost his job and went crazy. He started drinking all the time, and when he would come home he would be upset."

"Okay, then what?"

"He started beating on Juanita."

Donna opened up the file and showed me some rather gruesome photographs. Juanita had black eyes, a split lip, blood all over. Pictures of the house showed papers and broken plates all over, tables turned over, chairs turned over, picture frames on the ground, and of special note for the prosecution, children in the background.

"Juanita, of course, is a victim of all this violence. The problem was, according to the prosecution, she had a legal duty to remove her children from this violent environment. She failed to do that," Donna explained.

I know about these cases. It's just incredible. A woman, a victim of abuse, can become a defendant in a criminal action because the abuse is endangering the children and she is not taking appropriate steps to safeguard the children from that abuse.

"How did she get convicted?"

"It was following a jury trial. The evidence was very clear that there were repeated attacks by her husband. The photos show the house in complete disarray. It was quite clearly a dangerous situation. Unfortunately, during the pretrial proceedings, a misdemeanor was offered and should have been accepted."

"Was there a time element?"

"Thirty days jail, three years probation, one misdemeanor conviction. Her attorney was very confident that he could win the case," Ramos explained.

"I see. And I guess he didn't."

"Nope. The jury was convinced that she allowed her children to be exposed to a very seriously dangerous situation."

"Okay, here's my question. Number one, the two children, where are they now?"

She started crying. I could tell by her tears what her answer was.

"They're with the father."

"Yes."

"The abusive alcoholic gets the kids. Isn't that just incredible?"

"Well, what happened to him? Did he get some kind of conviction?"

"He followed his attorney's advice and plead guilty to a misdemeanor. He got 30 days in jail, he's now out, and because she's a felon, they have deemed him to be the better and more fit parent."

I shook my head in disbelief. Sometimes the law truly is an ass.

"Okay, I get the picture. So, under the immigration law, the felony conviction gets you a deportation if you are a green card holder."

Ramos nodded his head yes. This was a statute that was nondiscretionary, meaning the immigration judge could not find some kind of a teary-eyed exception to the rule. It's that simple: you got a felony, you go home. But here is a further problem.

"The children, they were born here?" I asked.

"Yes."

"So they're U.S. citizens."

"They are."

"So they're going to be staying here."

"So if she's sent back to the Philippines, she'll be permanently separated from her children."

"Exactly."

I looked out the window at the other people walking by the office. Parents with kids, people in normal walks of life. I looked back at Juanita and wondered how we could ever get her back to that life. I knew, of course, the first step.

"You want me to file a motion to convert her felony conviction to a misdemeanor."

Donna and Ramos nodded yes.

"Very well."

"And one more thing, we kind of need this done right away. If you file it immediately, it will become the basis for our stay of deportation."

"Okay. Well, you've got the criminal file right here?"

"I do."

"Donna, let's get busy."

This was not the first case that Donna and I had worked on. You could tell by the way she touched her hair, moving it off her shoulder, that this was a woman who was highly available. I shouldn't have, but I fueled the fire by smiling at her. She smiled back. All this went right by Juanita without a glance. We filed the motion the following day, arguing under penal code section 17, that a court has discretion to convert a felony conviction to a misdemeanor upon a finding that the defendant has led a lawful life and that it is in the interest of justice to convert the felony.

Generally, this kind of motion should be made after a defendant has completed the terms of probation. The problem was Juanita had been convicted recently. The deportation proceedings occurred on the heels of that conviction. Not only was she not done with probation, she had really just started it.

We explained in our motion papers that there was an emergency in light of the deportation proceedings, and that it would be a tragedy of justice to allow this victim of domestic abuse to become permanently separated from her children. You would think a judge would find such a case to be a no-brainer. Oh my goodness, we can't allow the mom to be separated from her child; the poor victim of abuse must stay here. Of course I'll convert the felony to a misdemeanor. Sorry we ever convicted you in the first place.

The first opposition I received was from the Probation Department. They had submitted a report stating in so many words, "Juanita has just started her probationary term. Although she has complied with all requirements to date, it is way too early to convert her felony at this point. We recommend deferring this motion until a minimum of one year."

I, of course, explained to the judge, "One year from now she'll be in the Philippines, permanently separated from her children."

"If she loses her green card and gets deported, then we later convert this felony to a misdemeanor, couldn't she come back then?" the judge asked.

"No, Your Honor," Donna explained. "She will have a five or a ten year exclusionary order. She will not be able to come back for that period, and that's the minimum time. An immigration judge would have discretion at that point to allow her back in, but they may very well just say no forever. So, if you let her go now, you let her go forever."

"I see."

Then the judge turned to the assistant district attorney.

"What do the people have to say about this? Do the people have a heart?"

This stopped the female prosecutor for only a second.

"Yes, of course the people have a heart. We have a heart for the victims of this case, her two children. They were made to endure insufferable sights of violence, of blood, of mayhem. This woman allowed that to happen—"

The judge stopped her right there.

"This sounds like your closing argument from the underlying criminal case."

"I didn't do that case."

"Okay, but it sounds like you're redoing your closing argument. Let me just summarize it this way for you. You oppose the motion."

"Vigorously."

"And I take it you support the statements made by the Probation Department?"

"We do."

"You understand that this mother will be deported and will be permanently separated from her children?"

"Your Honor, she should have thought about that when she subjected them to all this abuse."

The judge shook his head. It was a sad day for justice. The problem was he could not properly grant the motion because of her recent conviction and her status of being early in her probationary term.

"I'm afraid I must deny the motion. It is true you are too early in your probationary term. I would later grant this motion, maybe after one year of successful completion of a probation. But right now, over the objection and opposition of the prosecution and the Probation Department, I cannot. The motion is denied."

The judge hit the gavel onto his desk. It missed the round coaster, hitting it on its edge. Interestingly, it flew off his desk, landing forward on the clerk's desk, nearly striking the clerk. It landed right in the middle of her desk. She picked it up and handed it back to the judge.

"Sorry."

The judge was apologetic, put the coaster back on his bench, and called the next case. I turned to my client Juanita, shook my head, and said ominous words.

"It's not over."

Chapter 23
ALLIANCE AGAINST DOMESTIC VIOLENCE

You've probably heard about Mothers Against Drunk Driving (MADD). There is a similar group, the Alliance Against Domestic Violence, that very commonly attends domestic violence trials to give juries an understanding that these cases are extremely important. They are located in Sacramento and operate as a clearinghouse for people all over California seeking assistance in domestic violence situations.

I did not know that Donna had contacted them. One of the things they do, just like their drunk driving counterparts MADD, is get the press involved. When I walked out of that courtroom, oh my goodness, the halls were packed with people from the local paper, news channels, cameras flowing, lights on, microphones in my face.

"Mr. Franck, tell us what you're going to do next. You are going to do something, aren't you?"

"Oh yes, this is not over," I assured the press.

"Okay, appeal?"

"Our first procedure will be to appear before the immigration judge to see if in light of the court's comments, they will continue the deportation proceedings by approximately one year. As you just heard, the judge appeared willing to entertain a new motion to convert the felony at that time."

"What about appealing this decision?"

"We will look into that. The problem is the court was well within its discretionary powers in denying the motion. I do not believe I could convince a court of appeals to reverse this judge."

"In other words, the judge was right in denying the motion, causing this woman to be deported and permanently separated from her children? How could that possibly be correct?"

The prosecutor walked out.

"That question would be better answered by her," I announced.

I pointed to the assistant district attorney, Carla Finney. She was rather gruff with the press.

"The answer is just what I told the judge: she should've thought about that before she subjected her children to abuse."

The press was incensed with this remark. I became oddly sympathetic to this prosecutor. It was as though she were about to be lynched.

"You better get out of here," I told her.

She understood that this civilized set of journalists were about to destroy her. She walked away without further comment. Twenty days later, Donna and I appeared in the immigrations court before the first level judge, called a hearing officer. This is your first chance to convince the federal government to give you a break from the jaws of justice.

Donna argued the case.

"As you can see from the transcripts of the state court criminal proceedings, there was a substantial probability that a motion to convert this felony into a misdemeanor would be granted."

"Yes, I see that. The problem is—"

"Wait, wait. I'm sorry to interrupt, but let me just say one more thing. This woman will be permanently separated—"

"I know, I know."

The judge interrupted her.

"Listen, this is a tearjerker of a case. I would first like to say that the criminal law allowing for such a conviction to me seems completely improper. I don't know who wrote that law, I don't know what they were thinking."

At that point, the immigrations attorney representing the federal government stepped in.

"Your Honor, I object your second guessing the laws of the State of California. It is not proper."

"I know I'm a little bit out of bounds here, but even you must agree that this law sucks."

The people in the audience were a bit surprised to hear the learned judge use such language. But she was dead-on right. And that would be the perfect sound bite for next morning's front page of the paper, which appeared in super-large font with a photo of me leaving the courthouse having secured a one year deferment of the deportation proceedings. The headline read, "Immigrations Judge: This Law Sucks."

Media frenzies will develop on a piggyback basis. Once a paper sees something of interest reported by another paper, they will naturally pick it up themselves. The "This Law Sucks" article appeared in the Philippines and then hit the international papers. It went on to Europe, to Australia, and of special note to me, made the Italian news.

Interestingly, a woman who had not spoken with me since that night in Milan when she was in Cannes happened to be watching the news while completely high on black tar heroin with her rock 'n roll boyfriend. He was strumming his guitar, smoking a cigarette. A syringe lay on the table. She was lying on the couch in a lovely silk negligee. The news was on. They were ignoring it, but then she saw something that she knew: she saw me. She sat up all the sudden. Her eyes couldn't believe herself. She quieted the guitar down, found the remote and picked it up, and listened to the case as described by the Italian press.

There are many coincidences that happen in life. It may have to do with the formation of the stars and the planets upon a person's birth. It may have to do with karmic forces or other forces beyond our recognition. It may just be fluke.

As it would happen, Sassafras had a very raw and similar experience as Juanita. After seeing that article on the news, her reaction was not to call me, but instead to call her father. She cried as she told him she loved him and would never forget the night she saw her mother smash him on the head. He fell into a bookcase, the bookcase came tumbling down and fell on top of Sassafras, breaking her leg. As she spoke with him, she touched the scar on her leg that was still there from the surgery of resetting her femur. She survived that incident, but the emotional scar would never go away.

Chapter 24
ABUSE OF DISCRETION

My victory for Juanita would be short-lived. The government attorneys appealed the one year deferment of deportation on the basis of abuse of discretion. Abuse of discretion requires a showing that no reasonable judge, in light of the law, would have ever made such a ruling. The appeal was made to an immigrations appeal panel of three judges. They all agreed: there was no statutory or other legal authority to support the trial court's judgment and order deferring the deportation proceedings. It was accordingly the judgment of this court to reverse that deferment and to order that deportation proceedings commence immediately. So ordered.

Oh, no. Oh, no. This can't be. You can't do this. Now what? I looked at the press. They were just shaking their heads. They couldn't believe it either. Okay, where do we go from here? I knew that would be the press's first question. Before they even asked, I had the answer.

"There is a process to review these immigration court decisions in the United States District Court. We will be there immediately seeking a stay of this order, so that justice may be served."

You might be wondering what was going on with the emotion of all this between Donna and I, especially in light of the urgency that the circumstances required us to work late nights together and alone in her office. We were printing out the complaint seeking immediate stay when she asked me.

"Are you still single?"

I know where she's going with that. But the fact is the answer was yes. Not married, no girlfriend, but—and I wouldn't tell her this—I had a rather spent or vacant heart.

"Yes, I'm single."

"You know I'm single."

"I do."

"You don't think I'm pretty?"

She fluffed her hair. My goodness, how women will be flirtatious.

"I think you're pretty."

"How come you don't want to kiss me?"

"Why do you think I don't want to kiss you?"

"Because you haven't. We've worked together so much on this. You didn't kiss me a single time."

I stopped that argument right there. I lightly took her neck and pulled her head to mine and gave her a big, wet kiss. Oh my goodness, did the emotions flow with that. She gasped for air as though I'd held her underwater for four minutes. She unleashed with her 30-something near-prime sensuality pent up, kept up, and frumped up, the tiger was released from its cage. There were law books, stacks of paper, pens, paper clips, and other items on her desk. Those items were now on the floor. For a little woman, she had a lot of love. I will not go into details here, other than to say in the aftermath, she had one question:

"When we can we do that again?"

I shook my head in disbelief. It was eleven p.m. I guesstimated my own rejuvenation time.

"Maybe by, say, one a.m."

"I'll wait."

Indeed she would.

Chapter 25
WHAT TO DO WHEN YOU GET DUMPED

There is a theory I have about what to do when you get dumped. I've said it elsewhere, but I'll say it again: getting dumped produces superhuman skills in people. This has to do with the emotional trauma that getting dumped generates. There are many examples of brilliant songs coming out of nowhere. Those songs would have never existed had the songwriter not been dumped. When things are going well, when everyone is happy, the mind's creative process is limited. When things are terrible, highly emotional, and spiraling downward into utter defeat, it is then that the brain comes up with abilities that we just don't have during normal times.

It is incumbent on the dumpee to exploit these superhuman powers to the hilt. Do something absolutely spectacular. Imagine what would happen to your circumstances if you came up with the most incredible dumpee love song with words such as:

"What did you think I would do at this moment, with you standing before me with tears in your eyes, and you told me that you didn't love me anymore?"

Imagine if you applied that song to tender music and performed it brilliantly, and it went off the charts, became number one, and made you thirty-five million dollars? Do you think the girl would come back?

Okay, so you're not a songwriter. You don't know how to play music. You can't do lyrics. There is something you can do. Maybe it isn't even artistic. Maybe you're an engineer and you will draw the most amazing building design on the planet. If you're a banker, you will invent a whole new banking service that your bank can now sell to its customers and make hundreds of millions of dollars on. If you're an accountant, you'll come up with an amazing new offshore corporation/living trust that is waterproof and airtight, and allows a haven for tax-free income.

And if you're a lawyer, you will take the case that goes to the United States Supreme Court and generates a landmark decision that will be in the front page of every newspaper and on the evening news throughout the world. When you get dumped, find your superhuman powers and exploit them to the maximum possibilities.

Chapter 26
EX PARTE APPLICATION FOR STAY OF DEPORTATION PROCEEDINGS

The complaint seeking a stay of the deportation proceedings, and an accompanying ex parte application therefore, was filed by Donna and I within five days. The government's attorney was present. I argued the case.

"You're requesting a stay of an order that lifted a previous stay, correct, Counsel?" the judge first noted.

"Yes, Your Honor. We originally obtained a stay of deportation in the form of an order granting a one year deferment. That order was then reversed. We are seeking this court's intervention in staying that reversal pending these administrative mandamus proceedings."

For those who haven't heard that phrase, administrative mandates are a form of judicial review of an administrative law judge's final order. The court can step in and reverse the decision if it finds that it is contrary to law, constitutes prejudicial error, and/or abuse of discretion. They are rarely granted, and are in the category of a 'Hail Mary' attempt to bring justice to a completely unjust situation. This one was somewhat in the typical way: we were on the right side of everything except the law.

The judge continued.

"Before I hear from petitioner's counsel, let me first ask the government attorney. Why are you so keen on having this woman deported?"

"Your Honor, there are laws against child endangerment which we are duty bound to enforce. One of those laws is that you cannot subject a child to an environment of domestic violence. There are plenty of published cases upholding that rule."

The judge was the only person in the room that was able to look down on the prosecutor.

"You understand this woman was a victim of domestic violence, correct?"

"She was a victim, but in allowing it to happen in front of the child, became a perpetrator of a collateral crime."

"Collateral crime? That sounds like a case where you prosecute a murder victim for the fact that their head got splattered on the sidewalk and defaced public property. Have you ever done one of those collateral crime cases?"

"First of all, we don't prosecute dead people, but no. I can assure we have not."

The judge continued in her futile effort to convince the DA to fix the matter.

"As you know, Madam Prosecutor, you hold a role on behalf of the State, and in that role, you are duty bound to seek justice, not just to win."

"I acknowledge that, Your Honor."

"Do you really think it is appropriate to sever the family bond between the children and the mother, and in so doing, leave the children with the perpetrator of the primary crime of domestic violence? You have to admit, it sounds a little bit crazy."

"Sometimes when you follow the letter of the law, strange results occur. But as far as dividing up this family, this mother should have thought of that a little more when she refused to do the right thing."

"Oh, and what is it she should have done while her head was getting bashed in by this man?"

"She should have called 911."

"I did."

Now, it's not quite right for the defendant to interrupt, but it worked here. The judge turned to the prosecutor.

"Okay, so strike that one off your list. Check the box for '911 was called.' And by the way, I think the police arrived, because after all, we know the husband was prosecuted, right?"

"Yes. But here's what she failed to do."

"What was that?"

"She failed to obtain a restraining order."

"But wait a minute, the police issued a temporary restraining order."

"The police issued a temporary protective order, which only lasts until the arraignment."

"Then whose job is it at the arraignment to continue that?"

"It is the victim's job to request it."

"Where was your office in this process? Don't you assist the victims in obtaining the benefit of the statutory protections?"

"The victim must ask for it. In this case, she forgave her husband and invited him back in the house. That's where she committed a crime."

"Okay, so your program is the family bond should be split up, there should never be forgiveness, and if a woman does forgive, the consequence is termination of all parental rights, severance of the mother-child bond, and exile from this country. That's the rule?"

The prosecutor proudly responded, "That's the law, Your Honor."

The judge couldn't believe it.

"Well, that law sucks."

Chapter 27
ROUND FOUR

Women can put a spell on men. The spell has a grip that won't let go. It makes it all that much harder when the woman happens to be a famous supermodel, with photos adorning magazines everywhere. I would not normally notice the cover of fashion magazines, but it seemed like everywhere I went, there she was. She liked bright colored dresses to accentuate her dark skin. She looked positively gorgeous, and reminded me every second of how lost I was without her. While I was tending to my modest law practice, she continued to catapult herself into the upper echelons of the A-list of supermodels. I stood on a rainy San Francisco day in front of a news rack and shook my head at the fashion magazines showing her photos. There she was in a canary yellow dress. There she was again in a white dress; my goodness, it was so light that you could see the backdrop of her dark nipples. Is that legal? The fashion world is getting a bit liberal in what it defines as a functioning wardrobe.

I, of course, continued to toil away at law. To be sure, the case of Juanita was hardly my only project. Indeed, I would not survive on her project alone, as she had zero to pay. Ramos and Donna had been feeding me a series of other green card matters. Their practice was focused on your typical Filipino girl meets American guy, gets married, gets a green card, and hopefully doesn't dump the guy three days later kind of case.

I have to handle the non-marriage green cards. There was the banquet chef from Canton, China, and his new employer, on a work visa. There was the rich but large Chinese girl whose student visa had expired upon her graduation and whose matrimonial prospects were rather slim. We set up a subsidiary of her father's construction company, for which she obtained a visa to manage. Of course, she didn't care about the construction business, but it kept her in the USA.

Then there were the divorce cases from the Filipino green card. The 'guess what, the marriage didn't work out' cases. Ramos and Donna had quite a paper mill going, from the initial green card papers to processing the divorce papers and beyond. I could tell Donna enjoyed feeding me these cases, as it kept me working with her. Unfortunately, I did not develop the deep connection required for marriage to her. She had not put me under her spell.

Donna asked me about our situation as we left round four of Juanita's case for the United States District Court for the Northern District of California. The judge took the matter under submission, and would get us his written decision in a matter of several days. In the meantime, there was the issue of what, if anything, was I going to do with Donna.

"I know you like me."

"Of course I like you."

"Yeah, but I mean I think you *really* like me."

See how forward these girls have become? I began walking faster without thinking about it. She was fairly quick, and kept up with me.

"So, where are we headed?"

"To the parking lot."

"That's not what I mean. I mean where are *we* headed?"

She held my hand. It was very cute. We walked by the Civic Center garage, looking so romantic in front of some of the other battle-minded attorneys. We continued to speak of our relationship in front of them, as though they weren't even there.

"I haven't figured it out yet."

One of the female attorneys correctly guessed that we were not talking about some pressing legal issue. The elevator door opened. No fewer than eight attorneys got in, plus Donna and I made ten.

"I think you have a pretty good opportunity to figure out where we're going," she responded.

"Oh, I know that."

"Then you should have an answer."

The girl seemed to coach Donna into not pressuring me like this. All women should know it never works. I think women do know this, they just can't help themselves.

"Okay, if you don't mind, let me turn the question back to you: where do *you* see us going?"

"Oh, let's think about that for a second. I'm a 30-something single mom practicing law...oh yeah, I think I'd like to get married again."

Several of the men were looking up into the ceiling of the elevator while others looked down. It stopped at the first lower level and nobody got off. I was wondering if some people needed to go there and just didn't get off to hear the rest of this conversation.

It's kind of hard to answer a question like this, or respond to a statement like that, when you are super clear that you do not want to marry this girl. What could I say, I'm stuck on Sassafras? And in the meantime I'd like to fiddle around with you? The other lawyers anxiously awaited my response. I would not let them down:

"You need to beat the love I have for this other woman out of me before I can find my way to marry you."

They were not expecting that one. Donna would take the challenge.

"How about I kiss it out of you? How about I suck it out of you? How about I—"

I interrupted her with the palm of my hand to her mouth. We got to the second floor, and again, nobody got out. This conversation was getting a little bit too interesting for them to miss.

"Okay, okay. I get it. I got the picture."

The thing is, as much as you might think a new woman can get you out from under your true love's spell, sometimes just the opposite can be the case. The new woman can prove to you just how stuck you are on the other woman. You're kissing the new woman and you're thinking about the old one. You're holding her and you want to be with the other. You're speaking to the new one and you would prefer being with the old one. You're reminded of the old one all the time, can't get her out of your mind, you're stuck on her, and the new woman only makes it worse.

Is there a point of surrender where a man finally gives up and says, okay, that's it, I am not in denial, I am going to move on? Sure, in about a hundred years. In the meantime, the man will continue to drive a series of other innocent women crazy, as well as himself.

But I wasn't going to waste away waiting around for Sassafras. It didn't help that the tabloids had to chronicle the play-by-play of her exciting relationship with her rock 'n roll boyfriend, all while she ascended to the top of the supermodel A-list. It's hard to move on from such a woman, even when separated by all that had come between us.

My plan continued to be to do something absolutely spectacular that would catch the world on fire. This was not so much to attract her back to me. This was to better myself, to move me forward, and to make it so I could have my life back and find a new love.

My hope was in Juanita's case; it had this huge potential of becoming a landmark decision. That concept became all the more divorced from reality when I received the judge's decision in my email: the motion for a temporary stay of deportation was DENIED.

Chapter 28
ROUND FIVE

This defeat could be compared to the plight of a poet that is unable to complete the poem that would win back the love of his life. It was the same as the painter who could not complete the sunset from the first day he had met his lover, and thus could not win her back.

As devastating as the loss was to me, I fought my own egocentric tendencies and brought my thoughts to Juanita. After all, she was the one that would be deported and forever separated from her children. Donna consoled her at the law office as we explained the court's terrible decision to her.

"Juanita, please don't cry. It's going to be okay. Mr. Franck is preparing our appeal right now to the United States Court of Appeal of the Ninth Circuit."

She looked over to me. I nodded yes. Indeed, I was. This would be round five, a direct appeal to the Ninth Circuit requesting an emergency stay of deportation proceedings pending our appeal. The Ninth Circuit has an expedited appeal process for denials of motions for preliminary injunctions, which was how we presented our request for a stay. We were requesting that the Citizen and Immigration Service (CIS) be enjoined from, or stop, the deportation.

Donna and I worked straight through the weekend on this project and had it ready for filing on Monday. From this flurry of legal activity, there were two back-to-back articles that hit the press. The first described the District Court judge's decision denying our application for a stay of deportation; the second described our appeal of that denial and our motion for emergency stay and expedited briefing process.

Both of these articles hit the European press, including the papers in Milan. Sassafras sat elegantly stretched out on her couch until she found the articles. She sat up, put her glasses on, and read them carefully. It was three a.m. California time, but that didn't bother her in the least. She phoned me. BRRRINNNGGG. I sensed it was her.

"Hello?"

"Hey, it's me."

"Me? I don't know anyone named Me."

"Oh, yes you do."

"How is Milan?"

"It is another beautiful day."

"I haven't spoken with you in awhile."

"Did you miss me?"

I was quiet. I wanted to cry.

"Hello?"

She thought maybe she had lost the line.

"I'm still here."

"Well, did you miss me?"

"Yes, of course I did. Are you calling to torture me?"

"If I was going to torture you, I would just come over and put you into a pot of boiling water. But I didn't do that, did I?"

"No, you didn't."

"What's wrong?"

"Nothing's wrong."

"You seem angry at me."

"I'm only angry that I have lost your heart."

"My heart does not belong to anyone but me."

"Do you mean now, or forever?"

"I mean now. At some point I will give it to someone, but I have not done that yet. You have not lost anything that anyone else has won."

"I follow you in the magazines. I follow you in the tabloids."

"And I follow you in the newspaper. I saw the article today about your immigrations case. You have to understand something: you must win that case."

"I know. I'm trying."

"You can't just try; you have to find a way to win."

"So far I keep losing, over and over and over again. It's frustrating."

"Would it help if I organized more media support?"

"No, it is already getting lots of attention. The judges won't be swayed by what's in the newspaper. They base their decisions on the law and the facts."

"What about the government? Wouldn't the government reverse itself if there was a certain kind of media attention?"

"What kind would that be? 'Supermodels for Justice'?"

"Yeah, something like that. I can organize a whole bunch of people very quickly."

My initial reaction to this concept was negative only because I had never been in the business of lobbying the government. I was a court person that knew how to file lawsuits and motions. It occurred to me, though, that if we could persuade the government to do the right thing, then we wouldn't need all this court process.

"Maybe a high level group of supermodels coming together to lobby the U.S. government could help Juanita."

It also occurred to me that this effort would place Sassafras back into my world. Her heart seemed still available, at least she said as much. She was offering to come back to my world; it would be self-defeating for me to say no.

She offered up an idea.

"We can do this in a non-glitzy way. It wouldn't be proper to help this poor single mother by wearing ten thousand dollar dresses."

I couldn't agree more.

"We will unite for her and show her that she is not alone in this battle."

"Would you like to meet her?"

"I would."

"You'll have to come to San Francisco. She can't leave the country. If she goes, she cannot come back."

"I understand. I will come out."

"Hopefully you'll come before she's deported."

"How long does she have?"

"The deportation is set for ten days from now. I'm hoping by then we will receive an emergency stay."

"I will organize an immediate flight. I will be there within a couple days. Keep your phone open."

"Okay, Sassafras. We're happy to have you on Juanita's team."

Two major things happened two days later. The first was that the United States Court of Appeals for the Ninth District issued an order granting our application for an emergency stay and motion for an expedited briefing process on the appeal of the order denying our request for an injunction enjoining the deportation. The second was that Sassafras arrived at the San Francisco International Airport on a direct flight from Milan. I, of course, was there to pick her up. I had not forgotten how beautiful she was. The magazine covers reminded me of her beauty all too often. But photographs never do a person justice. Seeing her in person was a whole other world. Wow, this woman had a hold on me like nothing else on this planet.

She walked up to me and placed her hand on my cheek and gave me a big kiss. She wore a long emerald green dress with Chanel sunglasses. Her hair was long, straight, and black in a natural Chinese way. I believe even a double-legged cast would not have kept my knees and ankles from going gooey.

There were two things her palm on my cheek taught me. The first was that I could never in a million years marry Donna. It just wouldn't even be close. The second was that I absolutely had to find a way to marry Sassafras. But how?

Chapter 29
A WEEK WITH SASSAFRAS

Amazingly, she stayed for a whole week. We had a perfectly lovely time. I took her around San Francisco, thinking she would like to see places like the Golden Gate Bridge, Ocean Beach, and one of my favorite spots, the Dutch Windmill. I learned right away that her favorite part of the city, perhaps quite predictably, was Union Square where all the fancy stores were. Just as I was at home in the courtroom, she was at home in these fancy stores.

This brought me to another important revelation about how to catch a supermodel: go shopping with her. There is probably nothing a woman prefers doing more than shopping. Don't even think about selecting something for her; the odds that you would correctly guess her tastes are about one in a billion. Instead, let her do the choosing, you do the paying. You can also tell if you're with a good woman who has your interests at stake, or a bad woman that doesn't care at all about you, based on the items that she selects while shopping.

Sassafras knew that I was of rather modest/middle-class means. I was not some famous rock star making a million dollars a month. I was a hard-working attorney with many clients that weren't paying me, and eking out a small, modest living. She knew all about that, and knew better than to select a ten thousand dollar dress. At least, I hoped so.

She found a pair of lovely cashmere gloves, tan with flowers, and amazingly enough priced at less than a hundred dollars. I was happy to be able to buy something for her that pleased her. Afterwards, we went upstairs to a restaurant for a late lunch.

There is really not much you can do about the issue of whether your looks, for whatever reason, attract the woman you desire. She is either going to enjoy your looks or not. The good news is that women do not base their decisions on who to marry predominantly on looks. Yes, looks of course matter, but other things also matter. Whether your particular mix of character, education, attitude, personality, conversation ability, ability to make her laugh, ability to hold her interest, ability to challenge her, ability to outwit her, ability to lead her, and to occupy clearly the status of an alpha male in the relationship; in other words, the entire ensemble of you, whether this is a good match for her is entirely out of your hands. All you can do is be your true self, show that true self, and hope on hope that it works.

Unfortunately, we are past the days when we can club a girl, knock her out, take her over our shoulder, and bring her back to our cave. Now, we actually have to win the girl's heart. Happily, I was able to make her laugh. Despite the serious-ness of my writings (in case it isn't self-evident), I am a funny guy. I wasn't telling her jokes, I was just saying things in a way that made her laugh. I also benefited from the fact that her typical conversation was with either a supermodel or a rock star. I don't mean to sound uppity about my quasi-Ivy League education, but it is really true that going to these universities does something for your brain.

The good news for very smart, well-educated, not-so-rich men is that a woman will very much examine you as a genetic vessel to pass on your intelligence to her children. Women naturally desire intelligent children, and will adore even a not-so-good-looking man who is hyper-bright. This came out in our conversation, in the form of quite a few questions about exactly how it was that I became a law-yer.

"I was born a lawyer," I explained.

I have a theory that we have a calling in life, some kind of thing we are sup-posed to do. This caught her attention.

"Was I born to be a model?"

"Yes, I think you were. And a movie star."

She smiled. She redirected me back to her questions about my career. Note that whenever you talk about yourself, you risk the problem of boring someone to death, especially if you are not all that exciting. At the same time, if you don't answer questions clearly, the evasion will be duly noted and will be a strike against you. To balance these two issues, it is good to answer the question, and then boo-merang it right back to her, requiring her to speak about how wonderful she is. It should be like a ping pong match, where you return the ball, she returns it back, and so forth.

Here is the other noteworthy point when speaking about your career with a woman. First of all, you need to pause just for a second. Men tend to define them-selves by their job and their career. This is perfectly natural, but don't overdo it. There is more to you than what you do for a living. At the same time, you need to understand that a woman wants a man in a high-powered career, who has found his place there, and who is not depressed or lost in his job.

Let's say you are a mid-level banker, and you hate your boss, you hate your job, you hate your life. If you explain all that to a woman, she will be extremely turned off. She will see you as a man that is not happy in his own life. She does not want to be the solution to your problems. She wants you to be the solution to her problems, not the other way around.

Another supermodel I dated told me, "I will never date a man that is not happy in his career. If he isn't happy with his job, he won't be happy in life, and I don't want to be around a man who is not happy."

It may seem cold, it may seem unfair, it may seem whatever. This is a reality check; the man must be in a career he has found, that he is good at, that is impressive, high-powered, showing intelligence, discipline, education, and that he is happy in. If you do not have these critical ingredients in your life, you will have an extremely hard time landing a supermodel, or for that matter, any woman.

So she liked this 'I was born a lawyer' business.

"Tell me how that happened?"

Note how my answer emphasized genetics. Her questions were all about genetics and the prospect of handing down my genes to her children.

"My grandparents were lawyers. My grandmother's brothers were judges. Their children are all lawyers. My brother is a lawyer, and I knew I would be a lawyer at about the age of 5. How about you? When did you first understand that you would be a supermodel?"

Note how I dovetailed my response to boomerang back to her to give her an opportunity to discuss how wonderful she is. But the thing about a totally successful person is that they don't really want to talk about it. So she dodged the question, which was fine with me, and continued on in her own inquiries.

"How long does it take to become a lawyer?"

"I think you mean how long is the school process, right?"

"Yes."

The answer to this question, mind you, deals with the area a woman likes to see a lot of: discipline and intelligence. Undisciplined men, party animals that just go out and have fun, never study, don't do anything productive, will not be interesting to a woman. The rare exception to the rule is if you happen to be a party animal that has become an extremely successful rock 'n roll star. Her own dealings with the philandering rock 'n roller had been bittersweet. She enjoyed his success, his good looks, and his excitement about his own career. But the man was entirely undisciplined, and in many ways unimpressive.

I did not consider myself to be an overly disciplined person, but it is true that I did manage to get through a rather lengthy prelaw and law education. I explained it to her.

"First you have to get a university degree. I received mine from UC Berkeley."

"Isn't that near here?"

"Yes, it's right across the Bay."

"What did you study there?"

"Politics and economics."

"You must have been a top student there."

She was searching for intelligence and discipline.

"No, there were many at that school that could run circles around me, but I was good enough to graduate with honors," I explained honestly.

She misunderstood my response, which was deliberate by me. I was trying to show her another aspect of my ensemble, that of being a humble person. It is a rather obnoxious and generally untruthful statement to say "I am the smartest person on the earth." It is far more intelligent to show humility, as most people know that however high and mighty you might think you are, in reality, you are not. Indeed, ratcheting yourself downward is itself a sign of intelligence. There is nothing more boring to a woman than a mentally challenged guy who thinks he's some kind of God to the earth. The rare exception to this rule is that of a hyper-successful rock 'n roll star. She continued in her inquiry.

"So where did you end up going to law school?"

"An East Coast school, Georgetown University in Washington, D.C."

She, of course, had no idea of this school.

"Is that a top school?"

"I can explain it this way: on the first day of class, my professor had a kind of joke to tell. He said, 'Welcome to Georgetown University Law Center, and congratulations on being admitted into one of the twenty law schools in the top ten.'"

She failed to see the humor in that. I guess you had to be there.

"So how long was law school?"

"It is normally three years. I did another degree, so I took four years."

"What was the other degree?"

"I got a masters degree in Economics."

I wouldn't want to suggest that you have to have these fancy degrees in order to win the heart of a supermodel. What I was doing here was simply dealing with the hand of cards that I had. There are many different attributes a person has. Whatever you have is what you need to emphasize in your discussions. If you are a great athlete, talk about that. If you are a great musician, show that.

Chapter 30
HOW A SUPERMODEL CAN HELP A COURT CASE

I really didn't think there was much Sassafras could do to help me in Juanita's court case. How wrong I was. Sometimes the best thing you can do in a court case is to allow another person, who has nothing to do with the legal profession, to take a look at it. They might come up with a pretty clever idea that completely solves the entire problem.

Here is what she did. First of all, it was not hard for her to collect up a group of supermodels to come forward to assist Juanita. The reality is that most supermodels are from immigrant backgrounds. They could all immediately relate to Juanita's situation as an immigrant woman in distress. On top of that, and unfortunately, the crime of domestic violence is one that touches people in all walks of life, including supermodels. The group of eight women that she pulled together were all immigrants who had experienced the tragedy of domestic violence. These women were behind Juanita one thousand percent, and formed a new group, with my help, called Supermodels Against Domestic Violence.

And just to make sure that everybody noticed, oh boy, look what they did. First of all, you have to understand these girls have major connections to the media. If they call, people answer.

On the cover of three major fashion magazines there was displayed the rather amazing photograph of nine naked supermodels with black eyes, bloody lips, hand marks on their necks, bandages on their shoulders, skinned knees, and angry looks. The caption read, "Look how ugly domestic violence is."

The cuts, bruises, black eyes, and bloody lips were all the result of the work of careful and highly professional makeup artists, so nobody beat these girls up. But it looked incredibly real.

This was like an atomic bomb in the media, with internet articles firing off left and right about this audacious display. The girls were very smart to do it this way. The initial concern which I raised is the notion that these privileged celebrity women could not relate to the plight of your average domestic violence victim. We agreed, putting them on the cover in a ten thousand dollar dress would not be a good public relations stunt. Putting them on naked with cuts, bruises, bloody lips, and black eyes became a major media sensation. And when people started asking questions, all of the answers led to Juanita's case. How ugly is domestic violence? Sassafras was interviewed on the news:

"Look at the case of Juanita Santos. Here she is, an immigrant from the Philippines, she has two children, and because her husband beat her and she did not have the power to remove herself from him, now she is being deported and will be permanently separated from her children."

I would have never thought of this myself, but this is often the way things work in the legal profession. Rather than writing brilliant legal briefs and convincing the United States Court of Appeals for the Ninth Circuit to reverse the district court, and to reverse the immigrations court, and all the complexities involved in that process, what I really needed was a bunch of beat up, naked supermodels.

Here is how it all went down. Our Governor of the great state of California is none other than Arnold Schwarzenegger, the famous movie star. His lovely wife is Maria Shriver, a member of the United States' most powerful political family, the Kennedys. Ms. Shriver was formerly a journalist, and has an innate ability to take on the cause of justice, to investigate a wrongdoing, and to make it right. The beat up supermodel photos hit her like a ton of bricks. Inside the Governor's office, one lovely Tuesday morning, there was a direct discussion about this issue between Ms. Shriver and Governor Schwarzenegger.

"Did you see this?"

Maria Shriver held out one of the photos. Governor Schwarzenegger responded:

"Yes, Maria. This is all over the internet."

"Do you know what it's about?"

"I understand that they have formed together to help out Juanita Santos, who is about to be deported."

"Well, we have to fix that!"

"Maria, this is a federal immigration issue. I am not president of the United States; I am Governor of the state of California."

"Arnold, her problem is that she's got a California conviction, a felony. You can fix that."

Arnold looked up and smiled.

"I see. You mean—"

"Yes. I mean a pardon."

"A pardon? I haven't given a pardon since I've taken office. I really don't agree with pardons. If you've been convicted, you're guilty, and it should stay that way. I want to stay out of the court business."

"Well, Arnold, I think this is one of those cases where you've got to get involved. The court isn't solving this problem. You need to solve it."

Arnold began to come back with a counterargument. Maria held up the picture and pointed at the girls.

"Arnold, don't even think about saying no. You need to say yes to this one."

He thought of another way out.

"They haven't applied for a pardon."

Maria solved this problem in two seconds. She took out her cell phone and called her assistant.

"Jan, listen. I want you to look up Attorney Herman Franck. Get me his number. I'll hold."

Within a matter of moments, her assistant came back to her with my number. Arnold had to stop the entire business of running the state of California while Maria gave me a call. BRRRNNG. BRRRNNG. My favorite sound is the sound of the phone ringing. You never know what it's going to be. I answered.

"Law offices."

You see what an important attorney I am. You can tell when I have to answer my own phone.

"Is Mr. Franck in?"

"Speaking."

"Mr. Franck, this is Maria Shriver."

"Maria Shriver, as in—"

"Yes. As in the first lady of the state of California."

"Good morning, Ms. Shriver, and thank you for calling me. I can't imagine what this is about."

"This is about your client, Juanita Santos."

"Yes, she's my client."

"How's her court case going?"

"Oh, just wonderful. I seem to lose at every juncture. Other than that, it's going great."

"Yes, I've noticed. When is the next decision due?"

"We are waiting any day now from the Ninth Circuit Court of Appeals. We're hoping they will reverse the district court."

"Mr. Franck, tell me, what are the odds that they're really going to do that?"

"Oh, probably something like one in a million."

"That's what I thought. How many other of these loser cases are you handling?"

"About a million."

"Great. Sounds like you have a wonderful law practice."

"In my next life, I'm going to be Governor of the state of California, but in the meantime, I've got to deal with all these cases of mine."

"Mr. Franck, I have a solution to your problem."

"You do?"

"I do."

I thought about it. How on earth could they solve this problem? And then before she answered, the light went off. A pardon! Of course! Why didn't I think about that before?

"Are you talking about a pardon?" I asked her.

"I am."

I looked out the window of my office. I was angry. Why didn't I think of this before? Of course, I shouldn't worry about how stupid I was not to think of this before. The good news was it still wasn't too late. There's no statute of limitations on a pardon.

"Ms. Shriver, I would like you to know I feel quite embarrassed. I should have asked for this long ago."

"Let me ask you something, Mr. Franck. Have you ever, in your entire legal career, submitted an application for a pardon?"

"As a matter of fact, no. I never have done one."

"Well, you've got an interesting opportunity here. This is what you might call a pre-packaged pardon. I've already got your answer, and the answer is 'granted.' Just a minute."

She then turned to her husband.

"Arnold, am I right? The answer is 'granted.'"

I could actually hear the Governor on the phone answer, "Granted."

Maria continued, "I will have my staff Federal Express the pardon paperwork. I expect it completely filled out and back to me within a matter of days."

"How about a matter of hours?"

"Wait until you see the forms. They're rather involved."

"I'm on it. Thank you very much, Ms. Shriver. I will tell Juanita about this immediately."

"Thank you, Mr. Franck, and keep up the good work."

The first call I made was to Sassafras. She was back in Milan.

"Hello, Sassafras. It's Herman."

"Hello, dear."

"I have some exciting news."

"You have exciting news for me? Well, I have exciting news for you."

I was wondering what her news to me could possibly be.

"What's that?"

"I love you."

I had not heard her say that before. It floored me and completely distracted me from what I was calling about.

"Oh, Sassafras. Do you mean it?"

"I do. I've thought about it, I've searched my heart, and I know that you are the man for me."

I shook my head in disbelief. Here I've got the first lady of the state of California calling me, offering to solve my endless legal battle, and one phone call later I've got the world's most beautiful supermodel telling me she loves me. I don't want to come down from this cloud.

"Well?"

"Well, what?"

"What is your good news for me?"

"Oh, see, now you've distracted me."

"I'm sorry if my love for you distracts you."

"Oh, no. It's a good thing. Believe me, it's a very good thing. You know I'm crazy for you, right?"

"I don't think I know anything. Why don't you explain it to me?"

"I love you, I love you, I love you a million times. You know I've been chasing you for over a year now. I've asked you to marry me, what, five times?"

"Six."

"Okay. And who's counting?"

"And what was my answer?"

"Yes, no, maybe, I don't know, I can't tell, I do know. The answer is no, the answer is yes, the answer is I don't KNOW."

My head, of course, is swimming. That's the kind of answer I did get from her, and I just sort of shook it off.

"Is that still your answer?"

"No, I have a new answer for you."

"You do?"

"The new answer is...I'll tell you later. First of all, you must tell me your good news."

"Okay. My news is that your domestic violence campaign completely one thousand percent worked."

"Oh? The judges have decided that you win?"

"No, not the judges, the Governor of the state of California has decided that I win."

"The Governor? How is he involved?"

"He has the power to set aside the felony conviction. Once that is removed, the whole basis for her deportation goes away and Juanita can stay here for the rest of her life."

Sassafras was silent. I heard her crying. I did not know quite what to make of it.

"Sassafras, are you okay?"

"Yes, I'm okay."

"Your tears are of happiness?"

"Yes."

Of the many successes in Sassafras's life, most of them were in the realm of the fashion world. And let's face it, nobody ever saved a life in the fashion world. This was the first time she had done something real, and it hit her like a ton of bricks.

"Please tell Juanita that I love her and that I want her to be the world's most perfect mother."

"I will. But Sassafras, I have a better idea. Why don't you come here and tell her yourself? I would like to set up a meeting with the Governor, Juanita, you and me."

"Just tell me when and where."

"The where will be Sacramento, California, at the state capitol. The when, I'll get back to you on that."

"Okay, lover. Put it together. I'll be there on a moment's notice."

The great thing about supermodels is they think absolutely nothing about flying anywhere on the planet to do a gig.

The first lady was quite correct that the pardon packet was rather ominous. It took me five days to fill out all the paperwork. I did nothing else during that period. I signed it, Juanita signed it, and then I drove it to Sacramento. It landed on the Governor's desk and went into a rather impressive inbox. They actually have a special office for the Governor's correspondence, so the inbox is actually an office staffed by six people that review the thousands of correspondence items. Mine would have been lost in that, had I not sent a copy to Ms. Shriver. She was good enough to contact the Governor's mail clerks and arrange to place that pardon application at the top of the pile. She called me to confirm.

"Mr. Franck, thank you for sending me a copy of Juanita's pardon application."

"Thank you for your help on this, Ms. Shriver. I can't tell you what an impact this will have on Juanita's life. Ms. Shriver, I have a question for you."

"Yes, go ahead."

"The application, and I hate to sound presumptuous, but you said earlier that it will be granted?"

"Oh, trust me, Mr. Franck. It will be granted as sure as the sun will set in the evening and will rise in the morning."

"Okay, here's my question. Could we have some kind of a ceremony or event at the state capitol about this?"

"Absolutely."

"I would like Juanita to be there and if I could, I would like some of the supermodels to be there."

"Okay, but there's one rule: they have to be in clothes."

"I'll make sure they dress for the occasion."

Ms. Shriver had no idea that the lead supermodel in Supermodels Against Domestic Violence was my fiancée, sort of. I thought about telling her, but then I figured this is something she really didn't need to know.

"Mr. Franck, let me contact you in the next couple days to schedule this ceremony. I believe there's a bit of rush on this item, am I right? The rush is muted by the current stay order in effect by the Ninth Circuit, but that stay order could be lifted upon their decision, which could happen any day. Rather than waiting for that disaster, it would probably be better to have the pardon issued. Is that right?"

"Oh yes, it would be much better. I would then submit a new brief to the Ninth Circuit telling that the issue has become moot."

"Let's do it just like that. I can tell you right now to start writing that mootness brief."

"I'll get on it. Thank you, Ms. Shriver."

Chapter 31
SASSAFRAS GETS REAL

It was a major media event. More than three thousand women showed up supporting Juanita and Supermodels Against Domestic Violence. The ceremony was initially scheduled to be inside, but the crowd made this impossible. On the capitol building lawn, on a gorgeous sunny afternoon, Governor Schwarzenegger signed, before a crowd of domestic violence victims, a pardon that would be heard around the world. He hugged Juanita. Ms. Shriver was next to Juanita and held her as well. I was standing on the other side of her with Sassafras and the other formerly naked supermodels.

It was a beautiful ceremony, with one surprise attendee. At my request, and with Juanita's approval, Mr. Agusto Santos, Juanita's husband, was also present. You might think this was a terrible idea, but let me tell you a little bit about his odyssey. Pursuant to his conviction for domestic violence, he spent ninety days in jail. During that jail term, and continuing upon his release, he commenced a fifty-two week anger management program. During this program, he was required to repeatedly acknowledge his crime, acknowledge the impact of that crime on Juanita and his family, and engage in substantial group therapy to analyze why he did what he did, the hot buttons of his character, and the solutions for assuring that this would never happen again.

I turned to Governor Schwarzenegger and asked permission to let him speak.

"Governor, if you don't mind, I think it will be useful to have her husband speak."

The Governor was surprised and turned to Ms. Santos. She nodded yes. She knew that this man was a changed man. The Governor spoke,

"Ladies and gentlemen, we have Ms. Santos' ex-husband, who wishes to address you."

The crowd hissed and booed. They knew what this animal had done. They would never accept him as a changed man. The Governor had to referee this situation. "Please, please. Give this man a second chance."

Agusto took the microphone. He was in tears. Sassafras watched this drama in complete amazement.

"I first want to tell Juanita once again how sorry I am for what I did to her. I am guilty of committing a series of acts of brutal domestic violence. My conduct was one hundred percent my fault, and I take full responsibility for what I have done to her, the impact on her, which includes the continuing impact on her emotional state, and the huge impact that I have put the entire family at risk as a result of what I have done. For doing these things, I am forever sorry. I take full responsibility for what I did. Juanita, I know the court, in what can only be described as a huge injustice, has granted me custody of our two children. Today, I give you what I know you deserve and what they deserve."

At this moment, Agusto's sister came forward with the two beautiful children of Juanita and Agusto. Two boys, ages 9 and 7, with short black hair, soft Filipino looks, and tears in their eyes, came running forward and hugged their mama.

"Mommy, Mommy! We love you! We miss you!"

It was impossible not to shed a tear. Even Arnold cried. It was a beautiful reunion between mother and sons. I was very moved by this experience. There are times when being a lawyer is truly a joyful experience. You can actually right a wrong, and in doing so, can achieve a level of fulfillment that is far greater than all the money in the world.

I looked over to Sassafras. She was crying like a baby. Tears just flowed from her eyes. The other supermodels were crying as well. Maria watched Sassafras as she walked away from Maria's side and stood next to me. Before this large crowd, Sassafras at last had her answer for me.

"By any chance did you bring that ring?"

The crowd had been giving a wild applause to this ceremony, which made it difficult for me to hear.

"I'm sorry? What was that?"

Sassafras rarely raised her voice, but this was an exceptional situation.

"BY ANY CHANCE, DID YOU BRING THAT RING?"

It didn't matter to me that Sassafras had gotten caught up in the emotion of this family reunion, of the importance of all this for Juanita, and of the impact on Sassafras's core being. This was the first time she had actually done something real. It was time for her to shed once and for all the rock star boyfriend and to begin the process of going from supermodel to wife and mother. She was ready for this. It took Juanita's case to bring it about.

Juanita turned and watched. Ms. Shriver was quite fascinated by this.

"As a matter of fact, I do have the ring."

I reached into my coat pocket and pulled out the one carat used diamond on a still brand-new gold setting. The applause had died down. People were starting to notice this sideshow, and had no idea how or why this was going on. They watched along with the Governor, the first lady, and our special guest of honor, Juanita. In front of this now silent crowd, I got on one knee.

"I love you, I love you, I love you. I love you a million times with more than all my heart, with more than all my life, with more than everything that I have and that I am. You are my whole life, my half life, my quarter life. Will you be my wife? Sassafras, will you marry me?"

She continued crying and smiled. She held out her hand for the ring.

"A million times no, but today yes."

She accepted the ring that I placed on her finger. She gave me a big hug. The crowd went absolutely wild with applause. Her supermodel friends came around and hugged her. It was quite beautiful.

I am the type of person that will not get lost in an emotional moment to look past some practicalities. I got this great idea. Knowing how Sassafras was and how she was subject to changing her mind, to say the least, I looked over to the Governor. The look was a rather odd one. I had a request. He could see that. But what was the request? I nodded and silently mouthed the word "now." He didn't understand. I then silently mouthed the words, "Will you marry us, now?"

Arnold did understand that. He gave one of his trademark ear-to-ear grins. Maria did not see this exchange and was looking over to Sassafras and her entourage of supermodel friends and Juanita. Governor Schwarzenegger gave me a thumbs-up. He asked me to come to him.

"Just make it real short and simple," I explained.

He laughed and nodded his head yes. I walked over to Sassafras and held her hand. I whispered in her ear.

"If you would like—and let me say that I would very much like—we can get married right now. Governor Schwarzenegger can do this for us."

She whipped her head around and glanced at Governor Schwarzenegger. It almost knocked him over. Her sheer beauty, determination, and intensity was almost enough to knock the former Mr. Universe right on his butt. She turned back to me.

"Yes, let's do this right now."

To Ms. Shriver's complete amazement, the Governor announced, "Ladies and gentlemen, we have a very interesting addition to today's ceremony. Juanita Santos' attorney, Mr. Herman Franck, is today, by me, going to get married. Does anybody object?"

The crowd was silent. He repeated, "One more chance: does anybody object? If so, state it now, or forever hold your silence."

No one spoke a word. Sassafras turned to Juanita and her children, and with her hand waved them to stand next to her. Juanita would be her bridesmaid. The other supermodels stood next to her. I did not have a best man at the ready, and looked over to Agusto. I beckoned him over.

"Please stand next to me. You may be my best man if you agree."

I figured, what the hell, he's part of this whole thing. He, of course, agreed. Arnold then proceeded.

"Do you, Herman Franck, take this woman, Sassafras Qin, to be your lawfully wedded wife, to have and to hold, in sickness and in health, for richer or poorer, so long as you shall live?"

I gave the biggest smile of my life.

"I do."

He turned to Sassafras.

"And do you, Sassafras Qin, take this man, Herman Franck, to be your lawfully wedded husband, to have and to hold, in sickness and in health, for richer or poorer, so long as you shall live?"

She looked at me right in the eyes as she spoke in a barely audible whisper:

"I do."

Governor Schwarzenegger grinned.

"That's a yes! With the power invested in me by the state of California and as Governor, I now pronounce you man and wife. You may kiss the bride."

As I planted an open-mouth wet kiss on Sassafras's medium-rare lips, the crowd went wild with applause. At last, Sassafras and I were married.

The next question, which as will be seen is a very complicated one, is how to keep her?

Chapter 32
AFTER THE MOVIE IS OVER

Most movies about love stories would end at the point where the couple somehow miraculously manages to overcome the many obstacles blocking their togetherness and have an end story at the point where the couple gets married. "And cut!" says the straggly-haired, bespectacled director, taking off his French artiste hat, wiping his brow, and smiling with the knowledge that he has just completed another wonderful romantic comedy/tragedy.

Not so with this one. Imagine the opportunity of following that romantic couple past the day of their marriage and during the ensuing years. No doubt most marriages don't make for good storytelling, what with all the challenges of home finance, mortgage payments, car payments, insurance payments, sick kids, demanding kids, work layoffs, career disappointments, in-law issues, and the myriad of other issues that challenge marriages throughout the United States and the world. These issues just aren't that fun and exciting to make for movie material. But these are the very issues that will grip us in a marriage teetering on the brink of split-aster. As will be seen, a central theme of this story is first we marry, then we stay together. How exactly that is done remains a work in progress, which, like all works in progress, begin with the road already traveled.

Our story will fast-forward a bit to a year and a half into our marriage. We had decided to move to Sacramento. After all, it had been kind to us and helped bond us together. It didn't hurt that the price of homes up here was about half that of the San Francisco Bay Area. Not that we were looking for a cheap home, but rather we were looking for a large home at the price of a cheap home in the Bay Area.

Our initial big stress points in the marriage arose from a combination of Sassafras's first pregnancy with our son Adam, the resultant impact on her career ('you clipped my wings'), and the reappearance, out of seemingly nowhere, of Karen the hooker (uh oh). Added to this mix of issues was something that I had only been vaguely familiar with, and was completely not ready for, the baby blues which followed the birth of our son. Sassafras was hit with a case of postpartum depression that catapulted her into the world of the psychotic. There was violence, there was slapping, breakage of plates, breakage of chairs, shouting, screaming, and a level of anger that I had thought was reserved for men against women. It became wicked, with Sassafras spitting on me, slapping me, and spewing out a host of insults ('you are a loser'; 'I can't believe this is the man I married'; 'you are a bad man'; 'you are a terrible father'; 'you are disgusting'; 'I do not love you'; 'I hate you'; etc. etc.)

I attempted to be patient, but did not know that the baby blues had sent her into a tailspin of depression. Instead, I incorrectly assessed that this was just who she was, what she was, how she'd become, and that I would need to just deal with this for the rest of my life, or get a divorce. After several months of this abuse, I began thinking right away about the divorce option, as she had become too evil, too sharp-tongued, and on top of that, physically violent. I was still pretty fast and could duck many of her slaps, but she was quite strong and would land a few. Several of them left red marks on my face, which were noticed in court. I saw attorneys looking at me, and thought of making the kind of lame excuses women make: "I fell down."

Or something like that. Instead of telling a stupid-ass lie, I just remained silent. Things got triply worse when Karen called, innocently enough, to refer a client to my law office. I had never mentioned Karen's name before, but somehow in one of these women's intuition/telepathic moments, she figured it all out: Karen was a former lover, now treading on Sassafras's unwanted territory. There's a certain oxymoron of a woman who hates a man, and yet is still extremely jealous of any other woman's encroachment on that man. Try to figure that one out.

I was not the least bit interested in Karen, but I did realize this negotiation between Sassafras and Karen could only end up in an eruption. Thankfully, the only fatality was my cell phone, which went smashing down to the ground into more pieces than my life had. I didn't like that phone anyway. With all these stressors present, our marriage balloon bursting at the seam, there was one event that finally set it all off and threatened to put our miserable marriage out of its agony before its second year.

Chapter 33
SUPERMODEL IN JAIL

I am not one to call the police on a whim. It was not the first time of violence or the second time or the third, it was the tenth time. This time it was just too much. I was holding our newborn son, an absolutely beautiful child, when Sassafras went off on me yet once again. We've all read about other violent supermodels in the press, the most infamous perhaps being Naomi Campbell. It should be noted Naomi, like Sassafras, is Chinese; well, at least half-Chinese. She's also African, the combination of which makes her a very strong, violent woman that has absolutely no control nor desire to control her anger and temper tantrums.

As a result, we have all read about Naomi in and out of jail, arrests in several countries, at airports, slamming into her assistants, and of note, her complete inability to stay with a man. To this day, she remains single and childless. Ever wonder how one of the most beautiful women on the planet stays that way? It's because she is absolutely crazy-ass angry, due to a very normal problem that afflicts many people, an anger management problem. If she would undertake appropriate regimens of therapy, it would likely solve.

Sassafras had the same kind of challenge. As I held Adam, I was walking away from her in one of her temper tantrums. I figured out I could not control who she was or what she did, I could only remove myself and my son from the danger. She was screaming, shouting, yelling, heaving, throwing, spitting. When she got this way, saliva poured into her mouth. She would foam, literally, like a rabid dog and give me a look that quite easily scared the bejesus out of me. I swooped up our son and was in the process of walking out of our house when she heaved an abalone shell filled with coins at me. This I would have forgiven, had I not also at the time been holding my son. I turned so that the abalone struck my back, and rained coins all about me. Happily, none of them struck our four month old son.

I continued walking away, thinking that the only course of action was simply to get the hell out of there. I was hoping that in several hours she would cool down, and things could remain at a livable level. How wrong I was. Upon my return, I saw the rather odd sight of broken dishes, broken tables, broken chairs, the house in complete disarray, and one added super-odd feature: there was blood everywhere. Apparently in the process of breaking one of the dishes, she managed to cut herself. This sent blood all over the kitchen sink, onto the kitchen floor (which was white tile and contrasted handily with her red, red blood), and blood in the garbage can. I could see from her Scott towels filled with blood that she had attempted to mop up her injury. I could see the droplets of blood leading out the door. She had vanished into the city. Who knows where she was, but somewhere out there was a supermodel with a cut hand or arm.

I decided that enough was enough. The attack earlier that day on me was probably her tenth or fifteenth; I had lost count. She was completely out of control, bonkers to say the least. She had no desire to check her anger and/or temper tantrums. She had a rather obvious anger management issue, which she had no intent of dealing with any way, shape, or manner, other than to continue spewing it out at me.

Now, with the added sight of blood everywhere, the dishes all cracked up, I decided to take some action. So, I called the police. They came over, a male and female officer, and looked at what appeared to be a crime scene right out of one of the "CSI" series. There was breakage and blood. One of the suspicions quite naturally held by the officers is how do they know that I didn't somehow cause this. They also noted that I was a book writer. Several of my books were on the floor.

"Is this you?"

The officer asked, looking at my photograph on the back of the book.

"Yes, indeed it is."

"So, you're a book author. And it says here you're an attorney."

"It does."

"You know, if you think about it, as a lawyer and a book writer, you could probably know how to exactly create a crime scene, making it appear that someone else was the guilty party."

The officer was right. I offered up this defense:

"What motivation would make me want to do such a thing? And also, think about this, why bother? All it does is cast suspicions on me, as is going on right now."

The officer thought about it and continued taking down his report.

"So, you say she threw something at you earlier?"

"I did."

As he was taking down my report, the female officer went to the neighbor and interviewed the neighbor's wife. I could not hear the interview, but later read in the report she had indeed confirmed that the screaming that could be heard from our house was all a female voice and not a male voice. I, for the most part, try to remain calm in an avalanche and storm presented by a clearly psychotic woman bent on violence and disaster. Her complaints were many, mainly the stress of having a baby, having the baby blues, an overall feeling of being trapped and imprisoned in a new life, in a new country, in a new place where she was unable to continue in her career, or at least thought she couldn't. The concept being that pregnant women don't make for good supermodels. I tried to explain that there must be some sort of post-pregnancy supermodel career, which usually received a response of a slap and a spit in the face. I actually didn't know what the hell to do, and found myself on this fateful day with two officers in my living room looking at a bloody mess.

It was just then that Sassafras arrived at the door. Uh oh. The female police officer immediately directed her to go right outside the door. It's protocol to keep the male and female apart in a domestic violence situation. This way, you get more truthful information, hopefully. The idea is that often a woman who is in the same sight line as the man may give a completely inaccurate version, for example downgrading something that was clearly domestic violence into some kind of accidental fall, due to the continuing powerful influence on the male over the woman.

Here we had a rather reverse situation, but the protocol was still used: they took her right out the door.

"Did you make the mess in this house?" was the first question I heard.

Now, she could have said right then and there, "No, I didn't, my husband did," and got me in the process. Had she said that, I would've been in major trouble. Amazingly, she admitted that she had done it, which had the rather unfortunate immediate impact of having her handcuffed. They placed her under arrest for the crime of "malicious mischief." They examined her arm and makeshift bandages and realized right away that the only appropriate and professional thing to do was to make a first stop at the local hospital.

I later learned that while at that hospital, one of the nurses had an unfortunate exchange with Sassafras. The nurse was uppity and said in a judgmental tone, "When will you people learn to control yourselves?"

Sassafras responded, while being monitored by the female police officer:
"You don't even know me."

In front of the attending physician, the police officer made the unfortunate decision to slap Sassafras right in the face and yelled, "Just shut up!"

This put the physician in a rather awkward position. Physicians are what are called mandated reporters, meaning they are required by law to inquire into any injury. If it turns out the injury was caused by some form of domestic violence, they must report it to the police. What, then, is a doctor to do when he witnesses a police officer commit an act of violence? The officer did this, of course, right in front of the physician, and couldn't give a damn. Perhaps, if it was the male officer that had struck her, the physician would have done something. In this case, he decided not to do anything, other than rub his hand through Sassafras's hair and try to calm her.

He proceeded to stitch up her cut, which required sixteen stitches. He then placed a rather nice professional bandage around it, and released her to the custody of these two officers. They then brought her down to the local jail, where she was fingerprinted, mug shotted, and booked in on charges of malicious mischief. Bail was set at twenty-five thousand, which would be easily posted by Sassafras. But it would still take a matter of twelve hours in the holding tank at the Sacramento County Jail. The last place a supermodel should ever have to be is in jail, but on this day, in this early evening, that is exactly where Sassafras found herself.

The fallout from this arrest incident would be a mess. As people like to say, there will be hell to pay.

Chapter 34
TRAGEDY IN TAHOE

There is a kind of ancient traditional dance practice in China. They call it Chinese Traditional Dance, or Classical Chinese Dance and Orchestral Music. It connects back to about 5000 years ago, and combines elements of opera, theatre, ballet, symphony, with bright out of this world costumes, and a caliber of dancing that few ever achieve.

The best way to fully understand this form is to see a performance, you will be in awe.

Here is how one critic, Mr. Richard Connema of *Talkin' Broadway* magazine described a group called Shen Yun, one of the greatest performers in this kind of dance: "mindblowing."

Mr. Connema gave his review in the *The Epoch Times*, Northern California Edition Special Edition for Shen Yun October 2009 front page]:

> I probably have reviewed over three to four thousand shows since 1942. A lot of reviewers use stars, you know, 1 star, 2 stars, 3 stars, 4 stars, 5 stars . . . I will give this production 5 stars. That's the top. . . .The dancers were absolutely fantastic . . . I found out that there was not only dancing in this but heart. You could feel that coming even from where I was sitting [in the balcony]—just a beautiful production. I found that those backdrop scenes and the way it was projected and the way it comes out is absolutely fantastic.

The costumes are bright yellows and reds, bright blues and emerald greens, and each look fit for a princess. The backdrop murals and videos show scenes out of ancient China, large scenes of expanded skies, rivers, mountains coming out of the ground into the sky, rivers gorging between them, and wild horses running through. The dramas are opera style, love and hate, war and peace, royalty and commoner, and show the themes of freedom, liberty, and the unstoppable force of nature known as the pursuit of love. The dancers have practiced endlessly for this performance, and without a doubt, leave the people watching absolutely in awe.

This kind of dance has now reached the United States, to sell out performances. One such group from the Beijing National Dance Academy came to perform in several cities in California, including a sell out performance in South Lake Tahoe. The Dance group came with 26 dancers. These promising dancers are in the category of Olympic stars in China. Spend one night watching them and you will see why.

Their next destination was Denver, Colorado. They were driving in a series of three transport vans from South Lake Tahoe back to the Sacramento airport for a flight to Denver. It was early December. The roads were icy, slushy in parts, wet in parts, and frozen in parts.

The dancers looked out the window at the beauty of the land. These parts are filled with rugged mountains, sierra style with large boulders expanding out of the mountains, and millions of pine trees everywhere. There are cliffs on the side of the road, in some places jutting down over 2000 feet.

One of the dancers, Pen Yi, observed to his fellow dancers, "It feels like we are gliding over the road."

Indeed they were.

Several continued sleeping. It had been a long series of performances and they were tired. Others talked about how they missed being home, missed their husbands or wives. One complained of how she missed her pet dog, Chi Chi.

The driver, from China, did not have enough experience in these kinds of roads. California's Sierra Nevadas hold a strange beauty, but can also be quite unforgiving. The path from the Sierras down to the flatlands of Sacramento has been sadly dotted with many deaths. Tonight would see another tragedy unfold, a tragedy in Tahoe.

On the tires of the vans were nicely placed snow chains. These chains work to keep the friction between the tires and the ice and snow. One of the chains had somehow come off the right side passenger tire. It made a large "womp" when it came off the wheel, and was sent upward into the wheel well, collected there for a bit, and then fell off to the side.

"What was that?" The driver had no idea, but could immediately feel the difference in the handling of the van. The driver in the van behind knew full well what it was. It struck his windshield, crashing it into a million pieces held together by the shatterproof glue. Shatterproof doesn't mean it doesn't shatter, it just means when it does the window still holds together.

The crashing of the chain into the windshield shocked everyone in the second van. They screamed. The driver instinctively turned the wheel in an attempt to avoid the chain, but it all happened too quickly. That van turned into the side of the road, which had a small ditch running along side. When the wheel was stuck in that ditch, it couldn't get unstuck. The driver then tried to overcorrect, finally got the van unstuck, but then went too far. He swerved over to the middle of the road, and struck the embankment separating oncoming traffic.

The third van was right behind this second van, and struck it from behind. This pushed the second van right into the first van. "AAAAAAAGGGGGGGGGH-HHHHHH."

The 'about-to-leave-this-world' looks on the dancers faces were frozen in eternity.

The front van pushed forward and swerved to the right. It smashed right into a large tree, which didn't yield. The panorama of the outdoors swirled by the windows of the van.

The first van came off the tree and pushed back into the highway. It was struck by the out of control second van. Several dancers in the second van went up and through the windshield, dying immediately.

The people in the first van were mangled beyond recognition. Before the two vans were at a point of rest, the third van smashed into both of them, forcing the second van to go up and over the first van, and crashing it into the same tree that had stopped the first van.

There was a three van accordion collapse and annihilation of one of China's top dance groups.

There was an eerie silence. The only sound was the wind through the trees.

It was still daytime, but a darkness surrounded the crash site. Heavy clouds covered the sun. Some not quite snow but not quite water was falling on the vans.

Other drivers stopped and were dazed at all the deaths. Bodies were lying outside the front of the vans, having crashed through the front windshield. A driver called 911. Within several minutes, the sounds of multiple sirens could be heard, police, fire department, ambulance, and a rescue helicopter were all on scene within minutes.

And of course with that, came the media. Several news choppers arrived to the horror of a scene that looked more like war than the beautiful Sierras.

Back in Sacramento, I was at the courthouse, second floor. I had gone over to the Jury waiting room to get a soda in the vending machine there. They have a television there showing the news.

Every prospective juror in the place was glued to the television account of what had happened to these dancers. The news played snippets from the previous nights dance production, showing a level of beauty and grace that most folks had never seen before. Then they segued over to the tragic scene of the accident, and showed what had happened to this incredible group of dancers.

I called Sassafras right away. She was not in a good mood.

"What?"

"You have to see the news. There's been a terrible accident involving a Chinese dance group. I think they need your help."

The phone hung up. I'm sure she was watching the news. Then she called me back. She was in tears.

"Can you find out where they are taking them?"

"Yes, I'll call you back."

I spoke with a nearby sheriff's deputy, who was connected up to the reports through his radio system.

"They are doing air evacs of the live ones. They are being taken to Sutter Hospital, downtown Sacramento."

Out of 26 dancers, 9 were still alive. They were carried three per helicopter to the rooftop helipad of the Sutter Hospital. We were there to greet them, and to provide whatever assistance we could.

We collected up in the emergency room lobby of the hospital. Quite a few members from the Sacramento Chinese community were present, all crying and sharing the sadness of this great loss. Sassafras and I arrived separately, she first. I could see her right away hugging and holding other Chinese people, crying, sobbing, and wondering what was going on with the surviving members of this dance group.

A nurse came out of the ER surgery area. "We need a Chinese translator." Without any hesitation, I saw Sassafras walk directly toward the nurse. There were certainly others present that could have provided this important service, but everyone was more than happy to allow Sassafras to be the appointed translator. She followed the nurse back into the surgery area, where she saw a terrible sight, the sight of Lau Zhi all bloodied up. He had a tube coming out of his mouth. He had broken arms, broken legs, broken shoulders, and a broken face. He had glass in his face, which had been removed to give way to some frightening scars. Sassafras continued crying. The nurse consoled her, and explained:

"He can't speak, but he is trying to tell us something. Look at his finger."

Sassafras saw that his finger was moving, it was painting something in air. She knew right what he was doing, he was drawing Chinese characters in the air to explain what he needed. Sassafras interpreted into English.

"His throat is clogged, he wants it unclogged."

The nurse was impressed, and smiled. "Very good." She brought over a vacuum type device, and sucked out of this man's mouth a bunch of bloody gunk. After that the Lau Zhi wrote with his finger the Chinese characters for "Thank you", which Sassafras translated to the medical staff.

Meanwhile, back in the lobby area there was the arrival of the Consul General of China. She and her entourage of diplomats had come at a moment's notice to see what could be done. She was there to share in the grieving, and to make immediate arrangements with the U.S. Government to provide quick travel visas for the families of the surviving members of the dance group.

The ER doctors worked miracles to save these nine members of the dance group. There had already been way too much death, no other would die. It was obvious enough, though, that these lucky nine would never dance again.

The hospital was kind enough to clear out a large meeting room. They removed the desks and chairs and replaced them with a series of cots. This room became an impromptu hotel for the ten families of the injured dancers. By the seventh day, family members from all parts of China had collected up and were able to visit their injured children on a regular basis. The mothers cried tears of pain and joy over the fact that their elite dancer children had been injured, but were also alive. The seven dead ones were placed into coffins and shipped back to China.

The Chinese people, even though a billion strong, will treat the loss of even one of them as a major tragedy. All of the parents, the consular officials, Sassafras, myself and Adam accompanied the series of vans taking the coffins one by one to the airport. The embassy had arranged for a special Chinese military transport, which had one mission: to collect up these coffins and deliver them back to Beijing.

We were allowed out on the tarmac at the Sacramento International Airport and joined in the salute of the entire Chinese community. There were many tears as the coffins were brought out one by one, a military attaché lifting each of them. Sassafras walked over to the lead one and placed her shoulder underneath the coffin. She waved me to join her, which of course I did. One of the soldiers moved back a bit to allow me to shoulder the side opposite Sassafras. One of the Chinese mothers held Adam and walked with us as we carried the coffin from the van onto the conveyor belt leading into the cargo door of the military plane. We gently placed the coffin down. One went on, and then two, and then three, and then four, and then five, six, seven, and sadly, an eighth one that had died at the hospital. They were all received by a group of soldiers on the plane. They secured them in a neat row, locking them into place for their last journey home.

We watched somberly as the cargo door closed. The plane taxied out to the runway, and within several minutes took off on its flight back to Beijing. We all returned back to the hospitals and turned our attention to the members of the dance group that were still very much alive. There were broken arms, broken legs, sliced faces, mangled chests, and the mangled lives of people that had been turned over and over in a crumpled up piece of metal that had somehow spared their lives. Some of them who healed up more quickly than others were allowed to leave the hospital and to fly home. There were a group of four, though, who were tragically injured, almost beyond repair. They had metal plates in their heads, metal screws in their legs, metal screws in their arms, but all this top caliber surgery would never put them back together as they were before.

A local Chinese dance group had come to the hospital to join with these injured dancers. The lead instructor was a graduate of the same Beijing dance academy, the top flight dance academy of all of China. There were many tears shed, but there was a certain joy in seeing the young dancers coming up in the world. For every tragedy on earth, there seems to be a matching miracle. The broken up dancers smiled at the young Chinese girls, and talked about dance. Though these broken dancers would never dance again, they would have a new role as teacher.

Indeed, these dancers were teaching the local teacher how to train the local girls and the local boys to become top level dancers.

Sassafras could see the beginning of her own role as a student of this local dance group. The instructor and the broken men explained it all to her. She would see that all these children and young adults would grow up with this Chinese culture of ancient dance to ancient songs, and ancient costumes with beautiful scenery on artwork behind them, to the lovely ancient operas of the Chinese dynasties long since past. This would all be shared in their new lives in the United States. It would also give Sassafras a major new post-supermodel career as a highly visible ambassador at large and an expert dancer.

Sassafras was a natural for dancing and quickly learned many of these fairly complicated ballet-style dance routines. It was not long before Sassafras was once again on stage, this time it was not the supermodel catwalk of New York or Milan; instead, it was the opera theater of downtown Sacramento, performing to a sold-out crowd of completely amazed Americans who had no idea what was in store for them that evening.

Sassafras came out as a lead dancer in a bright yellow outfit, looking a little bit like a genie. By the end of the evening's performance, Sassafras showed this crowd that China had much to be proud of. At the end of the performance, a still on crutches Lau Zhi, his legs permanently mangled up, barely able to walk him across the stage, came over with his crutches. A small girl, a Chinese-American, carried a beautiful bouquet of yellow roses. These were handed to Sassafras. She bowed before the clapping crowd. She then took apart the roses and handed them one by one to the other members of the dance performance.

Some American kids took the stage, a local dance group having no connection to this Chinese group, but they had decided to make a small performance in memory of their fellow dancers from China. Sassafras and her Chinese dance group watched. In the backdrop were the photos of the entire dance group from the Beijing academy, not as they looked following the accident, but instead as they looked in the full glory of their top abilities. A film showed them in action, which was nothing short of absolutely extraordinary. The film was from a performance in Beijing and showed the backdrop of a beautiful Chinese mountain scene with costumes that were yellow, blue, and red, and simply out of this world.

The American children had studied this dance for several weeks and copied it. It wasn't anywhere near perfect, but was a beautiful rendition of what these dancers used to be able to do. At the end of their performance, the crowd gave a standing ovation. Sassafras and her newly adopted dance team came out with each of their yellow roses and handed them to the children. They all held hands and roses together, and bowed before the wild ovation of the crowd.

Chapter 35
SECOND SON

There came a time of peace between us. It could have been due to several factors, the main of which was the natural passage of Sassafras's postpartum depression and reentry into a stable psychological state. She very naturally glided into the role of a good wife and an excellent mother. Adam and I were among her biggest fans at her dance performances, which were occurring several times a month. She was quite a talented dancer, graceful and elegant like a dark swan. Her local dance group was called The Red Shoe Dance Group. They prospered with her addition to the group. She became their lead dancer, which helped to raise Sassafras's spirits. Being connected in a community is no doubt essential to the emotional well-being of a wife. Separate her, segregate her, keep her alone in the world, and you have a recipe for disaster. Let her spread her wings and flutter about her own people, let her rise up within that community, and you will have a highly stable marriage. All husbands should heed this rule: do not under any circumstances block your wife's attempts into her own social world.

Though her dancing did not earn money, it was not without its professional benefits. Her rise in the local Asian community was noted not only by the dancers, but also by their husbands and others who were local businesspeople. It became well known within the Asian community that Sassafras's husband was an attorney. Quite a few of these local business owners became my law clients. This also developed a working relationship between Sassafras and me. She would assist in the translations in the discussions between my Chinese clients and myself. There was an excellent synergy here. The Chinese immigrants turned entrepreneurs turned American dream holders very much appreciated the fact that I had an Asian wife.

At the same time, when it came to legal matters, they generally desired a white attorney. This was not due to any negative feeling among their own people, but was instead due to practicalities. The Chinese are eminently practical. Many of them, as it turned out, believed that if you are in an American court, you should have an American attorney. I thought to myself, if I had some kind of legal problem in China, I would certainly want a high-ranking Chinese attorney to represent me.

We placed a series of ads in the Chinese community newspapers, with a photo of myself and Sassafras, inviting business clients and others to engage us in various legal matters. I did not think Sassafras would enjoy any aspect of the practice of law. I was wrong in this. She very much enjoyed the networking, the telephone discussions, the meetings with so many new people. She also appreciated the importance that they would attach to their relationship with us. Most of their law matters would be the most important thing going on in their business lives. They would entrust these matters to us, and in doing so, gave both of us a huge vote of confidence. With this came respect, prestige, and further recognition for Sassafras in the Asian community. She became a "go-to" girl. If you had a problem, call Sassafras, and she and her husband would help you with it.

All of this propelled her into an excellent psychological state which brought about a period of family harmony. Sassafras prospered, the law office prospered, the family prospered. During this period, we had our second son, Alex. He is an absolutely beautiful boy, sure to catch his own supermodel one day. He was born much whiter than Adam, who shares Sassafras's darkish Cantonese features, except with an Anglo-looking face. Adam was long, thin, and dark. Alex was white, stocky, and had more of an Asian face. I refer to this as a genetic crisscross. You never know what you're going to get when you have children.

The two boys are completely different not only in looks, but in personalities. Adam seems more Chinese, obedient, thoughtful, pensive, and intellectual. Alex is more of the wild white man, preferring worldwide wrestling to kung fu, giggles to pensiveness, and has an endless series of entertainment for us.

Perhaps fitting of Alex's kickass personality was the drama that surrounded his birth. About eight months and three weeks into her pregnancy, Sassafras woke up one morning feeling extreme pain in her abdomen.

"It hurts!"

"Are you having the baby?"

"No, it's not that kind of pain. It's up here."

She showed a higher part of her abdomen, near her solar plexus. I called the hospital and spoke with a triage nurse. The nurse gave me some very simple advice.

"Bring her here NOW."

That was simple enough to understand. I grabbed Adam and helped Sassafras down the stairs and to the car. We were at the hospital within a matter of twenty minutes. Her pain grew more and more as we got closer and closer. The doctor brought her right onto a gurney and into an ultrasound room. He allowed me to be present. He turned the ultrasound on and saw little Alex, busy as a little bee. The doctor quickly saw the problem.

"His foot has punctured the womb."

You could see it plain as day. His foot was dangling outside the womb. This was quite a serious situation and caused huge blood loss to Sassafras. The doctor went right into action with "emergency C-section." They wheeled her into an OR room. I stayed outside with Adam. Within the period of an interrupted phone call to my brother, Alex was pulled out of Sassafras. He was perfectly healthy, though a little bit hyper in the feet. The doctor explained to me that Sassafras had lost about half of the volume of her blood in the process, and would have to stay in the hospital for observation.

I had court the following morning, which stops for no one. The case had to do with an intrafamily real estate squabble, son stealing house from mom. Just lovely. Adam and I arrived at the hospital in the afternoon. You should've seen how beautiful Sassafras looked in her light blue hospital gown, her much lighter looking complexion, apparently caused by the loss of blood, and her newborn son Alex with an ear-to-ear grin. What was one became two, became three, and now four.

Chapter 36
THE HELL BEGINS

I figure it's much more interesting to hear about marital tragedy rather than marital bliss, so I will fast forward from the bliss part and get to the tragedy part. We go forward eight years. Adam is 8, Alex is 6. They are incredibly handsome young men. They are learning kung fu, Chinese, and piano. During this period, Sassafras continued in her dancing and became quite advanced.

Meanwhile, I continued to toil away as a lawyer. I had also continued in a sideline career as a writer. This created a bit of a conflict between Sassafras and I. The problem was that my writing wasn't really getting me anywhere. I wrote a screenplay called "The Debt." I had given my heart and soul to this project and presented it to the powers that be in Hollywood. The good news, it got me in the front door, I got some interviews, and made some progress. The bad news, it didn't get picked up by anyone.

The story was about an American lawyer and his lovely Chinese wife who were having tons of bad luck. It turned out that in a past life the two of them had lived in Australia, during the turn of the century. They had headed up a medical/social experiment (based on real historical events) whereby the Australian government decided to force interbreeding between the white settlers and the aboriginals. The concept was after approximately five, six, or seven generations, the aboriginals would be gone. In the present day life of this lovely couple, they were suffering from the karmic results of this past life holocaust. The question presented by the story was how on earth could they possibly pay off this debt?

One of my purposes in writing this story was to allow a further opportunity for Sassafras to have a role in a movie. The process went quite similar to my experience with the Shanghai twins: close, but no cigar. I did not mind so much that Hollywood was not accepting my scripts. It's always a long shot whenever you try show business. But Sassafras reacted to it in an unexpected manner. Had I known of her reaction, I never would have tried. Her reaction was that of 'you are such a loser.' She had a big issue with failure. To me, living in the mode of an American entrepreneur, failure was a byproduct of making attempts at success. I look at failure as being part of the process. You don't always connect. To be sure, if you teach people that failure must be avoided at all costs, one of the dangers is that out of fear of failure, people will just stay home and never leave the house. Obviously, this is not a good thing. You have to have courage and fearlessness in your attitude toward life or you will never get anywhere.

Sassafras had a different attitude, perhaps due to her hyper-success as a su-permodel. Or coupled with her hyper-success as a dancer, she did not understand failure, had not experienced it directly herself, and did not relate or accept the no-tion that failure was just part of life. For her, failure was not an option.

"You are such a loser. You are so stupid. Look at you."

These were the words and phrases I started hearing on a regular basis. Mean-while, my law practice was such that it was making money, but not in a hyper way. Most people figure lawyers make big bucks. The reality is they make moderate bucks. We were living a middle class lifestyle. Here is the problem: a supermodel does not aspire to the middle class. This, of course, is the understatement of this entire story and generated a huge conflict between Sassafras and I. She simply would not accept our middle class suburban life. She lost respect toward me, and began to see me as somebody that was a pathetic loser. On top of that, I made a personal mistake in devoting my time to the law practice, and devoted completely insufficient time to her and our marriage. A combination of an undesirable middle class lifestyle, a lack of focus on the marriage, coupled with a lack of focus on my own physical appearance, began the process of unraveling our marriage.

I say these things in retrospect, having lost her to these circumstances. I had become a couch potato, engaged primarily in the legal practice and book/script writing, neither of which present physically challenging activities. Rather than sweating on the weekends, I was writing on the weekends. I became large, and ballooned up to two hundred and ten pounds. I am only 5'11", and became the worst thing in the world for a supermodel: a middle class chubby attorney.

Meanwhile, Sassafras continued to rise as a dancer. She looked absolutely gorgeous; trim, fit, beautiful, talented, and a kind of wunderkind in the dance community. Our marriage went from blissful to doldrums to tragedy when she was noticed by some Hollywood producer types that arranged for the ultimate invitation for a hot 30-something Asian former supermodel turned dancer: an in-vitation to appear on the hit reality series, "Dancing With the Stars."

Uh oh. I'm about to lose my wife to a movie star.

Chapter 37
I LOST MY WIFE

I lost Sassafras to, of all people, Brett Clawney, the famous movie star. She had already had photos of him that she posted in her work area at my office. I did not take offense to it; every girl should have her fantasy date. The trouble was when fantasy met reality. Of all the movie stars for the show to match her up with, they had to pick Brett Clawney. He was an exceptionally handsome man, winner of *People* magazine's sexiest person alive three times, holder of no fewer than three Academy Awards, had become not only a leading actor, but now was transforming himself into a director, a producer, and more recently, a totally cool social activist on par with Angelina Jolie. He was being hired for various green environmental causes, was giving moving speeches about how we need to save the planet for subsequent generations. He was quite simply the perfect man.

And then there I was: chubby, middle class, unable to pierce into the hard outer shell of Hollywood and, in the eyes of Sassafras, a total loser. I could see it in two seconds on TV. The way they danced was unbelievable. He was quite talented, she was brilliant. The two of them looked so perfect together. I would be the first to admit that they belonged together. Their chemistry was awesome. The way he looked at her, the way he held her, the way she danced with him. She and I could never do that in a million years.

I thought to myself, uh oh. I'm going to lose my wife to a movie star. She was constantly flying down to Los Angeles, leaving for weekends at a time and then weeks at a time. The boys and I meanwhile stayed up in our middle class suburban home. I drove them to school, got them ready for school, dropped them off at school, picked them up at school, went on my way to work, went to court, wrote legal briefs, and continued in my apparently pathetic life.

Soon enough, the tabloids were reporting the romance between Mr. Clawney and Sassafras. Photographs showed them in Beverly Hills having romantic dinners together. It was bad enough having a wife that is having an affair, but triple now that this affair was being widely reported in the Hollywood press. When she would return from Hollywood, she would look at me with complete disgust. It was pretty hard to go from the Beverly Hills hotels, Rodeo Drive, and dining with movie stars, to then return to her middle class suburban lifestyle.

I knew the score. She was sick of me, didn't want me, and wanted to leave. The problem was mine. I was obsessively in love with her and did not want to let her go. How could I re-catch her? How I could I keep her? How could I possibly win her back from this movie star?

Chapter 38
STEP NUMBER ONE: CAPITAL ATHLETIC CLUB

The first thing I did was cry. I cried like a baby. There is nothing that brings a man so low as to lose the woman he loves. I was in the dumps and I knew it. I was debilitated by this loss. My boys saw it. They were my companions and supporters.

"When will Mommy come home?"

Adam wondered.

"Is she gone forever?" Alex asked.

"How come she doesn't like you anymore, Daddy?"

"It's because you're fat," Alex noted.

Hearing this from my son was traumatic, but the fact remained he was one hundred percent correct. I knew, of course, that this would not solve all of my problems, but it would solve the problem of my physical appearance. So I decided to do something smart. I joined a local gym, the Capital Athletic Club. One of the things I learned is that working out is, like many things in life, a matter of habit. Once you start doing it, you never want to stop. I saw this right away with the fellow members of this co-ed gym. They were down there absolutely all the time. You should see the place at quitting time, at approximately 5:30. It is teeming with people arriving in suits and little gym bags. They come in, get into their workout clothes, and hit the stair climber, the elliptical, the stationary bicycle, and the treadmill.

My first time on, I about killed myself. First of all, just running in place on a conveyor belt takes a little bit of getting used to. I was off-balance, fell a couple times, I sweated profusely. I was able to do it for about twelve minutes before I had to stop and take a break. I then went over to the elliptical. This device is one where you run in place, plus hold onto a couple handles that are a bit like ski poles, and push them forward and backward with your hands. This way you get an upper body and lower body workout. I lasted about eleven minutes on that before I nearly died.

I could see that this is something that took a little bit of getting used to. I noticed that the other people on the ellipticals, the stationary bicycles, and the treadmills were running nonstop for close to an hour. These are people, mind you, that are well over the age of 50. I don't want to call them old because they aren't old. They are strong, vibrant, and to my way of thinking, quite impressive. I felt like a piece of garbage being blubbery and sweating like a pig. Guess what, the second time I went, the following day, I moved up to fifteen minutes, and then twenty, and then twenty-five, and then forty-five, and then an hour. Within a month, I was sailing on the elliptical without any trouble for one hour straight. By the time I was done, I was soaking wet. I enjoyed the feeling getting off the elliptical, my legs wobbly, tired, a little bit like getting off a horse.

The other interesting aspect to this workout regimen is that the room had a television. I don't usually watch daytime TV, but of all the shows in the world for me to be watching, there were episodes of "Oprah" and "Dr. Phil." Perfect. There were sessions on being overweight, how to lose weight, the psychology of obesity, and the need to break the cycle of endless eating, zero exercise, and vegging out. A kind of depression can take over from this which can create a terrible circle of further obesity, less attractiveness, the feeling of rejection, the receipt of the emotion of hate and disgust, leading to more depression, more eating, et cetera.

I saw right away there was a simple way to break this cycle: get down to the gym and kick some butt on the elliptical. And what better place to listen to episodes on obesity than right there at the gym? I also started eating differently. Part of it was my stomach was feeling sick due to the loss of my wife. This put my stomach in knots. I have a fairly acidic stomach naturally. When I'm worried, the acids flow. The good news is this makes me less hungry. I completely stopped eating junk food. No more McDonald's, no more Burger King, no more Taco Bell. Instead it was salads, fruits and vegetables, with an occasional soda.

I noticed the sessions of "Oprah" where they talked about soda. It is a completely useless beverage. It adds tons of calories with zero proteins. It does nothing good for the body. The bubbles actually make you thirstier, so when you drink one, you want a second one. It fills you with sugar, it's bad for your teeth, it is nothing but bad news. The only thing good about it is it tastes just swell.

I broke out of the soda habit and adopted instead a water habit. I started buying cases of water and drinking them one after another. I could not go entirely cold turkey; I had the occasional soda, and tried to work myself down to one per day. One of the nice byproducts of getting dumped is it puts you in a tailspin where you are willing to re-examine your life and do things completely differently. I thought about my relationship with Sassafras and what I could do to try to make it workable again. Of course, none of this could happen until she got home from Beverly Hills.

Chapter 39
STEP NUMBER TWO: FOCUS ON YOUR WIFE

Within several months, I had managed to lose an impressive twenty-five pounds. This actually made a huge difference to me, not only externally, but internally. I felt better. I felt more agile. If you think about it, losing twenty-five pounds is like getting rid of two bowling balls. I could move faster, I could run up and down stairs, I was athletic for the first time in years. There was a time, when I was a kid, that I was extremely athletic. I was a competitive swimmer, I was a football player, I did competition judo, I was a wrestler, I was a boxer, I was in awesome shape.

But those days had long passed and I had succumbed to a life as a lawyer, pushing papers and pencils, instead of lifting weights and running miles. I used to run three miles to school every day. Now I was back, running the equivalent of five to six miles per workout session. I was sweating out. Something that I saw on "Dr. Phil" was that "you have to break a sweat." I did just that every day. I was trying to go religiously to the gym and I noticed a simple reality: once you get in the habit of where you want to go, you go. I saw the same people there day after day doing the same thing, running for their lives. I could see right away that none of them would want to skip even a day.

During my sessions at the gym, I continued to watch "Oprah." How pathetic is that? But reserve your judgment. There is actually wisdom to be learned from her show. One of the therapists talked about a need for people in troubled marriages to refocus their energies on the marriage. Too often they have their focus on the many other aspects of their life. There's the obvious distraction of work, and as Shakespeare said, "The law is a jealous mistress." How true, but how typical of all careers. I don't care if you're a banker, an accountant, an engineer, or a garbage collector, a career occupies one's attentions, and sometimes excessively.

Then there are family matters: children, going to school, getting them dressed, getting them fed. Mundane things. Shopping for food, taking the garbage out, cleaning the house. All these things can get in the way of one's focus on a relationship. You have to stop at some point and ask yourself, what percent of my time am I spending on paying attention to my wife? Is it three percent, five percent? Is it even measurable? Do you need decimal points to calculate it? Is it something that you have to place on an atomic weight machine to truly measure?

You get the idea. We men will often lose our focus on our wives. Make no mistake about it, when you do that, you run the risk of losing your wife as I did.

I did this awkwardly. I picked Sassafras up at the airport and asked her questions about how she was doing. You can see for yourself how I made quite a few mistakes in this process.

"Hi, hon. How was your trip?"

"Fine."

She was abrupt and did not want a bunch of questions.

"How's Beverly Hills?"

"Beverly Hills is so much nicer than Sacramento."

"How is your dancing?"

"Are you checking on me? Why don't you just stop."

As you can see, this would take some time. My attempt to focus was being misinterpreted as spying on her. I thought it would be good to ask about her instead of talking about me, but then I started to understand that to turn this around, she had to see something about me that was changing. She didn't need to know about herself and wasn't even near interested in impressing me with any aspect of her life. She'd given up on me. She had tossed me into the garbage can of dumped husbands. My new name was Humpty Dumpty.

She once made a comment to me that I was frightfully in agreement with: "Once the mirror is shattered, it cannot be put back together."

But guess what, ladies and gentlemen, I would not go quietly into the night. I would fight for this woman. I would find a way to catch her again and to save my marriage.

"Your focus on me is not helping things. Don't you have a book or something you're writing?" she told me as I followed her around the house.

She wanted me to leave her alone, to ignore her and just let her fly away. You are probably quite naturally thinking, 'Why don't you just do that?' But here's the issue: I love this woman. I'm going to find a way to catch her back. So I showed her,

"As a matter of fact, I am just now finishing a book. Would you like to see it?"

I showed her the manuscript. It was five hundred and ten pages long, a beautiful story called *Katie Cranberry: Book Four*. This was the fourth book in a series that focused on a young Native American girl, Katie Cranberry, who has a group of fruit friends. These fruit characters, in the realm of veggie tales, except a little older and without emphasis on the Bible, travel with Katie Cranberry throughout the world. In each country, they are visited upon a conflict based on some type of race-based hatred, religious-based hatred, or other example of people hating each other based on their status. Katie and her fruit entourage would learn the art of diplomacy by breaking these cycles of hatred and finding ways to make friends out of enemies.

In Book One, Katie goes on a whirlwind castle hopping adventure with her fruit friends, Katarina Apple, Razzmatazz Raspberry, Jorge Banan, Valentino Orange (from Italia), Ivano Grape (from Ukraine), three Persian apples, and a pomegranate from Samarkand. They meet up in Eastern Europe, Central Europe, and along the Silk Road, where they learn about hate and how, through diplomacy, hate can be eliminated.

This story is set at the time of the Mayflower pilgrims in the year 1621. The initial scene is at the first Thanksgiving held sometime in November 1621. Katie is of the tribe that befriended the Pilgrims, and is whisked away by a magical swan. Book one takes her through several countries of Eastern Europe, Central Europe, Persia, Tajikistan, Uzbekistan, Kazakhstan, and ending in Zian, China. She is then whisked home back to Plymouth, Massachusetts. During the process she gains a couple years.

In book two, she journeys to South America, where she learns, to her horror, that the Spanish conquistadors have annihilated the Native American populations. This occurred about a hundred years before the arrival of the Pilgrims. She saw firsthand that the Spaniards stole the gold from these natives, stole their land, stole their heart and culture, their way of life, their everything. They imprisoned them and, much to her astonishment, managed to poison them with diseases that wiped them out. What few were left became slaves or prisoners. On her return to North America, she vowed to never let this happen to her people.

In book three, she begins her mission by marrying the Governor's son, a nice white boy by the name of Isaiah Brettford. In book four, *Katie's North American Peace Adventure*, the book I am just now finishing, Katie begins the mission of making it so that the annihilation of the Native Americans of North America never happens.

I showed the manuscript to Sassafras.

"Look here. It's quite a work. What I did was to find Native American legends, such as *The Tale of Little Man With Hair All Over*, and integrated them into a diplomatic adventure story that took Katie and her fruit entourage through various Native American tribes throughout North America. Their attempt to avoid annihilation began with the help of an extraterrestrial being by the name of Octobearagator, who taught Isaiah and Katie the first step of how to avoid annihilation: create a medical college that teaches Native Americans how to avoid the holocaust of European diseases."

She was not listening even for a second.

Chapter 40
CONVERSATIONS WITH THE WOMAN WHO DUMPED ME

Now this will sound really pathetic, but while working out and listening to "Oprah," one of the things I learned is how communication can be the anchor to a successful marriage. So I thought I would give it a try. Sassafras had just arrived back from one of her trips down to Beverly Hills with Mr. you know who. I was at the dining room table reviewing my five hundred and ten pages of *Katie Cranberry: Book IV.* She walked by me as though I didn't exist. I shook my head in amazement. Not that she didn't like me, but at how cold she could be toward me. I turned to her.

"Can we talk?"

"No."

She put her bags down in a corner not far from me. She went to the refrigerator and found some kind of odd-looking Chinese food. I think it was a hazelnut of some sort. She grabbed a handful and went upstairs. It didn't help matters that she looked positively gorgeous. I was in the throes of her spell, an obsessive love that I could not get unstuck from. This was my problem. I followed her upstairs. I watched her little ass move up the stairs, an impressive sight. I was now getting in pretty good shape, so I could fly up the stairs just as quickly as she could.

She went into the master bedroom. It didn't bother her to take off all her clothes in front of me. She prepared the bath and laid down in it. I came in and sat next to her. I didn't want to be in any way annoying, but the first words out of her mouth proved otherwise.

"You are so annoying."

This was something I had heard on quite a few occasions from her. If I say something, I'm annoying; if I don't say anything, I'm taking her for granted. I'm in one of these tight spots of you're damned if you do, you're damned if you don't. But I continued on.

"Can you tell me what is your biggest problem with me?"

Talk about a loaded question. This is a question I hardly advise anyone to ever ask their cheating spouse. You may not like the answer. Rather than answer me, she took her hands up out of the bathtub and flexed her fingers outward. It was an interesting maneuver. It was a way, I think, of her telling me, would you please just leave. I don't want to talk to you. YOU ARE ANNOYING. I got that communication, probably accurate enough, but decided to defy her.

I looked at her fingers, I looked at her naked body. Wow, she really is gorgeous. It's very hard to leave a woman like this. It's even harder to break up with her, even when she's having an affair completely out in the open and not making a secret of it, et cetera. Great, I thought to myself. She doesn't even want to talk. But me being the lawyer, a blah-blah-blah guy, I pushed on.

"Oh, go ahead, let's talk. Don't you think we should talk about this?"

One of the other things a therapist on "Oprah" stated was that in order for a troubled marriage to make it, the parties have to want it to work. It is similar in any other kind of psychological issue, if you don't want to stop drugs or stop alcohol or stop gambling or stop eating, you are never going to stop your drug addiction, alcohol addiction, gambling addiction, or food addiction. You have to begin by understanding there is a problem, and then by adopting an attitude and desire that you want to fix that problem.

Well, we all knew the problem was there. That part, phase one, we had long ago passed. The trouble was that she absolutely was not interested in fixing it. Without her motivation, were we doomed beyond extinction? Watch and you shall see.

I egged her on.

"Come on, just talk to me. What is the problem?"

She finally started to respond.

"First of all, you're a complete dick and an asshole. You abused me, you took me for granted, you treated me like shit, you yelled at me, you don't listen to me, you don't do the things I ask you to do. On top of that, you're ugly, you're fat—"

I looked down at my weight. My goodness, I had lost twenty pounds.

"Yeah, you're still fat. And on top of everything else, you're a loser, you're poor, and you're never going to be rich. You want me to go on?"

I thought about the list of things she had just said. The one I was puzzled by the most was the abuse part.

"How did I abuse you?"

"Oh come on, you know. You yell at me all the time, you shout at me all the time, you treat me like shit. That's abuse, you dickhead. Don't you know? Don't you understand anything? Did you really go to college? Do you remember when you put me in jail, you asshole?"

Oh. That, all of the sudden, reared its ugly head.

"Do you remember what *you* did on that day?"

"Oh, fuck you! You are such a dickhead. You are being such a piece of shit. All you're doing is focusing on yourself. You're just listening to what you need. You are not doing anything for me. It's all about you. And then you put me in jail; fuck you for that!"

Ooh, I thought. We have issues.

"But let's not even focus on that," she continued. I had her on a roll. I figured any kind of talking from her is better than no talking at all.

"Let's get to the real point: we are not compatible, okay? I don't like you, I don't love you, I fucking hate you. I think you are a loser, you will always be a loser, you are never going to be a rich guy. Let's be clear about this: I need you to be rich. You're not. And if you're not rich by now, you never will be."

"I'm not poor, right? I mean, I'm kind of in the middle."

"Yeah, and guess what, I don't want to be in the middle. I never wanted to be in the middle. That was your stupid-ass idea. I want to be one of the super-rich people. Don't you get that? You need to just let me go. You're not going to be what I want, you're never going to convince me that you are anything other than a piece of shit loser, so let's get real with it. You need to just shut up and let me go."

Gee, I thought. Don't sugarcoat it.

"Wait a minute, just a minute. You need to be rich? You are rich! You've got all kinds of money."

"No. Listen, you dickhead, you still don't get it. I need *you* to be rich. I need *you* to be a star, not a loser. And let's face it, you're a loser and you're always going to be one. As long as you are a loser, I'm not going to want you. It's that simple. Now, is there anything about that you don't understand?"

"Yeah, here's something I don't quite understand—excuse me for being such a stupid-head loser—why did you ever marry me in the first place if this is how you feel? You knew I was just a lawyer, I'm not some movie star guy, never would be a movie star guy."

She looked up at me and shook her head.

"Because you convinced me to make one of the biggest mistakes of my life to marry you. You did that, and it was a huge mistake. I want to fix that mistake. You need to let me go."

"Why do I need to do that? If you want to go, go! I'm not going to be able to stop you. This is a free country. You don't need my permission to go; you can just leave."

I started thinking to myself, everything she said made such perfect sense to me. Why wouldn't she just leave? Why would she stay with me? She hardly needed my permission, she could go out and hire a lawyer, divorce my ass in two seconds. She didn't need anything from me to do that. All she had to do was check a little box on the Petition for Dissolution form that says "Irreconcilable differences" and she's free of me. She could walk out the door, go to Beverly Hills, be with her Hollywood boyfriend, and have fun and games for the rest of her life. Interesting that she didn't just do it. So what's up with that?

As I was talking to her, the beeper on her phone went off. She grabbed it with great excitement, opened the phone and saw that she had received a text message. She looked over to me.

"Do you mind?"

Great, I thought. A text message from Mr. Handsome, Mr. Perfect, Mr. Movie Star, Mr. Rich Successful Man, Mr. In Perfect Shape, Mr. Everything, and here I am, Mr. Nothing. I got up and left the room. True, I thought. I am a loser. I am stupid. I am fat. I am all of those things, and I did need to let her go. But in the ultimate act of selfishness and stupidity, I didn't want to let her go, and I wouldn't let her go. I should just file for divorce, right? Put the misery out of this totally failed marriage? I couldn't do it. I wouldn't do it.

So I explained it to her when she got out of the bath.

"Listen, let me make something clear to you. You want a divorce, you go file divorce. I am not going to do it."

She looked at me with these killer eyes, black, not brown. They darted through my head and told me, "I am emotionally dead to you. I will never be in love with you. Why would you want to stay with me if I'm like that?"

I looked back to her and told her the God's honest truth, "Because stupidly or not, I am in love with you and I don't want to give you up."

She shook her head in amazement and walked away, sat on the piano bench, and proceeded to play piano.

Chapter 41
DON'T TRY TO BE LIKE THE OTHER GUY

I was smart enough to know to not try to be like the other guy. As a rather strange coincidence, I kind of sort of look like him. We have the same salt and pepper hair, I have kind of a square jaw, I have a boyish-looking waspy face. To my credit, and if I may say so myself, I am somewhat handsome. I am also quite witty and can out-talk, out-argue, out-debate just about anybody on the planet.

So I figured out right away, I'm not going to compete with this guy. He makes about twenty million dollars per film. He is a lot more handsome than me. He owns homes all over the world. How can I fight with that? I figured right away, I've got to just be me. If I can't lure her back by being who I am, truly the marriage is lost. But it wouldn't hurt if I became a millionaire.

As it happened, a case of mine that could make me not two million, but about nine hundred thousand, was coming up for review by the United States Court of Appeals Ninth Circuit. Here was the situation. Long ago, I had this advice from my grandfather, an attorney from way back, and a Stanford Law grad. In the pecking order of attorneys, there are the Harvard grads and Stanford grads, and then there is everyone else. As a Georgetown Law grad, I was in the category of everyone else. He was quite polite with me, me being his grandson and all, and gave me some very simple advice.

"You want to get as many trials under your belt as quickly as possible. There is no substitute for trial experience. You can't read about it, you can't watch others do it; you've got to do it yourself. Until you've done ten or so, you're really not going to know what you're doing."

Great, I thought.

"Tell me, Grandpa, where can I pick up some trials?"

"Oh, here's a simple one. Go down to the jail. There are all kinds of people in there that need a lawyer to do their trial. Don't worry about getting paid; just do them for free and get them done."

In the process, I started representing some pretty heavy duty felons: robbery, rape, attempted murder, major car chase, bang 'em up, hit a cop, drunk as a skunk, ran, fled, threw a screwdriver, hurt the cop dog, sixteen counts, seventeen felonies, the works. You name it, I did it.

"The plea is not guilty to all counts."

Then the game was on. Pretrial discovery, pretrial motions, motions to exclude evidence, all of which were denied, and ultimately a full jury trial where the evidence was hugely against my client: eye witnesses, fingerprints, blood samples, DNA evidence, confessions on tape, everything working against me. I was fearless. I would go to the jury and explain to them that the prosecution had not met their burden of proof beyond a reasonable doubt, that there were other explanations for the circumstances, that there were holes in the evidence, that everything did not add up to my client's guilt.

To my credit, the juries were staying out for a significant amount of time. Indeed, one judge commented, "I don't know what you did to confuse the jury. It would've have taken me five seconds to find your client guilty as sin."

Well, I thought, I'm glad you're not on the jury. For the most part, my clients were found guilty. Maybe not of everything, but enough to send them off to prison. Here is where I got involved in a rather remarkable and indeed extraordinary aspect of the law: prison civil rights litigation. This is an area of law that involves not what sent the prisoner to prison, the so-called commitment offense, it involves what happened to the prisoner while in prison. And believe me, all kinds of stuff can happen in prison.

I did gang set-up killing cases where prison guards would purposely stage a fight between members of opposing gangs, bet on those fights, and gee, guess what, one of the inmates got severely beaten, hurt, or even killed. Although I lost the criminal cases that got the people into prison, I was able to win almost all of the civil rights cases. These were total loser cases that no attorney in their right mind would ever take in a million years. But me, interested in getting significant jury trial experience, and indeed, federal court jury trial experience, I was game. Sure, I'll do the case. Next thing you know, I'm in front of a federal court jury arguing about a prisoner's right to do his time in peace and tranquility. The jurors would hardly shed a tear, but after they heard what the correctional officers and correctional management did to them, they found it in their hearts to agree to award damages and victory to our side.

One of the cases I handled was one that could've, should've, would've won me big bucks. I refer to it as "the interest case." This is the one coming up for review to the Ninth Circuit Court of Appeals. The prisoners have bank accounts within the prison systems; they're called inmate trust accounts. Now, each prisoner, of course, doesn't have very much money, maybe a matter of sixty dollars or a hundred dollars, but there are a hundred and seventy thousand of these inmates. Collectively, the account balance was in the neighborhood of thirty million. It earned interest; not a lot, but it added up to about five or six thousand a year. Guess what: the prison system simply handed this interest over to the state and placed it into the state treasury account. It went WHOOSH into the state budget.

This may seem like a fair idea, as inmates are receiving substantial expenditures of funds to keep them up, room and board and all. I read somewhere that it costs something like thirty thousand per year per inmate, so making them pay over their interest earned on their inmate trust account may seem like an appropriate thing to do. But strictly speaking, under the U.S. Constitution, the government is not allowed to take property that belongs to a private citizen and use it for a public purpose, without paying just compensation therefore. This arises from the Fifth Amendment to the U.S. Constitution, the same amendment that gives us "you have the right to remain silent," also gives us the right to not have our property taken by the government without just compensation.

The district court judge had disagreed with my analysis. One of the points she made was inmates have no constitutional right to interest. I tried to explain that interest is a part of the principal, and that the owner of the principal is thus the owner of the interest. She did not agree, and dismissed my case.

On appeal, I was hopeful that the Ninth Circuit would reverse this and order a full trial on the issue of damages. I was half right. Here's what the Ninth Circuit did, which unfortunately meant no multiple millions for me: they ruled that oh yes, "interest follows principal, like the shadow the body." How cool is that. However, as this case presented a case of first impression, meaning that no attorney had ever been crazy enough to bring such a challenge before, and because of that there was no published opinion in the Ninth Circuit stating that the prison did not have the right to take the interest, in such cases a court-made immunity, called a qualified immunity, applied.

Now, you may have heard elsewhere that ignorance of the law is no excuse. Well, guess where that doesn't apply. It doesn't apply in a civil rights case involving state officials doing things that violate the Constitution. The qualified immunity applies where whatever right you are challenging has not been nicely laid out in a published court opinion. In such cases, there is immunity from damages, not immunity from liability. What the court will do is agree that a constitutional deprivation occurred, and will issue appropriate injunctive relief. This means the court will order that whatever the state officials did, they must stop doing that now.

But, they wouldn't award me one-third of six hundred thousand for four or five years. Oh crap. And this was how I was going to come back to Sassafras and say, look, I'm not a loser, I'm not a poor guy, I just won a million bucks. Aren't I cool now? Won't you love me now?

How pathetic is that? You're trying to win back the heart of a woman based on some crazy-ass federal civil rights case? That's exactly what I was trying to do. Not surprisingly, it completely did not work.

Chapter 42
MAYBE I WILL TRY TO BE
LIKE THE OTHER GUY

Having failed to win my millions in the law case, I then had a new opportunity. Amazingly enough, a producer had picked up on the Katie Cranberry book and was interested in it. Ooh, I thought. Imagine that, Hollywood has come knocking at my door. Here was the deal. The producer worked with Lions Gate. Now, this is no small company. They're located up in Vancouver, British Columbia, and are a major player in the film business.

To understand this fully, you have to appreciate the plight of the lonely and lowly wannabe script writer. For the most part, nobody gives a crap about what I wrote, none of my writing ever went anywhere; it was all serially rejected. The strange thing is some of it was actually pretty darn good. I only know this based on feedback from others who have read it that aren't in the Hollywood business. They would say things like wow, that's a really cool story. And I thought, it is a cool story. I've been around the world, I've been all over the place, I've been in highs, I've been in lows, I've seen the rich, I've seen the poor, I've seen the worst of the world, I've seen the best of the world, I've bottled it all up into these books and I've told these imaginative stories and I'm screaming out to the world, look at what I have! And the world is often saying, I don't care. Well, this time, the producer called me and talked about Katie Cranberry.

"I love it," she said.

Imagine that. A major Hollywood producer—well, okay, Vancouver producer—loving my work. I thought, ooh, now what if suddenly, at long last, one of my books made it to Hollywood and became some kind of big movie production? Would that have any impact on Sassafras's attitude toward me? Here is the rub of all this. It endlessly upset Sassafras that I spent so much time and energy on my books. She stated to me countless times, "You are delusional. You are wasting family money on this stupid hobby of yours that's never going to go anywhere, that's never going to be successful. You are taking care of your interests and not mine."

Okay, how many times have I heard that? Let me say eleven million. I thought, well, should I just stop writing and kowtow to her? But then I thought, how come my interests are somehow contradictory to the family interests? Why is writing a book somehow antithetical to the concept of raising a family?

"Because, shithead, you're spending on these stupid books. That's money that could be spent on either a better house, more food, better clothes, or other things for the family. That's the problem."

I thought, well, I don't spend very much on these books. It costs me a couple grand. I mean, come on. Is that going to make the difference between our kids starving to death or not? She looked up at me coldly.

"You're wasting money, time, and effort on these books. As long as you're going to do that, I'm not going to have any respect for you."

And then I thought, isn't that a weird idea. Why would a wife dislike the fact that her husband likes to write books? It just seems like something a wife would be proud of. Hey, my husband's a book writer. How many husbands write books? I don't think there are that many.

Anyway, Sassafras, being the particular woman she was, the bottom line was she hated it. But of course she only hated it because none of them ever did make it. My goodness, if one of them made a best seller list and made us several million dollars, believe me, her attitude would be completely different.

So I thought, here I go, I'm onto something. Lions Gate has come calling, they like my Katie Cranberry book; hallelujah! This is my path back to Sassafras. I'm going to win her back not for being myself, but for being like the other guy. Now I'm going to be a Hollywood superstar: handsome, flat stomach, owning houses all over the world, yachts, boats, schmoozing with the Beverly Hills group, walking around with fancy Italian loafers that cost more than my entire automobile. Is that really going to be me?

I thought about this for a second. Can you be jilted by a woman because she prefers another type of man and somehow, in an effort to fight back, become like that other man? Is that just the stupidest thing in the world? It seems to me any self-respecting person would say oh no, I'm going to remain myself. The way I am isn't acceptable to the woman I love. Therefore, I must change the way I am. I must become a different person, a person she will respect and love.

One of her Chinese friends explained this to me.

"Look, the minute she started dating other men, your marriage was over. It means she lost her respect for you, she lost her love for you, she lost everything. And trust me, once it's gone, it's gone and there's nothing you can do. Just forget her. Get over it."

You might wonder why I would eschew quite available, and interested women. Ooh. For some reason, I was stuck on Sassafras. This can happen even harder when you have had children with a woman. The connection goes to the bone, and is hard to break. I was stuck on Sassafras. I couldn't get excited about any other woman. In fact, seeing the other girls convinced me all the more that I just had to have Sassafras. I had some kind of addiction to her that I couldn't let go of.

The producer happened to have a daughter who was also an associate producer with the cable TV company, USA. Ooh, I thought. How cool would it be to have a cable TV series based on a Native American story, involving fruit characters and a Native American girl that travel throughout the world to solve diplomatic problems. And in the process, solve their own problems and dilemmas. Save the world, save yourself. That was the theme.

With the Lions Gate calling card, and the benefit of a mother-daughter relationship at USA, I had a major in to this cable network. The Katie Cranberry series was presented at a boardroom filled with executives. They were looking at about eleven million other impressive projects. The Katie Cranberry series was discussed. I had an artist that had drawn about twenty-five pictures of Katie and her fruit entourage traveling to Hungary, Poland, Ukraine, the Silk Road, South America, all over the place. They looked at the artwork, they saw the story summary, I had written a one-hour pilot script; it was all there for them to review.

I was close. I want to say that I was about three inches from the top of their projects—maybe two inches—but in the end, sadly, like so many Hollywood dreams, they said no. Oh crap. That was my great shot at Hollywood. This was my best project, my premier project, the one that I had poured my heart and soul into. Indeed, the title could have aptly been changed to "Everything I Know," by Herman Franck, Esq. It was my everything. It was all I had. It was my best, and Hollywood gave me a final no.

Now how am I going to get Sassafras back?

Chapter 43
I BUY A DOG

The worst part of my failure in Hollywood was that her movie star boyfriend found out about it first. Of course he would know. He's an insider and gets to hear all of the shows that have come forward. He's the one who gets first dibs on everything. Not that he would ever play a fruit character, though I'd love to see him in a banana outfit, but he knew and he told her. "Too bad, your husband's project failed." Ha ha, gloat gloat.

Now one thing he could've done, just to help the underdog guy, the failing husband, he could've helped out. He could've given it a boost somehow. In the eat and be eaten world of Hollywood, he didn't help out. He was quite happy to learn of my failure. Sassafras was a bit surprised to even learn it had gotten as far as it did.

"Herman's project got all the way to the cable network?" she asked him.

"Yep."

"Who was promoting that?"

"Lions Gate."

"Lions Gate? Aren't they kind of big?"

"Yes, they are."

She was amazed to see that my book was even a contender. She had to ask,

"In order for it to have gotten to the point of rejection by USA, did it have to be at least a little bit good?"

Her boyfriend turned to her.

"Oh, yes. You wouldn't even get into the Los Angeles County region unless it was good. That meant it got past many filters. It had to be good."

She smiled and thought, okay, he actually can write. As a further example of just how pathetic my life had become, they were having this discussion in Portofino, Italy. He owned a lovely villa there, right by the sea. I've actually been to this city. It's quite lovely. I would be more likely to stay at a youth hostel at twenty-two dollars a night. The mansion he had there must be worth somewhere like four million. The yacht he had at the harbor was worth well more than my modest middle class home. They were boating and having this discussion. Great. She had her sunglasses on, she was wearing a scarf, she was wearing a white bathing suit. I only know this because I could read about it in the Hollywood papers. Some men have to hire private eyes to keep track of their wives' affairs; not me. I just had to buy copies of the Hollywood tabloids to see her gallivanting in the Italian Riviera with Mr. Perfect and Handsome.

Her Chinese friends here in modest Sacramento tried to console me, and urged me to give up on her.

"You have to understand, she's not in love with you anymore. She's miserable with you, she doesn't like you, and she never will. Herman, you've got to move on," one of them explained.

I couldn't disagree with this very simple analysis. But something in me told me I had to stay on. I couldn't just say no. I had a hot air balloon worth of despair that was about to burst. I thought, where can a guy go to eliminate an addiction to love? I had done enough criminal law work and family law work to know that there were all kinds of therapeutic programs for people with addictions: Alcoholics Anonymous, Narcotics Anonymous, Gamblers Anonymous, sex addictions, other addictions. There seems to be some kind of rehab therapy for just about everything. But what about Love Anonymous? How do you get rid of an addiction to a particular woman? How can you somehow free yourself from the grip of your love for her?

I bought a book about obsessive love. Of course several PhDs have written all about it. Unfortunately, their books are more about how damaging it can be. They describe what it is, how you get there, and how it can destroy your life if you don't eliminate it. Missing from the analysis is what to do to get out of its grips.

First of all, obsessive love is just like anything else that's obsessive. It means excess. Way excess. With love, it can be particularly dangerous because it is not returned. As much as I wanted Sassafras, as much as I would die for her, the fact remained she wanted nothing to do with me. She was off in Beverly Hills, Rodeo Drive, the Italian Riviera; places far more interesting than my modest home in Sacramento. Meanwhile, I was avoiding other women, I was not interested in new dates, I could not pay attention to anyone else. I was stuck on her.

So what could I do to somehow pry away from this stronghold on me? I got an idea. It was actually my son's idea. He wanted a dog, and I thought to myself, what a wonderful concept. I'll get a dog and the dog will somehow help me break away from her. Right? So here's how we went about it. The first thing I did was I got Alex a book about dogs. It was called *One Hundred and One Salvations*. I thought that was rather cute, and it was also a precursor to the type of dog that he ended up wanting. The first dog on the cover he absolutely loved and he pointed to it and he said, "I want that dog!"

I opened up the book to show the next photo of a dog.

"I want that dog!"

And then the next page:

"I want that dog!"

He basically wanted every dog on every page. Then we turned to the page with the Dalmatian.

"Oh, that's the dog I want!"

He was such a cute Dalmatian. He was a little puppy, black and white all over, lying on his back with his little paws folded right under his chin. He looked so cute.

"Forget about all these other dogs, that's the dog I want," Alex told me.

"Okay, Alex. I like the Dalmatian too."

I showed it to Adam. He laughed.

"Very cute dog."

So I decided we would wait a week and we would return to the book *One Hundred and One Salvations*, and I would see if he would again agree that that was the dog he wanted. I hardly had to wait a week. He came up to me almost every day with that book in his hands, open to the Dalmatian.

"Daddy, Daddy, when are we going to get the Dalmatian?"

I was now convinced a Dalmatian it would be. So I went about trying to find a Dalmatian. Now, where do you think you find them? Let's start with a Google, "Dalmatian California." I was thinking for some reason there would be a whole bunch of them on offer. The reality is, they're quite difficult to find. I found a Dalmatian breeder down in Palm Desert, which is by Palm Springs. He told me that he had some Dalmatian puppies, but he was quite far from me and it might be easier for me to go to a place in Madera, about three hours south. There he knew a Dalmatian breeder that he actually had bred one of his male dogs to, a female dog. He gave me the contact information and I contacted this breeder.

Her name is Jessie. She has a ranch in Madera that raises Great Danes and Dalmatians. As it would happen, one of her Dalmatians just gave birth to eight lovely Dalmatian puppies.

Leave it to me to get involved in a situation like this. Something as simple as buying a dog can become so convoluted you have no idea. Here's how it went.

"I have a lawsuit right now against a veterinarian for veterinarian malpractice."

"Oh."

"The problem is their attorneys are filing all these motions and I just don't know how to keep up with it all."

"Did I tell you what my day job was?" I asked her.

I like to use that phrase "day job." My other job is a book writer, but my day job is attorney at law.

"No."

Indeed, she didn't have any idea that I was an attorney. I figured she did and she was somehow inviting me onto her case.

"Let me tell you, I happen to be an attorney."

"Do you handle veterinarian malpractice cases?"

I knew the answer to that one.

"Oh, no. I've never done one. I don't think anybody does those. I've done medical malpractice cases."

I'd done quite a few prison medical malpractice cases where the facts were so egregious that no matter how bad my convict client was, the jury had no choice but to find against the doctor. In these cases, the major part of the case is proving through an expert witness that the involved doctor breached the standard of care owed to the patient. A veterinarian malpractice case would not be any different. You would have to find a veterinarian expert who would give an expert opinion that the doctor made a mistake.

"I already have a Great Dane veterinarian expert who will testify that the doctor screwed up," she informed me.

Ooh, I thought. That's half the battle right there.

"Listen, maybe we can do something here. I want a dog; indeed, a very specific dog. I want a Dalmatian dog. You have Dalmatian dogs and you need an attorney to do your case. Doesn't it make sense that you and I could do some kind of trade?"

Okay, here we go. What could happen, right? A simple trade, Dalmatian for a lawsuit? Within a couple weeks, me and my boys were driving down to Madera to pick up our beautiful Dalmatian. We arrived at the ranch and I met Jessie, the 50-something owner. She's a former correctional officer. Her ex-husband, a former correctional lieutenant, lived on the ranch as well. Here was the part I wasn't quite expecting: she had a young, vibrant, lovely, and completely single dog handler by the name of Tiara. Tiara, for reasons that will always escape me especially since she was such a fresh young lady, only 20 years old (did I say 20?), started to have a crush on me. I didn't do anything, I didn't flirt with her, I didn't try to flirt with her; I was just there with my two boys in my Mercedes SUV, looking a little bit more fit, hopefully handsome, and being very excited about our new dog.

Alex got naming rights. He immediately gave the name "Spots."

Of course that's the dog's name. He's got about a million spots all over him. He's a beautiful dog that was having fun playing with the gigantic Great Danes. One of the Great Danes, Dreamer, took a liking to me and gently placed her head and neck on my shoulder.   We left about two hours later. She gave me a bunch of paperwork on her law case and it was agreed, I would do the case on a contingency, equal to one-third of whatever I won, plus an upfront payment of one Dalmatian puppy.

Chapter 44

ONE WOMAN'S TRASH IS ANOTHER WOMAN'S JEWEL

One of the things I liked about taking on this case was that it was already set for trial. There was a big job to do to defeat a motion for summary judgment. This is a motion that says the plaintiff's case is not a case and should be dismissed without the right of a trial. I prepared a declaration of my client and a declaration of our expert witness, Dr. Story.

The situation was rather unique. The dog was Sam the Great Dane. He had gone in to see this Japanese veterinarian for a hip X-ray. Here's what went wrong. The receptionist/office manager decided to play pharmaceutical clerk and vet assistant that day. She selected the wrong dosage of a pre-anesthesia, and gave a very small amount. This was supposed to relax the dog to permit the placement of a mask on his nose. The mask would then bring the dog the general anesthesia known as SEVO. SEVO would put the dog under. This was necessary, not because of a surgical process, but because you simply cannot hold a Great Dane still while you take X-rays.

Unfortunately, this Great Dane had previously had a splenectomy. This is where they remove the spleen. Now, mind you, a Great Dane's spleen is about two and a half feet long, half a foot wide, and maybe half a foot thick. So it's a major piece to remove from a dog. When removing that large organ, it creates a void in the dog's abdomen. On this particular day, as unluck would have it, the dog did not have enough pre-anesthesia and went into an excited state when they tried to put a mask over his nose. He began to struggle. A struggle with a Great Dane is nothing anybody wants to get involved with. Even when they're calm, they're pretty hard to deal with. These are like small horses. This Great Dane had four people trying to calm it. In the process, there was twisting and turning of the dog's abdomen. In the process of that, a very rare event occurred: the dog's liver twisted. This is known as a liver torsion.

Here's the problem with the liver torsion. The liver is a cleanser of the body. It takes out the toxicity in the blood. It's like a giant garbage can of sorts, and when you twist it, it is rather like a crimp in a hose; the blood no longer flows through and no longer gets cleaned. The dog becomes entirely toxic. This dog was having an extremely bad day. He was lethargic, his eyes were droopy, he looked positively drunk. He couldn't get up, he couldn't walk. Tiara and Jessie had to carry him into their van. On the way home, they called the doctor several times to find out why he was in such bad shape.

"It's just the SEVO," The doctor's assistant opined.

Then the dog was returned to the hospital. When the doctor saw the dog, he saw right away that there was something very wrong and he gave the first good advice he'd given all day:

"Take him to the ER."

This would have to be another hospital about half an hour away in Fresno. In Fresno, they took the dog to an ER hospital for dogs where a doctor performed a partial liverectomy. Part of the liver had gone gangrene and had become black. The only thing to do was to remove it. He correctly diagnosed a liver torsion, the twisting of the liver, with resultant gangrenous effect. He removed the gangrenous part. This basically solved the problem. Thankfully we don't need our entire livers, and neither does a dog.

The dog would remain at the ER for several days. Later, upon arrival at home, it was noted that the dog had suffered some kind of back injury in the process. His lower back had some visible signs of trauma. It had become out of joint; his walk was not right; he was not standing squarely on his back feet; his tail was kind of humped down and curled underneath him; his butt, rather than being straight, flat across, curved downward. It was as though he was about to sit down as he walked. He was in great pain and, of all things, had to be taken to a dog chiropractor. After sixteen sessions with this chiropractor, this dog was still not healed.

As a result of all this, this dog could no longer breed. He could no longer be shown. This was a champion Great Dane that could have become a major player in the international competitions. Instead, he was stopped at a midpoint in his career. He was previously able to obtain stud fees of two thousand dollars per event. He was able to win all kinds of blue ribbons. Now he would have to be put out to pasture. He was no longer a champion dog, no longer interesting to anyone for stud services, the dog was through.

All of these points were argued to the judge to convince the court that the summary judgment should be denied. The court agreed, and denied the motion for summary judgment. This cleared the way for a trial on the merits.

The trial was in Fresno County Superior Court. Tiara was there every day of the trial. This is probably similar to the concept of a student having a crush on a teacher, but Tiara fell for me. I noticed her outfits were getting steadily sexier and sexier each day. She wore tight blouses that made her chest look compact and about to burst out. She showed her cleavage to me. She had very pretty green-blue eyes, and a lovely face. Her body could be described in one simple word: hot.

She was way younger than any girl I would ever even imagine chasing after, but I wasn't chasing after her; she was interested in me.

I suppose part of it would have to do with the opportunities that exist for a farm girl, a dog handler that lived in the tiny city of Madera, approximately thirty miles north of Fresno. I suppose part of it would have to do that, during the trial, I was somewhat of a hero in bringing this veterinarian doctor to task for what he had done to Sam. It got a little bit more exciting when the local CBS affiliate picked it up as a news story. Suddenly Sam, Jessie, and the trial became a film entity and was on the news.

"ABC News has filed a motion requesting permission to film parts of the trial. Are there any objections?" the judge announced on the second day of trial.

I, of course, had a big ear to ear grin. In my own efforts of shameless self-promotion, nothing was more exciting than the notion of being on the evening news, even in Fresno.

"No objection from the plaintiff, Your Honor."

"Well, I haven't given it much thought—" the defense announced.

"The motion will be granted."

Within minutes, the film crew loaded their equipment and set it up. They had many questions for me. I was cooperative in giving them trial briefs, medical records, photos of Sam before the event, during the event, and after the event. They interviewed me, they interviewed my client, they interviewed Tiara. Tiara was the dog handler that showed Sam. Her efforts were the ones that resulted in him earning the series of blue ribbons. She's the one at the dog show that walks him out into the area, runs him around as the judges scrutinize the way he behaves, the way he runs, the way he holds his head, the way he stands, the flatness of the line between his shoulders and his butt, and whether or not he is indeed a perfect dog.

We made *The Fresno Bee*, we made the nightly news, we were even on the news commercials. I thought to myself, it must have been a slow news day. The trial proceeded for four days. During this time, I got to know Tiara. She got to see me in action. I suppose, to my credit, I actually looked pretty good in a suit and tie, white shirt, salt and pepper hair, boyish waspy face, bluish-green eyes, arguing comfortably in front of the judge. In court, I am at home.

I think I was kind of like a hero to her. This is my own self estimate. She started touching me in the hallway. My goodness, I thought. I'm just not used to having a woman touch me. She would put her hand on my shoulder when she sat next to me. I started figuring out it was not by accident that the sides of her thighs were touching mine. She was very warm and soft. I looked at her and she looked at me. She stared into my eyes, she smiled. She put her hand on my chest.

She checked my tie to see its label. She put her hand again on my shoulder and I thought, ooh, I'm in big trouble now. I stayed at a local hotel in Fresno. She and Jessie went home to Madera, about a half an hour away. She called me at night, supposedly to talk about the case, but our discussion went far afield.

"So Jessie tells me you're married," she said.

"Yeah, I'm married. Sort of."

"What do you mean, sort of?"

"Well, it's a sad story, but my wife wants to leave me."

"Oh?"

She found this quite interesting.

"How come?"

"Because she thinks I'm a piece of shit."

"How could she think that?"

"Well, you gotta call her and ask her."

"But you're not a piece of shit. You're a really cool guy and you're quite nice-looking."

"She thinks I'm a loser."

"How could you be a loser? You're a successful trial attorney. Who's ever heard of that person being described as a loser?"

"She likes movie star types."

"Oh great. That's stability. Who is this wife of yours?"

" Sassafras. You know her?"

"Oh, the one with the movie star? With Brett Clawney?"

"Yeah."

"*That's* your wife?"

"Yep."

"Oh, boy. What are you going to do about that?"

"What can I do? Probably nothing. I think she's gone. I mean, everybody's been reading about that."

"I know. So she's tossed you out to sea?"

"Yep."

"You want to know what I think of that?"

"What's that?"

"One woman's trash is another woman's jewel."

Chapter 45
TRAGEDY IN TORINO

There is a place at the foothills of the Italian Alps, just south of Switzerland, in the northerly parts of Italy, known as Torino. Turin, to the Italians. This was not one of Italy's most quaint cities. Indeed, it is a bit industrial for such an arts-focused country. But every country needs to make a living, and Italy made its in Torino. This is the home of Ferrari, of Fiat, and of its automotive industry.

In the countryside, Torino has some beautiful Baroque-style castles. One of those castles, complete with marble floors, rounded columns, extremely high ceilings, lovely artwork, filled with Asian art, was the home of a youngish man by the name of Fabio. He had a beautiful young daughter by the name of Sassara. It was not just a coincidence that Sassara was half-Asian and half-Italian. Coming from these near-Swiss parts, her father, Fabio, was actually half-Swiss and half-Italian. He was a fairly handsome man with a babyish face for his 38 years, and large Swiss style bright blue eyes. His daughter inherited his mother's gorgeous looks, with brown eyes, long brown hair, lightened by the Swiss influence. She was 15 years old, at that awkward age where a girl is beginning the process of turning into a woman.

On this particular day, there was a rumble, and then another rumble, and then a very large rumble. Fabio ran outside to the porch overlooking the vineyards below. He saw several of the grape trestles rock considerably more than the columns in the front of the castle were. One of them fell down. He looked back and saw that one of the columns was about to fall down, matching the small impact of the trestle with a very large impact of several tons of marble. He screamed out for his daughter:

"Sassara! Sassara!"

She was in a safe place, in the front of the house, but became scared by all the movement on the ground. Had she stayed put, it would've been much better for her. Instead, out of fear, she ran to her father.

"Papa, I'm coming! I'm coming!"

She ran up the drive area, over the garden flowers, showing her own athletic ability in some impressive leaps over a couple hedges. He saw that he had made a big mistake and had actually attracted his daughter to the danger.

"No, stop! Stop! Stay where you are!"

He tried to come running down the porch area to the stairs. Right then, a piece of the ceiling in the outdoor porch area came down and struck Fabio on the forehead. He fell down. His daughter saw it and screamed.

"Papa! Papa!"

She came running up to him. He was trying to shoo her away, but it was no use. She held him. The columns started to shake more as the ground below shook. He had been knocked unconscious. Sassara pushed him and brought him back. He was out of focus, blurry, but then recalled his desperate circumstances. He saw something else coming from the ceiling and pulled her out of the way. It barely missed her head, and smashed on the floor. Dust came up, making both of them cough. One of the columns was wobbling and was about to give. He grabbed her and turned over, barely escaping its crushing fall. A piece of the fallen column broke off and rolled over on his leg. He screamed,

"AAAAHHHHHH!"

His daughter screamed. She tried to pull him away from it, but it couldn't be done. His eyes got big as he saw behind her another column about to fall forward. He grabbed her, pushing her under the protection of the fallen column. He put his body up to secure her, and used himself as a shield. She screamed out,

"Papa, no! No!"

The column was teetering. He watched it. When things like this happen, time slows down. What happens in a matter of seconds can seem like minutes. He took out his cell phone and punched Sassafras's number. This was a rare weekend when she was home with me and the boys. Her phone rang and she picked it up.

"Hello?"

She was quiet. She could hear the rumble. She knew who the call was from. The only word was, "Come."

She then heard a crashing sound, and the worst sound a mother can ever hear, that of the shrieks of her daughter. The column came crashing down, struck the already laid down column, shattered into boulder-size pieces. One of them tragically struck Fabio on the head and killed him. The other struck his abdomen so hard it broke his back. This pushed him in stronger to his daughter, who was pinned in between this boulder-size piece of column and the other lying on the floor. One of the pieces, sharp like a knife, solid like a sword, pierced Sassara's abdomen and cut into her several inches. There was an eternal quiet.

Sassafras listened to the phone. She could hear the shuffling and crying of her daughter. She screamed, "Sassara! Sassara!"

Her daughter tried to reach for the phone but couldn't. It was too far away. She tried to push her father's body off of her, but he was packed down by one of the pieces of the column. She was stuck. Sassaras screamed, "Mommy! Mommy! Come quick!"

Sassafras yelled, "Where are you?"

"I am at home. There's been some kind of earthquake. Help us! Help us!"

There's probably nothing worse for a parent than to be so far away from a child who's in desperate need of help. She gave me a look that I will never forget. Without saying a word, it was a look that said, do something.

"It's my daughter. She's hurt."

"Daughter? What daughter?"

You think you know somebody when you've been married to them for almost ten years, but the reality is people have all kinds of secrets about their background that they don't share.

"What daughter are you talking about?"

"I have a daughter. She lives in Italy. It's a long story. Right now she's having a big problem."

I explained to Sassafras, "Keep her on the phone and talk to her. Don't let her go unconscious."

She turned back to her daughter.

"Sasssara, can you hear me?'

"Yes, Mommy. I can hear you."

"Stay with me. Are you hurt?"

"Yes, I'm hurt. I'm bleeding."

"Ask her where."

"What part of you is bleeding?"

"My tummy."

"Tell her not to move."

"Don't move."

"Ask her if she has another phone."

"Honey, do you have another phone?"

"Yes, Mommy. I have it right here."

"Have her call emergency. She needs an ambulance."

"Sassara, call emergency."

Italy has its own 911 system. Unfortunately, on this day they were busy saving tens of thousands of people.

I asked Sassafras, "Do you know the neighbors?"

"There are no neighbors. It's a castle in the middle of the countryside."

"Do you have any friends in Torino you can call?"

She thought about it. Indeed she did. She had a friend in the city. Her name was Jackie, a Malaysian gal married to a nice Italian man. She called Jackie on her cell phone. They spoke in Italian.

"Jackie, it's Sassafras."

"Hello, Sassafras. Oh my God, have you seen the news?"

"I know, there's some kind of big tragedy."

"It's an earthquake. The whole town is crumbling."

"How are you?"

"I'm fine."

"And your husband?"

"Giuseppe is fine. Luckily we were outside when it happened. Our entire condominium complex has collapsed."

"Oh, I'm so sorry."

"Oh my god, Sassara!"

"Yes, that's why I'm calling."

"Is she okay?"

"No, she needs help."

"Where is she?"

"She's at the castle."

"We will go there right now."

"Oh, thank you. Please stay in touch with me. I'm so scared for her."

"Don't worry. We'll solve everything."

Jackie had a small Fiat car. She and her husband were luckily out shopping when this whole tragedy occurred, otherwise the car would've been smashed down as well. They bee lined it to the countryside. It was not a pretty sight on the way. Buildings were crumbled everywhere. Major telephone poles had smashed down onto the street, several buildings had collapsed; it was a complete mess.

While Jackie was making the twenty minute ride out to the countryside, Sassafras and I made quick arrangements to fly out there. I was on the phone speaking with Air Italia.

"I'm sorry, all of our flights are closed down now due to the earthquake."

Oh great, I thought. Next I called Air Lufthansa. All their flights to Italy had been cancelled. The nearest flight I could piece together was Air Lufthansa flight from San Francisco to Munich, Swiss Air flight to Lugano, Switzerland from there. This would get us within a couple hour's driving distance. We would rent a car and get down the Swiss Alps into Torino. There was a flight leaving in a matter of a couple hours. We didn't have any place to put our dog for what could be a week's stay. We had no choice but to bring Spots. The entire family—Sassafras, me, the boys, and Spots—packed rather quickly, flew out of the house, and drove down to the airport. Within several hours, we were on the place en route to Munich, and from there to Lugano, and from there, Torino.

Our family was about to grow by one member, maybe.

Chapter 46
STREGA NONA

There were two sharply contrasting women at the hospital. The first was Sassara, supermodel in the making. She was the perfect example of the phrase "drop dead gorgeous." I wouldn't say that out loud since her father had indeed just died. The Swiss-Italian/Chinese blood mix was a rather wonderful recipe for an Italian supermodel. Even lying in a hospital bed, all bandaged up, IV in her arm, black and blue marks on her shoulders and head, still ailing from a bloody lip, eyes filled with tears welled up from grief over the loss of her father, this girl was still looking good.

Her face lit up like a light bulb when Sassafras came in.

"Mommy! Mommy!"

Sassafras came running to her bed and hugged her tight. Though these two hadn't seen each other nor spoken in years on years, the love was obviously still strong. The bond between mother and daughter is never lost. Sassara then looked over to see me, and our two boys, Adam and Alex. We had to keep Spots downstairs with a security guard at the hospital. No dogs allowed in the ICU.

Sassara pulled back from her mother and asked, "Are these my brothers?"

Sassafras was crying.

"Yes. Please come to know them."

She asked with her hand in a sweeping motion, completely accurately read by Adam and Alex. There was a telepathy between them. They came over. The only people closely resembling the extreme beauty of Sassafras and her daughter in the room were Adam and Alex. As much as they were beautiful, these two were handsome. The three of them together were absolute dynamite. She looked at them.

"I am Sassara."

They could know right away by her name that there was an obvious mother-daughter relationship. Adam explained, "I didn't know I had a sister."

Alex laughed.

"Either did I."

"Wow, Mommy, she's beeeeautiiiiful."

He gave her a big American-style bear hug. Alex is a stocky little guy with a wall-to-wall smile. Once they connected up, there was no separating them. She held Alex's hand. He's the cutest little guy in the world, the perfect little brother for a 15-year old girl, especially one growing up in a castle as an only child to a single dad. She then asked Adam, "Is this your papa?"

Adam was a little surprised to hear the word "papa." This is very Italian, of course.

"He's our dad."

I stepped forward.

"Hello, Sassara. I am Herman."

"Very nice to meet you."

"How are you feeling?"

She looked down at the bandage wrapped around her stomach, at the IV in her arm.

"I am going to live."

She said it in such a definite way, I could see she had that survival part that Sassafras had. You cannot keep a woman like this down. You cannot defeat her. You have to win with her, not against her. I was very impressed by the certainty of her life.

Just then, the ugliest, darkish, witch-looking old scraggly woman, with the kind of shoes with tough heels that make so much noise when walking on linoleum, entered. I had never seen Sassafras afraid of anything, but this woman, I could see, scared the bejesus out of her. This ugly woman had the following rude greeting.

"So the little whore is back."

Luckily she had said this in Italian so I didn't get it, but I could see the impact on Sassafras. She looked down at her feet. She felt a very unusual emotion, that of shame and humiliation. I'm used to seeing her as a total star, at the top of the world, everything in a very beautiful and perfect way for her. For the first time, I see that she has this dark relationship with this old grandma, the mother of the recently deceased father of Sassara, a woman that I would come to know as *Strega Noña*, which roughly translates to "Witch Grandmother." And as could be seen by her introductory remarks, this was not the good witch from the East, she was the very evil witch from the castle on the mountaintop. No doubt she had flying monkeys and fireballs from her fingertips capabilities.

"Do you speak English?" I asked.

"Why, of course I do. All educated people in Italy speak English."

"Congratulations on that. I'm afraid I don't know Italian, so please excuse me if I introduce myself and my sons in English. This is Adam, this is Alex. These are the two sons of Sassafras. I am her husband."

"Yes, I know about your pathetic story."

I was a little bit surprised that she would dig into me. After all, what issue did this bitch have with me?

"You know about my pathetic story? How do you know anything about me?"

"Oh, my dear American boy, you have had the same plight as my dearly departed son. You have married a whore."

I was a little bit surprised at the vulgarity of this *strega Noña*.

"Excuse me, ma'am. I would like to ask you to please leave. If you're going to be speaking this way, I don't want to be anywhere near you."

"Actually, sir, it is you that should leave. I am Italian, I have a right to be here. This is my granddaughter, and now that her father is deceased, she is completely my child."

Sassafras walked forward. She was shaking. I was so surprised to see her in such a weakened state.

"I am her mother. She is my child."

"Oh, we'll see about that, my little pretty. We'll see about that."

Chapter 47
THE FUNERAL OF PAPA

We stayed by Sassara's side for the next several days, interrupted only by the funeral of her papa. The hospital let her go in a wheelchair on condition that a nurse accompany her, that her IV remain in her, and that she be brought right back for immediate observation. She had suffered some pretty serious abdominal slicing, and attendant complications with the sliced intestinal tissue having become affixed to her peritoneum, the sac that holds the intestines and other abdominal organs.

Unfortunately, scarring tissue is rather like magnets to other tissue, and connects up with that, and fuses. This causes a problem in that the intestines, once they fuse, become crimped, rather like a garden hose. What is stopped by the crimp goes up instead of down. Unfortunately for little Sassara, she had a major problem of puking up her partially digested food. It was quite disgusting to see it. It made me wonder how nature could create such beauty and such ugliness all at the same time.

It also gave Adam and Alex something to think about. At any time, no matter how wonderful things are, there can be a major change that degenerates and decomposes your life. Poor little Sassara was fighting for hers, with the help of the excellent doctors at the Santa Maria Novella Hospital in Torino. She had had several surgeries to disconnect the intestine from the peritoneum. Unfortunately, as the doctor explained, it is naturally gravitating back to the peritoneum, fusing again and crimping again. The solution was to remove this part of the intestine and insert in it an artificial connection made of a kind of surgical plastic. This plastic would not fuse with the wall, and would be a permanent fixture inside Sassara. The good news is that she was going to be okay. The bad news is that there were many unpleasant barfing scenes.

I was extremely impressed to see Sassafras in action, the way she cared for her daughter as she barfed up what was essentially fecal material right into a bowl. Sassafras was right on it. She held her daughter's head as the disgusting barf came up. Anybody else would've been just sick by it, but not Sassafras. Her daughter cried and cried and cried with this.

"Oh Mommy, I feel so sick. I wish it would all just stop."

Sassafras took the bowl away, dumped it in the toilet, and flushed it. She came back with a toothbrush and toothpaste and brushed her daughter's teeth, tooth by tooth. She had her spit it out in a cup, gave her some water, and had her spit it out again. Unfortunately for Sassara, this process would be repeated several times.

I think we all have this tendency to have songs pop up in our minds. As I was wheeling Sassara's wheelchair across the lawn at the cemetery, getting closer to the place where they had the coffin just next to the hole in the earth, where Fabio would be returned to the earth, the song "*Summertime*" by Janis Joplin came to mind. I used to hear this song all the time, and wondered what had happened to the songwriter that created that tune, what sadness became of them, and what sadness had come to Janis Joplin to sing it in such an earthy, sympathetic, tear-jerking way.

Suddenly my brain was filled with the song "*Summertime*."

"Summertime" by Janis Joplin, used with permission
Summertime, time, time,
Child, the living's easy.
Fish are jumping out
And the cotton, Lord,
Cotton's high, Lord, so high.

Your daddy's rich
And your ma is so good-looking, baby.
She's looking good now,
Hush, baby, baby, baby, baby, baby,
No, no, no, no, don't you cry.
Don't you cry!

One of these mornings
You're gonna rise, rise up singing,
You're gonna spread your wings,
Child, and take, take to the sky,
Lord, the sky.

But until that morning
Honey, n-n-nothing's going to harm you now,
No, no, no, no, no, no, no, no, no, no, no, no, no, no, no, no
No, no, no, no, no, no, no, no, no, no, no, no, no, no, no, no
No, no, no, no, no, no, no, no, no,
Don't you cry,
Cry.

I looked over to see none other than *Strega Noña* weeping over the coffin of her dead son. Next to her, amazingly, was one of the *Strega's* older daughters that had become in her own right a real live Italian supermodel/movie star. She was stunningly beautiful, on par with, believe it or not, Sofia Loren. Her husband was one of these top airline executives, wearing about a nine hundred dollar suit with crisp British-style napkin in the coat pocket. He looked positively gorgeous with his jet black hair combed straight back, sunglasses, and some form of Italian loafers.

I looked at the two of them, and then I looked over at the terribly ugly *Strega Noña,* and I could only wonder, how could that come from this? It just seemed impossible. Then I looked over to see Sassara and wondered the same thing. How do you get such beauty from such ugliness? This is the way of nature, the duality of what is marvelous and what is awful. There's not much to do about it other than to thank the earth for its good parts, and do as much as possible to mitigate against the bad parts.

A Roman Catholic priest gave Fabio his last rites. It was a sermon that, as they always do, ended with the phrase: "dust to dust, ashes to ashes." Fabio's coffin was gently placed into the earth. Sassara cried from her wheelchair, as the nurse and Sassafras held her. *"Summertime"* was playing in my head.

Afterwards, we wheeled Sassara back to the limousine and proceeded to the safety of her hospital room. *Strega Noña* walked slowly behind us. She had a bit of a limp, probably caused when she kicked some little boy or something.

Just before we closed the car door, she pointed her ugly little finger at Sassafras, and screamed out.

"Don't you think even for a minute that you're taking this daughter back to America! She's staying here with me FOREVER!"

That forever mark hit Sassafras like a ton of bricks. She looked over to me. Now, here is a supermodel that for the last several months hasn't needed me for a thing. But her eyes were filled with the phrase, "Help me! Help me!" I looked back at this *Strega Noña.* What a bitch. I told her something I'd been meaning to say for several days now.

"We'll see you in court."

Chapter 48
SASSAFRAS VERSUS STREGA NONA

Strega Noña would have no idea that, as it would happen, I am somewhat connected up to the Italian legal community. I was on the phone with Alfredo immediately.

"Alfredo, here's the deal. Remember Sassafras?"

"Oh, yes."

"We've got a rather complicated child custody case brewing."

"I've got just the guy for you. His name is Giuseppe Salvatori Giuliani. He is here in Milan. You and Sassafras need to come here and meet with him."

"We're on our way. Would you please be there as well?"

"Of course, my friend."

"Is it possible to meet him today?"

"Absolutely. He is a very close friend of mine. Not to worry. Come on over, when you get here, come to my office, I'll take you right over. His office is just a few blocks down the street."

"Thank you, my friend."

I explained this to Sassafras. As much as she hated leaving her daughter's side, it was necessary.

"Sassara, we will be back in one day. Mommy has to go to Milan to see a lawyer. He's going to help us make sure that you can come with us."

I watched intently. I was curious about Sassara's attitude about all this.

"I get to come with you and my new brothers to America?"

"Oh honey, I hope so. This is what I'm going to try to arrange."

"Oh Mommy, please do your best. Please get a wonderful lawyer who can beat *Noña* in court. Please get me out of her grip. Please let me come with you to America!"

Adam and Alex were old enough to understand that this girl was pleading for her life. They walked over and hugged her. Alex said it very nicely.

"You're coming with us."

Adam nodded his head.

"We're not going anywhere without you."

She smiled. She looked at me.

"You're the lawyer? Go to court, win this case."

I smiled.

"Don't worry, we will win."

Spots, Adam, Alex, Sassafras and I continued into our rent-a-car and made the several hour trip over to Milan. We arrived at Alfredo's office. He gave me a big Italian hug. I love this guy.

"Here is Sassafras."

"Oh, yes. Hello, Sassafras. It's wonderful to meet you."

"And my two sons, Adam and Alex."

"Hello."

"And here is Spots, our Dalmatian."

In a rare bark, Spots let one go. Something about Alfredo reminded him of a running jack rabbit.

"Before we see Giuseppe, Sassafras, I have one question for you."

"Yes?"

"Do you have Sassara's birth certificate?"

I was quite impressed that Sassafras had this document in her possession. She opened her purse, opened up her wallet, and in her wallet, neatly folded up into a small square of about one inch by two inches, was a fourteen year old piece of paper called "*certificato*." She carefully unfolded it and handed it to Alfredo. He saw right there that Sassafras's name was listed as the mother.

"This is Exhibit A to your case. With the passing on of the father and you being the surviving mother, it would be only an extraordinary matter that would keep you from having full custody of your daughter."

I was a little bit worried about that exceptional case possibility. I lived a life where virtually everything I touched was one of those exceptional, extraordinary circumstances. Would this be such a circumstance?

Just then, Alfredo's phone rang. He answered and spoke in Italian. Sassafras smiled. She could tell what was going on. Within about two seconds, the perfect example of the phrase "pompous lawyer" in the form of one Giuseppe Salvatori Giuliani entered the room. Of course, he kissed Sassafras's back hand French style, turned to me, looked me dead in the eyes, and shook my hand with a strong, manly grip. If I were a woman, I would've melted. He was one of these super-handsome Italian guys. We would call him a metrosexual in the United States. Here in Italy, he was just one of those darkish, dark-eyed, dark-haired, dark-suited, olive-skinned, natural beauties of a man who, in a parting with the ways of the Italian leisure/aristocracy, did the huge effort of attending law school at the University of Roma.

He was a natural attorney, and had found his way into the path of representing the rich and famous in their endless family law disputes. He was the perfect lawyer for Sassafras in her upcoming battle with *Strega Noña*.

Chapter 49

ORDER TO SHOW CAUSE RE. TEMPORARY ORDERS ON CUSTODY OF SASSARA

"We must move quickly into the night to file immediate court papers seeking immediate temporary orders giving Sassafras primary physical custody of Sassara. I'm sure the grandmother is already speaking with attorneys in Torino. In fact, I can almost predict the very one she will hire," Giuseppe explained.

He turned to Alfredo.

"Pietro?"

"I believe it will be."

I looked up.

"Who's Pietro?"

"He's the guy that represents all the rich people in family law cases in Torino. He knows the judges very well. His father is one of the high-ranking judges, and for several years was president of the court. His brother is a judge."

"Ooh. They sound rather connected."

"Not to worry. So am I. And remember, this is still a country where justice counts for something. There's not going to be any kind of corruption in this case. It's too famous for that. We have an Italian-American supermodel, we have her daughter, we have a deceased father, and then we have kind of a crazy grandmother. I think there's a very strong case that Sassafras will have custody."

I thought about that phrase, "very strong case." I know how I explain to clients that there's always a possibility that we will lose. Lawyers don't ever like to say one hundred percent guaranteed victory on anything. You never know what might happen in court, especially in an Italian court where the opposing counsel's brother happens to be a judge. No corruption? Give me a break.

Three days later, we were in court in an order to show cause re. temporary orders granting Sassafras primary physical custody, pending further custody proceedings. The first thing that shocked me was the judge himself. In contrast to the totally handsome Giuseppe, the totally beautiful Sassafras, the gorgeous up and coming supermodel Sassara, and if I may say, the somewhat handsome nature of myself, on the one side, we had the awful-looking *Strega Noña* and her disgustingly ugly but apparently well-connected attorney Pietro Venenzia, counsel to the rich and famous of Torino, and a judge who was best described as super-ugly. He had one of those large Italian noses that was overtaken by some kind of acne piled up growth. His nose looked bigger and uglier than Karl Malden's from "*The Streets of San Francisco*" series.

It was quite apparent from the get-go that he identified with the ugly side of the courtroom, and not the beautiful side. I saw the contrast immediately and looked over to Giuseppe. He put his hand up.

"Don't worry. The judge is subject to a statute that gives Sassafras primary rights as a matter of law."

The court session began with the hammering of the gavel. I would have to sit back and wonder what was being said, as all proceedings were in Italian. The court was listening intently to Giuseppe make some kind of explanation, no doubt of the Italian civil code section that gave the surviving parent the primary right of custody. I noted the judge's fingers tapping on his court bench. He was bored with the explanation of the law. This, of course, is always dangerous: a judge that gets bored with the law.

He put his hand up and stopped Giuseppe mid-sentence. He made a sentence that had the word Sassara in it. Sassara lit up. She nodded. I wondered what was going on. Sassara was wheeled over to the witness stand and was asked a series of questions. They were later explained to me by Giuseppe. The court asked the questions. This was a little bit similar to the French civil system, where judges, rather than lawyers, do the interrogation of witnesses.

"Young lady, first of all let me tell you how truly sorry I am for you over the loss of your father."

"Thank you, Your Honor."

Sassara was an elegant young lady and treated the judge with appropriate respect.

"I hope you understand what the proceedings are about today. The big question here is where are you going to live? Are you going to stay here in Torino with your grandmother, or are you going to move to the United States with your mother? This is the question."

"I understand that."

"The question I have is what do you want to do?"

Sassara looked at *Strega Noña*. There's this kind of power a witch holds over people. It's a kind of black magic. She looked at her beautiful mother and looked at the extremely ugly *Strega Noña*. There was a pause that seemed like a thousand hours, but in reality was just a matter of a couple minutes. *Strega Noña* smiled, showing her uneven teeth. Her lips were dry and chapped with little nodules on them. She basked with confidence that her *strega* powers were telepathing over to the young Sassara.

Sassafras saw this interconnection. I could see the worry in her face. Sassara turned to the judge, then turned to her mother.

"I'm sorry, Mama. I love you, but really, I prefer to stay here with *Noña* in Torino."

Giuseppe was floored by this. He had just spoken with Sassara. She had made it very clear to him that she wanted to come to America to live with her mother and her new family, her brothers; it was all a wonderful fairy tale story that just got ruined by some kind of weird interaction between the grandmother and the granddaughter.

"Objection!"

You can't really object to a judge's question. They are the rulers of the courtroom.

"What is the basis of your objection, Counsel?" the judge asked.

Giuseppe looked around.

"There is something going on here that's not quite right. I request that the court take a recess and ask the same question again in the court's chambers, without any of us present. I think there's some kind of undue influence going on here."

The judge looked over to Pietro.

"Any objection to that procedure?"

"None, Your Honor. I think it's a wonderful idea."

He smiled with the confidence of someone who already knew the outcome of the proceeding. It seemed so unfair.

Sassafras explained what was going on to me. I looked over and I noticed something about *Strega Noña* that gave me a very interesting idea. I looked at her purse, and you know what I saw? She's such a cheap multimillionaire it's disgusting. It was a knockoff Chanel purse. I could see right away the stitching just wasn't right. Chanel would never let that kind of product out of its factory, to be sold for twenty-five hundred dollars, with uneven stitching. I could see right away that this woman had some illegalities that, if closely examined, could foil her attempt at custody.

I explained to Giuseppe.

"Before you break, ask the following question of the court: can the grandmother financially support the granddaughter?"

Giuseppe looked at me incredulously.

"What are you talking about? The lady's worth probably twenty million dollars. She lives in a castle. She has three Ferraris in her garage. How can we even wonder about that issue?"

"Trust me, you want to go there," I told Giuseppe.

Giuseppe went against his instincts and agreed to ask my question.

"Your Honor, before you take the child into chambers, I think there is a fundamental question that needs to be asked of the grandmother, that of whether she is financially capable of supporting the child."

The grandmother laughed out loud.

"Oh, my heavens! Do you not understand who I am? Do you not know who I am? Do you not know what I have? Have you not seen my castle, my Ferraris? Have you not seen my bank account?"

I smiled as the *Strega Noña* began her demise. The judge explained to Giuseppe,

"I realize, Mr. Giuliani, that you are not from here, but Ms. Romano is well-known in the city as being fabulously successful. I can't imagine there is a true issue about her ability to financially support the granddaughter."

The grandmother spoke up again.

"Plus, I've been supporting her all along. I provided everything for her."

The judge turned to Giuseppe.

"I just don't think you're going to get anywhere with that argument."

Giuseppe looked back at me with an 'I told you so' look. I came back with a look that said, 'stay tuned.'

Chapter 50
SUBPOENA DUCES TECUM

It turned out that the in-chambers further questioning of Sassara did not change the telepathic hold of *Strega Noña*. She gave the same answer without anyone present. Giuseppe was amazed at her answers and walked out of the courthouse dejected. Sassafras gave me this other look: "Help me."

I turned to her and assured her, "I have a plan."

I turned to Giuseppe.

"Here's what we've got to do. I will guarantee you that this woman is dirty. She is conducting business in some kind of illegal manner. I don't know what it is, but there is something to it. We need to start digging. First step, let's do a *subpoena duces tecum*, a request for production of records of her income, of her taxes, of her business, of everything. I want to show the court that she's a corrupt woman, an illegal woman, and a woman with no morals, and who is completely improper as a candidate to raise Sassara."

Giuseppe smiled.

"This sounds like American-style litigation."

"This is how we do it in my country, but the same rules should apply here."

"Oh, they do. If you can show some kind of illegality, some kind of moral corruption, that is entirely relevant to these proceedings."

That day, we issued a *subpoena duces tecum* on the *Strega Noña*, requesting the production of her income tax filings, of her income expense statements from her business operations, of a balance sheet showing her various holdings, and of her bank statements showing the inflows and outflows of cash.

Pietro filed a motion to quash the subpoena as being an invasion of her right to financial privacy, as being overly burdensome and over broad, and as being an artifice of revenge and having no bearing of any sort to any aspect of the current proceedings.

The trial court had a hearing on this issue within five days. The judge looked at the subpoena and asked Giuseppe, "Why are these records relevant? You don't really believe that Señora Romano doesn't really have the kind of wealth that we think she has? Are you trying to show that she's poor?"

"Your Honor, if I may, the issue isn't that she's poor. We do not contend poverty. This is a woman that we know lives in a castle, has three Ferraris, and multiple millions. The issue is that she is a corrupt woman, does business in an illegal manner, a fraudulent manner, and has the kind of morals that are improper to raise a child with."

Strega Noña stood up and screamed at Giuseppe.

"How dare you!"

She pointed a finger at him. If lightning could have come out of that finger, it would have struck him in the heart. But there were no fireballs or lightning that morning. The judge saw the anger expressed by the grandmother as a "hot button."

There are many motivations of public servants. Some love to kowtow to the rich and famous, some love to hang out with movie stars, then there is the "I don't make very much money as a public servant and I'm tired of seeing rich people get away with bloody murder" type of judge. Although this judge was not really in that category, on this day he was pushed over to that corner. He announced a rather unusual finding.

"At this point we do not need to make any conclusions about whether or not the Señora is engaged in any type of corrupt practices. We merely need to reach the conclusion that the matter is a proper issue for this court to investigate. Indeed, if it were true that she was corrupt, this would bear on her ability to serve as a proper custodial guardian of her granddaughter. Accordingly, I am going to deny the motion to quash, and I am ordering Señora Romano to produce the documents requested in the *subpoena duces tecum*. So ordered."

The judge then slammed his gavel. The *Strega Noña* would have to fork over her financial records, and God knows what they would show.

Chapter 51

ORDER ON APPLICATION FOR TEMPORARY CUSTODY ORDERS

Our euphoria was short-lived. The following day, we received a call from Giuseppe. He had received a written order from the court on our application for temporary custody orders. Sassafras and I eagerly awaited a review of this order. Since it was in Italian, Giuseppe provided a verbal translation. The order read as follows:

"Order on Application for a Temporary Custody Order.

The Court has before it petitioner's application for an order to show cause on the issue of temporary custody orders. Having heard the testimony of the parties, and of the involved minor child Sassara, and having considered the arguments of Counsel, the Court hereby ORDERS as follows:

A. The Court is not prepared to grant the application for temporary custody for Sassafras Qin at this time. The Court requires further information, and hereby APPOINTS Dr. Feliciana Montevelli, a noted child psychologist, to commence with a series of therapeutic sessions with Sassara and Sassafras and Ms. Romano, to investigate the following issues:

1. Would it be in the child's best interest to have primary physical custody with Ms. Romano or with Sassafras Qin?

2. Is the child's stated desire to stay with Ms. Romano due to some kind of undue influence or other improper circumstance, committed by Ms. Romano?

3. In light of the lengthy period of time of a lack of contact between Sassafras Qin and Sassara, is there a need for reunification therapy; and would it be in the child's best interest to commence with a program of reunification therapy?

4. If the Court determines that primary physical custody of the child shall remain with Ms. Romano, what type of visitation schedule and conditions on visitation, including possible reunification therapy sessions, would be in the best interest of the child?

B. Pending Dr. Montevelli's review of the circumstances, the Court is of a view that the child's best interests are served without any kind of further upheavals and large changes in her life. Accordingly, Ms. Romano is granted temporary custody of Sassara, and is ordered to cooperate in providing Sassafras with liberal visitation and open telephone, email, text messaging, and other communication with Sassara. The Court is of a view that Sassara's best interest will be served by reunifying her relationship with her mother, and trust that the grandmother will cooperate in that process.

C. The Court is of the further view that Sassara's best interests will be served by having a healthy relationship with her two half-brothers, Adam and Alex Franck. Accordingly, Ms. Romano is further ordered to cooperate in providing liberal visitation between Sassara and her two half-siblings.

D. This matter will be reviewed by the Court in thirty days, during which at least four therapeutic sessions with Dr. Montevelli should have occurred. Dr. Montevelli is directed to prepare a written report of her findings and recommendations.
SO ORDERED.

Sassafras had a million questions.
"What is this about? Why do we have to have a child psychologist involved? What is this reunification therapy? What does the judge mean by—"
Giuseppe put his palm outward to Sassafras.
"Stop, stop, stop."
She stopped. She was agitated but collected herself. He spoke calmly.
"Let me explain. The court is understandably concerned that Sassara has had a huge jolt to her life. Her entire world has been turned upside down. The passing of her father and the introduction of you into her life, these are two major events. The court wants to slow the situation down to make sure that the process is done in a good way that does not harm the child."
"Harm the child? What would I do to harm the child?"
"You aren't going to do anything to harm the child. The court wants to make sure that the introduction of your relationship with the child is done in a way that progresses in a beneficial manner. Look at it this way: you do these four sessions, you make a favorable impression on Dr. Montevelli, she prepares a favorable report, and the judge will then grant your application for temporary custody. If you don't cooperate, of course the judge will hold that against you."
I put my hand on Sassafras's thigh.
"Honey, you need to follow the order exactly as it is written."
She looked at me and gave me something I rarely saw from her anymore: a smile.
"I will."
Giuseppe called Dr. Montevelli's office to schedule the first session.

"Hello, Dr. Montevelli."

"Yes?"

"This is Giuseppe Salvatori Giuliani. I am the attorney for Sassafras Qin."

"Oh, yes. I was expecting your call. I have already heard from Pietro Venenzia. I take it you have received the court's order?"

"I have. Doctor, let me ask you of your idea of how to proceed."

"First I want to meet with the mother, her husband, and their two boys. I want to get a better understanding of their family dynamics, of how stable their family is, toward an overall picture of whether their household would provide a proper environment for Sassara."

Of course Giuseppe had no idea of the upheaval that had been in our household. He thought the doctor's concept made perfect sense.

"Yes, of course, Doctor. Could you see them right away?"

"I could see them this afternoon if they are available."

He looked over.

"Are you available to meet with the doctor this afternoon?"

Sassafras, of course, would do anything and everything to progress the circumstances.

"Oh, yes."

I nodded yes as well.

"She wants you to bring your two sons."

"Then we will."

"Yes, Doctor. How about two p.m.?"

"Two p.m. will be fine."

"I will send them over."

"Thank you."

Giuseppe explained to us,

"You need to be very honest with the psychologist. What she is looking for is a stable home environment. She wants to make sure that Sassara will be taken care of in a good way, and that everything is going to be safe, sound, and healthy. Capiche?"

Of course, Sassafras understood what she was looking for. She looked over to me and gave me another big smile.

Chapter 52
DR. MONTEVELLI

Dr. Montevelli was a calm, professorial, grayish tweed jacket person on the outside, with a Brooklyn homicide detective's suspicions on the inside. Her warm smile and graceful ways easily disarmed Sassafras into thinking she was a nice, polite, elderly woman. Nothing could be further from the truth.

"Let us begin by having Sassafras explain to me how it came to be that she became separated from her daughter for so long."

This, as it would turn out, would be the main focus of her inquiry. After all, it is unusual and irregular for a mother to become separated from her daughter. Sassafras was not surprised with the question, and responded with the first layer of the onion.

"Fabio's mother hated me from the moment she first saw me."

"Oh, my dear, I don't wish to interrupt you, because I want to hear all of this, but I want you to understand, this is not about Fabio's mother. This is about you and your daughter. I want to know why you have chosen not to be with your daughter."

"I did not choose this. Fabio's mother chose it. She stole my daughter from me."

The onion began to unpeel.

"She *stole* your daughter? How did she accomplish that?"

Sassafras explained.

"Right away, she accused me of becoming pregnant to marry her son. She called me a gold-digging whore."

"Where were you when she said this?"

"I was in China, at the wedding."

"Where was the wedding?"

"In Shen Zhen, where I'm from."

"How did you and Fabio happen to meet?"

"Ms. Romano owns an art business that exports art out of Shen Zhen to Italy. She owns an art store in Torino. She and Fabio were in Shen Zhen looking for art items. That's where we met."

"I see. Did you find him to be attractive?"

"I did."

"Did you fall in love with him in a real way, in an honest way, in an emotional way?"

"I did."

"So you were not simply gold digging?"

"I did not know he was wealthy. He did not appear to be wealthy, he didn't even have a car, his mother didn't give him any money; he was actually kind of poor as far as I knew. I did not know about his mother's castle until after we were married."

"You must have been a bit stunned."

"I was. I had no idea."

"Okay. After the wedding, did you move to Torino?"

"Yes. I was pregnant and it was agreed that living in Italy would be better for all involved."

"Where did you live?"

"We had nowhere else to live, so we moved in with her at the castle."

"With his father and mother?"

"Yes."

"Tell me about your relationship with Fabio at the castle."

"It got off to a terrible start, all because of his mother. She treated me like a servant. I had to cook, clean, do laundry, and look after all of them. I was not her son's wife, I became the family maid."

"And during this process you also somehow became a supermodel?"

"It has always been my dream."

"How did you escape away?"

"I insisted that we move out of the castle. Fabio reluctantly agreed. I was still pregnant. I managed to get my first modeling assignment right here in Torino."

"Oh?"

"I really believe the glow of being pregnant helped me in my process of becoming a model."

"Oh, I'm sure it did. You must have looked quite gorgeous."

"Before I knew it, I was on the cover of several Torino magazines. Then I received a call from Milan, and received a further assignment there. Not long after that, my pregnancy was too obvious, so I had to take a short break from modeling."

"How did that make you feel?"

"It was kind of strange. I had been dreaming of being a model and had started down that path, when suddenly I had to stop."

"Yes, and what I wonder about is whether you blamed your child for that."

"Oh no, I didn't. I saw it as a short-term situation only. I wasn't giving up my career, I was just giving up three months of my career."

"Did you resume modeling after your child was born?"

"A couple months later I got my next assignments. They were for some magazines in Milan."

"So you had to go away?"

"Yes. And that is when Ms. Romano started the process of taking my daughter away. She hated me for being pregnant, but once she saw the baby, she absolutely fell in love with her. She wanted her, and began the process, slowly but surely, of taking her from me."

"What happened to you and her son? Why did you two break apart?"

"He became subject to the same influence of his mother. She hated me, and her hateful influence was handed down to him."

"What did he do to hate you?"

"He was just not there emotionally. Then—"

She started to cry.

"Then one day I found a letter."

"A letter?"

"Yes. From another woman. It was terrible. He was having an affair."

"How old was your daughter when you learned of the affair?"

"She was 4."

"So you were with your daughter on a regular basis up until that point?"

"Oh, yes. I held her, I nursed her, I cared for her every day."

"Even when you went to Milan?"

"Except when I went to Milan. During those days, I left her with Fabio."

"And his mother?"

"Yes."

"I see. What did you do to try to save your marriage?"

"I didn't really save it. I left Fabio. It was during this time that I met Herman."

"Oh, so rather than work to keep your family together and to solve whatever problems were going on between you, you simply abandoned them?"

"I did not abandon them. They abandoned me."

"Oh, wait a minute. Did he kick you out?"

"No."

"Did he ask you to leave?"

"No."

"Did you leave?"

"Yes."

"Did you go to the United States?"

"Yes."

"And did you never return for over ten years until now?"

She looked up in the air and realized what a terrible answer she had to give.

"Yes."

"Then you abandoned them, didn't you?"

"He had an affair."

"Okay. So what? You can always fix a relationship. You don't have to just leave them. Anyway, that's what you did. So you and your husband got married after that?"

"Yes."

"Did you get a divorce from Fabio?"

She looked up rather nervously. I, of course, didn't even know she was married to this guy. I had no clue about any of this.

"Not exactly."

"Oh, not exactly? What does that mean?"

"Well, I didn't. You see, under Italian law—"

"I know. It's not easy getting a divorce, it takes multiple years, blah blah blah. So you just kind of skipped that?"

"I did."

She looked over to me. I explained.

"Now we don't need a divorce from him. He's dead."

"Yes, I suppose you're right on that, Counselor."

Sassafras's eyes went up at that comment.

"And the two of you live in California?"

"Yes."

"What city?"

"Sacramento."

"That's in Northern California?"

"Yes."

She took out a map.

"I see. It's not too far from San Francisco."

"It's about an hour and a half away."

"Okay. And you are a lawyer there?"

"Yes."

"And Sassafras, what do you do there? Are you still modeling?"

"No, my modeling career is basically over. As you may know, this is a young woman's job."

"Okay, so what do you do to occupy yourself now?"

"I help Herman run his law office and I'm involved in dance."

"Dance?"

"Yes. I'm a member of a local dance group. We do traditional Chinese dance."

"I see. Sounds lovely."

"She's quite good. I wish you could see her," I explained.

"Well, maybe someday I will. And you have two boys?"

"Yes, Adam and Alex."

"I will be meeting with them later. I want to discuss with them the family dynamics. I want to get a full understanding of the stability of your current relationship and family life. Why don't you go ahead and summarize it for me?"

She looked to me for guidance. I gave her a look of 'don't worry, I'll cooperate.'

"We have a stable family," she explained.

Gee, I thought. I'm glad your name isn't Pinocchio. Dr. Montevelli scrutinized Sassafras's facial expressions. She was looking for some body language or facial muscle that gave away the actual truth. Sassafras could see this search for the truth, and compromised her last remark.

"That's not to say we're not without troubles. I think all marriages have trouble."

"Tell me about the troubles your marriage has."

Sassafras looked up to the ceiling for answers. Her eyes then came back down to the level of Dr. Montevelli's.

"I want him to pay more attention to me."

"Oh?"

"Yes. I want him to adore me more. I want him to respond to my needs."

"Your needs?"

"Yes."

She looked over to me.

"Do you know what she's talking about?"

"I know exactly what she's talking about, and I'm trying."

"Okay, and how about your relationship with your sons? How is that going?"

Sassafras became jubilant in her response.

"Oh, they're just wonderful. They are the light of my life."

"How old are they?"

"Adam is 9, Alex is 6."

"How are they doing in school?"

I responded to that one.

"They are doing quite well. Adam received a math medal, Alex received an academic excellence award."

"Do they have friends?"

"Oh yes. Our house is generally crowded with neighborhood boys and girls."

"So it sounds like they're socially successful?"

"Yes."

"Academically successful?"

"Yes."

"Healthy?"

"Yes."

"Everything sounds good."

"Everything is good," Sassafras explained.

All I could think of at this point was 'thank God for earthquakes.'

Chapter 53
ASIAN DREAMS

As it happened, the therapist's office was not that far from Ms. Romano's art store. Sassafras pointed it out to me. I couldn't resist going in. She refused and waited outside. The store had a sign in Italian that translated to "Asian Dreams." Inside, it was filled with all kinds of Asian art. There were screens, beautifully framed with dark lacquered wood. The paintings showed long-legged herons, bamboo, and those jagged mountaintops that can be found in the northern parts of China. There were jade lamps, the bases made of lions removed from the tops of a nobleman's gateposts, and transformed into a lovely lamp. There were furniture items, tables with glass tops and amazingly intricate wood carvings under the glass. They were painted with gold metallic on black lacquer. There's something about black and gold that works quite well together.

A youngish Italian woman worked in the store. She approached me and spoke in Italian.

"May I help you?"

"Thank you, I was just looking," I told her.

"Oh, American?"

"Yes."

She knew some English. Something then caught my eye. I looked over and saw an intriguing statue, most definitely not of Chinese origin. It was a bronze statue of a dancer, and had a small plaque on the stand with the name *Isis*.

She was of the French art deco style, with a sharply cut haircut, pointed at either side, and going down just a bit below her earlobes, showing her elegant neck. She was long, and wore the clothes of ancient times, perhaps of ancient Greece. It was a sheet turned into a dress that draped her thin body. She looked down with one arm in front and one arm in back.

I don't know why this statue registered with me, but it did. Perhaps it was its obvious European origin, found in this shop of Asian dreams. So I asked the attendant, "What's the story on *Isis?*"

"I don't know. She did not come from China. Actually, she did, but I'm sure she came from Europe first, made a trip to China, Ms. Romano found her and then brought her back here."

Interesting, I thought. I tried to pick up the statue, but it was quite heavy. She was cold and metallic. Everything else in the store had this soft Asian flair to it. She left this metallic smell on my hands. I lifted her just for a moment, about three inches off the cherry wood table she was placed on. Just then I heard the tapping on the window. It was Sassafras. She looked quite urgent. She pointed down the road. She was obviously ushering me out of the place.

I was a bit caught up in looking at the art items. Then I saw what Sassafras was worried about: in came the wicked witch of Italy, Ms. Romano. God, she was ugly. The first thing she said, predictably, was, "You must leave at once."

"Yes, yes, I'll go."

"Go now!"

As I walked out, I wanted to stare her down, but she refused to look at me. She turned away. We would have our face-off later.

Chapter 54
THE DOCUMENTS

Of course, receiving a couple bucket loads of documents from a subpoena is not the sort of activity that makes for great theatric drama. These are the things we lawyers deal with in real life. One person's boring stack of records is another person's revelation of truth.

As most lawyers do, Giuseppe had a war room, a place where stacks of records could be placed in neat little piles, and where scrutinizing eyes could examine them carefully. These documents provided a special challenge for Giuseppe. First, many of them were in Italian. No problem there. But many of them were also in Chinese language, which of course created a big problem. Some of them were actually in Chinese and in Italian, which also created a problem. There were shipping documents, bills of lading, invoices, bank statements, all coming from Chinese sources, with handwritten Chinese characters all over them.

As it would happen, Sassafras, of course, happened to be fluent in Italian and Chinese. We had the perfect supermodel legal assistant on our team.

"Okay, Sassafras. Here's the deal. What we're looking for is evidence of some kind of illegal activity."

"Like what?" she wondered.

"Look at it this way: a castle, several Ferraris, all that kind of money, do you think that cute little art store is producing that wealth?" I explained.

"I don't know."

"There must be some kind of scam, some kind of criminal activity. We need to find it."

"Okay, why don't we start with this stack right here. These are bank records."

Sassafras saw right away,

"There's something odd about this one."

"What's that?"

"First of all, the bank she's using is an agricultural bank."

"Okay, what's wrong about that?"

"It should not be the bank used for an art business. That is a Chinese government-owned bank that does loans and other banking for the agricultural sector."

"I see."

Giuseppe wondered,

"What does it mean?"

I thought out loud.

"It means she probably has a friend at that bank, a friend that is doing her favors."

"Okay."

Sassafras put the bank records down and went over to the stack of art invoices. She looked at them. Right away I could see she had a big question mark on her face.

"What is it?"

"These invoices."

"Yes?"

Now, first of all, Sassafras knew what an invoice was. She had been helping me prepare my own office invoices to our law clients. She knew what to expect to see on one: the date, the name of the client, the description of the transaction in question, the amount, any applicable tax, any other conditions. She also knew that typically the invoice would not be signed by the client. She also knew that invoices in China would be handwritten, especially invoices concerning art items. An industrial goods factory might have automated invoice systems that type them out, but an art dealer in Shen Zhen, where these invoices were from, probably would not.

"The strange thing is that they're in Mandarin."

Giuseppe was confused.

"So?"

I explained to Giuseppe.

"It's from Shen Zhen, isn't that right?"

"Yes, it is."

"Well, down in those parts, they speak Cantonese."

"Oh. So what does that tell you?"

"It tells me one of two things."

Sassafras then interjected, "The art dealer who prepared the invoice is not originally from that area. Or a completely different person is doing the invoices."

I asked Sassafras, "For example, many people move to Shen Zhen from the northern parts of China."

"That's true."

Indeed, Sassafras's grandmother came from Shanghai.

"But still," she explained, "the language of business in Shen Zhen is definitely Cantonese, not Mandarin."

I looked at the invoice. I could not make out a word of it, but asked Sassafras, "Does this give the phone number and fax number of the dealer?"

"Yes."

"Why don't we send the guy a fax? Why don't we call him up? Let's see what's going on."

Giuseppe asked a nice question.

"By any chance does the invoice state the name of the person that wrote it?"

Sassafras looked all over the invoice. There was no name on it.

"Here's what we're looking for: some man or woman working at an art dealer in Shen Zhen that speaks Mandarin."

Sassafras interjected.

"And is probably a banker or has a connection to a banker at the agricultural bank of China."

I am sort of a simpleton when it comes to doing investigations. If I'm looking for a person, I call 411 and ask the operator for the name and address. You'd be surprised how many people are listed. If I want to find out what's going on with an art store in China, I don't put on a cloak and dagger, I just phone the guy.

"So let's do it," I said. "Call him."

Giuseppe brought us his phone.

"Please do."

Sassafras called the number. It rang, and happily someone answered. They spoke for a moment about God knows what, but the conversation seemed to be going in a pleasant tone. That is, until it abruptly ended. She hung up the phone. Giuseppe and I were both at the edge of our seats.

"Well?"

"There is nobody there that speaks Mandarin. They all speak Cantonese."

"Well, somebody must speak Mandarin. How did they get these invoices?"

"The man wanted me to fax a couple examples to him. He can't believe it himself."

"Let's do it."

We prepared a short cover letter in handwritten Cantonese:

"Enclosed you will find some examples of invoices that were given to us by Ms. Romano of Turin, Italy, and which purport to show transactions with your shop.

Please confirm if these invoices are authentic. We have reason to doubt their authenticity because they are written in Mandarin. This will also confirm that you just advised me that no one in your store speaks Mandarin.

Regards, Sassafras."

She left her cell number, email contact, and Giuseppe's fax number. We faxed off ten invoices covering a period of four months. These transactions totaled about 1.2 million dollars worth of art.

After the fax was sent, Sassafras had a question.

"Let's suppose the invoices are somehow fake. How will that help me in my battle with Ms. Romano?"

"It goes like this. If we show her to be involved in some kind of criminal activity, the court will have a different view of her serving as the guardian over Sassara."

Sassafras looked over to Giuseppe for confirmation. He nodded.

"Okay. What do you suppose fraudulent invoices would show?"

Giuseppe knew the answer to this.

"Typical deal with international transactions involving a fraudulent invoice goes like this: there is a desire to reduce the level of profit in the incoming country, in this case Italy, due to the substantial higher tax rates in Italy. In China, the tax rates are relatively low, so it is much better to show a higher purchase price in China, and thus a lower profit level in Italy."

I continued, "At the same time, they wish to show a lower price in China for purposes of custom and export duties. So no doubt there is a real invoice showing a much more modest pricing of the art products. As a result, the export duties would have also been quite modest. Then they prepare a new set of invoices for the Italian tax authorities which show her making only a slight profit."

Sassafras smiled.

"Aha! So this is the game she is playing. She is evading taxes."

Giuseppe explained.

"And if there's one thing the Italian government will not tolerate, it is tax evasion. We even put Sofia Loren in prison for it."

I explained,

"And if they're willing to put Sofia Loren in prison, they'll be more than happy to put Ms. Romano in prison."

Just then the fax machine printed out a transmission paper showing that the exemplar invoices had made their way to the art store in Shen Zhen. Sassafras wanted to call to confirm, but I stopped her.

"Let's not be too overanxious here. We might scare the guy away."

Giuseppe nodded.

"Let's let him get back to us. He will have his own motivation to correct these circumstances."

Sassafras was puzzled.

"You see, what will upset him is the idea that he's selling something for a low price, which is actually worth quite a bit more. He will feel cheated as well."

I smiled.

"You can always count on human nature to assist in the process of uncovering the truth."

Chapter 55
THE REPORT

While we were basking in the glory of unraveling the onion of Ms. Romano's nefarious business practices, Dr. Montevelli was busy as a little bee preparing a very nasty report about Sassafras. She had interviewed Sassara, had interviewed Ms. Romano, and of course had interviewed Sassafras, myself, and our two boys. The only family member that was missing was Spots the Dalmatian.

Two days later, we were in court receiving a copy of the typewritten report. It was just terrible.

"Ms. Sassafras suffers from a psychiatric disability known as narcissism. This is an extreme case of selfishness, which can cloud a person's mind, and can influence the mind's process in correctly receiving and interpreting information. For example, a person can say one thing, but it can be received as something completely different. This is a significant problem in the process of raising a young girl, who will be saying many things to her mother, which will all be tragically misinterpreted. This problem of communication will create many insurmountable problems, the major one being an impasse over whether the daughter wants to be with the mother, whether the daughter loves her mother, and whether the mother loves her daughter. These basic fundamentals of a relationships will likely never be resolved between them.

"On the other hand, Ms. Romano does not have this kind of disability. She has a very free-flowing relationship with Sassara. They communicate openly, directly, and with what would appear to be one hundred percent understanding. They have a very strong bond, a bond that would be disastrously broken apart if primary custody was given over to Ms. Sassafras. Ms. Sassafras does not recognize that she in effect abandoned her child and chose a modeling career over motherhood. The daughter fully recognizes this, and though expresses a willingness to forgive, has to date not found the circumstances of forgiveness.

"The general circumstances would include a full acknowledgment by Sassafras of what she did, a promise not to do it again, a heartfelt apology, and a request for forgiveness. None of these elements of forgiveness have come to pass, and likely never will. Unfortunately, one of the problems with narcissistic people is that they don't understand the impact of what they do unto others. They are so busy thinking of themselves; basically their self-centeredness precludes any type of sympathy to the plight of others.

"Based on these findings, it is my professional opinion that primary physical custody of Sassara should remain with the grandmother, Ms. Romano. I do believe that limited visitation of the mother would be beneficial to the child. To start, I would like to be present at any such visits just to assure that Sassafras's psychiatric disabilities do not adversely impact the child. If at some point I am convinced of the child's safety in this regard, I would then prepare a further report to terminate such supervised visits. I expect the supervised visits to take place for some time, probably as much as one year."

The judge had an easy decision to make in the face of this damning report. Before he let the gavel fly, he allowed a small speech by Giuseppe. Giuseppe explained.

"Your Honor, unfortunately nowhere in this report is there an analysis of the rather odd stranglehold that the grandmother has over Sassara. There is some kind of impropriety here that needs to be investigated. Until that is done, we request that the court make only temporary rulings, and that no permanent rulings of custody be given at this time. We also request that the court allow Sassafras a full opportunity to establish her relationship with her daughter. We will cooperate in any supervised visits needed, and will have her fly here as often as possible to have those visits. I trust the court will allow that."

The judge then turned to Ms. Romano's counsel. The shark was already eating.

"It's unfortunate that Sassafras cannot see the harm that she has done to her daughter. It's true what the doctor says; basically, she chose a modeling career over motherhood. Now she wants to turn back the clock, as though that could be done. We believe the disruptions in Sassara's life have already been tragic enough. We believe the best course for Sassara is for the court to issue a final order giving primary physical custody of Sassara to Ms. Romano. We do not disagree with the doctor's suggestions about visitation, and will cooperate in allowing the supervised visits described by the doctor. Whether or not they can be completed in one year will remain to be seen."

The attorney sat down. Ms. Romano looked over to me and gave me a witch smile. If she could've laughed out loud in the way that witches do, she would have. The judge looked over to Ms. Romano and smiled. That was the smile of death for our case. He explained.

"It is a rare case where the court will not give custody to a mother where the father has passed away or is otherwise not available. This is one of those rare cases. The court will adopt the recommendations and findings of Dr. Montevelli and hereby issues an order as follows. Number one, this is a permanent custody order in which primary physical custody of Sassara is hereby ordered to be with Ms. Romano. Number two, Sassafras will be allowed visitation conditioned on the findings set forth in Dr. Montevelli's report, that they begin with supervision. Upon receipt of a further report by Dr. Montevelli in which she gives further recommendations that supervised visits are no longer required, at that point the court will entertain a motion to modify visitation to allow for unsupervised visits. SO ORDERED."

The judge slammed the gavel down, and that was that. Sassafras lost custody of her daughter to the ugliest, meanest, most fraudulent Wicked Witch of the West imaginable. She looked to me. Her eyes had welled up in tears. This would either destroy her, or would make her a stronger, better person, all depending on her own reaction to it.

Sassafras stood and stared Ms. Romano down. She said something in Italian that I, of course, would not understand until Giuseppe explained it to me: "This isn't over."

Chapter 56
GOING HOME

The following day, we received a most revealing fax back from our friendly art dealer in Shen Zhen. He faxed back eight pages of invoices, written in Cantonese, which matched the series of Mandarin invoices in date and in product description, but had one glaring set of differences: the prices for the art items in the Cantonese version were substantially lower than the prices set forth in the Mandarin version.

"Aha!" was my reaction.

Giuseppe was pleased. Now we had the witch in a bind. We could prove a significant tax fraud and tax evasion. Giuseppe explained this to Sassafras.

"She will likely go to prison for a minimum of one year."

I noticed Sassafras did not share our jubilance. This was a surprise to me. I thought she would be happy about the notion of putting the witch in prison, and its resultant impact on the court's custody order. Giuseppe explained.

"It is highly likely that the court would transfer custody to you. I can't imagine why the court would not."

Sassafras was still pensive, and then announced a rather surprising decision.

"Let it go."

"Let it go?" I wondered.

"'Yes. Let it go."

"What do you mean, let it go?"

"I mean take that fax and throw it away. Let's not do anything with it."

"Oh, I see. And why not?"

"I just think that putting her in prison is the wrong idea. This will further shatter Sassara's situation. She's already lost her father; now if she loses her grandmother, well, the impact could just be disastrous."

"Is that really what you're thinking?"

"Yes, it is."

Wow, I thought. There was a rare example of Sassafras thinking of someone other than herself. She explained.

"The psychologist explained to me that much of my daughter's anger toward me and willingness to stay with her grandmother is due to her own feelings of abandonment by me. She's angry that I left her father, angry that I destroyed the family. She's holding that against me. If I do any more damage like that, and it may already be too late, that will make a permanent scar and cause her to be irretrievably lost. I would much rather hold out the hope that someday my daughter will come back."

Giuseppe's eyebrows went up. He looked over to me. I shrugged my shoulders. This was all new territory for me.

"Okay, dear. If that's what you want to do."

"That's what I want to do."

So the bombshell was kept under wraps. We did not fire it off. But just for good measure, in case she changed her mind or some other occurrence transpired, I had Giuseppe neatly fasten that fax together, double hold punch it, and affix it into the law file. You never know what might happen.

The following day, we headed off to Milan. Not for a modeling gig, but instead for a one-way return flight to California. We took the nonstop Milan-San Francisco flight. The boys and Spots slept on the way to the airport. There's something about driving in a car that puts them right out. We arrived at the airport with plenty of time to board the flight. In the back of the car was that statue of Isis. I returned to the art shop when Madam Witch was gone and purchased it for a fairly obnoxious price. For some reason, this statue, with its travels from West to East, East to West, and now to California, had found a connection with me.

On the airplane home, we were all asleep. I woke up and looked over to see quite a lovely sight. Sassafras was being hugged by the boys. They so adored her. Whatever problems she had with her daughter, and with me, one thing was clear: these boys would never let her go in a million years. They each had a head on her shoulder and slept with a look of comfort. She slept with the serenity of knowing that whatever losses she had suffered in the past, she had gains for the future. A woman has a strong desire to have a loving family. Give that to her, and you have made huge progress toward keeping her.

This is one of my further lessons on keeping a supermodel wife. You can try to give her fame, money, social standing. All these items will pale in comparison with the biggest thing you can give her in her life: a loving family.

While they all continued sleeping, in the dark of the flight, I penned a dance story to the melody of *"Comedown."* I called it *The Dance of Isis*. I hope you find in it some of the answers to the big question of how to deal with a mid-wife crisis.

"Comedown" by Bush
Used with permission

love and hate get it wrong
she cut me right back down to size
sleep the day let it fade
who was there to take your place

no one knows never will
mostly me but mostly you
what do you say do you do

when it all comes down

cause i don't want to come back down from this cloud
it's taken me all this time to find out what i need yeah

i don't want to come back down from this cloud
it's taken me all this all this time

there is no blame only shame
when you beg you just complain
the more i come the more i try
all police are paranoid

so am i so's the future
so are you be a creature
what do you say do you do
when it all comes down

cause i don't want to come back down from this cloud
it's taken me all this time to find out what i need yeah yeah yeah

i don't want to come back down from this cloud
it's taken me all this all this time

shoot up, shoot up, shoot up you're high
love and hate get it wrong
she cut me right down to size

sleep the day let it fade
who was there to take your place

no one knows never will
mostly me but mostly you
what do you say do ya do
when it all comes down

cause i don't want to come back down from this cloud
it's taken me all this time to find out what i need yeah yeah yeah

i don't want to come back down from this cloud
it's taken me all this all this time

why did you
why did you
why did you

why did you
why did you
why did you
why did you
why did you
why did you
why did you
comedown

i don't want to come back down from this cloud
this cloud
this cloud
this cloud
this cloud
this cloud
this cloud
this cloud
this cloud

The Dance of ISIS, by Hamen

Introducing
Sabrina Q.Chen

The Dance of ISIS by Hamen

The goddess ISIS is before her earthly husband
He adores her, and shows it by dancing around her,
placing his arms out before her ,trying to pull her into
him. They are in the wilderness ,where trees,flowers,
streams of water and beautiful sky all meet in
harmony.

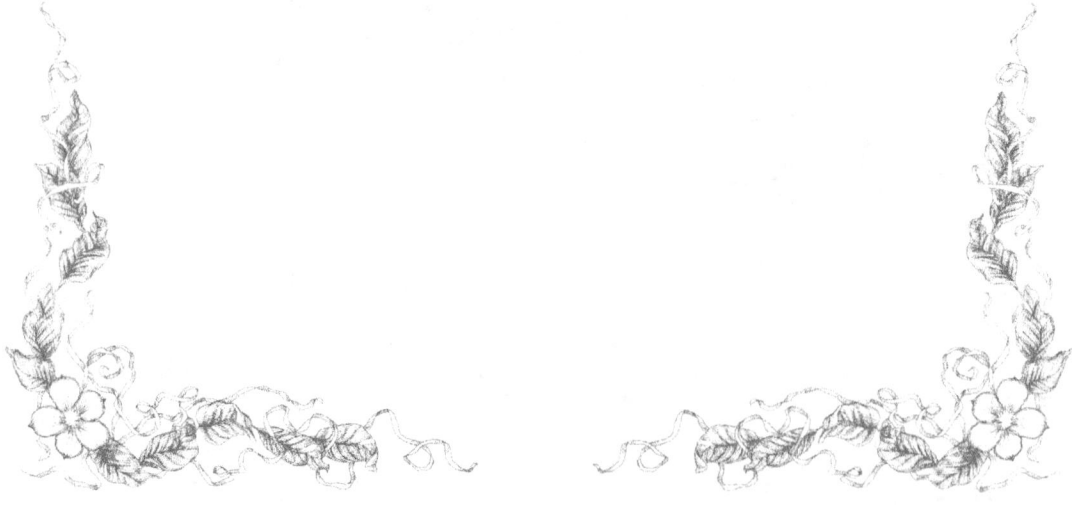

She is not coming to her husband , and instead dances is circles away from him. She goes into a stream of water and gets her feet wet. She jumps out of the stream, shakes the water off her foot ,and continues dancing away.

He stands still watching her as she circles away from him. One two three one two three, she dances away and away.
Her hands are in the air, moving around her head.

Another man enters this wilderness. He sees her moving hands, and comes to her. She is quite alluring. He holds her hand, and she twirls about. She smiles at him, and goes into his arms.

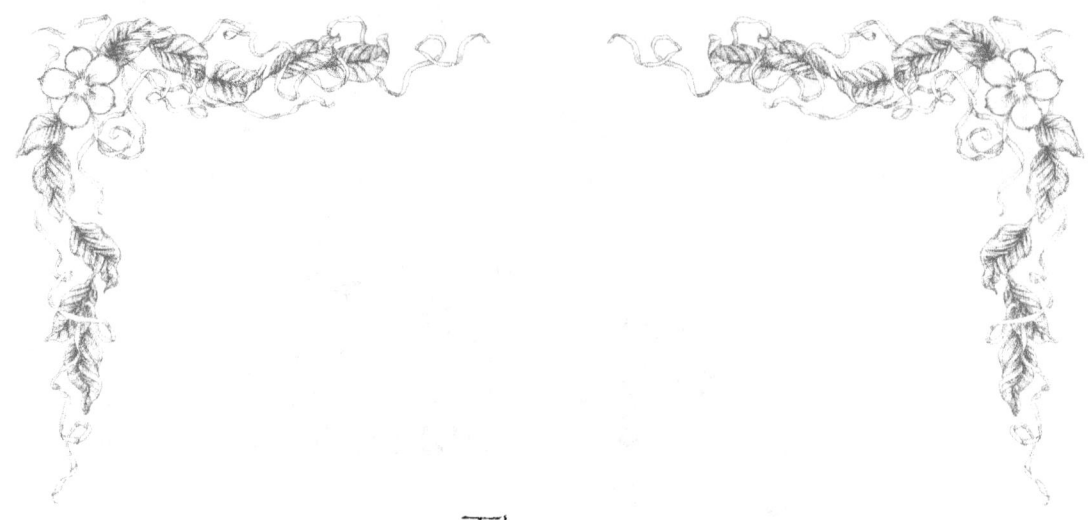

The man
is so happy to have found her, he stops and cries in
happiness. At last he has the woman of his dreams,
now he can settle down and be a husband and father.
He tells her he loves her, she tells him she loves him. It
isn't a true love, but she likes to see the blood boil.

Her husband sees all this and lays down on the
ground, head first. He is still, and looks dead.

But it isn't meant to be . ISIS moves away from this new man, and finds another . The first man is upset, cries, throws his hands up into the air, circles around, runs around, and kicks the husband, as though it were somehow his fault.

The husband takes the kick without a problem, he is dead.

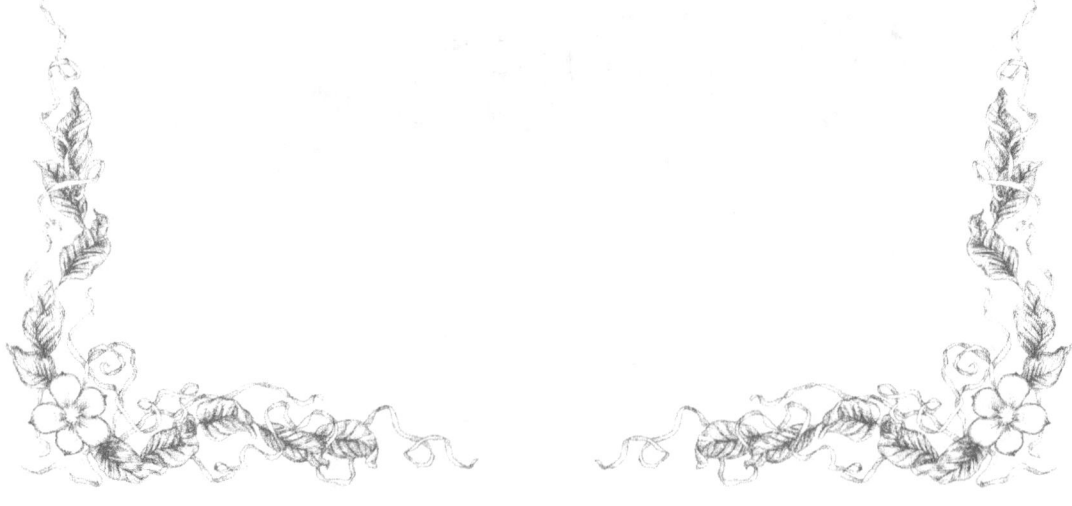

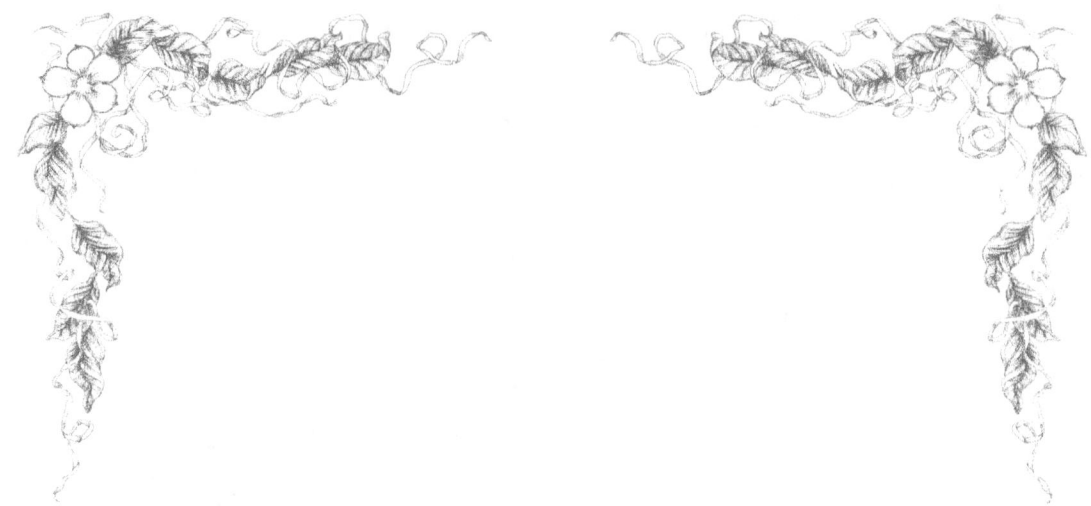

ISIS sees this and comes over to her husband. She checks him, holds his wrist to see if his heart is beating. With her touch, he comes back alive.

The man is not happy to see ISIS back with her husband. He finds another woman, and dances away with her into the wilderness. ISIS watches just for a second as this new couple twirls away.

Her husband gets to his knees, and faces her. She cries, he cries, they wave their arms around in communications. She is angry, and decides to leave again.

She dances in circles away from him and into the arms of a second man. Oh NOOOOOO.

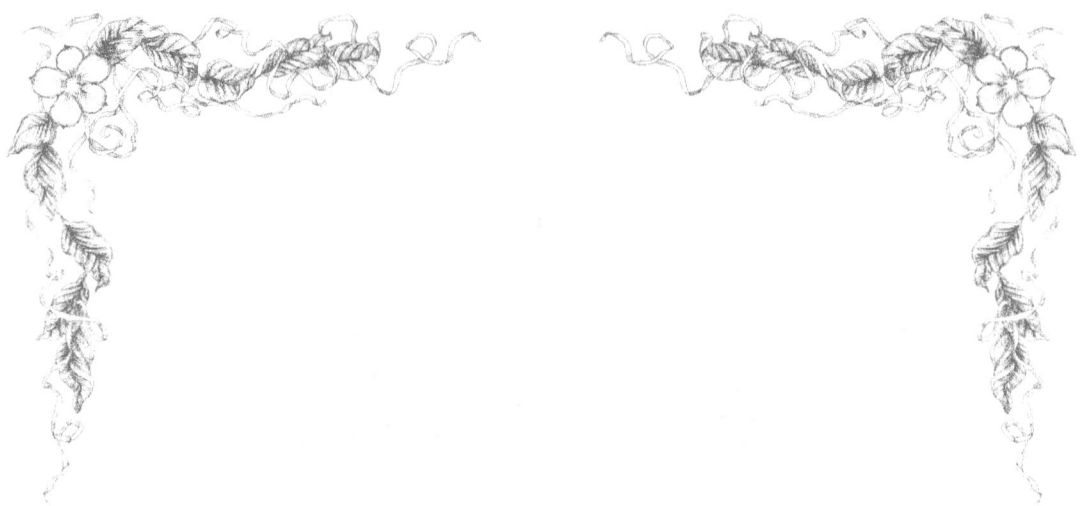

This man is so happy to see her, at last he has met the woman of his dreams. He loves her, wants her, dances with her under the moonlight. She is so happy in his arms, she rests her head on his chest. She kisses his neck, and places her softest hand onto his cheek. He melts.

She tells him "I love you, I love you, I love you." He looks up into the sky and thanks the gods for delivering such a goddess to him.

Her husband sees all this and dies a second time. He lays down with his head facing the ground. This time he will never get up.

ISIS comes over to check on her husband. She touches him. He lays motionless. She stands while the second man puts his arms up in anger. He wants her back. He walks over to her dead husband and kicks him in the head. Blood comes out his nose, but it doesn't hurt him. You cannot hurt a dead man.

ISIS is not happy about this man's kick to her dead husband. She holds her arm up to him, finger pointed, and tells him he should not have done that.

This man dances away into the arms of another woman. She is slow to take him at first, but slowly accepts his passion. They dance together, and leave into the wilderness.

ISIS is now in the middle of the wilderness with a dead husband. She walks over to him. She doesn't seem sad over his passing, just sad she can't do anything else to him. She yells at him, slaps him, shakes him, but he is dead.

ISIS dances away in sad long circles, going away from him, and then coming back to him. She checks him again, and then goes away for the last time. She realizes, he is gone.

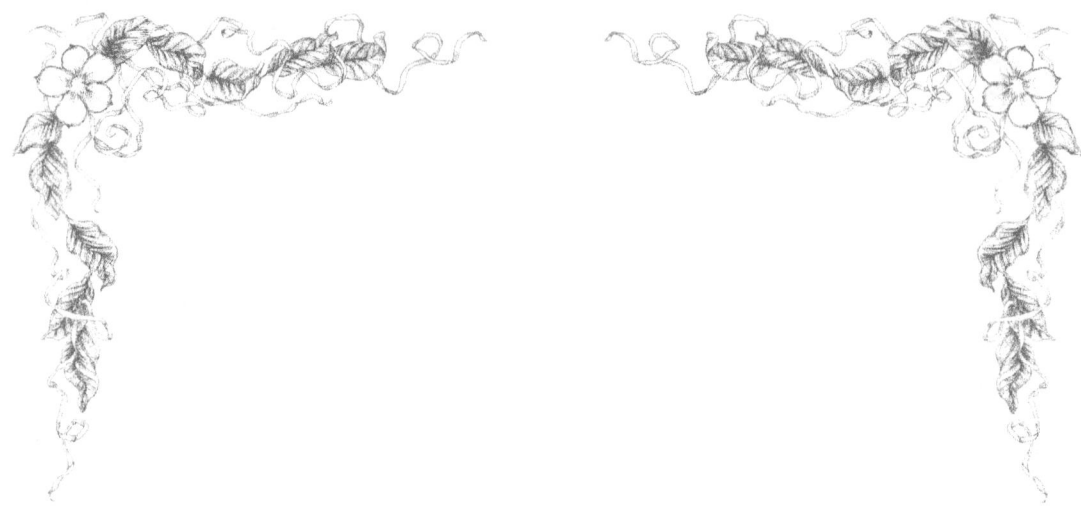

A third man comes. ISIS falls into the third mans arms, showing her beautiful smile. She touches his face. This goes on again and again, as she is held by each man. One two three one two three one two three.

She tells each of them,"I love you, I love you, I love you." She is so happy to say those words as she hasn't said them in years. Even fake love has power.

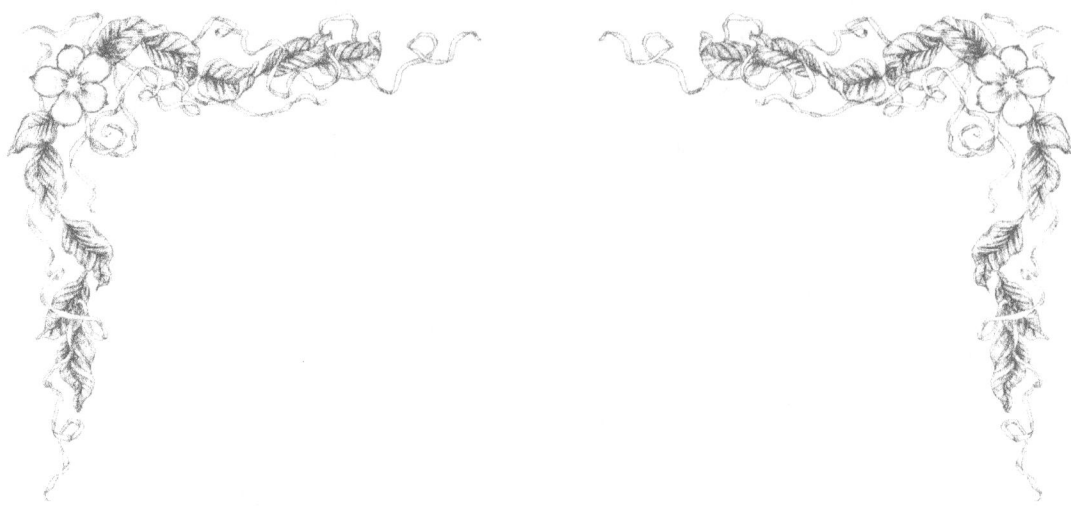

The man is so happy to hear of her love. At last he finds the woman of his dreams, and asks her: "You are the most beautiful goddess in the skies, and I want you to be my wife. Will you have me, will you merry me, and live with me forever and forever?"

He is on his knees, hoping on hope ISIS the goddess will say yes.

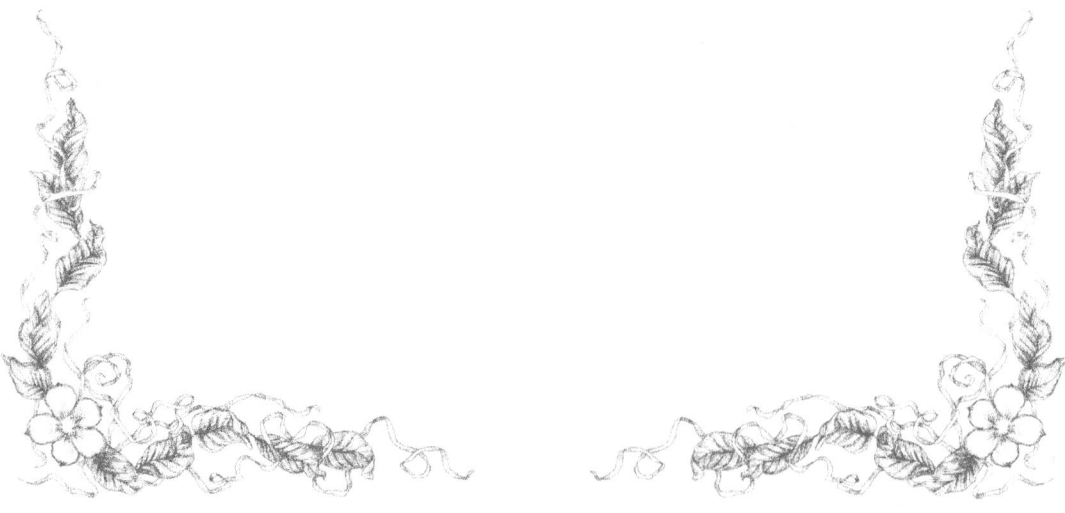

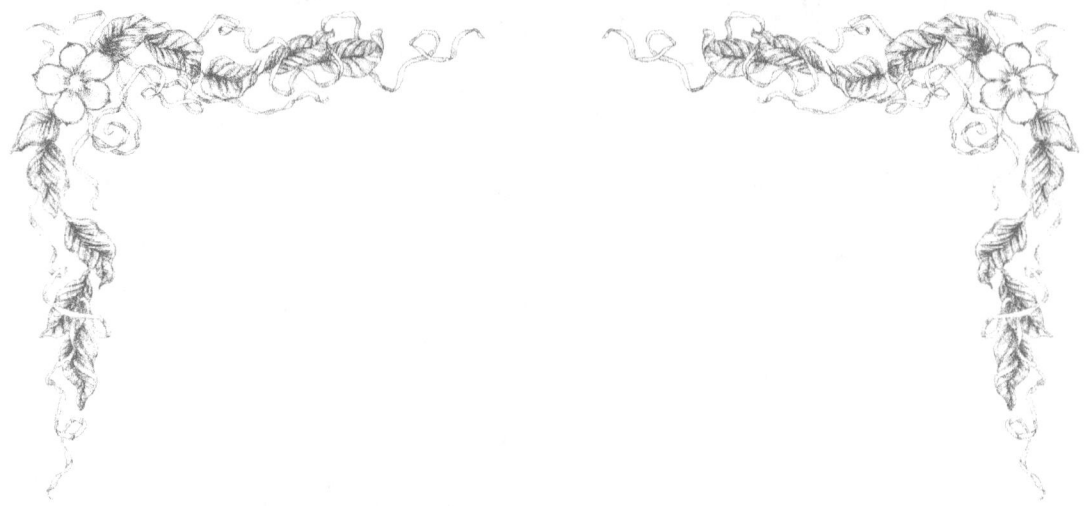

But she says no. There is some block on this, she doesn't quite know what it is. She dances away from him, leaving him shaking in the cold wind. A tree is blowing, a branch falls down. The noise of the falling tree scares ISIS. As the dead branch falls to the ground, she studies it.

An owl is sitting in the tree, and says "who who."

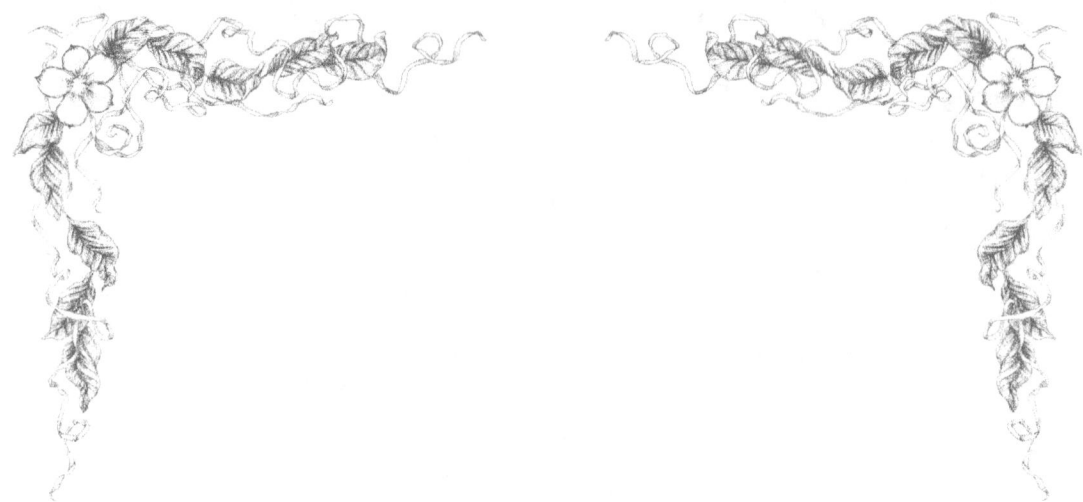

ISIS looks up to the owl, and smiles. The owl is a friend, and is wide eyed. The owl turns his head backwards without moving his body. The owl can see ISIS dancing around, and can see back where her dead husband lies.

The owl is sad to see the man lying face down. ISIS should at least bury her husband, and place him so his face is upward to the skies. She knows this, and agrees to bury him properly.

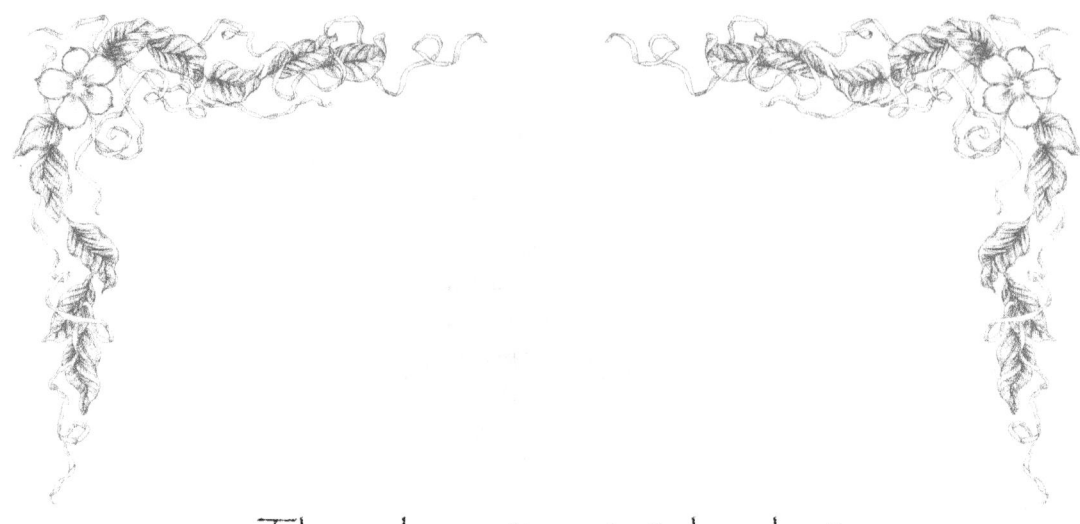

The owl says it again "who who."

She doesn't want to bury him, She wants to bring him back to life. She is a goddess so she can do this. She comes to him. The owl watches as ISIS begins the life restart process.

Now his clothes are torn. She rolls him over and sees his ripped shirt, tattered and torn. His pants have holes in them, he has no shoes.

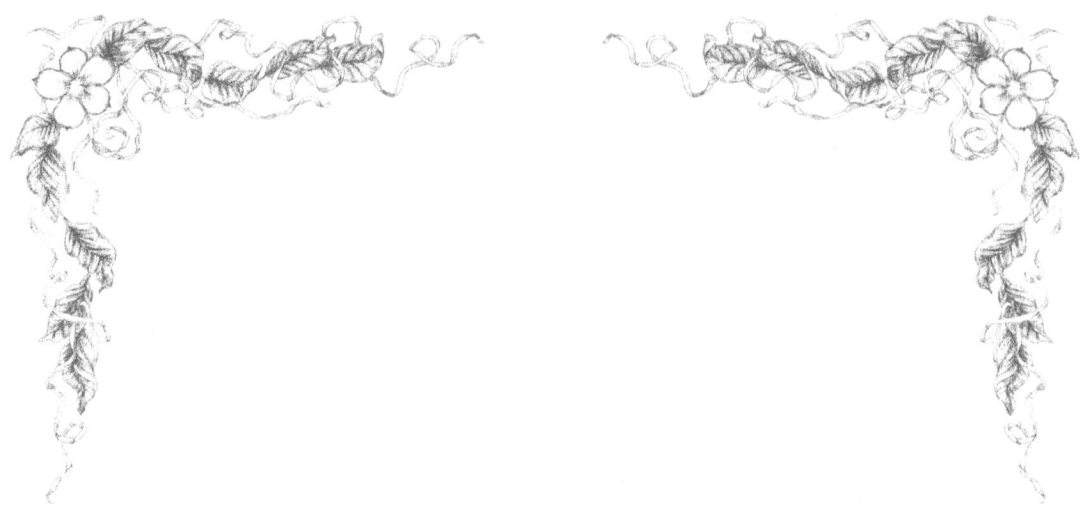

She commands him to rise up. It doesn't work. She
dances around him as lightening is striking the sky.
Loud thunder scares away flocks of birds. The rain
comes down, and washes the two of them.

She cries out to the gods to bring him back. But the
gods aren't listening.

She isn't going to give up. She yells out louder. She shakes her hands up to the sky, and commands her family of gods to do what she wants and let her husband live and love again.

At last, he rises. He smiles at her, thanking her for bringing him back to life. They dance.

Somebody like this isn't the same as they were in life. She dances in front of him, but he looks the other away. He tries to dance but has forgotten how. He dances in the direction of the clock, she dances counter clockwise.

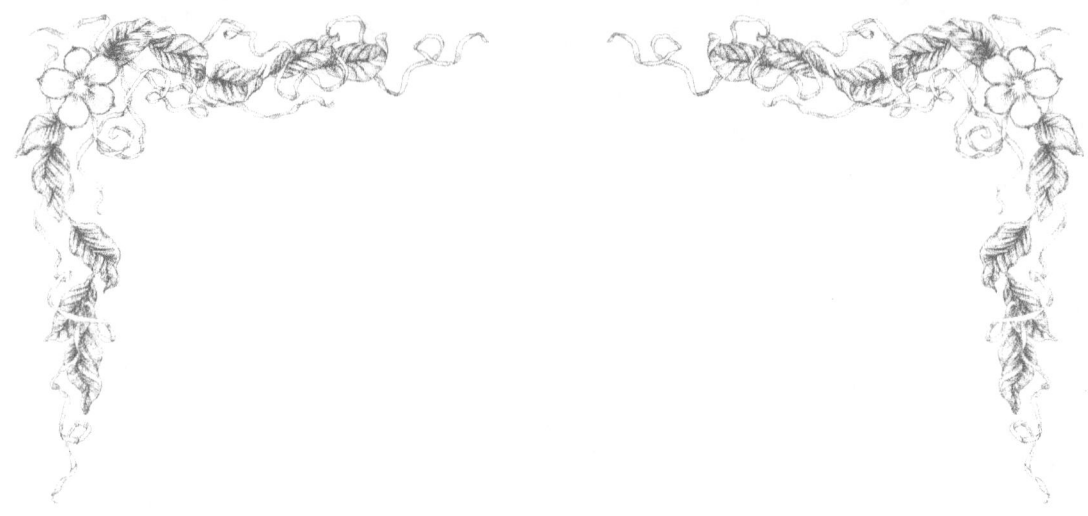

One three two three one two two three one, it is all
messed up. Their dance is not together, and she
floats away into the wilderness.
He stands alone before the broken tree and a full
moon. He sees the owl and waves.

Over to the side of the tree are the three dead bodies of her other men. Their clothes are also torn and tattered, like his. Behind them are three more, for a total of six. Six men and one husband, these are the dead men of ISIS.

He shakes his head. None of their other girlfriends worked out. Once they had a touch of ISIS no other woman would do. They would all live out thier lives in loneliness. They died in the same way as her husband, alone and cold.

They wished they had never met ISIS. Her spell kept them from ever falling for another woman.

He skips over each one of them, dancing over their bodies once, and then twice. He understands how and why they died. He is, of course, the same.

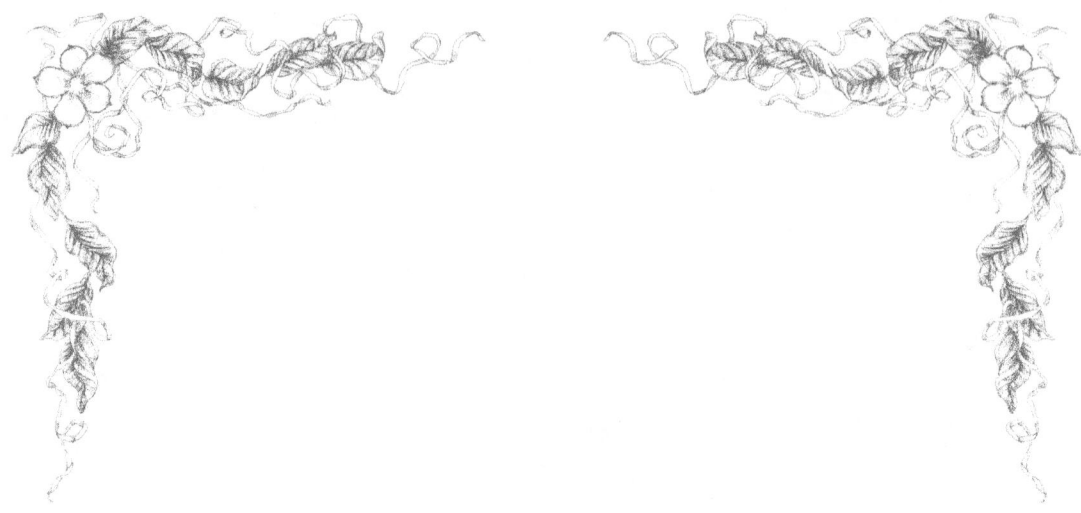

One two three one two three one two three. He is getting his dance back. He tries and tries and slowly remembers how well he can dance. His dancing takes him all over the wilderness. Animals of the forest watch as he jumps over streams, leaps over flowers, and takes in the warmth of the night.

ISIS comes back and sees him dancing. She is so surprised to see him like this. He never danced like this before, at least not with her. She is first happy, then sad; where did he lern this dance? She yells at him but now he is numb. He can't hear her yelling, and instead continues to dance circles around her.

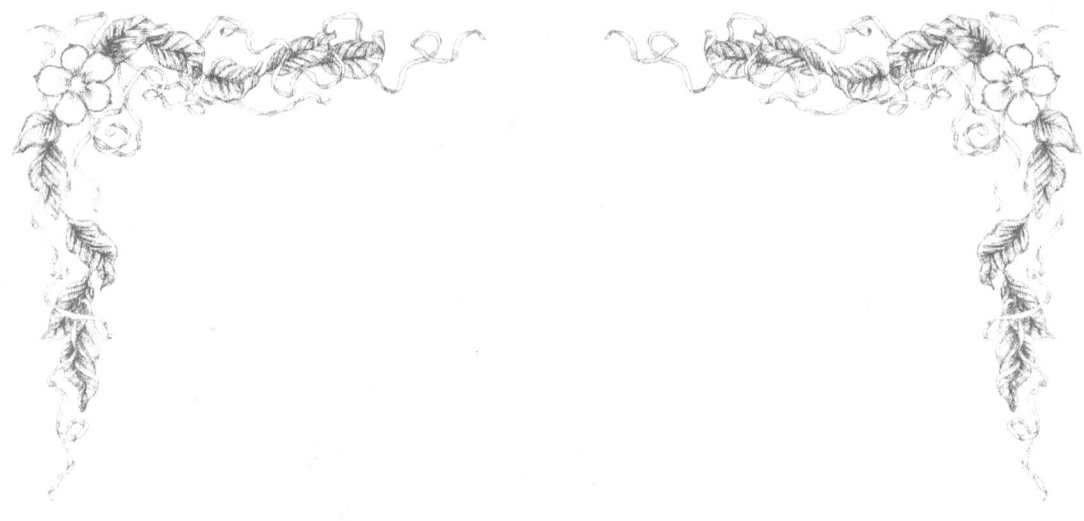

She watches him. She tries to join his dance but he is dancing alone, not for ISIS, not with ISIS, but just alone. She doesn't like this, and breaks into his dance.

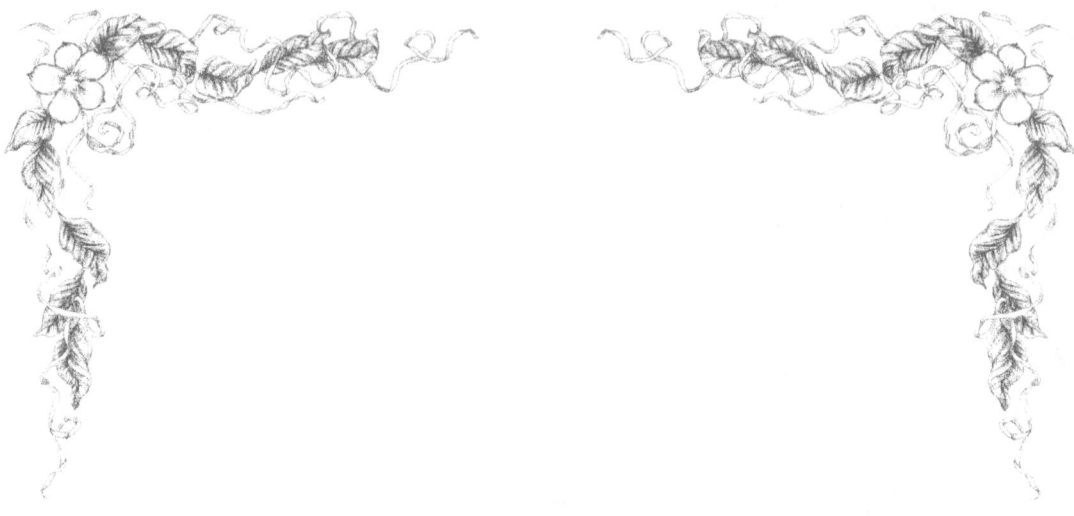

He smiles, he will let her do whatever she wants to do.
They dance like this until the early morning, when the
owl finally goes to sleep.

One two three one two three one two three.

Chapter 58
MID-WIFE CRISIS

It is with some trepidation that I begin the process of ending this story. It is not out of a love for this story, or unwillingness to let it go. My trepidation has more to do with the way the ending finds itself. As will be seen, it is completely incongruous to the rest of this. We will leave the realm of a romantic tragedy and enter the realm of the part of life that I know all too well, that of criminal violence, mafia hits, and murder in the first degree.

Before we get there, a short explanation of how this tragedy unfolds is appropriate. It is very likely nothing less than a force of nature that is afoot here. Let's become social biologists just for a second, and explore what Charles Darwin, the biologist/evolutionist, would say about the observable pattern of women ditching their husbands for another man.

Think about it from this perspective: we have many instances of women dumping their husbands for another man. This is not a mistake, it is not a coincidence, it is not entirely due to some simple foibles committed by many men. "I forgot to pay attention to my wife." Keep in mind, it is often the case that having your eyes glued on a woman is the most certain way to lose her. Excessive attention, excessive inattention, whatever you want to call it, women stray not so much because of all the reasons relationship-focused psychologists will tell us, but due to a whole other set of reasons that they likely want to hide from us, to give us hope. If there is something missing in a relationship—for example, "I feel unappreciated; unloved; you don't listen to me; I need a shoulder to cry on; I need your emotional support," items such as these—these things can be fixed. Perhaps too late, a point of no return is arrived at, when the wife finds another avenue toward that emotional support. She has an affair.

But let's step back for a second and ask ourselves, is it really because we were unsympathetic? That we were not loving, not appreciative? Or is there a much grander scheme involved, the scheme of Mother Nature? Of the ways of the human being as an animal, and as Darwin would put it, of species protection, or to put it in another way, species advancement.

So how could a woman straying from a marriage help the species advanced? It goes like this: nature loves a successful mating. The production of offspring is critical to the advancement of a species. Generally speaking, the more procreative events, the more offspring, the better the species. As economists like to say in their fundamental assumptions on their economic models, "more is preferred to less."

There are limits to this; overpopulation of an area, for example, can mean some need to reduce all this mating. But for right now, let's put the overpopulation aside for a second and realize that women and men have a program in them, a program much larger than any therapeutic regime could ever eliminate. Let us not deny the mandate of the programming of Mother Nature in all of us.

So why would Mother Nature want to force a family apart? How could that possibly be better for the species? The answer is in breaking up the family, as tragic as it sounds, the man will be released to the arms of another woman; as will the woman into the arms of another man. The procreative phases of a middle point marriage are generally over. For example, Sassafras and I had two children, and for whatever reason, we called it quits. There would be no more successful procreative events between us. Mother Nature steps in and says, "Oh yes there will be." And the method Mother Nature chooses, a method that we as humans cannot do a damn thing about, is to break up that couple and to send them to new mates, and with those new mates we will have successful procreative events. We will make new children. We will make additions to the population, and in doing that, we are adding to the genetic diversity of the planet.

Mother Nature loves genetic diversity. It is the keystone to species protection. Too much closeness in DNA between the mating couple will produce low level results. Create diversity, such as an interracial marriage, and you will create top level offspring. The example of just the opposite is seen with a simple trip to the banjo toothless playing lands of the Appalachians, where cousins commonly mate with cousins, and the results are barely human.

The other example which can bring proof of this point is in the offspring of a typical interracial couple. Take the white trashiest woman you can imagine. She weighs 185 pounds, she's all muscle, she's got six tattoos. You see her in the grocery store line; she's buying condoms, whiskey, and she's with her very large, strong black man who's got a bottle of grape juice. You don't even want to ask what they're going to do with all that. The black man is in and out of prison. He's got a criminal record as impressive as his biceps. You know from the width and length of his nose that he is extremely well-endowed. You look at the white woman and think, oh god, she loves this guy. You look at the black man and you think, oh man, he just loves this trashy white woman.

And you think about what kind of offspring they would produce. Would it be completely triple trashy? The answer is no. The kid's a genius. He's born with blondish curly hair, an odd color of aquamarine eyes, he is an honor student, he plays chess, he plays incredible violin, he goes to Harvard. From trashy parents to Harvard alum: one interracial mating can produce an extremely successful procreative event. Mother Nature will insist upon this whether you like it or not. You just have to step aside and let it happen. There is a need for this, there is a mandate for this, and there is nothing that is going to stop it.

As tragic as the loss of a wife may seem to a man, it has this happy consequence: after you pick up the pieces, scoop your heart off the ground, put it back into your chest cavity, you go to the gym, you work out, you lose weight, you make yourself look better. You buy a better belt. You get rid of your old shirts. You buy new shirts. You shave more often. You trim your hair. Your clothes need to be better fitting, and you realize that. You buy new shoes. You start doing things you weren't doing before. All these things make you more attractive to members of the opposite sex.

And remember this: there is oddly something very attractive to a woman to find a wounded man. The wounded puppy, devastated by the loss of his woman, will create a noticeable aura of hurt around him. Leave it to women to sense this like a dog can smell meat. And when they see it, they see certain things they look for in a man. You may think they're looking for strength, they're looking for money, they're looking for a river of gold, and in a very real way, yes, they are. But there's all kinds of men out there with money. There's all kinds of men out there that are successful. There's all kinds of men out there that have gold.

So if that's all you're offering and that's all you have, you're going to find yourself competing with many others that have the same thing. You show that vulnerable side, that hurt side, you show her that you were devastated in love, that you were devastated with the loss of the woman that meant everything in the world to you. I wanted no other woman, I wanted no other life, I wanted no other existence; there was only one woman I wanted, and that was the one, and I lost her and I am obliterated as a result.

Probably you won't have to say a word to get that concept across. She'll just look at you and see it. You'll be putting your hands over your cheeks. It's the way you hold your head, those droopy eyes, that saddened face, the tears coming down into your soup, plop, plop, plop. She'll see it. Now, you may think, why would a woman want such a broken man? Don't they want strong men, men that can stand up and fight? Don't they want a fearless warrior?

I've got news for you: there's lots of fearless warriors out there that get zero from women. There's a feminine side in every man. There's this molecular femininity in us. You find that, you bring that out, cry tears of love lost, of life devastated, of emotional obliteration, and all you've got to do is walk down a busy street and you're going to see that other women pick up on that, and they're going to pick you up.

It was probably one month into our return from Italy when she got back with the movie star. This whole thing of give her a family, lose weight, pay attention to her, show her you appreciate her, guess what, it all takes a backseat to this power of Mother Nature. This force of nature would not stop. The interesting thing: Mr.

Clawney got married. I read about it in the tabloids. It was really cool. He met a waitress, not really the kind of woman I would think he would end up with. She was blonde, blue eyed, tall, and it kind of scared me into thinking, this is not the woman he wants; he wants Sassafras, a dark Cantonese supermodel. So he settled for something he really didn't want, which meant he was still very emotionally available and needy.

There was another thing that happened that was most unfortunate, and I read about this in the tabloids as well. I thought, ooh, here comes trouble with a capital T. It was now a new administration in Sacramento running the government, and Mr. Clawney, who was often quite vocal about various public causes, was appointed as an advisor to the Governor. This was a situation that required him to actually move to Sacramento. The tabloids described his home. I know the neighborhood well; I used to live there. It's a gorgeous neighborhood called Land Park. It is the Beverly Hills of Sacramento: beautiful lawns, beautiful houses, beautiful people, all living side by side in lovely rows of wide streets with gorgeous large trees on either side, their little fingers arching around the road and touching each other, mingling with each other, bringing shade down on each other. It was a beautiful neighborhood, and he bought an absolutely gorgeous home there.

Well, here's what happened. I had to go to a county superior courthouse in an off the beaten path location known as Calaveras County Superior Court. It is located in San Andreas, California, in the foothills of the Sierras, about fifty-seven miles south and east of Sacramento. The case is irrelevant to this story, but let me give a quick summary. It involved elder abuse. An elderly woman owned a fifty acre ranch up in these parts. Gorgeous territory, tall pine trees, creeks running through, alfalfa growing high, horses running around, a barn, another small building, and a modest fourteen hundred square foot home.

The woman, oddly enough a former Bud girl and a model in her own right, looked as though she had just been placed into a washing machine and was not given one of those fluff-n-fold inserts. Her hair was kind of upright, short, scraggly. She had suffered what doctors refer to as a mild stroke. Her IQ had declined as a result from an impressive 128, which puts her into Harvard Law category, to a moron state of 78. The ranch, impressively enough, was owned free and clear. No debt, no mortgage, just a grant deed and what we lawyers refer to as fee simple absolute.

Add to this a couple of out of towners: a San Francisco Bay attorney and his development-oriented friend. Somehow these dogs sniffed out this elderly woman and convinced her to deed over the entire ranch, lock stock and barrel, on an agreement where they would develop it into fifty one acre homes. They would build her, and I'm sure they used their hands to show some Taj Mahal concept, a dream home. She would end up with a dream home on one acre and would be surrounded. Unfortunately her second generation Bud model daughter had moved out of there and was living nearby, but it might as well have been a million miles away. Nobody was looking over her. Without any advisory team, no lawyer, no real estate broker, no accountant, no daughter, no son, no nothing, she was convinced by this smooth-talking lawyer and his development team to deed over her property to them.

They went down to county planning, made this impressive application for a permit to subdivide to build up all these lovely homes, and of course they were doing this with zero down, a general plan to use "other people's money." As is often the case, these sheisters have absolutely nothing except a victim.

During the process of applying for the permit, they learned something that they were not expecting. The road going into the property was a modest road. Guess what, that modest road was sufficient for one family, but it was completely inadequate for fifty families. So the county folks required a new road at a cost of about two million dollars. This was unexpected, and was devastating to the construction development budget. As a result, the development never went forward.

What would the lawyers do? Say, 'sorry about that'? They would do nothing. Instead, they owned the property, and as property owners they were allowed to place a loan against the ranch. You might think, what kind of person would do this to an elderly woman that had suffered a stroke, which was obvious enough from her appearance, and the answer is who gives a shit what kind of person would do it, let's just go out and get the motherfuckers.

Enter attorney Herman Franck. We filed fraud charges, elder abuse charges, financial abuse charges, the works. We filed a lawsuit with a simple mandate given from the client. Even with her 78 IQ, she had one very clear mandate for me: "Just get me my ranch back."

The court appearance I spoke of earlier followed a series of motions to dismiss, filed by the fancy lawyers. They were making claims that there could be no fraud, that the fraud claim wasn't adequately specified, that I needed to be more specific about what exactly these sheisters did that constituted real estate fraud, elder abuse, financial abuse. The good news is the good judge ruled motion to dismiss DENIED. A fraud claim has been adequately stated.

You may think, can a lawyer survive a verdict of elder abuse, of fraud? The answer, of course, is no. Any such verdict would require the immediate revocation of his law license. Once it became clear that the motion to dismiss was denied—I might add, denied twice—the lawyers were forced into a mediation process to make a deal. It was this process that brought me to court on this occasion, during which we reached a basic concept of a deal: give her the ranch back, pay the debt on the ranch, and we will let you off the hook for all other consequential damages, emotional distress damages, treble damages, other punitive damages and attorneys fees. We will also not require any admissions of liability, you will not be convicted of elder abuse crimes, and we will basically sweep it under the rug. Just deed it back over. They saw the light, and that day we began the process of unraveling this terrible deed through agreement of a new deed transferring the ranch back to this disheveled, semi-moronic former Bud girl. She would get her ranch back.

I was euphoric, as any lawyer who experiences a victory would be. I got home, ready to explain my victory to Sassafras, but she wasn't there. That was a bit anticlimactic, but no problem. So here's what happened. I decided, time to check emails, I wanted to see what was going on back at the office, stuff like that. I went to my computer and brought up my Yahoo account. This is when I received a jolt that I'll never forget. This was the worst day of my life. Unfortunately, she was a bit careless and had been on her own email account and left it open. I saw an email from Mr. Clawney, the movie star.

Okay. The best thing to do would've been to not read it. But there's something in me that said, I gotta know. If it's bad, so be it. Sometimes you really do need to know the truth. So I opened the email. OH MY GOD. It was unbelievable. It was one of those chain emails that you get when you reply to another email, so I actually got about ten days of emails. I will not replicate it all here, and instead will summarize. He says to her, I love you, I love you, I love you. She says to him, you're the most wonderful man I've ever met. I love you, I love you. He says to her, I enjoy our times together. I love how your naked body looks, especially when your shirt is off and you're arching your back into my arms. There is nothing that has been more exciting than this in my entire life. She says to him, I love your touch. I love the way you make me feel. I love you. I'm crazy for you.

I read on. Oh, god. What has happened? I have completely lost my wife.

Chapter 59
WHAT TO DO WHEN YOUR WIFE FALLS IN LOVE WITH ANOTHER MAN

First, cry. Don't be ashamed. Don't feel like you're some kind of sub-man. Just cry, and cry hard. Admit to yourself that you love her more than anything in the world. Admit that there's no other woman you want to be with. She is the only one. You are hopelessly, directionlessly in love with her, and like it or not, you've lost her. She is in the throes of loving another man, a man that is madly in love with her. This force of nature has no recipe for reversal. You are cooked.

One of the things you have to do is hold your chest. Feel the beating of your heart. Smell your hand. Take in who you are. Look at yourself in the mirror. By this time, I had already been working out quite a bit, so interestingly, I actually didn't look all that bad. Okay, I'm no movie star, I'm not some multizillionaire guy with a gorgeous home in Land Park who's handsome, connected, a politician, a famous A-list actor. I am a mild-mannered attorney at law, madly in love with my wife, and oh my God, I've totally lost her.

Do not fight to get her back. You've already lost the battle. You have to understand this force of nature thing. Nature wants to bust up your family, and one thing about Mother Nature, believe me when I say this, she always, always win. You can mow down and forest and burn it up and I'll tell you right now, it's going to grow right back. Come back in a hundred years and it's there again. You can try to fill up the Grand Canyon with dirt and I'll tell you right away, that Colorado River is just going to wash it right away and you're going to still end up with the Grand Canyon. I don't care what you try to do, you cannot and will not ever in twenty million years of geological movement win over Mother Nature. Ain't gonna happen.

So you've got to go. You've got to pack your things. You've got to move out. You have to shake your head. Like a dog that's been in the water and shakes his body and the tears go up into the air, you shall do the same. You need to realize that there's this odd purpose in all of this. Your job is to follow the mandate of

Mother Nature and to go forth and get a new woman and procreate with her. That is your only job. You are not to try to fight for her, you are not to try to be infected by petty thoughts of intense jealousy, rage, anger; all these stupid male reactions, they're going to come, but just let them pass. Okay, if you want to act on them, go ahead and make a total ass of yourself while they are having dinner together, and make a scene. But trust me, it'll do nothing for nothing, and you'll just create a last memory in her mind of being the stupidest man on the planet.

She's not going to care that she hurt you. Why are you doing this to me? Hey, get it through your thick skull: she's not doing it to you. This is not about you. This is about her being in love with another man. Why did she do that? Because she's programmed to do that. Why is she programmed to do that? Because Charles Darwin says species protection, species advancement is what evolution is all about. Mother Nature is an expert on this and has designed a program to obliterate families at a midpoint, toward the overall goal of requiring the man to go out and find a new woman and to mate with that woman and to have new children with that new woman. More babies are born, the species is advanced.

Don't even try to fight it, don't yell about it, and don't feel bad about it. Look around you. Look at the sky. Look at the grass. Look at the flowers. Look at the rivers. Look at the oceans. Look at the mountains. You think they're rather impressive? Well, move aside. This is Mother Nature at her best. Don't question her, don't criticize her, don't be insulted by her. Realize that her magical design is the greatest design, it is the only design, it is an unstoppable design, and you must get with it. Get into her current. Don't go against it; it'll never work. Trust me, I know. I've been there. I did everything humanly possible: I changed myself, I tried to be nice, I tried to be appreciative, I tried to be more loving, I tried to make more money, I tried to write better books, I tried to write better songs, I tried to get better looking, I did the workout thing, I lost the weight, I got lucky and got new business into the law office, interesting cases, money-making cases. None of it stopped Mother Nature's design.

This is going to happen whether you become a multizillionaire, whether you lose two hundred pounds, whether you become president of the United States. You can win a Nobel Prize, you can become the best seller, the best star, the best politician, best lawyer, best lover, best whatever; mark my words, you're still losing your wife. Walk away. Walk out that door. Don't pack your bags. Come later. Just walk out the door.

I had a good friend that happened to own an apartment complex that happened to have an available unit. I moved right in. It was a small room, but it was my room, and I sat there in my furniture-less room in a beautiful part of town. There were gorgeous trees, people walking about, people having fun with their lives, people at a point when there was no tragedy. They were doing well. I saw that and thought to myself, there is an afterlife that begins today. I will start that afterlife. I will move forward, I will pick my heart out of my liver. I will separate the kidneys. I will pull it out. I will put it back in the upper part of my chest where it belongs. I will sew myself up. I will stand up. I will open my apartment door and I will stand on that sidewalk where there is a current of single people walking to and fro.

One of those persons is going to become my new soul mate. I will find her. I will be patient. I will realize that these women like the injured, wounded, vulnerable, hurt man that I am. I won't have to say a word. I'll just be me. They're going to see it, they're going to adore me, and I will survive.

Chapter 60
WE WERE JUST DANCING

I often find myself writing during these depressed moments, often with super-human ability. A song came to me, which is so very real and raw that I now share it.

"We Were Just Dancing" by Herman Franck, ESQ.

We were just dancing
My arm on your waist
In the moon light.
And everything was right.

You kissed me
Twisted your hips
Showed me your lips
and hugged me tight.

Everything was right

Then you left me;
Gone out of sight.
With all my might
I called you twenty
But you didn't answer
You just left.

I was going to say
Come back to me please.
Let me make it right.
But you said no way.

Dance with me again
Let me make it right.

You said no way.
Never again.
The answer is no;
Repeat: No, No and No.

I've got to go
Into a new life
No longer as my wife.

Head hanging low
Tears flow.
Elbows on the table
Chin in my hands.
I am half a man
Even a third.
When you don't take my call
I'm Not a man at all.

Nothing to eat
No water to drink
One pillow on the bed,
Nothing is said.

We were just dancing.
And everything was right.
And now you're gone;
It's all so wrong.

Chapter 61
BRRRRRIIINNNNGGGGG

My cell phone rang. BRRRNNNG. BRRRRNNNG. It was Sassafras.

"Where are you?"

"I'm somewhere else."

"Where is somewhere else?"

"I'm in an apartment."

"Whose apartment?"

"My apartment."

"What do you mean, your apartment?"

"I got an apartment."

"Why did you get an apartment?"

"I have moved out."

"What are you talking about?"

"Sorry, darling. I thought we were doing well, you know, I really did. We were talking, we were holding each other. I thought we were passionate, I thought it was genuine."

"What are you talking about?"

"I got home, you know, you made a mistake. You left your email account open. I read an email from Brett."

"Ohhh."

"Yeah, ohhh."

"You know, maybe we should just get a divorce."

"Yeah. I mean, hello, absolutely. You're in love with the guy. You want him in a big way. You're having a completely physical relationship with him. You're sneaking out all the time. The email talked about last weekend. I remember that, you were gone and then you just showed up again. I was like, where did you go, and you told me not to talk to you about it. Well, now I know why. You're having a complete sleepover affair with a man that is madly in love with you and you're madly in love with him. So should we get a divorce? Oh yeah. Absolutely. Don't worry, I'll handle it. I'll do it first thing in the morning."

"Yeah, we should."

"Okay, I will."

"Bye."

She hung up the phone, and then I hung up the phone. All the love we had would not put Humpty Dumpty back together again. I still wanted her, though.

This is the hard thing. How do you move on when you don't want to move on? How do you go forward when you want to go backwards? It's probably similar to what an alcoholic or a drug addict must go through, and unfortunately, there does not appear to be a Love Anonymous. There should be. I want to invent it. I want to invent a place that lovers can go when they've been dumped.

I thought of a club that would be really cool to create. It's called Humpty Dumpty. It's a place where dumpees go to mingle. And women love dumpees, so it would be a great place for women to go to find a man who will be a completely loyal lover. It would be a great place for men to go because for the most part, dumped men don't want to go to some hot-shot club where everyone is looking good, wearing all black, fancy shoes, gold chains, lots of money, oozing success, feeling good about themselves, looking magical, having the power, and you go there and feel like a piece of crud. You have no money, you don't have that black shirt, your belt is worn out, your shoes have a hole in them, and you feel like crap.

That's not a place you want to go to. You don't want to be surrounded by a bunch of strong, egotistical, mover and shaker men. You want to go somewhere where the devastated collect, and within those that are similarly devastated, there are opportunist women who will collect up and say, 'I like a man who's been hurt. I like a man who's vulnerable. I like a man who's not afraid to cry. I like a man who's been humiliated. I like a man who's down to the ground and is ready to come up and know the power and importance of a love for a woman who once he grabs onto a new one will never let go.'

I sat in my room and I thought about a few things. Now, this may sound really petty or stupid or whatever you want to call it, but I did something I probably shouldn't have done. I called one of her good friends, one of her dance mates. Her is Pe-ye. I explained to her.

"I am just devastated. Sassafras is in love with another man. We're going to get a divorce."

She told me this was all wrong, I've got a complete misunderstanding.

"Sassafras loves you. I know this because she's told me this over and over again. She wants the family together, she does not want to lose you, you've got to believe me."

As much as I wanted to believe that, I knew it couldn't be so. So I asked her to do something for me.

"Will you talk to her?"

"I will."

About one hour later, my phone rang again. BRRRRRRIIIINNNNG. I answered it. It was Sassafras.

"Can we talk?"

"Yeah, we can talk."

"I want you to know I'm really sorry about what I did. I really don't want to lose you. I love you, I love our family, I don't want to give that up. I don't want this all to be destroyed. Will you give me another chance?"

My legs are actually quite strong, with substantial muscle. They've always been that way. I was a swimmer, I was a wrestler, I was in competition judo, I was a boxer, I was a runner of miles and miles and miles, I played football, and more recently, I'm doing an hour on a stair climber. I'm going miles and miles and miles. I have muscular, strong legs, but I'll tell you, right now they were made of spaghetti. I am panting. I am holding my head. My poor little heart is back in my liver, surrounded by my kidneys. It's in a cesspool of poison, of toxic poison. It isn't pumping and bumping; instead, it is sucking in poison. It's in the wrong place. I stand up. I sit down. I'm like a pogo stick.

"Listen, Sassafras. You don't have to do this to me. You don't need to torture me. You love him, he loves you; why don't you two just get married?"

"No, I don't want that. He asked me to marry him. I said no."

I thought about that. How odd. Why would two people send each other emails that say "I LOVE YOU" a million times—in all caps, no less? Why would they have secret rendezvous and have wild sex? Why would they sneak around on this, but when the opportunity comes where they can be married and do it in a proper way, then they don't?

She explained, "All these things this man has, the beautiful house, the beautiful car, the money, the fame—"

I had to interrupt her.

"Can you just stop? I don't need to hear all this crap. I don't want to hear it."

"Let me explain. I have something to tell you."

She had that tone of voice where I had to listen. Great.

"So go on and tell me how wonderful he is and what a piece of shit I am. Continue."

"All these things he has, none of them are mine. They're just his things. They're not my things."

I tried to explain to her that this doesn't have anything to do with things, this is about love.

"It doesn't matter. You love him. It's what's in your heart. You love him. He loves you. That's all that matters. You've got to go with that. If you don't, and you stay with me, you're going to hold it against me for the rest of time, to the next Ice Age, to the next interglacial period, to the next geological period, to the next era when the dinosaurs come back, when the world is taken over by plant-eating giants; you will still be realizing and remembering the day that you gave up a movie star for me, and you will never forgive me for a thousand million years. You will hate me forever, and I will tell you right now, that kind of life, trust me, I pass."

I hung up the phone. I knew this could not be. I knew I was doomed. I had to walk out the door of my apartment and get into that current of single people walking up and down that sidewalk. Good people. Nice-looking people. Vibrant people. Healthy people. People who were not doing these weird things to me. People who didn't want to hurt me.

I walked out. I walked down to a local bar. I don't really like drinking, but I went ahead and ordered a beer. It was kind of a weird interchange I had with the bartender, a woman. For some reason, she was wearing surgical gloves. I thought that was rather odd for a bartender.

"What's that about?" I asked.

She told me she put some hand cream on and didn't want to let a bottle slip out of her hands. And then she showed me on the bottle how her hand would slide up and down it. I'm looking at her going, are you just fucking with me? And she looks at me with this smile and says, "You bet."

Okay. Maybe single life will be fun. So let me give this a little bit of a whirl. I asked her a simple question, "I'd like a Becks."

She gave me what I thought was a rather ridiculous response: "You want a non-alcoholic Beck?"

"Do I look like I need a non-alcoholic beer?"

"Yeah, you do."

"Really? Well, I want a regular beer."

"Well, we don't have a Becks with alcohol. We only have the non-alcoholic one."

Okay. This bartender with surgical gloves that wanted to jack off a bottle of beer was starting to get on my nerves.

"Tell me, do you have a Heineken?"

"Yes."

"With alcohol?"

"Yes."

"I'll take one."

She gave one to me.

"That'll be six dollars."

What a rip off. I gave her six plus a two dollar tip. She said thank you and put it into a cup that had lots of other dollar bills in it, a communal tip cup. How cool was that.

Sitting down at the end of the bar was an Asian girl with one of her Asian friends, another girl. I was obviously a hurt puppy, and they quite obviously saw it. She smiled at me. Ooh, I thought to myself. Amazingly enough, there is life after bust up. A woman will like me. As one of my friends told me, "Sassafras is not the last pretty Asian girl on the planet." And this is what all men need to realize: your wife is not the last woman on this planet. You will find another. Don't have this "I will somehow win you back" mandate. Instead, remember the current of Mother Nature. Swim with it, not against it.

BRRRRIIINNNNNG. Oh god, here we go again. I look at my caller ID and there it is, Sassafras. Here we go. Now, normally I just take a call outside, but I expected this to be a rather short one, so I took it inside. It's not very polite to talk inside a restaurant on your phone, but I had one of those earphone sets. They look rather geekish, but I decided fine, I'll put it on.

"Hello?"

"Where are you?"

"I'm at a bar."

"What do you mean, you're at a bar?"

"I'm at a bar. What do you think men who have been dumped by their wives who fall in love with movie stars do afterwards? We go to bars. Hello."

"Well, that's ridiculous."

"My life is ridiculous."

"I want you to come home."

"I'm not coming home. I'm staying out."

"We need to talk."

"What do you want to talk about? You're in love with another guy. He loves you. Isn't that just it? I mean, haven't you done enough? Do you really need to do more to me?"

"You know, if you weren't such an asshole to me, I would've never been open for this new love."

"Okay, I don't need to know about that. You've already told me eleven million times all the shitty-ass things I've done to you. I know all about them."

"You were such an asshole. You didn't appreciate me. You didn't protect me. You insulted me. You told me I had a chicken brain. You said I didn't have any talent. You told me I was stupid."

I thought to myself, when did I say that? But I don't even want to go there, because it will just be a litany of complaints. So I responded to her.

"Look. You don't need to beat me up anymore."

"You need to understand, I'm getting my revenge against you. I don't give a shit about you because you're such a dick, and that's why I'm having this affair. That's why I'm doing him. And let me tell you something, that email isn't even one one-hundredth of what we've done."

Okay, so now I'm on the ground, I'm bleeding, I'm unconscious, and she wants to kick me in the teeth. What's up with that? I looked at her name on my phone. I just studied it. I was quiet. I didn't say a word.

"Are you there?"

"Yeah, I'm here."

"Did you hear what I said?"

"Of course I heard what you said. I have stereo earplugs, so I get to hear this kind of crap in stereo. I've got the volume turned up to seven, so it's like being at a rock concert where the singer is telling you what a dick you are."

I looked over and saw that woman with the surgical gloves. She frowned at me.

"Sorry."

"Who're you talking to?"

"Just a girl."

"What girl?"

"Oh, never mind. I just said that too loud. You know what, hold on a second. Let me walk outside a second so you can yell at me a little bit more.—I'm sorry, I'm having a problem."

"Who are you talking to?"

"This girl. Don't worry about it, I'm walking out right now."

The other Asian girl watched me as I got up and walked out. It would've been really cool if she would've followed me and given me a big kiss right then. These things don't happen in real life. I walked out.

"Okay, continue berating me. I just love to hear this after I learn all the shit you're doing with this guy. Oh yeah, I need to be insulted. I need to be leveled again. I need to be just destroyed now because you haven't really hurt me enough yet, have you?"

"I want to hurt you."

"Well, congratulations. You have. You've destroyed me. I'm devastated. I have a knife in my stomach and now you're twisting it. What's up with that? Haven't you done enough?"

"No, I haven't done enough. I want to do more."

"Okay, listen. Here's how it's going to go. You're not going to do any more because I'm cutting it right here. We're done. You can't kill me again, because you've already killed me. We're done, so don't worry about it. You can now be with him, he can be with you, you guys can live happily ever after and you will not be able to hurt me anymore."

CLICK. I hang up the phone. I am just beside myself with anger, with hurt, with envy that this man would have her, with envy that he could love her and she could love him, and I couldn't. She'd never told me she loved me like she did in those emails. She never was crazy for me like she said about him. She never fantasized about sex with me like she did with him. She didn't want me anywhere close to how she wanted him. It was so unfair, so wrong, so bad. I was wanting absolutely to die.

BRRRRIIIINNNG. BRRRRRIIIINNGG. My phone rings again. It's Sassafras.

"Yes?"

My voice is very meek. When I'm in court, I bellow. I am at home and I take charge and I speak in a loud, forceful way. Today, this evening, on my cell phone with this woman who has fallen in love with another man, I don't bellow. I barely whimper.

"I'm sorry, honey. You have to understand, I just get so upset with you. I say these things, I don't mean them."

My strong, stocky legs are once again turning to spaghetti. My soul is more like flattened ravioli. My legs are spaghetti. Imagine a piece of ravioli flattened out, supported by two strands of spaghetti. The ravioli has red sauce dripping off, the blood of my heart. Inside there was meat, but it is now cheese only. My flattened ravioli with red blood flying off supported by two spaghetti limbs starts to waver, a little to the right, a little to the left, a little forward, a little backward. I'm going to fall down.

Just then, one of the Asian girls amazingly enough does walk out of the bar and she sees me. She sees me crying. I'm so embarrassed. My eyes are red, my cheeks are red, I'm faltering, I'm wavering, and she walks up to me and says, "Are you all right?"

"No. I am not all right."

"Who is that? Who are you talking to?"

"It's a girl from the bar. Don't worry about it."

"Who's this girl from the bar?"

"You want to talk to her yourself? I'll put her on."

"No, I don't want to talk to that bitch. You tell her to get the fuck outta there."

"Okay, just a minute, I'll tell her that. Uh, my wife says to get the fuck outta here, how about that?"

The girl just shakes her head and walks away.

"There, I got rid of her. Are you happy now?"

"What are you doing there? Are you picking up women?"

"No, I'm not picking up women. I'm devastated. I'm dead. I'm picking myself off the floor, at least I'm trying to. I decided to go to a bar and have a beer, and in the process some girl saw me. That's all. What do you give a shit? You're cutting me loose, what the hell?"

"You know, even as a trashy piece of shit that you are, it still bugs the crap out of me that some other woman will scoop up your trashy self and take you for herself."

I thought, yeah, well, that's it.

"Someone probably will, but whatever. It ain't happening tonight."

"I want to get you to come home."

"No, let's not do this again. You're just going to kill me. I can't handle this hurt anymore. I've gone up and down with this. Can we please just not do that? Don't hurt me anymore."

"I'm not going to hurt you anymore, I promise."

"Oh yeah, you promise. What are you promising? Tell me."

"No, you tell me, what do you want me to do. You tell me what you want me to do and I'll do it."

I hung up the phone. Back in the bar they played one of the greatest dumpee songs ever, *"Black"* by Pearl Jam:

Chapter 62
RESTORING BALANCE

I am not a Buddhist. I am not Asian. I don't understand that whole yin and yang thing. I don't understand Confucius, I don't understand Zen, I don't understand Tao, I don't understand the psyche, the methodology, the approach; I don't know any of it. I've been with a Chinese woman for ten years now; I feel like I've learned about as much as I had when I first met her.

But there's something I do know. It's part of my ancestry. I am a sliver of Cherokee, and they have a concept of restoring balance. There is a legend of a rattlesnake told in Cherokee lore. It has to do with a snake that kills a member of another tribe. The rule was the imbalance had to be corrected. There was a minus one, and there needed to be a positive one to bring it back to zero. The method was to kill that rattlesnake. This is a little bit of "eye for an eye," with the danger of eye for an eye. The main danger, as pronounced by Mahatma Gandhi, to the effect: "The trouble with an eye for an eye is pretty soon everyone is blind."

Sassafras called me back and asked me what she could do to get me to come home. I explained it to her this way, so that we didn't all go blind: "You will need first of all to get rid of him. You know we cannot survive if you have a lover. Are you understanding that?"

"Yes. I will get rid of him, I promise you."

"I promise you that you can't. You're in love with him. How are you going to get rid of this man who now lives in Sacramento and that you're madly in love with?"

"I will. I did before, but unfortunately I ran into him again and it started up again."

"Great. And it's going to happen again. You're going to be running into him here and there. I can't live on knowing that all you need is one chance encounter and bam, you're right back to loving him."

"I will get rid of him. You have to accept that."

"I don't accept that."

"Well, let me just tell you, I will. I'll get rid of him. What else do you need from me?"

"You getting rid of him is basically getting rid of a negative. What I need is for you to restore balance by adding a positive. You need to do something positive, something specific, something obvious, something concrete, something very real."

"Like what? You want to have an affair? You can do that and I'm not going to complain about it."

"Oh, right. You're not going to complain about it? You just told me to ditch some girl that I don't even know. Listen, you can't handle me having an affair. Let's get real with that. Beyond that, I don't want an affair. I don't want another woman. I want you. You are the only woman I want."

"This is what I need to hear. This is what I needed to hear before."

"Don't go there. Let's not go down your path of all the crappy-ass things you need from me. You asked me what can you do for me. I've already done things for you. I've done very concrete things for you. You know what they are. I've been a nicer man, I've been a more appreciative man, I've told you I love you, I've shown my love for you, I've been exercising, I've lost weight, I've tried to clean up more around the house; I've tried to do all this shit you need me to do, and you're still in love with this other guy. So hey, guess what, I give up. All these things I've been doing, the good news is they make me a better person and make me in a better way to go out and start the next phase of my life. I don't consider any of it to be a waste of time. I just consider it to be a lesson that this isn't going to work."

"What if I did something positive for you? What if I was a better wife to you? What if I got rid of him? What else would I need to do?"

"You need to want me. You need to be there in a real way and to want me. You need to love me like you love him, and I just don't think it's even remotely possible. You don't have room in your heart for two loves. You only have one love, and you've got that love. How are you ever going to have room for love for me?"

"I do love you. I love our family."

"Wait, I'm not the family. I'm a guy. I want you to love me one on one. You are equating your love for the children and your desire to have this family go forward as a love for me. That's not what I'm interested in. You can't have it both ways. You're going to have him, then you're not going to have the family. You want the family, then you're going to get rid of him, but you're not going to have me unless you're truly back to me. You've got to be with me in a real, genuine way, and I just don't think you can do it."

"Is that what you want from me?"

"That is absolutely what I want from you. I want to see you give me tender moments. I'm not talking about sex here. I'm talking about you walking up to me, holding my arm, holding my hand, putting your hand on my cheek, kissing me on the cheek, telling me I love you and meaning it, holding me. I want to give you a picture. We're in the kitchen. You're cooking. There's broccoli, there's cauliflower, there's spam."

She laughed at that. She actually does use spam in some of her otherwise completely healthy Chinese foods.

"I come behind you. I put my hand on your shoulder. Now, let me tell you how this scene works out right now. You turn around and say, 'Leave me alone. Don't touch me.' You snap at me; I walk away rejected. I know you don't love me. I know you're disgusted by me, you can't stand me, I walk away. Here's how I want that to play out. You turn to me, you look me in the eyes, you smile, you kiss me, you hold me, you let me hold you, you say, 'I love you.' I tell you I love you, and we both mean it. And then I walk away and I leave you alone, and I feel like a man again, and you feel like a woman again, and we both feel real, like we're in a loving relationship. We have a family, a house. We have all these things that all of us are supposed to want and need, and we have it in a real way and we feel good about it and our heart glows. Our head glows. Our eyes are lit up and we feel wonderful. That's what I want from you."

"I can give you that."

I take my glasses off. Oddly, across the street the Asian girl is still over there watching me. I wave at her. She waves back. I shake my head. She shakes hers.

"Are you there?" Sassafras asks.

"Yeah, I'm here."

"Did you hear what I said?"

"I heard it."

"Will you give me a chance to do that?"

Here's one of those forks in the road. You love the woman more than anything in the world. You can't imagine life without her. There is no other life you want to live. You love her, you have to have her, but you can't have her. You realize that you need to move on. You know that right across the street, there's that opportunity, just sitting right there, a smiling pretty girl. Available, interested; what's the problem with me? Hang up the phone, go across the street, and say hello. But no. In a typical completely stupid, irrational way, I'm not going to do that. Instead, I agree.

"Okay, dear. I'm coming home."

Chapter 63
I AM A HOTTIE, TOO

The Asian girl looks at me as I walk across the street. I walk on the other side of the street, and she follows. I go down to my apartment, turn off the light, turn off that air conditioner that's in the window, walk out, and there she is. She is pretty, a much whiter Mandarin Asian from North China, with long legs. She wore a zebra dress and had straight black hair.

"Hello."

"Hello."

"What's your name?"

"I am Tang."

"Hello, Tang."

"You've been crying?"

"Oh—sorry."

"No need to be sorry. Why you cry?"

"I lost my wife."

"Did she die?"

"No, she found a new man."

"You need a new woman. That's what you need."

Duh.

"Okay, how about you?"

"Maybe me, maybe another girl."

I looked at her. She smiled. She is smart to know she can easily have me.

Just a short drive, but I don't get home for three hours. The entire time I am speaking to Tang. I come in. Sassafras greets me and doesn't ask what delayed me.

"I love you. Please believe me. I really do."

I am flattened ravioli with spaghetti legs. I fold over onto her. I cry. She wipes the tears from my eyes.

"I'm so sorry. Please believe me when I tell you that."

I don't believe her, but I can't leave her. I hold her. I cry some more. She pulls back and sees me crying. One thing that is attractive to a woman is when she sees a man hopelessly in love with her. This is a very strong aphrodisiac. She also is smart enough to know that these movie stars are players, and it's here today, gone tomorrow. There's no certainty in it, there's no long term; it's a flash in the pan kind of relationship. Hers, however, has been already a year, so let's call that an explosion in the pan.

She takes me upstairs and shows me as best she can that she will love me for the rest of my life. I accept her. I feel I have no choice. My heart is driven by a love that is stronger than Mother Nature's current against my family. Mother Nature may want to bust us up, but my heart says no. I will forgive, I will try to forget, I will find a way to get over this pain, this agony. I will take my wife back. I will fight for her. I will convince her to dump this movie star guy, to stay with me, and to let our family live.

"You don't have to do a thing. I'm already there. I want our family more than anything in the world. I want this house more than anything in the world. I want you more than anything in this world. I want us to stay together. Please give me the chance to show you I can be the wife you want me to be. I know you can be the husband I want you to be. You're doing it, I see it, and I love you for it. You've made the changes I've asked for. I will now make the changes you need from me."

That night, for the first time in months, Sassafras was able to sleep well. She had had major problems sleeping at night, and it occurred to me that part of the problem she was having was pangs of guilt over this torrid affair while still wanting a family. This all somewhere makes perfect sense in love and life, that the woman has this fantasy date, a fantasy love, and her reality husband, and she wants both. She doesn't want to go with the movie star. She just wants to do him every now and then.

She realizes at some point that obviously she can't do both, but how can she pull away? How can she give it up? It's such a temptation. How do you stop? And I want to know the same thing; how do I stop? Just like she can't stop her love for him, I can't stop my love for her. Now she's seeing how real my love is. I don't think she ever expected me to fight so much for her, and once she finally sees me throwing in the towel and giving up, that's when she's going to finally come around to me, stay with me, and fight for me.

I look at her as she's sound asleep. I feel so uneasy. I feel so—I don't know how to say it, but agitated, intense, angry. The next morning we wake up. I go down and make some coffee. I'm downstairs. She comes down, and just like the picture I described for her, she kisses me and says, "I love you. I love you. I love you. Please believe me, I do."

She holds me. She caresses me. She puts her palm onto my cheek, onto my neck. She tickles my ear. She puts her finger into my ear. She takes it out. She scratches my back. She scratches my butt. I am flattened ravioli with spaghetti legs, blood dripping off of me, cheese only inside.

Chapter 64
ANOTHER REASON MEN HAVE AFFAIRS

There are studies out there done by qualified psychologists, including such as Dr. Gary Neumann, that look into the reasons behind the practice of men having affairs. [M. Gary Neumann, <u>The Truth About Cheating: Why Men Have Affairs and What You Can Do to Prevent It</u> (Wiley, John and Sons, 2008)] Dr. Neumann has interviewed two hundred men, and learned that, for the most part, affairs are not about sex at all, but are instead a response to emotional detachment between the husband and wife. The men need roughly the same emotional support as women do. They want to be validated, appreciated, they want someone to speak with, to share their trials and tribulations with, to obtain emotional support from, and to be told those magic words, "I love you, I care for you, I appreciate you, I value you, I need you, I want you."

Women may think they are the only ones in the relationship that need these important statements and actions, but the reality is that men need it equally, and in the same exact manner. As stone-like as men are supposed to be, the reality is that we men are as emotionally needy as our female counterparts. If a woman stops the flow of emotion towards her man, stops saying "I need you, I want you, I value you, I appreciate you," etc., closes her heart to him, she can expect a rather obvious consequence: the man will stray.

Dr. Neumann's study interestingly noted one rather dramatic result: the clichéd vision of a middle-aged man having a midlife crisis and driving off in a red convertible sports car with a youngish blonde bimbette is actually not grounded in reality at all. Most men that have affairs do so with women who are not younger than their wives, who are not as pretty as their wives, who may weigh more than their wives, but do something the wives won't do: they appreciate this man. They marvel at his accomplishments. They know what he does for living, and think it's wonderful. They tell him, "Wow, you did that? That's incredible!" They kiss him tenderly. They hold his hand. They caress him. They look him in the eye and tell him, "You are lovely."

When a man is receiving this type of attention from a woman, during a period when his wife has closed off, during a period when the wife has basically taken him for granted, it can be pretty well assumed the man will stray. Now, you can call the man a louse, you can call him a cheater, you can call him whatever you want, but the real title should be: "emotionally needy." If you don't feed a man, he'll go down to a restaurant and get food. If you don't give him the emotion he needs, he'll find it somewhere else.

I would like to add one more item to the list of reasons why a man will stray from his wife. It is a rather obvious one not covered in Dr. Neumann's book, but which I will put out here: if a man's wife is having an affair, the man will be highly likely to respond in kind and have an affair of his own. This is not necessarily a "revenge affair," or an affair meant to create jealousy in the wife toward the overall goal of getting her back. Instead, this could very well be a rather obvious reaction to a disastrous set of circumstances, where the man has come to recognize that no matter what he does, he has lost his wife to another man, he will never get her back, and his only choice is to move on into the arms of another woman.

In other words, this is not a game. This is about getting a new woman, a new wife, and a new beginning to the next Chapter of the man's life. It is exactly here that I found myself on this interesting evening with Tang at my door. She was 42, older than my wife, and I don't mean to degrade her in any way, but I have to say, she was not quite as pretty as her. The good news is you can be not as pretty as a supermodel and still be very beautiful. Though Tang was no supermodel, she was still babe-alicious. She had lighter skin, Mandarin from the North, she was skinny, lanky, with somewhat oddly formed strong arms. She must have lifted weights, almost to the point of where Madonna has found herself. There was something about her semi-manly arms that I found oddly attractive. They showed the veins, veins of strength.

You never know when you might connect with a woman. You can go out with a hundred women and not be interested in them, or they will not be interested in you. But every now and then, in those beatable odds, perhaps one in a million, you will find that other woman out there that likes you, and you like her. It is this equivalence of desire that will at last draw two fish swimming in the sea together into a union. For reasons I don't understand, Tang was attracted to me. The way she stood in my doorway, with her elbow on my doorframe, her other hand on her hip, her body angled into a semi-K; her smile; her confidence from weight lifting or something; her maleish aggressiveness; her willingness to quite literally pick me up off the ground; it was extremely attractive to me.

She wore a zebra dress. I don't know why women do this, but they are dead right to do so. There's something about animal skins that bring out the jungle in us. When we're married, we're like domesticated dogs. When we're single, we turn back to a wolf state, the state of a hunter. Put on a leopard print, a zebra print, a python print, or any other kind of wild beast, and somehow that call of the wild will bring us forward, panting.

I was about to go out the door, back to Sassafras, for another period of betrayal, fake reunification, endless cheating, berating, belittling, and disappointment. Why I would want to do such a thing has more to do with the unfortunate concept of obsessive love, the concept of being stuck on somebody, than anything else. The psychological bond between Sassafras and I was part of the spell that started the minute I saw her, and wouldn't let go. The fact that we had children together made it all that more strong. It was a bond that went into the marrow of our bones, and wouldn't let go. She could spit on me, she could pee on me, she could kick me, she could have a lover, she could have ten lovers; I would still go back to her. I would never let her go.

Until, that is, I found Tang in my doorway.

"Why you look so sad?" she asked me.

There's something about that slightly imperfect Asian English that just drives me crazy. Add to that the zebra dress, her long, athletic legs, and I'm done. I tried to be strong for her, but didn't want to be fake.

"I'm having a problem."

"Problem? I can help solve all problems."

And how. She looked at my rather pathetic apartment, and couldn't help but laugh. I had no TV, my child's bed mattress had artwork of hot air balloons all over it, and there was a quilt covering it with one pillow without a pillow case. There was a plastic fold-up table, and on the table were two books. One was *The Law of California,* what we refer to as a "five-in-one," that has the civil code, the code of civil procedure, the evidence code, parts of the government code, and parts of the probate code, all collected up into one handy collection of statutes. The other was a red book of California civil jury instructions. These are the instructions the court reads to the jury about the law that applies to a particular case. The jury instruction book is rather large, about fourteen hundred pages, and sets out instructions for all kinds of cases.

She saw the books and knew right away what I did for a living.

"You're a lawyer?"

"I am."

"Civil law?"

"Yes."

"You do any construction law?"

"Some."

"Oh? How about mechanics lien?"

I thought that was a rather funny phrase for a lovely Asian girl to know.

"Mechanics lien? You know about those?"

"Oh yes. I deal with them all the time."

"What do you do?"

"I'm the office manager of a general contractor here in town. I'm the one that files and records mechanics liens any time we don't get paid."

"Oh, I see."

"I also manage the lawyers who file the lawsuits to collect the money owed to my boss."

"Well, I guess your boss must really trust you in doing all that."

"Actually, it's more like this: he doesn't trust the lawyers as far as he can throw them, so my job is to keep a hot eye on them."

One thing I could tell about this girl is she had a rather eagle eye. She had scoured my small apartment in a matter of seconds and picked up my whole life story, mainly by seeing all the things I didn't have.

"You just moved out?"

I couldn't possibly start denying the obvious.

"I did."

"Married?'

I nodded.

"Children?"

"Two. Two sons."

"Looks like you took his bed."

"He sleeps in a king size bed, so he'll be all right."

"What's the problem?"

"You really want to know?"

She moved her positioning from the doorway. She didn't respond. She was searching for an invitation, and I wasn't numb. I looked at my pathetic little place, and knew right away that I didn't want to invite her in.

"You want to go on a walk?"

"I'd love to."

I was so happy to hear those words. She wanted to be with me, she wanted to listen to me, she wanted to hear me, she wanted to share my situation. I would not question even for half a billionth of a second her motivation. It didn't matter. She was obviously exactly what I needed.

So, we went on a walk. It was a lovely night. There are very large trees on this street. It has a sidewalk that is a little bit jutted up and down where the roots of the trees have grown into the concrete. This means you have to be careful as you walk, or you'll stub your toe. I could see she was quite agile, walking down the sidewalk missing all the jutted up concrete, and it occurred to me, she must live around here.

"Are you from this neighborhood?"

"I sure am. I live just right over there."

She pointed to a house that could not have been more than two hundred yards from my new little pathetic apartment. Say what you will about my studio – no living room, family room, dining room, TV, computer, small kitchen, no back-yard – but it was one hundred and eighty-seven yards away from a lovely Mandarin whitish maleish Asian chick by the name of Tang. And she was hot for me.

Would you say I was emotionally available? That I was in a position where I might open my life and heart up to another woman? Oh, please. We talked. We walked. We strolled. Two hours later, it felt like we had just started. I noticed that she was not the least bit tired. In two hours, you can walk several miles, so this was all good energy. Our hearts were pumping, the blood was flowing, we were getting exercise, we weren't drinking and getting drunk. Instead, we were just talking and sharing our lives.

I had completely forgotten about my recent phone call with Sassafras and my agreement to come home. My phone rang. Tang listened to it and noted I didn't want to answer it. She smiled.

"Your wife?"

"It is."

"How do you know if you didn't look?"

"Because no one else would call me right now."

"You better get it."

"I don't want to get it. It's not going to be good."

The phone stopped ringing, and then it rang again. Sassafras has this telepathic ability to know when something isn't quite right. She knew that I was at my wit's end, that I was out on my own, in the great beyond, that the domesticated dog had been reintroduced into the world and was sprouting wolf hairs. She knew this. I think she sensed something, because she called again and again. I decided to just turn my phone off.

Now, here is the cool thing about this.

"Does she know where you live?" Tang asked.

"No. I just got this place. She has no idea where it is."

"So she's not going to make a surprise visit?"

"Nope. She couldn't find me."

We stopped at a bench and sat awhile. It was near midnight. The moon was half full and it lit up the sky, not as much as a full moon, but enough so that I could see how pretty Tang was. I loved the way she looked at me. It was as though she had been searching for something for so long and, at last, had found it. I don't know what it was about me that connected with her, but something most definitely did.

She smiled, and then she did something that I'll never forget. She caused me at last to come out from under the spell of Sassafras: she put her head on my shoulder. It is these tender moments that can mean more to a man than endless hours of raw sex. You have no idea of the chills that went up and down my backbone, down to my pelvic bone, my femur bone, splitting up in my fibula and tibia, going down to my metacarpals in the ankles, down the metatarsals to my little toe bones, down to my big toe, my little toe, and all toes in between, flowing out into my shoes and down to the sidewalk and the tree roots that grew below the sidewalk. The tree shimmered, perhaps due to the wind only, but as far as I knew, it was just connected to my own shimmering.

It was completely nonsexual. She was not saying "do me." She was saying "I'll love you." And I could tell she was saying it in a way that was like this: "I will never cheat on you, I will always love you, I will never leave you." I got all that from the simple act of Tang's head being on my shoulder. It was done in such a cuddly way, and I just took it in.

I held her hand. I wanted to be very clear to her that I was open to her. I did not want her making a move on me, which I somehow would not reciprocate. I don't want to make any kind of unmentioned incorrect intent. I don't want to cause any confusion, I don't want to make a mistake. I want to let her know right here and right now, you want me? I want you!

When I held her hand, she took her head off my shoulder and looked at our hands together. At first I thought wow, I wonder if she didn't like that idea. But then, she looked back at me and smiled. She held my hand tight, like she was never letting go. I found myself oddly attracted to her strength. There was a definite maleness in her. I can't really explain it other than to say, you should see this girl's arms. She's strong, gazelle-like, to be in a post-Olympics phase for all I knew, and had a grip that wouldn't let go.

She was very careful to keep her legs completely together. I could tell she was a proper girl and would not want to get overly sexual with me. This was not even a date, so we couldn't go too far. I felt as though we'd gone all the way around the universe and right then and there had fallen in love—before our first date.

We sat silently and enjoyed each other. No kissing, no heavy duty touching, just holding hands with a male-on-male grip that would never let go. She adjusted her legs a few times. I could tell something was going on in her pelvic region. It was uncomfortable but comfortable. It was restraint but it was flowing. She was adjusting her hips, moving herself, crossing her legs, bending forward a bit. It was a self-pleasuring maneuver that I don't think she consciously knew she was doing.

I smiled. Then it seemed she caught herself. She was a bit embarrassed and stood up.

"We should go."

I laughed silently. She was going too far for her own comfort. Though I was one horny man, it was not sex that I was searching for. I was searching for an utter and complete replacement to my wife, and I had found it in Tang. I walked her home. I looked at her face carefully. The happiest hundred and eighty seven yards I have walked in my life was the distance from her house to my little studio apartment down the road.

Chapter 65
YOU CAME JUST IN TIME

Back in my studio apartment, no longer pathetic, I sat at my plastic fold-out table, moved the jury instructions and the five-in-one civil code to the side, took out my legal pad, and wrote the following poem: *You Came Just in Time,* by Herman Franck.

Perfect time can be many things
When the fall removes the leaves
When the moon takes out the tide
When you found me just in time.

In the wet lit street reflections of rain
And out of the home.
Thinking of life, living alone.

Naturally I fight
I was not meant to be just one.
Not where I'm going,
Not where I'm from.

Under a spell
Living in hell
Struck by a witch
Such a bitch.

Walking small steps
Not looking up
Eyes to the ground
Ears turning in
Not taking it in
Not seeing two
Then understanding
There is an after,
Now I'm after you.

Chapter 66
HONEY, I'M NOT HOME

Meanwhile, back at the ranch, I checked my voicemail. Uh oh. Seventeen calls from Sassafras. She's probably out driving around, wondering where on earth I am and what I'm doing. Oddly, the messages went from initially friendly to "Where are you?" to "Where the fuck are you?" to "Call me," to "Call me now, you motherfucker," to a hysterical "What are you doing? Where are you? Come back to me now! You promised me you would come back. You said you would. How come you're not doing what you said you would? What's going on?"

Uh oh. Sassafras went telepathic, and totally sensed that something had interfered with the radio waves between her and me. There was a distortion. Her spell had been squelched, and there would be hell to pay for that.

I called her at approximately 1:30 a.m.

"Hello?"

"Sassafras, it's me."

"Where are you?"

"I'm at my apartment."

"Which is where?"

"It's in Sacramento."

"But where in Sacramento?"

"Why, you want to come and see me?"

"No, but I have no idea where you are."

"Well, I don't think you need to know where I am."

"Tell me where you are."

"Okay, I'm just going to make up an address: 1000 N Street."

"Oh, I think that's the Capitol Building. I don't think you are in there."

"Whatever. I'm not letting you know right now, though. I'm going to have this place to myself."

"I thought you were going to come by."

"Yeah, I decided against that."

"How come?"

"Because I think it's better if I just stay away from you. You're bad news."

"I'm not bad news. I'm trying to come around to you."

"You know the problem, though, you're so hooked on this guy, and I just can't do anything about it."

"I will let him go."

"I think the best you could agree with right now is you will *try* to let him go. But it's a little bit like an addiction. It's almost like you're a drug addict. I just don't think you can do it. You need him, he needs you; you want him, he wants you. I just don't see you ever giving him up. I really don't. And I just don't want to go through this anymore, so I need to just kind of stay away."

"Where are you? I'm coming over right now."

"No, no, no. You just let me stay. I want you to know that I am completely, one hundred percent of a view that you can't do it. And as long as that's going on, I'm just going to stay away. You have to accept that. I've got to go."

I hung up the phone. Five minutes later she called back. She was crying.

"You can't do this to me. You have to come back. We have a family together, we have a house together, we have our whole lives together. We've been together for so long, we cannot end this right now, not over this man. It's not right."

I listened to her sob and cry and I thought to myself, "What a psycho, crazy-ass bitch."

"Look, you've got to understand something: I don't want to do this anymore. You're just going to put me through this on a daily basis. Those emails I saw, they have completely, one hundred percent convinced me that you are lost in love."

"You can't believe those emails. You know, people just write things in emails that they don't really mean."

"I wouldn't know, Sassafras. I've never received any kind of email from you like that, so you're talking to a guy that doesn't know anything about anything as far as that goes. I look at things at face value. You want me to read between the lines? What does 'I love you, I love you, I love you' mean? If I read between the lines I'm supposed to somehow say, what that really means is 'I don't love you, but I'm just saying that because it's fun to write'? Is that what you want me to believe?"

"Yes, that's exactly what it is! You've got to believe me, I'm just saying that! Look, we're not together, this isn't a real thing. This is like a fantasy man to me. Don't you understand that?"

"Your fantasy has become a big reality. No, Sassafras. It ends here. I'm not doing this anymore."

I realized, of course, she would just call me right back, so I did the only appropriate thing and turned my phone off. I then retired onto my son's hot air balloon printed bed, my pillowcase-less pillow, and looked out a tiny window to a half moon that lit up the sidewalk leading down the street a hundred and eighty seven yards, to the house where Tang slept.

Chapter 67
MY VERY BAD, SUPER AWFUL DREAM

We all have dreams, some good, some bad, and some that are very bad and super awful.

I normally wouldn't set out a dream of mine for public review, but in this case, I will make an exception. Mainly I wish to show people the impact that these affair situations can have on a person and a family. The impacts can be quite large. While the folks having the affair can laugh over martini lunches and suave dinners, the others are suffering in ways that they would never imagine.

To assist that imagination, and to provide a clue as to the many ways of the twisting and turmoil caused by these situations, I will share my very bad super awful dream.

I should first point out that we don't control our dreams. Our dream state is a rather unique example of a part of our brain at work when we are absolutely not in control. In a way, we are all super creative geniuses when we are asleep. We return to regular human status when we wake up.

Imagine how the world would be if we thought during the day the same way we think at night.

A case I handled on behalf of a state worker subject to a workplace violence restraining order taught me a bit about this fact of life. This state worker had a dream that he came to work with an AK-47 and starting shooting people. For some reason, he decided to report this bad dream to his supervisor, and of course, all hell broke out for him.

During the ensuing workplace violence restraining order trial, the State brought an expert psychiatrist witness having an M.D. and Ph.D. This man was a super brain during the day and night.

Anyhow I asked this super brain M.D.-Ph.D. a simple question, which went to the issue of whether my client had engaged in any voluntary and intentional violent act by having a super violent dream.

I asked: "Do we have control over what we dream about?"

The M.D.-Ph.D. answered, "No."

Of course we don't. There is a chemical released into our dream state, quite literally, called DMT, that is a super hallucinogen. This DMT, for some reason, appears naturally and organically in our bodies, and is released when asleep. It brings about many odd and amazing stories that appear as motion pictures during our sleep.

Lest the reader think I am making this up I provide the following from http://en.wikipedia.org/wiki/Dimethyltryptamine:

> **Dimethyltryptamine (DMT)** is a naturally-occurring tryptamine and potent psychedelic drug, found not only in many plants, but also in trace amounts in the human body where its natural function is undetermined. Structurally, it is analogous to the neurotransmitter serotonin (5-HT) and other psychedelic tryptamines such as 5-MeO-DMT, bufotenin (5-OH-DMT), and psilocin (4-OH-DMT). DMT is created in small amounts by the human body during normal metabolism[1] by the enzyme tryptamine-N-methyltransferase. Many cultures, indigenous and modern, ingest DMT as a psychedelic in extracted or synthesized forms.[2] Pure DMT at room temperature is a clear or white to yellowish-red crystalline solid. A laboratory synthesis of DMT was first reported in 1931, and it was later found in many plants.[3]

* * *

Several speculative and yet untested hypotheses suggest that endogenous DMT, produced in the human brain, is involved in certain psychological and neurological states. DMT is naturally produced in small amounts in the brain and other tissues of humans and other mammals.[18] Some believe it plays a role in mediating the visual effects of natural dreaming, and also near-death experiences, religious visions and other mystical states.[19] A biochemical mechanism for this was proposed by the medical researcher J. C. Callaway, who suggested in 1988 that DMT might be connected with visual dream phenomena, where brain DMT levels are periodically elevated to induce visual dreaming and possibly other natural states of mind.[20] A new hypothesis proposed is that in addition to being involved in altered states of consciousness, endogenous DMT may be involved in the creation of normal waking states of consciousness. It is proposed that DMT and other endogenous hallucinogens mediate their neurological abilities by acting as neurotransmitters at a sub class of the trace amine receptors; a group of receptors found in the CNS where DMT and other hallucinogens have been shown to have activity. Wallach further proposes that in this way waking consciousness can be thought of as a controlled psychedelic experience. It is when the control of these systems becomes loosened and their behavior no longer correlates with the external world that the altered states arise.

[citations omitted]

Note two of the series of articles cited in the above passage:

Callaway J (1988). "A proposed mechanism for the visions of dream sleep". *Med Hypotheses* **26** (2): 119–24. doi:10.1016/0306-9877(88)90064-3. PMID 3412201.Wallach J (2008). "Endogenous hallucinogens as ligands of the trace amine receptors: A possible role in sensory perception". *Med Hypotheses* **in print** doi:10.1016/j.mehy.2008.07.052. PMID 18805646.

One of the wild cards of what we dream about is the fact that during our dream states we have something akin to an 8 hour LSD trip given to us by our own bodies. So whenever you are wondering why you had such a bizarre dream, now you know.

Which brings me to my very bad super awful dream.

I was on a trip in a hotel room. For some reason, the hotel was pink. The room was quite nice, with a large bed, a mirror behind the bed. The bed was sitting at an angle to a corner, forming a kind of diamond. The room had a large space between the bed and a nice balcony. The balcony overlooked a pool area. There were palm trees outside, all in a nice row. The rest of the room was typical hotel style, a desk with a chair, and another sitting area by the wall. The room did not have wallpaper, and instead had a mauve pinkish paint.

I was there alone, at the desk. I had a laptop computer open, and was doing some work. I was wearing a white dress shirt with thin royal blue sweat pants on. I was not wearing shoes or socks.

It was daytime, still light out. It was hot, summer time, so the window to the balcony was closed. I like super cold air conditioning, which brought the temperature to the room to about 66 degrees.

There was a hard knock at the door. I didn't sense any danger, so I got up from the desk area and opened the door. By the time I realized the danger, it was too late. Brad Clawney was in my room in the fit of a steroid rage.

Oh my goodness, the first thing I couldn't help but notice was how large he was. This guy is about 6 foot four inches, extremely muscular, and ten times as tough as me. I'm basically a geek guy that hadn't been in a fight in about a hundred years, so I'm easy to take down.

And boy, did he take me down. He immediately grabbed me by the neck and started to choke me. This made it impossible for me to scream. I was far from the hotel phone, and my cell phone was over by the laptop. So I couldn't call 911 or anyone else.

He didn't want to kill me. He held both hands to my neck, and cutoff the blood to my head. He had some kind of battle field training, this much was clear. It was so quick and easy, the next thing I know I lost full consciousness.

In my unconscious dream state, I watched my unconscious self get raped by this man. It was awful to watch, but here is how it went.

First he threw me on the bed so hard I bounced up and off the bed, on to the floor. He picked me off the floor and threw me again onto the bed, stomach down, butt up. He placed a pillow under my stomach to prop my butt up a bit. He used both hands to pull down my pants and white boxer shorts in one swoop.

He pulled off his pants, and brought out his dick. It was not hard. As would be seen, getting this steroid-raged-permanently-soft dick hard would be a major ordeal for him. He brought out some hand cream. He actually had a small bottle in his pants, so this was all premeditated. He proceeded to jack himself off, but the dick just wouldn't get hard.

He looked at the mirror on the wall, and smiled at his body. The ultimate in self fantasy, this man used his own pornographic image to get excited.

He finally got his cock about half up, and proceeded to plunge it in to me. He had to use both hands, crouching down a bit behind me, moving me, adjusting my position, and finding the perfect angle to dive in.

Now, for those of you who have ever tried to stick a soft dick into something, you should know right away that it is no easy feat. Especially when the item it's being stuck into is not, shall we say, made for this kind of thing. He really worked it up, placing the contents of the cream bottle on my ass, rubbing his dick in it, getting it all lubricated, and trying over and over again to get it in.

It wouldn't go in, which increased his steroid rage. He banged on my back, yelling, "You piece of shit, I am going to fuck you!"

He said this several times.

In my dream I regained consciousness, to find this huge man with a soft dick roaming around my asshole. My head went up. I twisted to get away, but he wouldn't have it. He smacked me in the back of the head, karate chop style, which again broke me out of consciousness. He turned back to the mirror and looked at himself again. He was triumphant, flexed his chest, which at last made him harder.

This time he was able to get his slightly-more-than-half-hard dick in a little way inside me. It made him smile. He rocked back and forth, knowing that he had succeeded in his mission. It didn't matter that he couldn't cum, that wasn't the point. The point was to rape me, and he had done just that.

He looked at himself in the mirror as he did this. The only thing that could really keep him even close to hard was his own image. How odd.

Just then the whole picture of this terrible sight vanished to an actual awakening. Sassafras had heard my heavy breathing. She woke me up with several pushes to my back, telling me, "Wake up, wake up."

I awoke. Wow.

I was actually at home, in my bedroom, with Sassafras. The kids were down the hall safe and sound.

She turned on the light and asked me, "What was that about?"

I explained it all to her, the entire dream. I was able to explain it much more vividly than here, as I had just experienced it.

She listened carefully and then hugged me. She started to understand that this affair of hers had caused some serious emotional damage to me. She held me like a police woman would hold a rape victim, and rubbed my back.

"There there, everything is okay, he is gone, he is not coming back, this will never happen."

Somehow, right then and there, I just didn't believe it.

Chapter 68
PRACTICING LAW DURING TIMES OF EMOTIONAL TURMOIL

The strange thing about all this is in the depths of all this emotional turmoil, I had a full load of law cases to deal with. There's nothing quite as challenging as to have a feeling that your entire life is about to evaporate. You're about to lose everything you have: your wife, your house, your children, every piece of furniture, every stitch of clothing, and at the same time, you need to show up at court at 8:30 a.m. and convince a jury in a powerful speech that your client is right and should be awarded damages.

The odd thing about me is that I can totally pull this off. There is something about the courthouse and me that connect. Put me into a grave, put the dirt over me, pack it down as tight as you will, put a tombstone on top reading, "Here lies an unloved man." Put me in a suit and tie and give me a briefcase, walk me or carry me to the nearest courthouse, and this zombie man will rise and make a speech that will bring tears to the jury's eyes, and will cause them to connect with my client in a way that they never dreamed of. I can do it dead or alive.

I have this associative psychopathology, it can be thought of as negative, but is the perfect ailment for a busy attorney, known as adult attention deficit disorder. It gives me the power to be engaged in a jury trial, and during a ten minute break call back to the office to get everybody as busy as little bees on their other projects.

This morning, I was not buried below packed earth. I rose up like a hot air balloon from my son's bed. I turned the one appliance on that I took from the house, the coffeemaker. I turned my phone on. It beeped. I figured it was a series of nasty ass messages from Sassafras. Instead, it was a text message from Tang. Ooh, I thought. It read:

"Good morning. Do you know what happened to us last night? Love, Tang."

Oh yes, I thought. Oh yes, do I ever know what happened to us last night. That was my exact text back. We weren't going to say a thing, but we were going to say everything. I didn't know if she was already at work, busy signing and recording new mechanics liens, or if she was luxuriating around her apartment or what. I expected to get a quick reply, but did not. That was okay. I had lots to do.

I then saw the text message from Sassafras: *"Call me."*

And then another: *"Call me now."*

And then another: *"CALL ME NOW!!!!"*

Okay. I guess the best thing to do before a jury trial is to get leveled at the knees by your wife, to have her emotionally beat the crap out of you, tear your heart out, tear out your stomach out, your liver, your spleen, put it out on the sidewalk, stomp on it, cut it up, put it in a box, and then bury it back in your gut and say, 'There, now go win your case.' Maybe I shouldn't call her. But I thought, all right, I'll call her. So I did.

"Good morning."

She was surprisingly docile. She had spent the night without me and realized that there was something serious afoot.

"You turned off your phone."

"I know. I had to sleep, hon. I've got a trial this morning. I've got to go. Please don't start yelling at me."

"I'm not going to yell at you."

"Okay, thank you."

"I'm not going to yell at you."

"Okay."

"Can we have lunch today?"

"If you don't mind, can you come down to the courthouse? We can have lunch down there."

"Okay."

"Listen, I've got to go now."

"Okay, call me at lunchtime."

"It'll be around noon."

I hung up the phone and then saw, ooh, good news, a text message from Tang. I opened it right away. It had four magical words: *"Can we have lunch?"*

Well now. Me, being a man who has been deprived of all love and emotion for the last while, any and all types of emotional support, appreciation, and devolving into a bitter internal rage of deprivation, annihilation, and extreme emotional neediness, my response was rather simple: *"Oh, yes."*

I got a quick reply: *"When and where?"*

Hm. Good question.

"Can you come down to the courthouse? I'm in a trial this morning and I have a lunch break from 12 to 1:30. I'd like to stay close to the courthouse if possible."

She got right back to me.

"What courtroom are you in?"

"Number 23, Judge Riddle."

Great name for a judge. It matched his personality perfectly. And then it occurred to me, wait a minute, is this a disaster waiting to happen. Sassafras and Tang both finding themselves at the courthouse? Uh oh. What was I thinking? Let's rearrange this a little. I called Sassafras.

"Hey, listen, I'll meet you at the office for lunch. I'm going to have to come back to sign some stuff, so I'll see you down there, okay?"

"Oh, okay. Are you leaving soon?"

"Yes. I've got a bunch of stuff down there to do."

"Okay."

"I've got to run off to court. Bye-bye."

I then proceeded to the courthouse, without thinking even for a second about what exactly I would say in my opening statement.

Chapter 69
NIECE VERSUS UNCLE

The white-haired judge called the case of Gloria Levantes versus Ralph Hernandez. I stood.

"Herman Franck appearing on behalf of the plaintiff, Gloria Levantes, who is personally present." The buzz-cut defense counsel stood and made his appearance. "David Placer on behalf of the defendant, Ralph Hernandez, who is also personally present."

The judge asked a question that there was only one possible answer to: "Are both sides ready to proceed?"

I responded, "We are."

Defense responded, "We are."

"Very well. The first issue we need to take up is the admissibility of the other alleged wrongful conduct of the defendant. I think your trial brief indicates there are three others?"

"Yes, Your Honor. We are ready to show the court that the defendant victimized three other family members."

Defense counsel objected to my use of the word "victimized," but that's exactly what it was.

"Your Honor, none of these allegations have been proven, so the use of this term 'victim' is a bit premature."

I thought to myself, "I wish he wouldn't use the word 'premature' in a sex case."

"Your Honor, the witnesses are all here to explain what happened to them to the court."

The judge explained, "Under the case law, I need to first conduct a hearing outside the presence of the jury to listen to each of these alleged victims, and to determine if what happened to them is similar enough to what happened to the plaintiff that the other wrongful conduct may be admitted into evidence under Evidence Code Section 1101(b), to show planning, preparation, motive, intent, lack of mistake, and identity. Counsel, do both of you agree that I need to conduct such a hearing?"

Both of us agreed. This was the law.

"Yes, Your Honor."

"Yes, Your Honor."

"Mr. Franck, I would like you to begin by calling your first witness on this point."

"Very well, Your Honor. We call Maria Ruez as our first witness."

Maria came into the courtroom. This would be her opportunity to face down her uncle, the first time ever. As the court would hear, what he did to her was criminal in every way, and had a huge impact on the rest of her life. Today would begin the healing.

I stood before I called the witness.

"Your Honor, there is an issue about the defendant and his English ability. I believe his first language is Spanish, and I'm not so sure he can understand what is going on here. I also believe it is essential that he does understand what is going on here."

"That's a good point. Counsel, does your client speak English?"

"He speaks a little bit of English."

"Oh, I need him to speak a lot of English. We need to get a translator here. Has any arrangement been made for a translator?"

"No, Your Honor."

"Madam Clerk, can you call the Translation Department and get a translator up here right away?"

"Your Honor, if I may—"

I knew this problem, as I had been there many times in the past.

"The translation service only provides translators for criminal cases, and although this seems like a criminal case, it is actually a civil case for damages. Because of that, they are not going to provide you with a translator."

"What if I order them to?"

"Well, that would be interesting. I just don't think they're going to do it. It's just not their program."

The clerk nodded her head in agreement. She knew. Clerks pretty much know everything about the operations of the court.

"I see. Well, Counsel, what do you recommend?"

"I believe the defendant is accompanied today by other family members that could provide an unofficial translation for him."

"Yes, that is true."

Mr. Placer pointed out that the defendant's son was present.

"The defendant's son is here, and he'll provide an unofficial translation."

"I'm a little worried about that, gentlemen, because I don't want any kind of appeal issue to arise from this so-called unofficial translation. Let me stipulate that this so-called unofficial translation will be in all intents and purposes a real translation and that you will waive any irregularity or inaccuracy thereof."

"I'm not sure if I will."

"If you're not sure if you will, I'm going to stop these proceedings right now and order you to go get an official translator. I am not going to have this entire case subject to appeal just because his son did the translation versus a court qualified translator."

"Your Honor, if I may, I don't think we should be the brunt of a translation issue on the defense side."

"Counsel, the continuance would be maybe for a day. I think we can obtain a translator in a day, don't you think?"

"Yes, I'm sure we can."

The defense spoke up.

"Your Honor, we'll waive all appeal issues and proceed with the son."

The problem was the defendant would have to pay for this translator, and they are generally about a hundred dollars an hour. He would need this translator for the entire trial, which was slated to take approximately four to five days, so this would run into some pretty significant money for a twelve dollar an hour pipefitter. So he waived the appeal issue and we were now ready to proceed.

"Okay, Counsel, we may now proceed. Madam Clerk, please swear in the witness."

"Please raise your right hand."

Maria quickly raised her right hand, almost in a salute.

"Do you swear to tell the truth, the whole truth, and nothing but the truth?"

"Absolutely, one hundred percent yes."

"Very well. You may take your seat."

The court spoke.

"Miss—"

"Excuse me, Your Honor, it's 'Mrs.'"

"I'm sorry. Very well, Mrs. Ruez, would you please state your name again for the record."

"I am Maria Ruez."

"Very well. Counsel, you may proceed."

"Mrs. Ruez, this man to my right, sitting at the defense table next to the attorney, do you know him?"

"I am pathetically and permanently related to this piece of shit."

The judge was completely unfazed by this remark. I was not, and did not wish to hear anything like that again.

"Mrs. Ruez, I would like to remind you that you are in a court of law and there is a level of decorum here that prohibits you from using such language. Will you agree to cease the use of such language?"

"I will, and I apologize."

"Thank you, Mrs. Ruez. What relation is the man to you?"

"He is my uncle. I wish he were my deceased uncle."

"I understand. I can see quite obviously that you are angry and upset with him."

"Oh, you don't know even the half of it."

"Why are you so upset with him?"

She then proceeded to answer in Spanish, in a guttural way, low sounds. I don't know what it meant, but it sure sounded awful. The son stopped translating. Martin responded by looking away from her. He would not face her down in her own language. In all this excitement, I had not noticed that just after Mrs. Ruez took the stand, Tang had showed up and was sitting in the audience.

Defense counsel then pointed it out, just as I was starting my next question.

"Excuse me, Your Honor, I just want to make sure that the young lady who is here is not a witness in this case. If she is a witness, we would of course request that she remain outside the courthouse during this testimony."

"Oh, yes. Ma'am—"

I, of course, had no idea what they were talking about and I turned around. Who did I see but the lovely Tang. She smiled at me. I smiled at her. My client could see right away that there was something going on between us. She smiled. It brought a bit of happiness to this otherwise extremely dark Chapter at the courthouse.

I spoke up, "Your Honor, she's not a witness. She's a friend of mine."

"Oh, I see you like an audience, Mr. Franck."

"Yes, Your Honor. It's part of my insecurity complex that I like people to come and validate my talent. I hope it's okay."

Defense counsel laughed. He was in the same position, but today had no audience. Tang, of course, would be busy comparing the two attorneys. Hopefully she would find I was the better.

"Very well. Counsel, you may proceed."

"Mrs. Ruez, you need to speak in English. Will you please describe what your uncle did to you in English?"

I barely finished the question when she proceeded with a rat-a-tat-tat answer that, if a jury ever got to hear it, would annihilate this son of a bitch.

"Let me first start by telling you that what happened, happened to me when I was 14 years old. I was just a little girl. I didn't know nothin' about nothin'. I was at his house, we were having a picnic. He found me in the bathroom. I didn't know the bathroom door lock didn't work. He opened it and he came in. I was sitting on the toilet. This disgusting man, he came over to me and he put his hands right on my shoulder. He opened up his zipper and he took out his little, tiny, ugly, disgusting penis and he put it in my face and he said, 'Suck it.' I spit."

And she actually did spit, which is actually not too good. The judge wasn't about to admonish her. It added a bit of a dramatic virtual reality to the situation. I wasn't about to admonish her either, and gave her a hand motion to continue.

"He put that little dick in my mouth. It was so disgusting. I can still remember the taste of it today. This man made me suck his cock."

I let it stop right there. I gave what we refer to in the law as a "pregnant pause" to allow that testimony to just sink in. I then went to the point of this hearing, to show the similarity of what happened to her and what happened to my client.

"You're a family member?"

"Yes."

"You were a minor at the time?"

"Yes."

"You were at a family gathering?"

"Yes."

"He's a relative?"

"Yes."

"You were in the bathroom?"

"Yes."

"And after this event, did he ejaculate?"

She looked at me with an extremely puzzled look.

"What?"

Oh, I thought to myself. That's an English word she doesn't know.

"Did he cum?"

"Oh no, he don't cum."

This is the thing about sex cases. They're not about sex, they're about power, humiliation, degradation, subjugation, and revenge against what someone else did to you, revenge taken out on a totally innocent other person. Whatever had happened to this man, it had obviously messed him up to the point where he would do these terrible things to three other women. And in each case, they happened in family gatherings in either a bathroom or a bedroom to a young girl, a family member, and in the aftermath, as Mrs. Ruez would explain, "He told me I'm a fat ugly girl that no man is ever going to want to touch, that he's the only man that'll ever touch me, and that I should thank him for that."

She spit across the courtroom area at him as she spoke. It wasn't spitting as in spitting, it was just that her mouth had watered up in her anger at this man. He again looked to the right. He refused to face her.

"Your Honor, that's all the questions I have right now."

"Okay, defense, you may proceed with cross-examination."

Mr. Placer remained seated as he asked several simple questions:

"Did you report this incident to the police?"

"I don't know nothin' about any police."

"So I'll take that as a no?"

"I did not call the police."

"Did you file any kind of civil lawsuit about this?"

"I didn't know you could sue somebody for that. If I had known, I would have certainly sued him."

"So I take that as a no?"

"No, I did not sue him."

"Did you file a restraining order against him?"

"No."

"I have no further questions."

"Counsel, any redirect?"

"Yes, Your Honor, just one question. So you don't have any money, compensation, or other claim here today, do you?"

"I do not."

"You stand to gain what from giving testimony here?"

"I want this man to face justice. That's why I'm here."

"Thank you, Your Honor. I have nothing further."

These Mexican families can typically be quite large. There were quite a few nieces as a result. I had two others present right then and there who gave stories tragically similar to Mrs. Ruez's story. One of them was in the bedroom changing into a swimsuit when he came in and invaded her innocence. The other was in the bathroom in a way quite similar to Mrs. Ruez. In each case, there was a sexual assault, a forced oral copulation, the absence of an orgasm, and an aftermath of insults. In each case, there was no police report filed, no civil lawsuit filed, no restraining order. Only my client had the guts to come forward with a lawsuit. Unfortunately, by the time she found herself strong enough to sue, so many years had passed that the district attorney's office declined to prosecute. She was left with but one form of justice: a claim for civil damages for sexual assault and battery.

I turned back to see if Tang was still there, and boy was she ever. This case was obviously a far cry from her typical claim for monies due and owing to a general contractor, and enforcement of a mechanics lien. After my last witness, the court asked me, "Any further witnesses?"

"No, Your Honor. We have the three other alleged victims and my client. Our request is that the three victims be permitted to testify to what happened to them based on the remarkable similarity between the incidents."

The court turned to the defense counsel.

"Your response?"

"Your Honor, the incidents are all fabrications, completely untrue, and are made up by a family faction that is completely against one side of the family. It's all a bunch of lies."

"Well, Counsel, I'll tell you this. If it's all a bunch of lies, they are dramatically similar lies. It is the court's decision that these incidents are similar enough to constitute admissible evidence of other wrongful conduct, under Evidence Code Section 1101(b), to show planning, preparation, motive, intent, lack of mistake, and identity. Accordingly, the court will grant the plaintiff's motion to admit these incidents into the trial.

"Okay, gentlemen. Now that we have that resolved, I believe we can proceed with bringing in the jury. They are all waiting outside in the hallway. Madam Clerk, will you please call in the jury panel?"

There were about sixty prospective jurors sitting in the hallway wondering why the matter was not proceeding straight ahead. The next step is called voir dire, which allows the attorneys to ask questions to the jurors to make determinations if any of them have attitudes or biases that won't benefit their client. Such as a bias against child molesters, imagine that.

Defense counsel had a little surprise for me, though. He stood.

"Your Honor, I request a brief recess to discuss settlement with plaintiff's counsel. May we have fifteen minutes?"

The court smiled. This was not unexpected. D-Day had come. Judgment was pending. The other victims would be a disaster for the defendant. It is one thing to call one young girl a liar; it is quite another to call three other girls liars. Say all you want about the absence of police reports, the absence of criminal cases, the absence of civil lawsuits, but the testimony with spitting anger is all so raw, the jury will believe it. And they're going to believe if three women had this problem, my client also had this problem, and they're going to award big damages. This asshole finally figured all that out.

"Counsel, you wish to allow an opportunity to settle the case?"

"Your Honor, we've been down this road before with the defendant. So far he has refused to acknowledge what he did, he has refused to offer any kind of confession, apology, or regret. These are the main things my client wants. If he is not prepared to do these things, I would prefer that we just go forward right now and call in the jury."

"Your Honor, if I may, I would like to suggest to plaintiff's counsel that the fifteen minutes I am proposing will absolutely not be a waste of time."

I looked over to my client. She nodded. I looked back at Tang, as if she should be giving me advice about this. She did give me advice, though, and the advice was take the fifteen minute break. Don't put the girl through the trial if you can avoid it. Let a settlement happen.

"Okay, Your Honor. I tell you what, I'll take the fifteen minutes. You never know, something good could happen. I would like to spare my client the trauma of testifying about what happened to her."

She unexpectedly spoke up: "I do not have any problem with telling the jury what happened to me."

However meek she once was, she had grown into a much stronger woman, and like her cousin, was ready for justice.

Interestingly, the room that we were allowed to use for purposes of a settlement discussion was the jury deliberation room. There were twelve chairs. We would only need four: one for me, one for my client, one for the defendant, and one for his attorney. We sat at opposite sides of a rather long table.

Before I even sat down, I announced,

"You know the terms of our offer. We have said it many times before. We need a written public confession, apology, and regret, number one. That is not negotiable. Are you prepared to do that?"

The defendant, in the same way as he did in the courtroom, looked to the side out the window. I got up to walk over to interrupt his view. I got into his face and asked him,

"Hey, I'm talking to you right now. I've got sixty prospective jurors ready to hear you and sit in judgment. My question to you—and look at me when I talk to you—is are you ready to confess right now, in writing and publicly?"

He looked over to his attorney. The attorney realized that if he would do this, the entire case would go away.

"I am."

"You're willing to say you did what my client says you did?"

"I am."

"You'll say it on the record in open court? And you will agree to the issuance of a judgment in the amount of two hundred and fifty thousand dollars?"

"I will."

"And you understand that this judgment will be for an intentional injury to her person, and as such, this judgment will not be dischargeable in bankruptcy?"

"I understand that."

"You're willing to do all those things?"

"I am."

"Counsel?"

"If he's willing to do it, I'm willing to go along with it."

"Gloria?"

"These are the things I want. If he will do those things, we have a deal."

"Okay, I'm going to ask you one more time before we leave this room: are you ready to do all those things?"

"I am."

We left the jury deliberation room and walked back to the courtroom. Now, here's where things got a little dicey. I had told Sassafras I was going to come down to the office for lunch. For reasons that will always escape me, and perhaps another Chapter in the operations of Murphy's Law, she decided to come down to the courthouse and watch me in action.

When I walked back to the courtroom, there was the rather amazing sight of Sassafras in the courtroom audience, sitting just a couple rows away from Tang. She had no idea who Tang was, Tang had no idea who she was, so the two of them sat there in a very civilized manner. When I walked in, both of them stood up, and for the first time understood that they were both there to see me. Uh oh.

I didn't quite know what to do. I felt like just turning around and running away, but of course that wouldn't work. I needed to put this settlement on the record. I walked over to Sassafras first.

"I didn't know you were coming down here."

"Who's this girl?"

"That's Tang."

"Who is she?"

"She's Tang. What do you want to know about her?"

"How come she's here?"

"She's here to watch the trial."

"Who invited her?"

"I did."

"How come you invited her?"

"I wanted her to see me in action."

"Why did you want her to see you in action?"

"Because I feel very much at home in the courthouse. It's a place where I belong and can shine, and it was my idea that if she saw me here, she would probably be impressed."

Tang knew the discussion. I thought she might escape away, but she didn't. She held her ground. She knew of the problems Sassafras had caused me, and knew that there was a huge opportunity for her to snatch me away from this evil, cheating woman of betrayal. So she wasn't going anywhere.

Before the drama could get too heated, the clerk asked me: "Counsel, do you have a settlement?"

I had to delay the further confrontation between Tang and Sassafras to answer this official question.

"We do."

The defense counsel and the defendant were looking over at this drama with great interest. I asked that the settlement be immediately put on the record. The clerk got a court reporter out. The judge came to the bench.

"I call the case of Ruez versus Hernandez."

"My clerk informs me that we have a settlement."

"Your Honor, amazingly it appears that we do."

"Mr. Franck, will you state the terms of the settlement?"

"Your Honor, we've reached a very simple agreement as follows. Number one, defendant Ralph Hernandez will right here and now, in open court, confess on the record that he committed a series of sexual assaults on my client, as alleged in her complaint, and including forced oral copulation, forced genital touching, molestation of a child under 14, and committed the civil tort of sexual assault and battery. Further—"

The court interrupted me.

"Wait a minute. Before we go any further, the first thing I want to do is ask defense counsel, is your client prepared to do this confession?"

"Yes, Your Honor."

"Well, before we do that, I feel duty bound to advise him of his Miranda Rights. Mr. Martinez, you have not been charged with a crime. I understand the DA has issued a letter explaining why they are not coming after you. It has to do with the running of statute of limitations. However, that could be subject to change, and because of the possibility of a future prosecution, I feel duty bound to advise you that you have a right to remain silent, that anything you say can and will be used against you in a court of law, that you have a right to an attorney. I understand that you have an attorney, but if you cannot afford an attorney, an attorney will be provided to you by the State. Do you understand these rights?"

"I do."

"Just a second. I want his son to translate these rights. Did you understand what I just said?"

Indeed, there were times when they were given to him on the street by a man in blue.

"Now, with those rights in mind, are you prepared to waive those rights and to give in open court, as counsel has stated, a full confession of what you did?"

"I am."

"Counsel, do you join in this settlement?"

"I do."

"Before we get this confession on the record, Mr. Franck, I would like you to set forth any remaining terms of this settlement."

"Your Honor, in addition to this confession in open court, he will also sign a written confession. I would like that to be prepared by counsel in the following form: we will have the court reporter prepare the transcript, and he will sign the transcript."

"Very well. Counsel, do you agree with that approach?"

"I do."

"Next issue?"

"There will be an apology given by the defendant, and he will do so right after his confession."

"Counsel, is that your understanding?"

"Yes."

"Is your client prepared to issue an apology?"

"Yes."

"I take it that an apology will help the plaintiff in her path of healing. Is that the concept behind this?"

"Very much, Your Honor. We need some healing here all around."

I turned back and looked at Sassafras and Tang. Sassafras understood that this was no game, that this time I meant it, she was done, and that she was in the process of being replaced. This whole comeuppance with Gloria ran parallel to my simultaneous comeuppance with Sassafras.

"What is the next term of the settlement?"

"The defendant does not have any money. He makes twelve dollars an hour as a pipefitter. He can't pay a settlement, but what he can and will do is stipulate to a judgment in the amount of two hundred and fifty thousand. It is agreed that the stipulation will be for the intentional tort of sexual assault and battery, and that as this is an intentional tort to the person of Gloria, that such judgment will be dischargeable in bankruptcy."

"Counsel?"

"Yes, Your Honor."

"Is that the agreement?"

"That is the agreement."

"Very well. Mr. Franck, let me begin by asking your client, you've heard the terms of that proposed agreement?"

Gloria spoke softly.

"Yes, Your Honor."

"And do you agree to allow those terms as a complete settlement of your case here?"

"Yes."

"And counsel, I take it as a further condition that this action will be dismissed?"

"No, Your Honor, it won't be dismissed. Instead, there will be a judgment and then it will be over."

"I see. No dismissal. Very well. And Miss Levantes, do you then agree to all those terms of the agreement as described by your attorney?"

"I do."

"Very well. I will now turn to Mr. Hernandez. Mr. Hernandez, you've heard Mr. Franck explain the terms of this settlement?"

"I have."

"And with all those terms in mind, do you agree to them?"

"I do."

"Let me then make a finding of a voluntary settlement. I will make order that this settlement is enforceable under the summary settlement enforcement procedures of CCP Section 664.6, which allows me to issue a judgment in the event that these settlement terms are not performed by both parties. Is everybody okay with that?"

"Yes, Your Honor."

Defense counsel responded, "Yes, Your Honor."

"Mr. Hernandez, I would like to now have you perform the first two and part of the settlement and give your confession.

There was a total deafening silence. Then the man spoke of things he did not wish to speak about.

He said sheepishly, "I did the things she said I did."

I did not like that confession at all. The confession should be freely given, should be much more detailed.

"Your Honor, I would like to request the right to question the defendant to bring out a full confession."

"Counsel?"

"Proceed."

"Mr. Hernandez, did you force your penis into the mouth of my client?"

"I did."

"And did you do so on six different occasions?"

"I did."

"And did that occur at your home?"

"Yes."

"And when you did that to her, was she under the age of 14?"

"She was."

"Did you touch her breasts?"

"I did."

"Did you touch her butt?"

"I did."

"Did you massage her vagina?"

"I did."

"Did you do that on multiple occasions?"

"I did."

"And in each case, did my client not agree to allow you to do that conduct?"

"I don't understand the question."

"Yes, I'm sorry. It wasn't worded very well. In each of the instances you have just described, isn't it true that my client did not want you to do those things?"

"She did not want those things."

"And you did it anyway?"

"I did."

"You forced yourself, your hands, and your penis on her."

"I did."

I turned to look at my client. She nodded. It was enough. The healing had begun. I turned to the judge.

"Your Honor, we're satisfied with that confession. I have one more question for the defendant. The court reporter will prepare a written transcript of this. You will sign it without any amendment or change to it?"

"I will."

"Then my last question is, is there anything you would like to say to my client?"

His eyes had welled up with tears. This time he was looking right at her. He was shaking. He was red-faced. His son was stoic. The court was dead silent. You could hear a pin drop from the court next door. The Judge attempted to help him.

"Please, Mr. Hernandez, take your time."

He was breathing hard. He fell down, smashing his arm and side against the table, landing on the ground. It was as though he had fainted, but there was no faint; he was still completely alert. The court bailiff rushed over.

"Are you all right?"

He picked himself up. The Judge was concerned about this.

"Mr. Hernandez, are you okay?"

"I'm fine. I'm fine."

"I think we should take a recess to let him regain his composure."

"No, Your Honor. Let me do this right now. I'm ready to do it."

He did regain his composure. He stood, he turned to Gloria, and he finally said the words that she'd been waiting for for over six years: "I am so very sorry for what I did to you. I beg that you find it in your heart to forgive me."

Gloria had tears streaming down her cheeks. She was forcing back a smile. This is what she needed to hear from her uncle. But she was also a very selfless woman. She looked at the audience and noticed her cousins Maria, Debra, and Patricia. She motioned with her hand and asked them to stand. Tang and Sassafras had to put aside their issues to watch this healing process. The three of them stood. Gloria turned back to Ralph Hernandez and told him, "And what about them? Do you also apologize to them?"

Defense counsel could have objected to this. It was not part of the deal. It was something of an add-on. But before the word "objection" could come out, Ralph turned to his nieces and told them, "Maria, Debra, Patricia, I'm so very sorry for what I did to you. Please find it in your hearts to forgive me."

At this point, it was four minutes before noon. The judge noted the time.

"Counsel, I believe you've got your confession and your apology and then some."

"Yes, Your Honor, we are satisfied with that."

"Then the next step is to prepare a judgment. I'll request client's counsel to prepare a form of judgment, submit it to defense counsel for approval as to form, we will then sign and file that. The court reporter is ordered to prepare a copy of the transcript and pursuant to the settlement agreement, that will be given to defense counsel who will then have his client sign it. With that in mind, I believe we are adjourned."

The judge hit the gavel. And then something happened that had not occurred in six years: Gloria walked over to her father and for the first time found a way to trust the touch of a grown man again, and hugged him. She said the words he had been waiting a hundred million years to hear: "I love you, Papa. I love you, Papa."

He cried, she cried. Hell, even I cried. I looked over and I saw two other women crying, Sassafras and Tang.

Chapter 70
SASSAFRAS VERSUS TANG

The court is pretty methodical about closing its doors at noon. This is due to the labor union contract with the courtroom staff, including the deputy sheriffs who act as bailiffs, and the clerk staff. They *have* to go to lunch at noon. It's the law.

We were ushered out of the courtroom by the polite bailiff. In the courtroom hallway, there were a series of furtive glances by my client Gloria to me, Tang, and Sassafras. You would probably have to be a bit numb not to know what was going on, in the same way Sassafras had picked up on the whole situation and went into battle mode. She took my arm, looked at me in the eyes, gave me a big kiss, and turned to Tang and said, rather impolitely, "Who's this bitch?"

I rolled my eyes. I waved at Tang, my own way of saying, "Please just walk away. I will get back to you later."

Tang could've been easy about this and just walked away, knowing full well I indeed would call her later. But of course, women are anything but simple and easy. She instead did something rather interesting that hardly helped the ever-escalating situation: she took the palm of her hand and gently caressed her cheek. She then caressed her neck, her shoulders, and her arms. She was massaging herself in a provocative manner. Without saying a word, she telegraphed to Sassafras the incident in which I massaged her neck, arm, and face.

Sassafras looked to me. I had a 'I am completely guilty' look on my face. Sassafras had a stern, warlike face—a survival look. She took my arm and walked me over to the elevator. Tang did not follow, but instead put her thumb and pinky finger out to make the symbol of a telephone, and placed that near her ear. She mouthed the words, "Call me." Of course, Sassafras saw this. I answered "yes" with my eyes and nothing with my mouth.

We entered the elevator. Thankfully it was packed with people, including several sheriff deputies. I could be safe here, but the ride would only take perhaps a minute. Once outside the courthouse, I expected a blistering exchange. It didn't happen. Instead, Sassafras invited me on a walk: "Can we go on a walk?"

I thought that was an absolutely wonderful idea.

"Certainly."

We proceeded to walk down to the area near the state Capitol. This was a beautiful building, white, statuesque, quite similar to the Congress building in Washington, D.C., including a fancy white dome top. It has a beautiful garden with lengthy sidewalks throughout. The perfect place to walk around and consider such matters as what to do about Sassafras. She proceeded in a salesperson mode.

"What's her name?"

"Tang."

"She looks like she's about 45."

"She's 42."

"She *told* you she's 42."

"Well, I didn't study her teeth, so I don't know for sure."

"I'm sure she's at least 45."

"Okay, so she's an older woman. I'm 50, she's 45, she's 42. That's about what I would call age appropriate."

"She's so white. You don't like white girls, you like dark skinned girls like me."

"I did not exactly seek her out. She found me."

"How did that bitch find you?"

"You want the whole play by play, or can I just conclude 'she found me'?"

"Whatever. Where does that bitch live?"

"On the moon."

"On the moon?"

"Yeah, I don't know where she lives. Look, I just met her. I don't know that much about her."

"You just met her and she's down here at court watching you?"

"She's just getting to know me. She wanted to see me in action."

"Action?"

"Yeah."

Chapter 71
I WILL MAKE YOUR PRETTY FACE UGLY

"And she's so stupid, she doesn't even know English."

"I can communicate with her."

"She's been here how many years and she doesn't know English? It's just ridiculous. How much better is my English than hers and I've only been here ten years? Okay, I'm so much smarter than her, I'm much more ambitious, look at all my successes; what has she done? She's working at a construction office? That's just pathetic."

"Okay."

"And look how she dresses. She looks like an old woman, she dresses like an old woman; she is an old woman! Obviously I'm a lot prettier and sexier, I have a much nicer figure. I'm hot and she's not."

I studied Sassafras as she made these statements. I shook my head.

"You know, Sassafras, all that is true. But none of it matters if I don't have you. You could be the most perfect woman in the world. You could have everything a man would ever desire: the looks, the personality, the smell, the sound of your voice, the touch of your hair, the smoothness of your skin, the erotic nature, how you look naked, the chemistry is perfect, your feet and toes can be perfectly smooth and alluring. None of that matters, however perfect it is, if I don't have you. And that's the difference. I've got Tang. I don't have you."

"But you do have me. I'm still with you, we're still married."

"We're still married, but you're in love with another man. You're seeing another man, and you're hopelessly lost with him. You'll never give him up, and that's what it is."

"I am not going to do that anymore. Period. So what's your plan?"

"My plan is to get a divorce and to start the next phase of my life."

"Are you going to marry Tang?"

"You know, I've only known Tang for less than a week, so don't think we're way down the road here, getting married or something. It's a new thing for me. It's not about Tang. It's about you, your lover, and my unwillingness to go along with that. That's what it's about."

"What if I give up my lover?"

"What if? What if this guy suddenly has two moons and three suns? Would it make a difference?"

"Oh yeah."

"But it's not going to happen, so I'm not going to be studying too much about your 'what ifs.' Pardon me for that."

"But seriously, I will drop him."

"The problem is you may wish to do that—"

"I do wish to do that. I don't want to break up the family. I want to keep us all in the house. I don't want to make all this go away. Listen, you've got to understand—"

"No, Sassafras, you need to understand. You may want to do that, but the problem is you can't. You are addicted to this lover very much like a drug addict is addicted to drugs, like an alcoholic is addicted to alcohol, like a gambler is addicted to gambling. You have an addiction to your lover, and you cannot give it up."

"But I can give it up. I gave it up before."

"Okay, how many times did you give it up before and then restart?"

She looked down at her feet. She was guilty of this.

"Look, I'm not trying to criticize you. Let's just understand what we've got here. You're in love with another man. The other man is in love with you. You want him, he wants you. There's nothing evil in that. Why don't you guys just do what you need to do? He should divorce his wife, you should divorce your husband, and the two of you should live happily ever after. Cut me loose in the process."

"I don't want to do that."

"Why not? I don't get it. Why would you want to not have this true love? True love is so rare, it's so unique—"

"No, it's not true love. That's the point: it isn't. It's more of a fantasy love."

"Whatever it is—let's just call it love, and it is a love, and it is in your heart, and you can't get rid of it and you're not going to be able to avoid this person, you're not going to be able to avoid this love, and you cannot have him in this marriage."

"You've got to understand me. I do want you to be happy and I'm going to stop."

"I don't believe you."

"I realize there's a huge trust issue."

"It's not just a trust issue. It's a problem that you just can't do it. You are saying you're going to do something that you are unable to do. The problem is you won't do what it takes to put yourself in a position where you can do it."

"What is that?"

"You need help."

"What do you mean?"

"Probably you need some therapist, family counselor, something. I don't know what."

"I don't want to share my problems with some stranger."

"You know, I get that. You and I have talked about this before. You should get a therapist. We were close to getting one; the last minute you closed down those discussions. So that's fine. Just don't get help. You don't need help, you just need a divorce and go with him. Don't even worry about it. And I'll just be a single man and you'll have a new husband and everything will be just fine."

"No, I don't want that!"

Just then, the buzz on my phone went off. It was the sound of a text message. I was pretending to ignore it. I was very certain it was from Tang. I'm sure she was checking on me. Sassafras grabbed the phone out of my top pocket. Indeed, right there, there was a message from Tang. She read it.

"I love you. I miss you. I want to come and kiss you."

She showed it to me.

"You see what this bitch wrote?"

I looked at it and smiled.

"Oh, you're smiling about that?"

"Sassafras, I've got to tell you, those are the nicest words I've heard from a woman in about a year. From you, I've heard endless shit. I've heard about how I'm ugly, how I'm fat, how I'm poor, how I'm a loser, how I'm stupid, how I'll never go anywhere in my life, that how I am right now is how I will be forever, that it will never get better, that everyone else on the planet is better looking, in better shape, and is rich and is famous and is perfect, and I'm just a piece of garbage. That's what I've been hearing from *you*. Now today I get this from Tang, so just take a wild guess: guess which message I like better? Guess which message I want to go with, and guess which message I want to dump forever."

She looked at me. She was not about to give up. I tell you, these Asian girls, they don't mess around. She went into survival mode. On my phone, there was a green button that can be pushed, which will call the sender of a text message. Sassafras pushed the green button. Tang's phone rang. Of course, poor Tang thought it was me calling her. Uh oh. It wasn't.

I could hear Tang's voice on the speaker system on my phone.

"Hello, dear!"

Oh boy, was that ever the wrong greeting.

"Fuck you, bitch. This isn't your lover. This is your lover's wife."

There was silence on Tang's end.

"Are you there?"

"I'm here. What would you like to talk about, dearie?"

"Don't call me dearie, you little bitch. I want to know why you're sending these messages to my husband."

"Let's see now. Because you dumped him, because you got a lover, because you don't like him anymore, because about a million reasons. He's completely available, he's cute, he's funny, and I like the way he smells."

Ooh, that really got her. She knew how important smell was to me, now she met a woman who had the same issue: good smell equals chemistry, and chemistry equals love, love equals replacement. And I'm talking total replacement.

Sassafras got that right away. She looked at me with fright in her eyes. She turned back to the girl.

"Listen very carefully, bitch: there will be consequences. I will make your pretty face ugly."

Chapter 72
CUMEPPENCE

Tang hung up the phone. She wasn't about to hear that kind of crap from anybody. She was a soft, fragile flower that worked in the construction industry, and was used to brutal people. But even the hard hat construction workers weren't as rough as this supermodel bitch that had turned on her.

The phone rang again. She saw it was Sassafras, using my phone. Sassafras then sent her a text message. She addressed it to "Herman's free whore":

"I don't know how much sex you've had with my husband, but you have to understand, he doesn't love you. You are just his free whore."

She texted right back: *"We haven't had sex yet, so don't worry about the 'free whore' stuff."*

Sassafras texted right back: *"Oh, I guess he doesn't really like you so much. You can't even get his dick hard."*

She fired right back: *"Oh? I guess that was just a cucumber in his pocket that I saw and felt."*

This enraged her. She turned to me.

"Did she touch your dick?"

I looked up in the air, searching for the answer to the question somewhere in the clouds.

"You leave my husband's dick alone. If you ever touch it again, I will hire someone to come and slice you."

Tang did not respond. Sassafras then transferred the number to Tang's phone over to her phone. Oh great, I thought. It would then be a campaign of text messages and phone calls between the two of them.

Sassafras commenced a bitter battle with her new rival, an innocent 42-year old Asian fragile flower by the name of Tang, weighing in at 101 pounds, long white creamy legs, straight black Asian hair, lovely complexion, those almond slanted Asian eyes that drive me crazy, a natural smile, and hands that love to touch. In the other corner was the darkish Cantonese bitch-on-wheels Sassafras, multimillionaire, hugely ambitious, does whatever the hell she wants to do, Hollywood lovers, A-list boyfriend, non-list husband, mother of three—of which two she has, one still in Italy – and a woman hell-bent to somehow keep her family all together while she carries on with her movie star boyfriend.

Oh, this ought to be good. Let's just sit back and watch the exchange. Sassafras continued.

"You are so stupid. You are so uneducated. I can see you don't even know English. Do you actually know how to write and read?"

Tang did not have a mean bone in her body. She fired back: *"I'm so sorry I'm just a small China girl, alone here in Sacramento with nobody to turn to but your delicious husband. Mmmm."*

Sassafras fired right back: *"He is not your dinner, he is not your lover, he is never going to leave me."*

"Oh, I'm so confused," she wrote back, *"I thought I saw his apartment, and if I'm not mistaken, the apartment is separate from your house, so couldn't we say he already left you? Ha ha ha. You're the stupid one."*

Uh oh. Now it's on.

"Look, don't you fucking laugh at me, you free whore."

"Hey girl, look, you've got to get real. You lost your husband. You had a boyfriend, congratulations on finding an A-list actor. Just go with him. I'm just a little nobody, your husband's just a little nobody, let the nobodies be together. What's wrong with that?"

I looked over to Sassafras. I was very curious to see what her response would be to that.

"You will never have my husband. You will not replace me. I will absolutely guarantee that."

A flurry of text messages continued.

"Free whore."

"Cheater."

"Bitch."

"Betrayer."

"Opportunist."

"Liar."

The list went on and on. I decided I had heard enough and walked away with my phone. I called Tang.

"Listen, Tang, I'm really sorry about this. She's just going crazy right now. I want to assure you I'm very sorry."

"What is with this crazy woman of yours? She's just crazy!"

"I know. And I can't control her, but I guarantee you this: if you don't respond, you will not hear from her again. Please just leave her alone."

"Hey, she started it."

"I know she started it, but why don't you end it. If you don't text her back, she will not text you again."

Of course Tang had to text her back. But Sassafras had already put her phone down and turned it off. It was later that evening at home, after dinner and when the boys were in bed, that Sassafras got the text message from Tang that had been sent several hours earlier.

"Women like you should not be allowed to have families, should not be allowed to have children."

Ooh, that was a tough one. Sassafras got right back: *"Sorry it took me awhile to get back to you, but I was too busy making love to my husband. As for your opinions about my ability to have a family, this must come from a woman who is barren, without children. You're just jealous."*

Tang fired back: *"I don't have children now, but all I need is one night with your husband and – oh goodness, I can just feel him right now."*

Sassafras fired back: *"One night and you'll make zero money. You're just his free whore."*

"Free whore? How about mother of his child."

"You're not having his baby."

This really got Sassafras going. It bothered her so much that I got laid. But another woman having my child, that would bother her big time. She turned to me.

"Are the two of you going to have a baby?"

"Hey, I just met this girl. We're not having anything. We're having conversations. We're having the very beginning of a relationship, that's all."

She stood up and walked over to me. Without any warning, she gave me quite a slap, right across the face. KABOOM. It has a stinging sensation, a ringing in my ear. I stood up. I didn't want to hit her back, and I wouldn't do that. Instead, I just left. This is an important lesson for all men: when a woman hits you, number one, I don't care how she hit you, why she hit you, where she hit you, how hard she hit you, and whether it was coupled with a spit, an insult, a reference to how her lover is more endowed than you, a reference to how small your dick is, I don't care how she does it, whatever you do, do not –– REPEAT – do not hit her back. Do not throw her down. Do not kick her. Do not slap her. Do not even touch her. Don't wrestle with her. Don't push her. What you should do is about face, 180 degrees, walk out. Don't even put your shoes on. If you're naked, walk out naked. Get in the car and drive away. Take off. Don't call the police, don't call anybody, just get the hell out of there.

Luckily, at this point I was in shorts and a shirt, it was not a cold night out, my shoes were actually by the front door, so I put them on. I got my car keys, I got my phone, and I took off. Now, if I didn't have my apartment, I would've just gone to a local hotel and stayed there. But I had an apartment, so I went there. And of course Sassafras knew this, and she also knew that this place put me into the immediate neighborhood of Tang. Uh oh.

She called me. Great. I pick up. I'm not going to avoid her call.

"Yes?"

"I'm sorry."

"You're sorry for what?"

"For slapping you."

"I don't really give a shit about the slap."

"Please come back."

"I'm not coming back. You're getting violent, you're getting crazy, you're going to beat up Tang, you're going to beat me up, you're going to beat up everybody. You've got to realize, these are just the consequences of what you have done, and rather than trying to punish everyone else for reacting to what you have done, you should instead fess up to what you have done, hold yourself accountable, and start to begin the healing process. You're not doing that. Instead, you're just attacking everybody. You're doing this all wrong and it's not going to work."

"Help me do it right. I'm just going crazy right now."

"Okay, what do you think you should do to make this right? What is the first thing I want to hear from you?"

"I'm sorry?"

"Yes. The next thing I want to hear?"

"I did something wrong?"

"Yes. The next thing I want to hear?"

"I will never do it again?"

"Oh, don't bullshit me. You will do it again. You've already flunked that test, so forget about it."

"Well, I don't know, what do you want to hear from me?"

Chapter 73
BUILD ME A MOUNTAIN

I explained to her,

"I want you to build me a mountain."

"What do you mean by that?"

"You need to understand that from this whole affair of yours, you have dug a large hole and you have put me in that hole, and it's caused me incredible hurt. So far, you've been justifying it and rationalizing it with a bunch of arguments about what a dick I was, what an asshole I was, how fat I was, how stupid I was. At some point, you may or may not stop and say, 'Enough about me, how about you?' Now, I don't know if you're ever going to get to that point or not, but I'll tell you this right now: you've dug a hole that has hurt me to the middle of the earth. I have a sense of restoring balance. If you want to keep this together, you need to restore the balance. You need to build a mountain that is at least as tall as the hole you dug is deep."

I stopped. I was curious about her reaction. It was silence. I was getting close to my apartment. She could not respond.

"Look, I'm coming up to my apartment now. You just think about what I said."

"No, don't go yet. Don't go yet. I don't understand."

"It's all about restoring balance. I need you to build me a mountain. I don't think you're going to do that. I don't think you can do it, I don't think you understand it, I don't think you care enough about the impact that this affair has had on me to even attempt to do it. So I'm just telling you my terms. That's what I need. If you don't want to do that, don't even worry about it. I will just stay at my apartment, I will date Tang, I will never turn back. That's how it's going to be. Goodbye."

I got out of the car. I looked down the road to where Tang lived. I didn't want to go there right now. Instead, I opened my front door, came into my hot air balloon mattress, and flopped myself down on my pillowcase-less pillow. The phone rang. This time, to my pleasure, it was Tang.

"Hello, Tang."

"How's the bitch?"

"Oh God, you have no idea."

"Where are you?"

"I'm at my apartment."

"Can I come over?"

"Sure, come on by."

I hung up the phone, and within a matter of minutes, Tang was there. Sassafras called again, and of course not in a million years am I going to take a call from that bitch while I'm going to spend the night with Tang. I let the phone ring. She saw who it was. I turned my phone off. The cool thing was that Sassafras had no idea where I was, so she couldn't come and yank my ass out of the apartment, shove me into the car, gag me, handcuff me, and drive me back home. Wow. That made me feel pretty good.

Tang became primal. She put her hand on my chest and rubbed it in circles. She explained to me, "That woman will never make you happy."

"I know."

"You need to understand. When a woman does this to her husband, when she has a lover, when she acts this brutally, it means she doesn't love the husband anymore. It means she has lost all respect for him. And once that happens, it's over. She will never regain that love. She will never regain that respect, and you will always have this problem with her, forever and ever."

I looked out the window above the air conditioning unit and saw the dark. Of course Tang was right.

"I know you're right. I'll never get her back."

"I know you want her back. I see your struggle."

"I don't know why I want her back. She's causing so much pain. I should just say see you later. But there is an issue here, Tang, I'll be honest with you. I have this weird idea of getting her back."

"It's only natural. You've been with her for quite awhile, you've got kids with her, you've got a family."

I have learned there's a kind of bond that goes between a man and a woman who have had children together. It is unlike any other relationship bond. It is very hard to sever. It is the kind of bond that goes down through the bone, through the skin. It goes into the marrow of the bone. It is a kind of connection that, short of an atomic bomb, may not be severed. Even an affair won't sever it. Even an affair that is done openly and notoriously, flaunted in my face, done in a way that humiliates me, in front of my friends and family, my social circle, my entire world. Put upside down, my head is the ground, I am buried in a hole, I am forever traumatized and injured, and amazingly enough, I still want that girl back. Go figure.

But then I realized it's like a sickness or something. It's something that should not be. It is a love addiction, and I explained this to Tang.

"I'm suffering from an addiction, just like a drug addiction. What do you suppose I need to do to be rid of this addiction?"

Tang smiled. Oh, did she ever have an answer. Her shirt went off. She was not wearing a bra. You could compare this to ending your addiction to alcohol by beginning a new addiction to heroin. Call it what you want; that heroin looked pretty damn good.

She looked down at my waist and saw I was immediately aroused. Okay, so I'm easy. She unzipped me. Oh my goodness, what that woman could do with her hands and mouth. Unbelievable.

She looked up at me in assurance.

"I don't care what that mean wife of yours has told you, this is not small."

I smiled. I then took a man charge about this, and brought her down. In the background were hot air balloons and a pillowcase-less pillow. We had our first step toward my healing process and getting over and beyond Sassafras. And oh, did it feel good.

Chapter 74
POST-INFIDELITY STRESS DISORDER

You may have heard the new and scientifically approved psychosis called "post-traumatic stress disorder." It is something that attorneys and psychologists refer to as "PTSD" for short. This was first uncovered among soldiers returning from Vietnam. Of course the horrors and traumas they experienced are unimaginable, and are about a thousand to a million times greater than anything that non-military folks would ever experience.

So let's divide that by a million and get to the non-military type traumas people experience here on planet Earth. One example: a man or woman is brutally beaten by another person. Another example: a woman or man is raped. Another example: police event, nightstick taken out, person clubbed. Person's home is invaded by cops or other persons.

In all these incidents, there will be a huge emotional scar. I've had several clients who've had their homes invaded by police officers who arrived without a search warrant, rummaged through the home, took things, and left. I can tell you, years later they still have nightmares about people invading their homes and taking things. It's just a weird idea, the idea that someone can just walk into your house under the cover of legal authority, go through your front door, flashlight and gun in hand, go through your entire home and do pretty much whatever they want to do.

Do you think that takes awhile to get over? Okay, how about this one: somebody rapes you. How long does it take for a woman to get over a rape? How about twenty-five million years? How about never? Assume for a moment the rapist never fesses up (they rarely do), never says "I'm sorry" (as though that would make a difference), and doesn't do anything to assist the victim in coming out of the tailspin caused by that traumatic event?

How do you suppose that woman would ever get it off? The answer is she doesn't. A similar but related issue has been coined "Post-Infidelity Stress Disorder" (PISD). [Dennis Ortman, Ph.D, Transcending Post-Infidelity Stress Disorder: The Six Stages of Healing. (Celestial Arts 2009)]. I like the sound of it because it sounds like "P-I-S-S-E-D." Suppose for a moment that Sassafras really would stop the relationship. First of all, I don't think for a minute she could, but let's just assume some kind of perfect post-affair situation where she actually did. How do I get over it?

Let's even go further and assume that she says, "I'm sorry. I really feel terrible. It was completely my fault. It was wrong to do and I'll never do again." Words, I might add, that I will never hear from her. But let's suppose I did hear those words. Do you think I would get over this? I don't think so.

So how do you get over it? What do you do? Therapy? I'm not so sure about that. I mean, come on, you show up to a therapist, you bleed your heart out, you tell them what a big impact it's had on you, and ultimately what can a therapist tell you? "Time will heal." I don't buy that. I've seen my clients several years later: they are not healed from the invasion by police into their homes; rape victims are not healed several years later; the people that went to Vietnam are not healed by even a decade of time passing. Something needs to happen.

I like my analysis that I gave to Sassafras: balance needs to be restored. When you have a huge loss, if you don't somehow get a countervailing victory, you may never get over the huge loss. If someone digs you a hole, they're going to have to build you a mountain or you'll never get over it.

I explained this ad nauseum to Sassafras. I sounded a little bit Native American about it. I told her the story of the Cherokee, of the legend of the rattlesnake. It's a story where a rattlesnake came over to a Cherokee tribe and bit the chief's wife. She died. He then had to go out and find his wife's killer. He, unfortunately, believed it was a nearby tribe, not a rattlesnake. So they went to the nearby tribe and explained, "My wife is dead, someone must pay for it." The other tribal leader realized how true it was. Even though the tribe was completely innocent, someone must pay. He went ahead and allowed it.

"Pick your victim."

The Cherokee chief looked and found the daughter of the chief, a lovely 17-year old girl, completely innocent, who hadn't done anything wrong. He pointed at her.

"We will take her."

The legend of the rattlesnake and its moral teaching, is that an eye for an eye is not the right way. As Gandhi said, "Pretty soon we'll all be blind." But this kind of thinking of a revenge to restore balance is only natural.

There must be a better way. For example, in the Cherokee legend, what if instead of killing that lovely 17-year old daughter of the chief, it was agreed that she would just be given over to the tribe and they would take her, care for her, raise her, marry her off, make her into a good woman, a good wife. This would be an example of "build me a mountain" instead of "an eye for an eye."

I liked the concept of a mountain for a hole.

Unfortunately, Sassafras just did not get this. I tried to explain to her what I wanted.

"What do you mean, build me a mountain? Can you be more specific?"

"Okay, I'll give you an example. I need tender moments from you. So far in the past what I've received is quite a bit of negativity. I've heard endless complaints, endless insults, I've seen the look on your face. It's a very cold look filled with hate. I don't want to see that again. Here's what I want to see instead: I have an image of you in the kitchen. You're cooking broccoli and cauliflower. I come down, I see you in the kitchen, I stand behind you. I put my hand on your shoulders. You turn around, you look at me in the eyes, you smile, you give me a lovely kiss on the lips, with tongue – or without, whatever – you tell me, 'I love you,' you pat me on the shoulder, you turn around and you continue cooking. Now, multiply that by sixteen thousand and you've got a mountain. That's what I'm talking about."

"Tender moments? That's what you want?"

"That is exactly what I want."

She responded by kissing me right then and there. She held me tight. She grabbed my cock.

I moved her hand away and explained: "Here's the trick about these tender moments. This is not about sex. This is not about letting me do it. It's not about letting me have my way with you. This is all about showing me part of you that I just have to have. You need to show me that you love me, that you want me, that you need me, and that you want to show that love and that need and that desire, and that you'll be willing to do it and that you do do it. You can't just have these thoughts in you and not show them; you need to act on them in an open manner. You need to show it to me and you need to do that all the time. Can you do that?"

She looked at me.

"I will do that."

She gave me another kiss. She left the room and just disappeared. We have a living room upstairs, so I decided I'll just stay here, stay out of her way. Then I walked downstairs and I saw what she was up to. She was in the kitchen, she was cooking broccoli. I smiled. I came over to her. I stood behind her. I put my hand on her shoulder. She turned around. She smiled. She looked at me. She gave me a big kiss and told me, "I love you."

She then told me, "Can I show you something?"

"What?"

"Come over here."

We walked to the computer. She brought up her emails. She went to the sent files and showed me an email she had sent to her lover. It was actually quite well-written. I was very impressed.

Dear Brett,

It is time for me to say goodbye. I feel very ashamed about what you and I have been doing and I realize now that I need to spend the rest of my life with my husband. You are a wonderful man. Your wife is lucky to have you. But I've got to go. Please understand my wish. Good luck in your life and good luck in your marriage.

Regards,

Sassafras

I saw that it had been sent the day before. There was perhaps some therapeutic value to be gained where the offending party sits down with his or her spouse and they co-write a letter to the affair. In this case, we didn't do that. Instead, she wrote the letter. It was probably better that way. There's nothing worse than a letter coming from the husband going to the affair. That's not as real. The letter really should come from the offending party. If you think about it, it's sort of like getting an apology from somebody that didn't commit the act in question. If you don't get the apology directly from the culprit, the apology is rather useless.

So it is the same with letters of closure. If they don't come from the offending spouse, they are at best dubious, and at worst, a complete waste of time. This one was written one hundred percent by Sassafras, and as far as I was concerned was perfect.

She turned to me.

"Now, how about you?"

"How about me what?"

"How about you write a letter like that to Tang?"

I smiled.

"You want me to get rid of her?"

"I do. I got rid of him, you get rid of her."

"Do you really think I need to get rid of her?"

"Yes, you do. I'm ready to go forward in this way, I'm ready to reconcile with you, to begin a new marriage, to start over with you. But we can't do it with another woman in our marriage. Our marriage has been too busy. So you need to think about that. Let me ask you: do you want Tang, or do you want me?"

It's easy to say 'dump the bitch' when you are the victim of an affair. It becomes easier when all your family and friends give you that basic advice. Everyone thinks you should get rid of her. But everyone isn't living your life. Everyone isn't in your shoes. Everyone doesn't have your family. Everyone doesn't have the bond that exists between you and your spouse, a bond that goes through the skin, the muscles, the bone, and into the bone marrow.

Nobody but you will understand that. You may not be able to describe it, you may not be able to explain it, you may not even understand it. You just know that it is what it is, and no matter how much advice you may get during these kind of times, you've got to realize that the number one thing you will ever do on this planet is to create a family. It's not about what you look like, the law cases you may win, the money successes you may have, the homes that you may own, the cars you may own. All that doesn't add up to an anthill when compared to the monumental triumph of creating a beautiful family.

So you want to be a tough guy and say 'dump the bitch'? Split up that family and have, what, visits every other weekend plus dinner on Wednesday night? Two homes, both of which will be quite a bit less than the current home? You want to have your wife permanently angry with you, bothering you for more and more child support, more and more spousal support, even if she is a multimillionaire? Or, even if you could get child support from her, is that really what you want? Do you want to be like one of these kept husbands and make fifteen thousand a month off your ex-wife?

Forget the revenge. Forget the anger. Forget about your male ego for a second. Go back to Mother Nature and realize that the number one thing Mother Nature wants you to do is make a family. Realize that you have a duty to yourself and to that family to keep it all under one roof. Don't violate that duty. You'll hurt yourself and your family. You'll make your children the victims of your own failures.

Go ahead and think about it. Think about the things that you did or did not do that got your spouse into the position where she decided to stray. Don't deny it, don't minimize it; embrace it, acknowledge it, and become better for it. Talk about it. Discover it. Feel it all out. Look at every little naked contour it has. Understand the woman's needs. The woman needs that emotional connection, the emotional attachment. She needs the compliments, she needs the validation, the appreciation. "Honey, I love you. Honey, thank you for what you've done. Thank you for this. Thank you for that."

Well, guess what, we men need the same thing. You can call us emotionally needy. So are the women; so are we. We're all human. We all have emotions, we all have needs. Do I need validation? Oh, yeah. Do I need to be appreciated? Oh, yeah. Do I need to be told 'I love you'? Oh, yeah. Does she need that? Of course she does. We both need that.

And if we can cut out all the bullshit and both sit down and realize that this is what both of us need in equal doses, we can fill up the hole and begin the process of building that mountain. We can do it together.

Chapter 75
THE INCONGRUOUS SIDE

Here's the part of the ending that is incongruous to the rest of the story. Remember I told you there was kind of murder involved? Well, here's how it went.

First of all, this movie star guy has a bit of a background that I did not know about. As a kid, he was not some geek studying in the library, making good grades, applying to Ivy League schools, getting top scores on the SATs, getting into those top schools, making his way through their to the top of his class, graduating with honors from a major university, studying for the law school admissions tests, placing in the top three percent nationwide, gaining entrance into one of the top law schools, suffering his way through that, taking the bar exam, and becoming an attorney. He didn't take that path at all.

Instead, he was part of a gang, a tough gang, kind of a Greek mafia here in Sacramento. These are tough guys. They have guns and drugs; they do all kinds of stuff. He actually killed a few people. I didn't know that. Nobody else did. There was a felony case brought against him, though. I found it. I had hired a private eye to check this guy out. Who exactly is this man? I'll tell you one thing about him. I go down to the courthouse and I see a two-count felony indictment for murder against Mr. Brett Clawney when he was 19. The charges were dismissed due to insufficient evidence.

I do a little Nexus research. I have a little Nexus program that gives me newspaper articles. I go back to the *Sacramento Bee* during that time period and I see that the main witnesses mysteriously disappeared. The defendant walked. It's easy to win a case when you kill instead of cross-examine. So now I understand I'm dealing with quite a thug here. Okay, so he grew up and became an A-list actor, but do you think he's ever left that gang, thug, mafia, Greek situation behind? Not on your life.

He's already simmering because Sassafras sent him a "Dear Brett" letter via email in which she informed him that she has made a new decision to stay with her family and that they could be no more. She also told him that he should seize this opportunity to reunite with his own wife and to make his own family. He would be a better man, a better person, and it would be better for all involved. He sent back a rather nasty email to her, "I'm going down to the courthouse. I'm looking for Herman."

She warned me, "Oh man, you don't want to mess with this guy. He's mafia. He'll kill you."

I told her, "I am ready to die. If he has a gun, I'll take my shirt off and he can shoot me right in the heart, no problemo."

She told me that was not the right way.

"Stay away from him."

I started to think about this asshole. I read the emails a little bit more. He was discussing how, since he's moving to Sacramento, he can be with her every day, he was discussing how he was going to keep her from me, how the whole idea that she was still with me disgusted him, and he was going to make it so that I was no longer part of her life. She was his soul mate, they were destined to be together, they would be together, and his new appointment as special advisor to the Governor would ensure that they would have an every day affair, instead of an every other weekend affair.

As I read that, I thought about his attitude and how God awful it was. He didn't care that he was going to totally screw up my life, my family, my children, everything. My sons had told me quite intelligently, "Brett will never be our father. He's going to hate us. He's probably going to kill us."

I assured them, "Look, he's not going to hurt you. He may not care for you—"

"No other man is going to want us. You know that, Daddy. And you know what happens."

And it's really sad but true, the stepfather ends up doing something really bad to the step kids. If it's a daughter, he rapes her. If it's a son, he beats the shit out of him or kills him or both. How was I going to protect them from that?

"Daddy, you can't let Mommy marry him!"

"Wait, wait, wait. Don't talk to me about that. Talk to Mom about that. She's the one going that way, not me."

We had already had all these discussions and I told them it was out of my hands. I can't do a damn thing about it. She's gone, she wants him, and that's that. Well, now she was saying no, I don't want him, I'm not going to have him. I'm going to stay with you. The idea was I was just supposed to do nothing to this movie star guy. I was supposed to just walk away and pretend like it didn't happen. Bullshit. This motherfucker is a bad apple and I'm going to do something to fuck him up.

Chapter 76
HOW TO DESTROY A MOVIE STAR

Real simple: step one, hire a private eye. Mine was a former cop, twenty-five years on the force, retired as a sergeant. Knows his way around town, knows police people, knows how to get them involved, knows how to make things happen. Here's all I had to do. I wrote a letter to his lovely little wifey-poo. Her name was Karen. Karen the waitress. How lovely.

"Dear Karen," I wrote. *"I am sorry to inform you that my wife, Sassafras, and your husband, Brett Clawney, are having an affair. It's been going on for over a year. They are hot and heavy. I have a solution to this problem. Please call me and we will discuss it. I'm sorry for my enclosed email, which I know will hurt you dearly, but I want you to know the truth so that you and I can talk about the solution. Regards, Herman Franck."*

I gave her my cell phone number, I put that and one of the emails into a package, and gave it to the private eye with the following instructions:

"Hang outside the house, wait until he leaves, ring the doorbell, give it to the gal. And please tell her not to tell him where she got it from, because he's probably going to kill me or something."

The private eye understood the situation. Three days later, he called me back.

"The package has been delivered."

How cool is that. This woman would go ballistic. Added to the fact was that she was pregnant. I thought of it this way. Revenge is truly a negative thing. It's not good, it's not smart, it's not mature, it's not anything right, but goddammit, does it feel good. He was going to bust up my family, he was going to screw over my kids, probably beat the shit out of them on a regular basis, he was going to destroy my heart and take my wife, and probably leave her high and dry down the road for some other girl. He would've destroyed us, left us both hurt, injured, devastated people and we would've never been able to pick up the pieces. We would've been permanently disabled by his asinine conduct. So did he need something negative to happen to him? Oh yeah, he sure did.

The wife went absolutely ballistic. That night when he came home, she flashed the email to him.

"What the fuck is this, you motherfucker?"

She slapped him right in the face. She tried to do it a second time, but he stopped her hand. The thug was coming out.

"Where the fuck did you get this?"

"Never mind where I got it, I got it! Look at this! You love this woman? Who is this bitch?"

Just as he was about to grab her throat, she pointed down to her stomach.

"Don't forget, you motherfucker, I'm pregnant. You fuck me up, you know the cops are going to take your ass away. How many days do you want to do in jail?"

He backed off. He wanted to kill her. But then his anger turned to me. He looked at that email. He knew where she got it. It was obviously from me. Motherfucker, he thought. I'm going to get that little piece of shit. I think I know where he is. Indeed, it was a fact that many afternoons at the end of the day, approximately seven p.m., I could be found out by a river where I regularly walk my dog. It was during these times that he had had email correspondence with my wife, and she explained to him, "My husband's at the river walking the dog." He knew where the river was. It's a very famous deep channel that goes between the Port of Sacramento and the Port of Stockton. My house is just a couple blocks away. It's a beautiful natural area where my Dalmatian Spots can run for endless hours.

Chapter 77

THE STUNNING CONCLUSION OF HOW TO MEET AND MARRY A SUPERMODEL

It is true that I am a creature of habit. I wake up in the early morning, approximately six a.m., I put on a cup of coffee, I turn on the television and watch old *JAG* and *Walker* shows. At around seven, I start doing law work, in the form of reviewing the output from the day before. This is largely an editing process, with some rewrites as necessary. Normally, court starts at nine, so I have to be out the door by about eight thirty. I go to court in the morning, I then do further law work in the afternoon.

On my return home, I methodically take Spots out to the river. More recently, he has adopted a rather interesting practice himself of not allowing his own bowel movement until I bring him out to the river behind my house. It's an interesting concept, which is connected to the dog's own idea of "living space," and the dog rule that you do not leave a bowel movement in your living space. A rather intelligent rule when you think about it.

So when I get home, he's triple anxious to get out to the river. I get out of my law suit, put on casual clothes, tennis shoes, shorts, during which he watches my every move, panting anxiously, moving from inch to inch. He is right next to me, literally head-butting my leg. When I go down to the cabinet door where we keep the leash, the noise of that chain leash coming against the wood brings him to a point of frenzy. He is at the door, he knows he's going out, and he's ready to go. I put the leash on him. When the door opens, he wants to fly like an eagle the two block distance to the river. I have to wait as he pees on just about every tree between my house and the river. Dogs are funny this way; their sense of territoriality is huge.

I go down the street, I take a right on another street, I walk to the dead end of that street, and suddenly I leave suburban USA for the raw land of a deep channel river, buttressed by a rather impressive levy. This deep channel was created out of an existing river, which was dug out to allow for large ocean bound vessels, and connects the Sacramento Port to the Stockton Port. It's a wonderful place for a dog to run. When I get there, I take the leash off and Spots goes tearing off. Dalmatians need lots of running time, literally five to seven miles a day, if not more. He chases birds, and his favorite fun, the occasional jackrabbit that bounces out of a bush and tears down the top of the levy. It's one of the few times I hear him bark. He's for the most part a non-barking dog, but when a rabbit pops out, he barks and goes tearing after it. Unfortunately for Spots, and fortunately for the rabbit, the rabbit wins every time. Spots is an extremely fast dog, but the rabbits are faster.

Mr. Brett Clawney, the movie star, was well aware of my predictable regimen, due to the simple reality that Sassafras told him so in her series of love emails.

"My husband's out on the river, so we can talk now."

This was her 'love time.' While I was out walking the dog, she was sending off romance emails to the love of her life. He also knew what the river place was, as she had described it to him in quite a few of her emails. She explained, "My husband is at a trial in Oakland. I am all alone on the river. There's a beautiful sunset. It is red. It is coming down. I am wishing you were here to touch me, to feel me, to make me feel like a woman."

So he knew where it was, what it was, and that I could be predicted to be there.

The other part about the river is it is where I find my time to write my books. You will find me out there with a tape recorder in hand, talking into the tape recorder, telling my stories. It was like this on the infamous day in June. Sacramento summers are exceptionally hot. I was in shorts, tennis shoes with white socks, one taller than the other. I was with Spots. When Spots and I walk, he just tears off in his own way, finding rabbits, birds, and the like. He is not right next to me, but periodically rejoins me. He will go as far away as a half a mile and then I will see him running back.

My walk had just started. I was holding the tape in hand and I was writing my twenty-first book, appropriately called *Ultimate Revenge: A Thing of Beauty Must Be Destroyed*. This is a rather doozy of a story about a man deeply in love with a woman who tragically gets raped. The man does a bit of a crime investigation and forensic job and very cleverly finds the culprit, and brings him to justice. The rapist, though, does a plea bargain and gets eight years. Meanwhile, his fiancée was rendered catatonic by a mixture of her own preexisting anxiety-prone psychological state, and the barbiturate, depressant, anesthetic cocktail of a drug administered to her by the rapist. That, plus the impact of the rape, left her without feeling, without an active brain, and she just stared blankly out the window in a mental institution.

The fiancé decided he would get revenge in a rather unique way. He found the rapist after the rapist had successfully completed an in-prison sexual offender therapy program. For the most part, they never get resolved, and can be predicted to commit another offense within twelve months of their release from prison. For this reason, they are placed into a halfway house that has very strict hours and reporting regimens. He managed to steal this man away from the halfway house and put him prisoner in his own house. He then proceeded to administer a series of estrogen-based hormone pills into the man, and turned that man into a woman. A she-male, to be exact. He forced her to exercise, forced her to eat good foods, and forced her to take these drugs. She developed small breasts, and all facial hair, leg hair, arm hair, chest hair, back hair, and butt hair disappeared. She became shapely, womanlike. He grew her hair, and within six months, he was ready for the ultimate revenge: he would take that woman out and get her raped. This was his evil plan.

Unfortunately, during this plan, something unexpected happened; after several rapes and victimizations of this rapist, he began to feel guilty himself. This is the thing about revenge, you become the very monster that you are fighting against. What is the difference between a rapist and a man who takes a rapist out to get raped? The answer is, there is no difference. He starts to understand that after about six rapes. On top of that, his own feeling of guilt and sympathy, plus the fact that his she-male turned into quite a beauty, caused him to fall in love with her. He then started a romance with this she-male, which replaced his desire for revenge and turned it into true love.

Miraculously, his previous fiancée was finally cured of her catatonic state, and came out of it. It was at this point, when the fiancé returned home with the rather surprising statement, 'Honey, I'm home,' that I was taping on this very hot summer day in June. I was proceeding to describe a process where the fiancé was explaining to his prior fiancée how he had to move on with his life, how he had a new woman, how he was very sorry about that, and how he wanted to get back with her. She was explaining how she understood, she didn't expect anyone to be on hold, and not to worry, she's going to pick up the pieces and move on and maybe they can still be friends. She met the woman and looked at her from head to toe, and got the idea that something wasn't quite right about her. It was agreed that the fiancé would move in, in a newfound platonic friendship. There would be a process where the reality of the new woman being the old fiancé's rapist would be disclosed.

I was in the process of dictating these final parts of the book when Mr. Clawney arrived with an aluminum baseball bat.

The other thing I'd like to report is that when I am writing, I'm lost in my own little world. There could be an atomic explosion that would go off just to the right of me, there could be a carnival just to the left of me, there could be a car accident right in front of me, there could be ten thousand naked women right behind me, and I wouldn't notice any of them. I am lost in my world. As I dictate, I walk around, I'm completely focused on that. There is no outside world. There is my handheld tape recorder, there was my brain, there was my mouth, and periodically there was my dog that circles back around to see me.

I was easy prey for Mr. Clawney. He was inappropriately dressed for this levy river area. As usual, fancy Rodeo Drive style black shoes, probably costing more than three of my car payments. He had pulled up in his slate gray, four door, 6 series Mercedes. Before he got out, he slicked his hair, put his RayBans on, went to the back of his trunk, and took out his baseball bat—a rather rough weapon, to say the least. He walked out and there's a hill area where you can have a good vantage point. He looked to the left, he looked to the right, and saw me. He saw the dog in the distance. He studied the situation and realized I was walking further away, so he'd have to get going to catch me. He proceeded. He walked. He held the bat in his hands and you could see the knuckles turning white. You could see the anger in his eyes. His lips were tight. He gave a false smile, as though this would make him happy. Revenge actually doesn't leave you happy, but sometimes, you just gotta do it.

He did not want to engage me in any discussion. He did not want to have any kind of a fair fight. In a true thug way, he walked up behind me and THWACK, smacked me with that aluminum bat right on the back of my head. The saying, 'he never knew what hit him,' applies. I went right down. The thing was, though, he didn't realize I had my tape recorder in hand and it was actually recording. He got me literally mid-sentence at the point where the man was describing to his former fiancée that this woman that's living with him is actually her rapist. It was quite an apex moment in the story, a point of revelation, a point of further revenge that she would want against this man, and a point at which the two of them would discuss maybe they've had enough and they don't need any more revenge. This was the arc that I was attempting in this story, that revenge actually was a bad thing, that we shouldn't do it, that we should just leave negative things alone and move on.

It was right then and there, that he got his own revenge. He was extremely upset at me for having somehow stolen my wife back from him, and on top of that, for destroying his own marriage. Ooh, that pissed him off big time. I went right down in a crushing blow. I was down on my chest first, my tape recorder still in my hand and playing. He started yelling, "You motherfucker! You think you're going to fuck my marriage up? You think you're going to fuck my life up?"

On the tape recorder his voice would be imprinted perfectly. He took the bat out again. WHAM, hit me right in the back. WHAM, hit me in the side. WHAM, hit me in the leg. WHAM, hit me on the arm. Had I been awake, it would've really hurt. He smashed me on the head again. Blood was coming out of my ears. Blood was coming out of my nose. There was a hemorrhaging going on where blood is being dumped from a cracked area of my cranium onto my brain and is pooling. This is known as a hematoma. The result is a point of pressure between an ever-growing pool of blood that gets caught between the lower wall of the cranium and the upper wrinkled portions of the brain. As it pushes down on the brain, an extreme headache forms, and ultimately, if the pressure is not released, death.

Luckily, if you could call it that, he smashed me again in the head. This forced that hematoma to be moved and displaced more evenly throughout my cranium. Instead of having a small pool building up in one focused area, instead I had a rather larger lake forming around the top of my entire cranium. This bought me some time. The small pool would've killed me in a matter of moments. This lake on my brain, a lake of blood from his revenge, would give me perhaps more than an hour to live. It also shifted my body just a bit so that I was on my side with my tape recorder down underneath my ribcage. He did not see it.

Now here's the part where you get an idea what a thug this guy is. Here I am looking dead, or near dead. You'd think that would be enough. You'd think he'd just say, okay, I did it, and turn around and walk away. No. Not so this guy. He took my arm and broke it. Unbelievable. He took the forearm part of my arm, held my wrist, placed his knee on the tibia, and cracked it like you would a tree branch. It's the worst sound in the world, that of a bone breaking. CRACK. God, if I were conscious, that would've hurt.

Now, you'd think that would've been enough. As I'm lying there with blood coming out of my ears, blood coming out of my nose, a lake of blood pooling on my cranium, a broken rib, and now a broken forearm, you might wonder, what else could he do? He proceeded to unzip his pants. What, is he going to commit a sex crime on me now? He pulled out his penis. Oh God, now what? Is he—? No. What's he going to do? Is he going to try to do me? Is he going to make me suck it? Because believe me when I say this: I am not in the mood.

No, it was not about a sex crime. It was about a toxic crime, the ultimate territoriality by a dog-human. He peed on me. Unbelievable. Here this guy steals my wife, does her every which way but Sunday, has a complete emotional affair with her, falls in love with her, she falls in love with him, he fucks up my entire family, destroys the family home, the family system of trust, puts in me a sense of betrayal that I will probably never get over. It hurts me to no end, he obviously doesn't give a shit about that, and when I screw him up, he just goes to pieces and goes off on me like this. And on top of beating me up, smashing me in the head, smashing me everywhere else, breaking my forearm, now he's gotta pee on me! Unbelievable.

He's done now. The pee's over. He zips up his fly, picks up the bat and studies it. He has to say it to me: "Motherfucker, if you're not dead and you ever get out of this, I'm going to hunt you down again and I'll make sure that you are fucking dead."

WHAM. He had to hit me one more time, right in the back, right between my shoulder blades. OOMPH. Again, if I were awake, it would've really hurt. He brought the bat over to a couple nearby bushes and did a bit of a job to clean off the blood. He then casually walked away, leaving me there with my growing hematoma, a broken arm, smashed up back, broken rib, and pee all over me.

Just then, Spots runs back. Now Spots, like most dogs, is extremely loyal to me. I would never have to worry about any sense of betrayal from him. When he saw me on the ground like that, he just went crazy. He'd never seen anything like it. First thing he did was smell me, and then he smelled that urine. What was that? He then did something that only a dog would do: he licked the urine. He put his face in it, he got his nose wet with it, he licked it. It was just disgusting. I wish I could've yelled out, "Spots, just stop it!"

I was hoping to be saved right then, saved by somebody or something. If I'm going to be out here for more than an hour, I'm going to be dead. Just then, a major oceangoing vessel cruises by. This has Chinese lettering on it. It had just left the Port of Sacramento where there are a series of rice elevators. It was filled to the hilt with rice from Yellow County, California, bound to China. Unfortunately, the people on the ship were focused on the ship, on going down the deep channel, and were not looking to the side. Spots did a great job of barking at them. He barked very loudly. One of the ship people actually looked at him and waved, but they didn't see me. I was horizontal to the ground, I was wearing beige clothes, the grass was beige; unfortunately I was beautifully camouflaged. That boat just kept going down. Shit. That would've saved my life.

Spots realized the situation was pretty serious. He also saw in the distance the culprit. He smelled the bush where my blood was, he also noticed my blood was dripping off that bat and left little droplets, one here, one there. He tore off after that son of a bitch. On the way up from the river, there's a small hill which forms a levy. On top of that levy, there is a road. On top of that road, there were two other people with their dogs. Spots barked and barked. The people did not know what they were so excited about. He then put his nose to the other dogs. They smelled the pee on his nose and they just went crazy. He continued to bark at the man walking away, but nobody really understood what he was communicating. Spots took off after the movie star. It was very impressive.

The movie star got into his car and made a big mistake. He should've just gotten rid of that bat. Actually, there were several mistakes he made. He shouldn't have peed on me, because that would directly connect his DNA to me. He shouldn't have kept that bat, because that also had my blood on it and would directly connect my blood to him. All these things would later end up convicting his ass and sending him to prison for a significant period of time. But that didn't help me survive the moment.

He did a u-turn and proceeded to drive down the road. Spots took off like a bullet train after him. It was quite impressive. The guy had no idea that in his side view mirror, passenger side, there was a non-ferocious, non-attack bullet speed Dalmatian fearlessly chasing his ass to wherever he went.

As Spots ran and I continued to lay out on the levy, I couldn't get a song out of my mind. It was a song: "Zombie," by the Cranberries (used with permission):

Another head hangs lowly,
Child is slowly taken.
And the violence caused such silence,
Who are we mistaken?

But you see, it's not me, it's not my family.
In your head, in your head they are fighting,
With their tanks and their bombs,
And their bombs and their guns.
In your head, in your head, they are crying...

In your head, in your head,
Zombie, zombie, zombie,
Hey, hey, hey. What's in your head,
In your head,
Zombie, zombie, zombie?
Hey, hey, hey, hey, oh, dou, dou, dou, dou, dou...

Another mother's breakin',
Heart is taking over.
When the vi'lence causes silence,
We must be mistaken.

It's the same old theme since nineteen-sixteen.
In your head, in your head they're still fighting,
With their tanks and their bombs,
And their bombs and their guns.
In your head, in your head, they are dying...

In your head, in your head,
Zombie, zombie, zombie,
Hey, hey, hey. What's in your head,
In your head,
Zombie, zombie, zombie?
Hey, hey, hey, hey, oh, oh, oh,
Oh, oh, oh, oh, hey, oh, ya, ya-a...

Spots ran and ran and ran. The street is a major artery to an even larger street called Jefferson. There's a big stoplight there with lots of cars. This guy barely made the green light, it was turning yellow. By the time Spots got there, it was red. Spots did an impressive rounding of that turn, and in the process caused a three car accident. BOOM, BOOM, BOOM. Spots flew out of the accident unharmed and continued in a beeline straight up Jefferson after that slate gray Mercedes.

Not far up the street there's a police station and a fire department. Word about the accident was quickly radioed in. One of the cars was on fire, so guess what, the fire department had to take action. Three long fire trucks proceeded out of the fire department, sirens blaring, firemen jumping on left and right, some with jackets buttoned, some with jackets flopping in the wind. They meant business. In the process, they held up the traffic at that intersection. Of course the rule is you have to stop for a fire truck. This caused a bit of a delay, a delay that stopped our movie star's getaway. In the process, Spots was able to catch up to the son of a bitch.

The three fire trucks then made it through the intersection and the light turned green. The man was highly impatient. He proceeded to pass the cars on the right and went down the highway about a mile, to where it goes on to an on-ramp to what is part of Highway 50 that merges onto Highway 5 South. Spots followed him up that freeway onramp. It was a surprising sight to see this slate gray Mercedes being chased by a beautiful, champion level black and white Dalmatian, but that's what was going on. Spots followed as he went up the rather steep incline of this part of the highway. It goes over a river, so it goes quite high, and then it comes back down. The next exit was Fifth Street, which Clawney took. That proceeded to take him onto a frontage road called X Street. He proceeded down X to a street called Broadway. He took a right on Broadway and proceeded into the neighborhood known as Land Park.

Spots was far behind, but luckily the residential area had quite a few stoplights and stop signs. He caught up. He ran after that car all the way to Mr. Clawney's gorgeous multimillion dollar home in Land Park, Sacramento. Spots was absolutely exhausted. He'd never run that fast and that far in his entire life. Clawney didn't expect a thing, came out of his car, looked around to make sure no one was watching, removed the baseball bat from his trunk. He must not have been thinking straight, because obviously the blood from that bat had rolled around onto the carpet of his back trunk. Just cleaning the bat wouldn't do it; he'd have to disinfect the whole back area, and of course he would never think of doing that. He took the bat out, walked inside the garage, placed it in a corner, and came in to see his still extremely upset wife. He knew not to even talk to her. He had done what he needed to do. He felt good, he felt accomplished. He had had his revenge.

Meanwhile, back at the levy, the other dogs followed the blood and the urine and found me. They began barking incessantly. Happily, their owners followed. They didn't know what it was at first, and then they saw they had a near-dead human. One of them was an Asian woman and an attorney of all things. The other was a person that worked for REI, an outdoor equipment company. These were perhaps the two perfect people to find me. The attorney took out her cell phone and called 911.

"We have a dead man on the river levy in West Sacramento, right by the end of Marshall Street."

Just then, I let out a moan. The REI guy pointed out, "Hey, he's not dead!"

He put his ear to my chest.

"He's alive!"

As he moved me a little bit, the attorney warned, "Don't move him. Do not move him!"

Just then he saw something in my hand. The tape recorder was playing the whole time. He shut it off. He put the tape recorder very gently into my top pocket. The attorney looked into the recorder and thought in a forensic manner right away.

"Was that on?"

"Yeah."

"Ooh. I bet it recorded the whole thing."

"Should we listen to it?"

"No, let's let the police handle that. Let's just wait for them to get here."

The police had already been quite busy with that car accident that Spots caused. They weren't that far away. When they got the radio call, three of them were dispatched in high speed fashion right down Marshall Street to the end of Marshall where the levy starts. They came running out. The Asian attorney waved at them. They came down and saw what a complete mess I was.

"Oh, shit! This poor guy."

The other one remarked, "He's not going to make it."

The attorney looked at me and then looked at the officer.

"He can make it. Let's get him out of here. Can we get an Airvac?"

"Yes, we can. Let me call it in."

He got on his radio: "We're out here on the levy. We need an Airvac. We've got a man near dead. Please send a chopper ASAP."

At this moment, my wife Sassafras had picked up the boys from daycare at the YMCA and had driven them home. She had no idea as she drove why there was an ambulance, a fire truck, and three police cars racing down Marshall Street. Adam looked up and saw a helicopter.

"Whoa, look at that!"

It was a sheriff's chopper. They had been brought in to help. You don't see this very often out here, a chopper coming down and actually landing. They do patrol the area, but you don't see them land. When this one was landing, they could see it right from the house. Adam and Alex got real curious. Sassafras was her normal cautious self: "No, stay away. Don't do anything."

They strapped me into the helicopter. Paramedics were very careful to place blocks around my neck. They checked my eyes, they put flashlights on my pupils to see if they were responding. They were. They checked my head wounds. They could see it was quite serious. One of them shook his head.

"He's a goner."

I was playing in my head the "Zombie" music. It wouldn't go away. I was in a kind of dreamland. The officer looked at my back pocket and found my wallet.

"His name is Herman Franck."

Oddly and coincidentally, the address on my license was a Land Park address where we had lived before. Before we bought our home in West Sacramento, we had rented a rather lovely Land Park home where we got a taste of that place. Someday we vowed to return, but we went to another place where we could buy quite a large house for about one-third of what it would cost in Land Park. We never regretted it.

They called in my driver's license and realized that I was not living in Land Park anymore, and got my new address. As the chopper took me away to the hospital, one of the officers was dispatched to my home just a couple blocks away. My wife was just in the process of getting out of her Mercedes and walking into the house when the police officers pulled up.

"Ma'am?"

"Yes?"

"May we have a word with you?"

"Certainly."

She walked over to them.

"What's the problem, officer?"

Adam and Alex could sense something was going on. They looked up and saw the chopper flying away. They looked at the police, and they were starting to put two and two together.

"Ma'am, is your husband Herman Franck?"

"Yes."

"He has suffered a very serious injury. Somebody tried to kill him."

Oh, you should've seen the look on Sassafras's face.

"Where?"

"Out at the levy."

She knew right away what was going on. I'd been walking Spots. Her first question, somewhat predictably,

"Where is the dog?"

This caused a bit of a suspicion with the officer. Here this woman's husband was near dead and she's worried about the dog? The officer responded, "There was no dog. Just your husband, near dead."

"Where are they taking him?"

"Mercy Hospital. Ma'am, if you'd like, we'll take you there right now."

"Yes, please do."

"These are your sons?"

They walked over.

"Hi, I'm Adam."

"Hi, I'm Alex."

"Boys, let's go. You get in this car, ma'am, why don't you get in this car?"

She was very troubled to be separated from her sons and they could see that.

"Okay, just a second. Officer, you ride with me. I'll let her go in the front seat of the other patrol car and the boys can sit in the back. How about we do that?"

She nodded her head. That was much better. You don't want to split a mom up from her kids, especially during a time of crisis. The officers put on the sirens and tore out of the neighborhood. Neighbors came out and wondered what on earth was going on. They proceeded to Mercy Hospital and arrived within a matter of ten minutes. It helps when you have sirens and can proceed downtown at ninety miles an hour.

Upon arrival, they went to the ICU. Oh my God, she was shocked to see me all bashed up like this. I had an oxygen mask on, I had an IV in, I had bandages on my head, I had a team of surgeons working on my broken arm, I had another team of doctors working on my broken rib, and I had a brain surgeon trying to drain off the hematoma from the top of my cranium. My heartbeat was fairly strong: BUMP-BUMMP, BUMP-BUMMP. They had a brain scanner to show brain activity; it was going off the charts. The doctor noted it.

"A lot of brain activity going on here."

He looked over to Sassafras.

"That's a good thing. His brain is working fine. His heart is working fine."

"What all has he gone through?"

"We've got a broken arm, we have a cracked cranium at the base of the skull, we have a cracked cranium at the top of the head, he has one broken rib."

She also noticed a nurse sponge bathing me.

"What's going on here?" she asked.

"One of the strange things we found is that his assailant, for whatever reason, urinated all over him."

Sassafras got really upset at that. First of all, she only knew of one kind of animal that would do such a thing. One of the doctors took her to the side.

"Ma'am, do you know who would do a thing like this?"

She was quiet, reserved. She didn't know what to say. It was like, if I know, aren't I going to be guilty also? She looked at the doctor and just started crying. The doctor then pulled out my tape player.

"We found this on him. You know what this is about?"

"Oh, he writes books. That's how he writes his books."

"Well, he was recording at the time of his attack. I want to play this back to you and see if you recognize the voice."

He went a little bit too far to the point where I'm still talking about this woman who comes home to find a new woman that turns out to be her rapist, and how she's dealing with her fiancé and his decision to get a new woman while she was catatonic. They had to fast-forward through all that drama and they got to the point where the voice of the man that Sassafras had fallen in love with was clearly heard yelling out, *"You motherfucker! You think you're going to fuck up my family? Take that!"*

And then SMACK, the sound of a bat could be heard. Just then, in my pocket my cell phone rang. BRRRINNNNG. BRRRRRIIIINNNNNG. The doctor removed it.

"Hello?"

"Yes, I'm looking for the owner of Spots."

"Oh, one moment please."

He handed the phone to Sassafras.

"Hello?"

"Hi. Do you own a Dalmatian dog by the name of Spots?"

"Yes. Do you have him?"

"Oh, ma'am, I'm sorry to tell you. The dog has been seriously injured."

"Where have you found him?"

"He's on the sidewalk in front of a home here in Land Park. I was going on a walk when I saw him."

"Oh my God, where is he?"

"It's at 2911 Tenth Street."

Sassafras put the phone down.

"Oh God, that's his house."

She realized right then and there that Spots was out with me on the levy and somehow had followed this man home, and somehow, when the man came out and heard Spots barking incessantly, the man did something terrible to the dog.

"Can you tell me what's wrong with him?"

"I can't. All I can tell you is he's lying down, he's crying, whining, and he needs help."

The police realized what was going on and took Sassafras aside.

"Who is it? Who did it?"

She told them.

"Mr. Brett Clawney. Our dog apparently followed him, and he's right there right now. We have to go get him."

"You want to leave your husband here?"

"My husband's in excellent hands right now. I want to go get our dog."

"Let's go."

Adam and Alex followed out to the parking lot near the ER entry area. They got into the police car and tore off to Mr. Clawney's house. They were there in a matter of moments. Several people had gathered around Spots. They were down on their knees petting him. He was whining. They were taking excellent care of him, but they didn't know what to do. Spots had suffered a beating very similar to mine: Clawney had smashed him in the ribs, smashed him in the back, smashed him on the head. Spots had been barking incessantly. He was trying to make a marker of this assailant of his master. In an attempt to get this guy caught, he risked his life and nearly died.

The good news is that he wouldn't die. He would be okay. Sassafras arrived and saw the state of affairs. She looked to the police with these eyes that said, I don't know what to do. Please help me. Officers are often quite good in situations like this. Now, they could've called Animal Control. It would've taken about fifteen minutes for an Animal Control officer to show up. During that time, Spots may very well have died. Instead, they gently lifted Spots up, put him into the police car, and tore off to the veterinary hospital not far from our house.

This place knew Spots well. The doctor came out. He was used to seeing Spots in a hyper mode, a gorgeous Dalmatian, a unique champion dog. Today the dog was near dead.

"Oh my god, what happened to him?"

"I'm not sure, Doctor. That's why we brought him here."

The doctor looked to the nurse.

"Anesthetics, X-ray, let's go."

They pulled out all the stops. Three nurses came out, two doctors, they put Spots on a small gurney, took him back to the X-ray room to see what the heck was wrong with him. Similar to my injuries, broken cranium, hematoma developing, broken rib. Unfortunately the rib had punctured a lung and the lung was filling up with blood. He was in the process of suffocating on his own blood. He had a collapsed lung. It was a very serious situation. They would have to operate immediately. They would remove half of his lung, suture it up, drain all the blood. He would have one and a half lungs from here on out. The good news is that you can live with one and a half lungs.

They drained his hematoma in the same way that the doctors were draining mine. They fixed and reset his rib, they taped his abdomen, and they put him under a deep anesthesia where he would sleep and sleep and sleep. It would be several days, but Spots would make it.

Sassafras and the boys returned to the hospital where I was. During this process, Clawney had been placed under arrest on one count of attempted murder, one count of assault with a deadly weapon, and one count of animal abuse. He would later be forced into a plea bargain that would fetch twenty-five to life.

That man was going away forever. Again, that would not help me in my state. I slipped into a coma. Days went by. The doctors had the sensors on my brain. The whole time, one thing that could be seen was my brain was highly active. The little readers that form an ink printout were going off the charts. Adam figured it out first. The doctors were quite puzzled at why a coma patient would be so mentally active.

"He's writing a book."

The music "Zombie" continued to play in my mind. I thought about the entire story that you're reading right now. And just so you know the somewhat happy ending of all this, the proof that I come out of this coma is the fact that you're reading this book right now. My brainwaves would continue like this for days and days. The doctor watched it and printed it out. Adam and Alex looked at the printout and saw all the little electrodes at work in the form of inkjet printers showing brain activity up and down and all around. There were points at which I would rest. It was like I was still having a day of work and a night of rest, and then I would get busy again in the day and start thinking about this entire story from start to finish.

I went through our entire relationship from the very beginning when I met this girl in Florence, when I saw her at the train station, when I tried to find her on the train to return that jade earring, when I started to call her all the time, when I went and visited her, when she dumped me the first time and she dumped me the second time and the third time and the fourth time and the fifth time. I went through the entire saga.

Chapter 78
FLY ON THE BED

You have probably heard the saying "I wish I could have been a fly on the wall."

The saying shows a desire to be present, but not visible, during a discussion between others. We want to know what they are saying, but we realize if we were known to be present it would impact what they say, and more significantly, what they don't say.

It is a desire to spy on others.

In the incident about to be reported, I was lying in my hospital bed in a coma, when none other than Mrs. Brett Clawney showed up to speak with Sassafras. Ooooh, I am so happy to actually be a fly in the bed to hear this discussion.

Here is how it went. She arrived, a full eight months pregnant, with a lovely bouquet of flowers. It was a tightly wound group of short cut white roses placed into a rectangular glass vase, six in a row times two made twelve. The vase had some kind of green tea leaves in it, so there was a mix of emerald green against the white roses. Quite lovely.

"Hello. I hope you don't mind, but I brought some flowers for your husband."

Any woman that is pregnant will not be the least bit threatening to another woman. She figured for some reason that Sassafras knew who she was. This was an incorrect assumption. Sassafras thought it strange that this large white woman would be bringing me flowers.

"Excuse me, what is your name?"

"Oh, I'm sorry. I thought you knew who I was. I am Laura Clawney, Brett's wife."

Oh boy, here we go.

Sassafras studied her up and down and examined every outward and inner curve of her very pregnant belly. She was at the point where he bellybutton had popped out; what was an inny was now an outy.

"I didn't know you were pregnant."

She was in a kidding mood, for some reason. "Honey sometimes I don't believe it myself. Somebody pinch me!"

I don't think Sassafras understood this idiom; she didn't smile at it. They awkwardly stood in silence for a moment, and then both said simultaneously, "I am so sorry."

Sassafras was puzzled at why Laura was sorry.

"I don't understand. I am sorry for having an affair with your husband. Please believe me when I say if I had known you were pregnant I would have never done that."

"Oh, it wouldn't make a difference if you had an affair or not; either way there would have been an affair."

"Why do you say that?"

"My goodness, I hope you don't think you are the only one. There have been at least three others. Do you know about the Russian girl?"

Sassafras spoke in a quiet tone. "Russian girl?"

"Oh god, she is just awful. Thick lips, way too much lipstick; I don't know what he sees in her. Plus she smokes, it's just disgusting. I swear to God I've kissed him and I can taste the bubble gum lipstick and cigarette smoke from his lips. How sick is that?"

They were silent as they pondered the bubble gum and cigarette taste. Laura continued.

"Then there is the Vietnamese cutie pie. Did you know about her?"

"Vietnamese cutie? No."

"Now, she was a pretty one. Hell, I wanted to sleep with her. Cute as a button. She wore these nice little shirts. Oh, what the hell."

Sassafras was saddened to learn of this. It is a sad reality of women that cheat with men that, generally speaking, the man they are cheating with is a complete cheater himself.

Oddly, there can be an anger by a cheater who cheats on another cheater. There is a similar parallel of a thief who steals a car, and then someone else steals the car from the thief. The thief will go crazy with anger. He is, after all, a victim of a theft.

It is a bit ironic, but a cheater whose lover also cheats on him becomes a victim. This irony does not stop the bitter feeling.

"Why does he have so many women?"

"It's hard to say. First off, his Dad was the same way. Perhaps it's inherited. His dad fooled around on his mom big time."

"I heard about that."

"Plus he has this guilt thing going on."

"What's that?"

"Did you know his Dad died recently?"

"Yes."

"Did you know just before his Dad died, he asked Brett, he begged him, could he please come live with us? I was more than happy to say yes to this. I believe in family, and family always comes first."

Sassafras smiled at her values.

"But Brett wouldn't have it. He told his Dad no. About one month later, his Dad died. Probably died of loneliness. Brett feels just awful about it. He thinks maybe he killed his Dad."

The discussion of death brought both sets of female eyes over to me. Laura said it again, "I'm so sorry about your husband."

"But this isn't your doing, it isn't your fault."

"In a way, it is. I received the copies of the emails between you and Brett, and I went berserk over them. If I had been a bit more calm, perhaps Brett would not have reacted in such an animal way."

Sassafras held her head low about the emails. They were embarrassing to her. She said so many things there she didn't want me to see, and certainly didn't want Laura to see.

"I'm so sorry about the emails. I hope you know they aren't real."

"What is real, what is not real, I don't know."

She patted her stomach. This much was clearly quite real.

"Here is what I know. My husband will be in prison for a long time. Unfortunately, 'roid rage' isn't a defense. Your husband may be dead. You and I may end up being single moms. All this over an affair with a serial cheater who abandoned his father during his last days. How pathetic is that?"

Sassafras realized an important and simple lesson: an affair can kill a family. She had seen the affair as just having a little fun; no big deal, just a little action on the side. But hear this: *An affair will absolutely kill your family.* You will end up a single mom, your family will be split up into two different, much smaller homes, and your entire life will be upended.

Before you go and do this, look at the endgame and ask yourself, is it really worth it? If you really want to end your marriage once and for all, go for it. If you just want to get some attention, talk to your husband about your issues, and maybe he will listen and do something about it.

Doesn't your husband at least deserve a chance to try to make things right?

Sassafras quietly thought about this lesson, and then reacted.

"I can't believe I risked my own family, everything I have, for this cheater."

I smiled to myself. One of the unexpected benefits of delivering that email to Laura was this meeting between the wives. Never in my wildest imagination could I have predicted this would occur.

The information given during this meeting brought Sassafras to a new state, a state of being completely and irretrievably emotionally over Brett. She wouldn't just refrain from seeing him; now she didn't *want* to see him. She was disgusted by him.

So I got two birds in one email. I managed to get a form of revenge on Brett. Say what you want about it, it helped me immensely. And as an added kicker, and indeed perhaps the best benefit of all, I had managed to get Sassafras into forever puking out her passion for him, even down to dry heaves. That man was burnt toast.

Sassafras was crying and crying. Laura hugged her.

"It's okay honey, live and learn. Hopefully it's not too late."

Laura came over to me, then turned to Sassafras. "He will come out of this, I just know it."

Sassafras continued crying.

"I did this. It's my fault."

This was a terrible burden for her. Laura tried to help.

"No, Brett did this, not you. It's like you just told me seconds ago: it's not my fault, it's Brett's doing. Let's you and I not beat ourselves up over this. Brett will have to pay the price."

Laura looked at me.

"Of course he will have to pay the price. Poor dear."

"Look at him, he looks so peaceful."

The two of them watched me in my coma, realizing that for every action there is an opposite and wholly unequal reaction.

Their conversation continued for about two and a half hours, interrupted only by Laura's need to pee. The baby was pressing against her bladder, and she had to go.

Chapter 79
HOW TO HELP YOUR HUSBAND OUT OF A COMA

I was now about a month into this coma. Sassafras felt just terrible about how her affair had caused all this grief, destruction, and serious injury. She looked over to Adam and Alex. They were more fascinated by my brainwaves. They didn't concern themselves with the idea that I was going to die because they knew I wasn't going to die. Instead, they watched.

The doctor then noticed something.

"Okay, Adam and Alex, I need you guys to wait out in the hallway. Sassafras, you stay here. Nurse, take them out."

Nobody knew what the doctor was talking about. The nurse took them out.

"Yes?"

"Sassafras, I've noticed something. Normally, in these coma patients, the process of coming out of it can be sudden, where a person's in a coma for years and then, voila, they open their eyes and they're back to planet earth. Other times, it happens gradually. This may be a gradual case where we're going to have some muscle movement to begin with. Maybe a leg will twitch, an arm will twitch. Generally what we do in this case is we want to rub that arm. If you bring touch to it, the body will react to that, and often it can twitch and move more. And as that starts moving more, other parts of the body start to move, and the whole process of coming out of the coma can start."

"Doctor, did you see part of his body move?"

The doctor pointed to my pelvic area. Sassafras hadn't noticed it, but the doctor had. I had a full erection. He could see it in the form of a small pup tent on the blanket. Sassafras was embarrassed.

"Ohh, I see."

The doctor explained to her, "Now, if this was his arm moving, I would be giving you the following medical advice: rub the arm. I would tell you to rub it and keep rubbing it and make it move more. So I've got to tell you, I want you to do the same thing to that. I might add, if it was his arm I'd probably have a nurse do it, but given what it is, I'm not going to have my nurse do it. You are the one who can do it. Here's what I'd like to do. We're all going to leave the room. I want you to rub him and rub him good."

He handed her a bottle of cream. He and the other nurse exited the room. She was alone with me for the first time in quite awhile. She shook her head.

"I can't believe I've got to jack off my comatose husband."

She put hand cream on me and proceeded to jack me off. Within a matter of a minute, she walked out of the room. The doctor was pacing in the hallway.

"Yes? Is there a problem?"

"No problem."

"Well?"

"We're done."

"You're done with what?"

"Doctor, do I need to spell it out?"

"That fast?"

"That fast."

And it would proceed the following day in the same way. I would wake up with a hard on. She would take care of it. Slowly I started moving my hips and gyrating to this sexual stimulus. The doctor asked her about it.

"Are any other parts of him moving?"

"Yes. His hips, now his legs."

And then it became my arms, and then it became my mouth as I started to pucker up, wanting a kiss. She also advanced the situation by using more than just her hand. She kissed me, she held me, she stroked me. She used her mouth, she got me going. There was a point at which she was actually getting on top of me. I started moving more and more, and finally, one day, I opened my eyes and looked at her. I had one question: "Do you love me?"

She smiled down at me as she was gyrating on my hips. I was no longer comatose. I would make it. I would live. I would live to tell this story. I would live to raise my sons, and I would live to stay with my wife and to keep us all as a family.

She stated, "I love you."

EPILOGUE

I have read about so many ways in which a writer will get their book or screenplay down to Hollywood. Somebody apparently slipped a script under a pepperoni pizza that was delivered to Harrison Ford. I don't know if that stuff really works, but there's always the question of how to get in through the Hollywood filtering system.

While I was in a comatose state, a period of approximately six months passed. While the cops were developing the case, they listened to the rest of my tape that had the story of ultimate revenge. Because the resultant criminal case involved an A-list actor, the contents of that tape became a public news event. It was shown on 20/20, CNN, Fox News, the works. There was even an article in the *Wall Street Journal* about it.

Well, guess what, a producer picked it up, and at long last, as I lay comatose, it would turn out that the book I hadn't even been able to complete would be my first book to make it to the big silver screen. Weiner Brothers picked it up, Tim Cruze would play the role of the victim fiancé, Silem Paltrow took the role of the rape victim, and Evan McGregen played the role of the rapist. What happens in Hollywood is like this: an unknown writer gets discovered, one movie makes it, and then some smart producer asks, "What else does this guy have?"

They went back and pulled out my *Katie Cranberry* book. It was in vogue right now. It was perfect timing, and at last it, too, would be picked up and made into a television adventure series. Don't worry, I won't quit my day job.

Brett ended up getting just four years in prison, owing to his highly skilled criminal defense lawyer. He received three years for the assault on me, and one year for the assault on Spots. As they were crimes involving violence with serious bodily injury, he would have to serve 85 percent of his time.

His attorney came up with a roid rage defense that the judge saw, not as something that created a lack of guilt, but which did go to the issue of a mitigation of his sentence. Brett made some nice promises to assist some charities, and agreed to come out in public about his roid rage issues toward the overall goal of convincing men all over to stop taking those dangerous drugs.

When he gets out, he will hopefully reunite with his wife and son, and live life as a better man. Sassafras and I both wish them the best of luck in keeping their family under one roof.

You may naturally challenge the following part of this ending as being a tad too perfect, but here is how it went.

Sometimes you don't have to lift a finger to make things happen. That *Strega Noña* in Italy finally faced justice. It seems she went a bit too far with the fictitious markups on the artwork from China, and at last, an Italian tax official figured it out. She was busted on sixteen counts of tax fraud, and did a deal that kept her out of prison for sixteen years, opting instead for a mere three years. Under Italian law she would do half of that time, and would spend three years on parole.

This created a custody hand-off situation with Sassara. Sassafras received a call from her Torino lawyer. The judge had called him and told him to contact Sassafras, and to ask her to come to Torino to pick up her daughter.

Oh my, we are getting a new daughter. An Italian/Swiss/Chinese supermodel in the making. She is 16 years old, has barely detectable Asian eyes, stands at five foot ten inches, and speaks Italian and a moderate level of English. Hello, *Sports Illustrated*.

We decided to send Adam over with Sassafras, so she could meet her brother again. Adam had just finished a three and a half week training session and a Kung Fu tournament held in China, and flew in on a flight from Shanghai with a gold medal and a silver medal. He left the same day with Sassafras for Milano, Italy, and took a train to Torino.

This time it was different; Sassara wanted to come to California. The dark influence of *Strega Noña* didn't reach out from inside the prison walls. She was freed from this terrible woman, and at last came to unite with her mother, Sassafras.

Spots made it through his ordeal as well, and gave me some telepathy that said in dog language, "I want a girlfriend." So we got him Diamond, a female Dalmatian. She will become his wife as soon as she grows out of her puppy stage.

We will have a big church wedding for them, and you are invited.

We present to you this special family: Herman, Sassafras, Sassara, Adam, Alex, and the Dalmatian dogs, Mr. and Mrs. Spots.

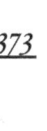

Appendix A:
Post Affair Book Resources

Post Affair Book Resources and Summaries

Books on Infidelity Issues, from Barnes & Noble website (www.bn.com)

Post Affair

1. **The Truth About Cheating: Why Men Stray and What You Can Do to Prevent It** *by M. Gary Neuman*

Wiley, John & Sons,

September 2008

From the Publisher

The *New York Times* bestselling look at the real reasons for male marital infidelity and what might prevent it.

Few events cause as much turmoil in a marriage as infidelity. It can shatter trust and breed insecurity and resentment from which some relationships never recover. People who think it won't happen to them are hit that much harder when it does. Why are men unfaithful? Can infidelity be prevented? What do men say they're getting from their mistresses that they're missing at home? Do a man's friends have anything to do with his willingness to cheat?

In this *New York Times* bestselling book, experienced family counselor M. Gary Neuman shares the revealing and surprising findings of a cutting-edge research study in which he interviewed men across the country who have physically cheated on their wives. Neuman shares many shocking discoveries, including the prominent role of emotional dissatisfaction in motivating husbands who stray and how small a role sexual dissatisfaction plays.

Based on a groundbreaking study of both cheating men and men who have remained faithful

Reveals surprising findings on the contribution of sexual and emotional dissatisfaction to male infidelity

Written by experienced family counselor M. Gary Neuman, coauthor of *In Good Times and Bad* and author of *Emotional Infidelity*

Neuman and *The Truth about Cheating* were featured twice on *The Oprah Winfrey Show*

Drawing on dramatic case stories of the author's own work with clients, *The Truth about Cheating* includes proactive strategies and action steps for married women to help them preventinfidelity and create a faithful and rewarding marriage.

Publishers Weekly

Neuman (*Emotional Infidelity*) attempts to arm wives with the tools to prevent their husbands from cheating by drawing upon questionnaires and interviews with 100 men who reported sexual affairs. According to the author's research, sexual dissatisfaction within their marriages rated fourth and emotional dissatisfaction first as reasons given for straying. Neuman notes that only "12% of cheating men said that the mistress was more physically attractive than their wives," thereby reinforcing findings that men were missing an emotional connection in their marriages (whether this is intended to serve as comfort to their wives is unclear). Neuman introduces "The Innervoice Recognition Formula" and "Quick Action Program," challenging women to revise assumptions about marriage, make immediate behavioral changes and forge new bonds with their husbands, thereby deterring future dalliances. While some wives might find this book helpful, it is perhaps more likely that readers will wish that the author had devoted more time to holding the cheating husband responsible for his actions rather than putting the onus on wives to take preventive-and dubiously effective-measures. *(Sept.)*

2. **Emotional Infidelity : How to Affair-Proof Your Marriage and 10 Other Secrets to a Great Relationship** *M. Gary Neuman* Publisher: Random House Inc

Pub. Date: September 2002

Synopsis

What's holding you back from a great marriage?

"I don't believe in 'okay,' 'decent,' or 'solid' marriages. I'm against them," says M. Gary Neuman. "I believe only in great marriages, and that you should expect and reach for no less." In the last fifteen years, M. Gary Neuman, marital therapist and architect of the Sandcastles Divorce Therapy Program, has helped thousands of couples in crisis. Couples who fight. Who've grown apart. Who are stuck in relationships that run more on routine and rancor than love and understanding. What he's found is that, contrary to popular belief, the problem is usually not poor communication. It's the failure to put most of your focus into your marriage. You've only got so much energy. Are you spending it by being emotionally unfaithful?

Take a quick check: Do you send that funny e-mail to your friends at work—but not to your spouse? Do you chew over all the problems on the job so thoroughly with your colleagues that by the time you get home, you just don't feel like going into it all over again? Do you get a secret thrill out of flirting with coworkers—thinking it's safe because you know it's not going any further? If so, you're committing emotional infidelity—and you're draining your marriage of the energy it needs to be great. Learning how to break this cycle is one of eleven secrets M. Gary Neuman shares in his provocative new book.

Based on the ten-week program he's developed in his successful couples counseling practice, the book offers guidelines that are often counterintuitive, even outrageous or shocking. But they work. Dare to limit contact with members of the opposite sex. Dare toneed each other. Dare to put in writing the nitty-gritty realities of a marriage plan. Dare to put your marriage before your kids or job. Dare to make love in a whole new way. Dare to change your focus: make the commitment to focus on each of the eleven secrets (ten plus one bonus secret) for one week apiece and you'll reap the rewards of a transformed marriage and a reconfirmed relationship.

M. Gary Neuman's program is guaranteed to challenge you and make you reexamine the myths holding you back from true happiness and satisfaction. It will change your marriage forever.

3.   **After the Affair : Healing the Pain and Rebuilding Trust When a Partner Has Been Unfaithful***Janis A. Spring, Michael Spring, Michael Spring*

Publisher: HarperCollins Publishers

Pub. Date: January 1996

Synopsis

For the 70 percent of couples who have been affected by extramarital affairs, this is the only book to offer proven strategies for surviving the crisis and rebuilding the relationship — written by a nationally known therapist considered an expert on infidelity.

When I was 15, I was raped. That was nothing compared to your affair. The rapist was a stranger; you, I thought, were my best friend.

There is nothing quite like the pain and shock caused when a partner has been unfaithful. The hurt partner often experiences a profound loss of self–respect and falls into a depression that can last for years. For the relationship, infidelity is often a death blow.

After the Affair is the first book to help readers survive this crisis. Written by a clinical psychologist who has been treating distressed couples for 22 years, it guides both hurt and unfaithful partners through the three stages of healing: Normalizing feelings, deciding whether to recommit and revitalizing the relationship. It provides proven, practical advice to help the couple change their behavior toward each other, cultivate trust and forgiveness and build a healthier, more conscious intimate partnership.

4. **Not "Just Friends" : Rebuilding Trust and Recovering Your Sanity after Infidelity** *Shirley P. Glass, Shirley Glass, Jean Coppock Staeheli*

Publisher: Simon & Schuster Adult Publishing Group

Pub. Date: February 200

Synopsis

You're right to be cautious when you hear these words: "I'm telling you, we're just friends."

Good people in good marriages are having affairs. The workplace and the Internet have become fertile breeding grounds for "friendships" that can slowly and insidiously turn into love affairs. Yet you can protect your relationship from emotional or sexual betrayal by recognizing the red flags that mark the stages of slipping into an improper, dangerous intimacy that can threaten your marriage.

5. **How Can I Forgive You?** *Janis A. Spring, Michael Spring, Michael Spring*

Publisher: HarperCollins Publishers

Pub. Date: February 2005

Synopsis

Janis Abrahms Spring's long–awaited second book expertly tackles the sensitive issue of forgiveness by giving real people a new model from which they can heal from interpersonal injuries, by debunking myths, and by controversially setting the record straight that forgiveness is not the only all–or–nothing sound response to injury

The topic of forgiveness is fast becoming one of the key concepts in psychotherapy. With illuminating anecdotes and case material based on nearly 30 years of clinical experience, Janis Spring controversially reveals that we have more options than just forgiving or not forgiving. From forgotten birthdays to deliberate sexual offences, infidelity and disloyalty, *How Can I Forgive You?* takes a bold new position that frees us from the corrosive effects of hate and helps us to make peace with both the person who has hurt us and with ourselves. By providing concrete, step–by–step instructions for both the hurt party and the offender, Spring brings to light a new, empowering model that is bound to change forever the way we think about forgiveness, regardless of whether or not the offending party is willing to apologize.

6. **Infidelity: A Survival Guide *by Don-David Lusterman***

Publisher: New Harbinger Pubns Inc

Pub. Date: January 1998

Synopsis

An expert with years of success in helping couples overcome infidelity shows how a marriage can not only survive but be stronger after couples confront the reasons behind indiscretions.

7. **Intimacy after Infidelity: How to Rebuild and Affair-Proof Your Marriage *by Steven Solomon, Lorie Teagno***

Publisher: New Harbinger Publications

Pub. Date: November 2006

Synopsis

While trying to cope with the pain of knowing that their partners have cheated, victims of infidelity have to wrestle with two big questions: whether to stay in the relationship and, if they do stay, how to best prevent experiencing this kind of hurt ever again. In this book, two relationship experts offer a new way of understanding the causes and types of infidelity and innovative new ways to "affair-proof" recovered or new relationships.

The book begins with an overview of the phenomenon of infidelity and the way a long-term relationship develops over times. The book develops a three-type model of intimacy and infidelity and analyzes each. The authors include a discussion of how to evaluate a relationship for infidelity risks and how to choose a partner that is less likely to be unfaithful.

8. **Transcending Post-Infidelity Stress Disorder: The Six Stages of Healing** *by Dennis C. Ortman Ph.D. (Celestial Arts 2009)*

Synopsis

A psychologist uses post-traumatic stress disorder as a model for the wounded partner to explore rage and emotional pain and learn the secrets of recovery.

The discovery of a partner's infidelity is heart-wrenching and traumatic. In TRANSCENDING POST-INFIDELITY STRESS DISORDER (PISD), Dennis Ortman likens the psychological aftermath of sexual betrayal to post-traumatic stress disorder (PTSD) in its origin and symptoms, including anxiety, irritability, rage, emotional numbing, and flashbacks. Using PTSD treatment as a model, Dr. Ortman presents steps to recovery from the pain of infidelity. With the author's PISD system, readers will find a structure to help them categorize emotions, face their rage, make important life decisions, and find wholeness, peace, and forgiveness.

9. **Obsessive Love: When It Hurts Too Much to Let Go** *by Susan Forward, Craig Buck* (Bantam Books 2002

Synopsis

Is it impossible to let go—despite the pain?

- Do you yearn for someone who is not physically or emotionally available to you?
- Do you believe that if you love him enough he will have to love you?
- When you feel insecure, does it drive you only to want her more?
- Do you find yourself phoning repeatedly or waiting long hours for the phone to ring?

Do you wish someone would let go of you?

- Does an ex-lover or ex-spouse refuse to believe that it's over?
- • Do you receive unwanted phone calls, letters, presents, or visits?
- • Is this pursuit of you creating so much anxiety that it affects your physical or emotional well-being?

In this invaluable self-help guide, Dr. Susan Forward presents vivid case histories as well as the real-life voices of men and women caught in the grip of obsessive passion.

Whether you're an obsessive lover or the target of such an obsession, here is a proven, step-by-step program that shows you how to recognize the "connection compulsion," what causes it, and how to break its hold on your life so that you can go on to build healthy, lasting, and pain-free relationships.

10. **Surviving Infidelity: Making Decisions, Recovering from the Pain** *by Rona B. Subotnik, Gloria Harris* (3rd Ed. 2005 Adams Media)

Synopsis

An all-new edition of a leading book on the subject, "Surviving Infidelity" offers nonjudgmental, compassionate emphasis on practical recovery from a painful experience.

11. **Divorce Sucks: What to do when irreconcilable differences, lawyer fees, and your ex's Hollywood wife make you miserable** *by Mary Jo Eustace, Joanne Kimes* (Adams Media 2009)

Synopsis

Hock the platinum. Take down the vacation photos. Cancel the joint checking account.

There's no question . . . Divorce Sucks. And perhaps no one knows that better than author Mary Jo Eustace, whose ex-husband Dean McDermott married Tori Spelling a mere thirty days after their divorce was finalized. One part tell-all and one part guide to get readers on their feet after a bitter breakup, this hilarious addition to the bestselling Sucks series tells everything readers don't want to know about divorce—from what a phone call with a lawyer will cost; to how to handle your newer, younger replacement; to what Hollywood divorcees are actually thinking when they watch their ex walk the red carpet with a millionairess. Sometimes horrifying, sometimes gratifying, and never merciful, this book will give readers an inside look at one of today's most public divorces while reminding them—hey, it could always be worse.

Appendix B:
I Remember, by Herman Franck, Esq.

This is a document that will give the reader some pause to think about how these occurrences can really mess a person up. If it seems a bit raw, it's because it is me.

I have learned this simple advice about the problem of remembering: wear a rubber band around your wrist [or neck, if you wish]. When you have these bad memories, pull on the rubber band and let it thwack you.

The memory will at least temporarily vanish.

I Remember by Herman Franck, Esq.

West Sacramento, September 2, 2009

I remember you going out to clubs and God knows where else, staying out to 3 a.m. in the morning. I remember asking you to come and kiss me when you got home, and you refused. I asked quite a few times, but I never got a kiss.

I remember going to a Felix's official function at the Rice Bowl during late September 2008, and you brought Tyrone. I sat at the table and met him. I saw his gold chain, gold watch, and giggled to myself.

The next night you came home late at night from Fairfield. At 1:20 a.m. you managed to get caught speeding. You little bandito.

So you brought him as a date to Felix's party. What a mean ass thing to do. That is what I thought.

I remember seeing him again at my birthday party. I thought it odd that Sandra was dancing with another man, Dr. Stuart.

I remember Tyrone oddly explaining to me how rich he was. His grandmother had come over from Italy as a poor immigrant. She purchased quite a bit of property in Elk Grove, property the family didn't even know about. When she died they found a group of deeds, and sold them all. The family made more than $20 million off of this. Not bad.

I thought it was odd that he was explaining all of this to me.

I remember the next night you came home at 3 a.m. I was sleeping on the couch, and saw you come in. I was so surprised. It was the night after my birthday, a Sunday night, and you were out until 3 am? What was up?

So I asked you. Instead of apologizing you said rather rudely, "The time passed." Then you proceeded to give me a series of insults:

"You are poor, fat, ugly, stupid, awful, mean, terrible, etc."

I would hear these same insults during the next several months.

I remember hearing you tell me, "this is the new me, the new Sabrina, and you better get used to it."

I remember moving out of the house, living alone in a group home in Sacramento. It was off of Watt avenue. I told you, as to the new Sabrina, thanks but no thanks. I'll pass.

I remember you asking me to come by and have a night with you. I agreed to do so. When I arrived you completely ignored me. During the evening you asked me two times: "Who are you, why are you here and why are you in my house?"

I remember leaving that night. You called me and left a voicemail. You said "I see you driving away. You just left. This is your way."

Indeed it is my way. When you treat me poorly I don't hang around for it. How simple is that. For some reason you want to give me a bunch of shit and expect me to hang around for it.

I remember in November when Lee got out of jail, and we had a nice meeting with Jorge and Anne. You didn't come. Instead you were with Tyrone. I remember coming home and seeing your phone with long calls to him. I remember speaking with you about it. You were very mean, angry, and insulting.

I remember understanding that every time you spoke with him you became super mean to me. I remember speaking with you about it, and you didn't care a shit about it.

I remember that Monday morning driving to depositions in the Lutge case. I called Tyrone. He told me you and he were just friends. A friend that he asked to marry, so what a bunch of bull that was.

I remember him telling me that you had told him not to speak with him any more. So this would have been break up number one for you two.

I know now that within a couple of weeks of that he asked you to marry him. During this time I was busy on a three week trial in San Francisco.

I remember you came and visited me during the trial. You brought Spots. We snuck him into the hotel in a duffle bag.

I remember you attacked me that night. You insulted me for a million hours over the same stuff I'd been hearing over and over from you:

"You are poor, you are fat, you are ugly, blah blah blah"

I remember the next day thinking you and I are forever done with our marriage, that I had lost you forever and that I would never in a million years get you back. I began the process right there of accepting this as a fact.

I remember Sandra telling me that this was the new Sabrina and that I had better get used to it because that was the way it was going to be. I remember thinking I don't want this new Sabrina at all. I want a divorce.

I remember seeing a video from a birthday party over at Peyee's house. Steve took it. During the video you are seen on it receiving a text message, excitedly opening it, and then going outside to make a phone call. I remember Adam explaining to me that you had a one hour phone call with Tryone that night.

I remember Adam telling me that you were in the bedroom with Adam and Alex, speaking with Peyee about Tryone. She was telling you to stop this. You told her you would.

I remember somehow during late November you became nice again to me, and for about 30 days remained nice. We went to Tommy's Christmas party, and Gina's New Year's Eve party. We had a nice time. You looked very beautiful.

Then during January or so it picked back up again. You became mean, angry, and started going out with Tryone again.

I remember receiving text messages from you: "I am not going to be your wife today." And you would be gone for the day, gone with Tryone.

I remember seeing your phone and text messages. I remember the one from the other man that wanted "to blow cum" on you. Strange stuff.

I remember you telling me that you couldn't help what these other men wrote you.

I remember you telling me you had to go to the hospital to care for Tryone. You spent the night at the hospital. Two nights. I had to take Adam and Alex with me to court in San Francisco. We left early in the morning. I had tried to reach you that night but you shut me out.

That was an awful night for me, a night I will never forget.

You and I got into some big arguments during this time. You told me you had three boyfriends and could marry any one of them in a snap. You may not remember this statement, but I do. I remember it as though you said it yesterday. I will never forget what you said.

Then that weekend you gave me the text message I will also never forget: "I am going away for the weekend. Don't worry I'm not sleeping around."

And you left for three days. We didn't hear from you. We couldn't reach you. It was the worst weekend of my life. I will never forget this weekend. I watched LMN movies about cheating and betrayal the entire time. I learned how women can do this, when they do it, why they do this, how they do this. I learned that there isn't much a man can do about it. We are hopeless, we must just move on.

You went to Las Vegas, and met up with Tryone there. You want me to believe you just happened to run into him at the airport. You must think the entire world is really stupid to come up with such a remark.

I remember understanding very clearly that our marriage was over. When you came back you were screaming at me about how much I spent on Kit Media projects and stuff like that. You are the only wife that hates her husband for writing books.

I remember you and I agreed that night to get a divorce. That was probably the smartest thing I've ever done with you. Not following through with it was probably the stupidest thing I've done.

The next day I prepared the papers, and was ready to file them. I managed to find an apartment from David our landlord. It upset you that I was talking to David about this.

I remember telling you that David had gone through the same thing with his first wife, and he is still very much hurting from it. I am sure his first wife never said sorry, never really understood the hurt she caused him. I am sure Naomi, Bruce's first wife, is the same way.

Women will do these things without any sympathy for the man.

I remember Gina telling me "when a woman does this to her husband, she has lost all respect for him, and has fallen out of love. She is gone forever."

I remember Sandra telling me "Herman, you have to understand, Sabrina doesn't love you anymore. She wants Tryone, and has him. He is the man for her."

I remember you oddly telling me not to file the divorce, not to move out, that if I did you "would act like a single woman." I thought, wow, how are you already acting? But I stupidly agreed not to file the divorce.

I remember we had a series of nice lunches, and had what I come to know as a fake reconciliation. You smiled, you were sweet. The entire time you were still dating Tryone and were sleeping with him.

You were also sleeping with me during this time. I got your second serving. I had to kiss your mouth where his cock was. I am sure I tasted his cock. I am sure I tasted his cock quite a few times when I licked and sucked on you.

I am sure I tasted his cock when he raped me.

I will never forget these things.

I remember coming home and your email was on. I read the series of emails between you and he. He said he loved you, you said you loved him. He talked about giving you orgasms, and how you and he were so perfect in bed together.

I remember the weird email where he describes how he is going to bring the boys to bed, kiss them good night, clean the house, and then come downstairs and make love to you. How weird is that! This man was taking over my wife, my two boys, my family, everything. You allowed that to happen, and I will never forget it.

I will never forget those emails! I have them printed out and every now and then I read them. They are so amazing, so much love between the two of you, and it made me wonder, why don't you just get married to him?

I remember understanding that you were lost in love with another man. I remember accepting this fact as a done deal. I remember how sad I was, how terrible it was to understand this. I cried a million tears. My heart went below my pants.

I will never in a million years forget these times.

The emails talked about your dates, about Saturdays away from the house shooting a gun, about making love at his house, about other dates, it was just terrible to read.

I will never forget the day I understood through those emails that you and I had a fake reconciliation and that you were endlessly in love with Tryone.

I remember the night you caught the text message from Serena. I was moving in with her the next day. I had filed for divorce. *Franck v Chen,* Yolo County Superior Court.

I was going away with a new love. She was so sweet to me, you have no idea. She used to look at me, smile at me, tell me she loved me, put her head on my shoulders, hold my hand, all the things I wanted you to do, she did.

I told the boys I was moving out with Serena, and that they had a choice to stay with you or with me. I told them I would love to have them with me.

The boys agreed to come with me. I told them this has to be their honest choice, and they told me it was.

We were all going to leave you in your little shitty house, to be free to have Tryone. We all knew that this was all you really cared about. You didn't need us, you didn't need our small life, the small law office, the small house, the old cars, you didn't need any of that. You just needed Tryone and that was that.

We were ready to all move away from you and start a new life with Serena.

Then you scared her away. You told her, "I will make your pretty face ugly." Nobody ever told her that before. I saw how Tryone and his violent ways had become your way too. I thought, wow, this guy really got to Sabrina. I thought that I can never get him out of her heart and soul, he is with her forever.

I remember telling you that you and I could only stay together if you agreed to build me a mountain. You promised me you would.

I remember the email you sent to Tryone, telling him how ashamed you were of your relationship with him, and how you needed to return to your family. I remember I didn't believe a word of it, I was sure you would see him within a week.

You agreed to build me a mountain. Then you received word from Lugano that your daughter was coming. This made you forget about your promise to build me a mountain. The shovel is still outside in the front yard, untouched.

Then we went to LA, and had our marriage recommitment. I remember during that ceremony hearing you tell the Rabbi how miserable you were with me. Did you know how miserable you made me? Insulting me all the time, all the bitter energy coming from your mouth every day? Having an affair with another man, etc, etc? You were miserable, but I was even more miserable.

You have issues with me, I have issues with you.

I remember on the way home from the ceremony you started screaming at me about your situation with Amy at work that happened about a hundred years ago. I was ready to throw my new ring out of the fucking window.

I asked myself how can I get rid of this endless bitching by this endless bitch? Of course, the answer is I can't. You will never be happy with me, you will always hate me, you will always think I am a terrible husband. You will never forgive me etc, etc.

I remember all of these things. I am not over any of them. Writing this has helped a little.

Today after court I will go visit Haini, Tryone's wife. Maybe that will help. You have to understand that I have to do something to make this right. So far you haven't done what I need you to do. You told me you won't do it. I accept that as my reality. You expect me to be over it, and to move on.

Well guess what I didn't get over it, I didn't move on.

www.ingramcontent.com/pod-product-compliance
Lightning Source LLC
Chambersburg PA
CBHW081140020726
47504CB00009B/1942